FOREVER BOUND

CYNTHIA EDEN

This book is a work of fiction. Any similarities to real people, places, or events are not intentional and are purely the result of coincidence. The characters, places, and events in this story are fictional.

Published by Cynthia Eden.

Copyright ©2011-2012 by Cynthia Eden

All rights reserved.

Cover art and design by: Pickyme/Patricia Schmitt

Copy editing by: J. R. T. Editing

BOUND BY BLOOD

CHAPTER ONE

The sexy little vampiress walked into the bar as if she owned the place.

Since Howling Moon was a low-rent dive hidden on the shadier side of Miami, a bar that catered to werewolves, well, the lady was very much out of fucking place. And, if she wasn't careful, she might just become the night's entertainment.

Jace Vaughn tensed when he saw her. He wasn't as drunk as the other wolves, not yet anyway, so he recognized the deceptively delicate woman instantly.

He could see the hint of her small fangs peeking out just behind the plump fullness of her too-red lips. Vamps' fangs always came out when they were about to fight or fuck.

So which one was the vamp about to do?

She stilled inside the doorway of the bar. Her long blonde hair tumbled behind her as her gaze raked to the left. To the right. Huh. Looked like she was hunting for someone—or something. In this place, the only thing she'd find was a pack ready to rip her to pieces.

Vampires and wolves weren't exactly playing nice these days. Or any days.

She *should* know that.

But then her gaze swept by him. Swept by, then came right back. Her blue eyes—bright with a vamp's power—caught his. She stared at him, and Jace found he couldn't look away. A vampire's trick of compulsion?

Nah...more likely just his own lust. Because the lady was hot. Most female vamps were, those pureblood ones anyway. And Jace knew he was looking at one of the elite pureblood Florida vamps.

A pureblood, in a werewolf hell.

He smiled. Fate must be laughing her ass off somewhere.

Then, *she* smiled too. A lick of heat shot straight through his body, and the beast that he kept chained inside stretched and growled.

Want.

She started walking toward him in her high, fuck-me or fuck-off black boots. Jace shoved away from the bar.

But the others had noticed her now, and they were closing in.

Three males. Big and hulking because that was the way of the beast.

"*Vampire...*" The snarl floated in the air, and the males reached for her.

"*No!*" His roar broke a second too slowly.

Two of the males crashed into nearby tables. They'd made the mistake of actually touching her. You didn't touch a vampiress who didn't want to be touched. Fools should know that rule.

Purebloods were especially strong.

Excitement had the beast inside yanking on his leash.

Every person in the bar froze for a moment, then instantly turned their attention on her. The vamp had the third wolf on the floor in front of her. He hadn't shifted, not yet, but his claws were already lengthening. She had one small hand at his throat while the other held tight to his hair, yanking his head back to better expose his neck.

Vampires always went for the throat. So predictable. Their hunger made them weak every time.

"Kill the bitch..." Ah, that mutter came from one of the guys she'd tossed a good ten feet. He was already rising with his claws out and blood dripping from his busted cheek.

Jace lifted his hand, staying the men even as they rose. "Not...yet."

He knew no one would disobey. They couldn't. He was alpha, and if they tried, he'd be the one kicking ass.

Even the shitty band stopped playing as he crossed the room. The few human females in the bar glanced around curiously, and he saw a couple of the shifters push them toward the back. The women came to play at Howling Moon. Or rather, the wolves played with them. Those women knew the score about the supernatural world, and they *knew* to keep quiet about the paranormal society.

The vampiress didn't release her grip on her prey. Jace took his time stalking toward her. Like most vamps, she had pale, ivory skin. Her features were…damn, pretty perfect. Wide eyes, high cheeks, small nose. Her chin was pointed a little, giving her a slightly stubborn edge, but then, bloodsuckers were not exactly known to be easy going.

Neither were wolves.

She wore all black. Tight black shirt, a *very* short black skirt, and those boots that oozed sex.

Sex and violence. Yeah, that was pretty much how vamps and wolves rolled.

As he closed in on her, Jace picked up her scent, separating the light perfume of her skin from the booze, sweat, and the cigarettes in the air. The vampire smelled sweet, tempting.

Her kind always did. The better to lure their prey in for that deadly bite. But she was—

More.

He inclined his head toward her. "Let him go."

"Of course." Her voice rolled lightly, soft, sensual, but had no accent. She dropped her hold on the wolf instantly.

Then Mike made the mistake of lunging back up and slicing at her with his claws.

Rage exploded inside of Jace, and he leapt forward even as his own claws broke from his fingertips.

Don't hurt —

She stepped back, ducked, then shoved her fist right at the wolf's heart. Her punch threw Mike back against Jace.

Jace grabbed the wolf and twisted him around. He lifted the other guy off the floor and glared at him. "I don't remember giving you permission to attack, Mike."

He heard the vamp's breaths panting lightly and knew she wasn't as controlled as she appeared. No scent of fear, not yet.

"B-bloodsucker...comin' in here..." Mike snarled. "She can't just...walk in..."

"I was invited here," she said smoothly.

Still trapped in Jace's grip, Mike twisted and glared over his shoulder. "Who the hell...would be dumb enough to invite a vampire here—"

"Your alpha." Her answer came with a shrug as her gaze lifted back to Jace. Then she inclined her head in the smallest of subservient gestures.

Submission. "I was told of your offer, and I'm here to accept."

Mike's head swung back toward him. "Jace?" His voice was stronger now. Wolves always healed fast. "What bullshit is she talking about?"

Jace slammed his forehead into Mike's nose. Bones crunched and blood spurted even as the smaller wolf howled. Then Jace threw the guy against the nearest wall, one that was about fifteen feet away. When Mike crashed, he didn't get up.

Silence. So thick it covered the whole bar. Jace stared at the vamp, trying to keep all emotion from his face. Then, slowly, he closed the remaining space between him and the woman who was going to change everything for him.

He caught her hand and turned her palm over. Hell, yes, the mark was there, cradled inside her left hand. Just like he'd known it would be. A blood-red rose.

He stood close enough to see the circle of gold in her eyes. The faint gold that marked her just as her hand did. She was something far more than an ordinary bloodsucker.

She was a vampire princess. His key to power, immortality, and she was the perfect weapon that he needed to kick the ass of the demons who'd come to town looking to wipe out his people.

Her lips parted as she stared up at him. He glimpsed her deceptively delicate fangs.

And he caught the scent of fear as it swept through her.

She was right to be afraid. Now that she was there, within his grasp, he'd never let her go.

Never.

"I'm Jace." He let her see his own fangs. "And you're mine." A claim made before all the wolves in the room. From now on, any wolf who touched her would face him—and death.

She swallowed and tilted her head back to better meet his stare. "Hello, husband."

The wolf within growled...*Mine.*

***

When you were stuck between death and hell, sometimes, you had to turn to a big, bad wolf for help.

The door to the small storeroom closed with a soft click behind Morgan LaBeaux, and she tried hard not to tense her shoulders.

Alone. With him. The werewolf's footsteps padded around the room.

She kept her chin up and knew that he'd smell her fear. Dammit, she hated being afraid. But the idea of bonding with this male and staying with him for the rest of her very long life—*hello, fear.*

Morgan didn't fear many things, but every vamp in lower Florida knew it was smart to step cautiously around Jace Vaughn. He hadn't earned the alpha title by playing nicely.

No, he'd earned it by cutting a bloody path through his rivals and leaving their savaged bodies in his wake.

And I get to marry him?

Some days, a bride was just lucky.

"I didn't think the vamps were going to accept my deal."

His voice sounded more like a beast's than a man's. Deep. Rumbling. He propped his shoulders against the wall in front of her and crossed his powerful arms over his chest. His eyes, so dark they almost looked black, swept over her once more. "A real fucking princess," he muttered as he shook his head. "I'll be damned."

Probably. They all would be. That's why they were *monsters*. Though she really hadn't been given much choice since she'd been one of the few vamps actually born to the blood's call.

She cleared her throat. "At first, the Council didn't plan to accept your...ah...offer." The Vampire Council—the strongest vamps in the area—hadn't exactly been keen on Jace's plan. But then the game had changed when their guards started showing up dead, courtesy of the demon bastards who'd come to town.

Once upon a time, the supernaturals had all lurked in the shadows, content to exist only in the nightmares of humans. Why take the spotlight? Death and persecution would only follow. The witch trials had taught them all that.

Vampires had never sought attention, still didn't.

Wolves, yes, they got a little wild and some rumors had been known to circulate about them, but they'd kept fairly quiet over the centuries, too.

But the demons—those assholes who were escaping hell in increasing numbers—they weren't in the mood for quiet. They'd amassed in Miami and were planning one deadly coming out party. But first, they wanted to prove they were the biggest, toughest prey in the night.

So they were eliminating their supernatural competition.

A war was coming. No, it had already started. Vampires versus demons. Demons versus wolves.

The enemy of my enemy…
Is my husband.

"The demons want to wipe us out," she said. "You want them stopped as much as we do." He still hadn't moved. Just stood there with his arms crossed. But at least there was no sign of his claws, not anymore. "You were right. The best way for us to end this battle is to team up."

He smiled, a half-smile that didn't lighten his face. It just made him look all the more dangerous.

The guy exuded danger like no one she'd ever seen. Darkly tan, golden skin covered a body hard with muscles. Jace Vaughn towered over her, easily passing six-foot-three or six-foot-four. He wasn't handsome, no, his face was too savage for that. His long, dark mane of hair brushed his shoulders. He had hard, tense features.

Not handsome. But...sexy. Dammit, *sexy*.

Wolves and their animal appeal. She hadn't thought that appeal would work on her. She'd been wrong.

"Wolves are holding their own..." Now his arms dropped as he stepped toward her.

"So far," she whispered. That would change soon enough. Once the demons started concentrating their full strength on them. "You know we have to find the doorway that's letting these demons out of hell and close it. If we don't, they'll take over."

And their coming out party to the humans would be a nightmare.

His eyes held hers. When he took another step toward her, Morgan held her ground. She had an image to maintain. *A vampire can't tremble before a werewolf.* But the slight flare of his nostrils told her that the wolf was drinking in her scent, and no doubt picking up on her fear.

Great.

When his hand lifted toward her, she tensed.

"Easy, princess," he murmured, "it's just a touch."

Right. And if they were going through with this bargain, he'd be doing a whole lot more touching.

What's one life versus the fate of your people? That had been the Council's big selling speech to her. Sacrifice yourself. Save everyone else.

Go be food for the big, bad wolf...because he can save our asses.

"My name's Morgan," her voice came out huskier than she'd intended, but his hand was on her cheek, smoothing over the flesh, and she wanted to shiver. *Don't.* She couldn't show that weakness. His hands were hard, but his touch felt whisper-soft. "Morgan LaBeaux." There was pride in the words because she was named after the first pureblood vampire ever to be born, Morganna La Fey.

The first, but not the last.

His gaze swept her face. "I can't believe...they'd really trade...you?"

She swallowed. In the end, it wasn't about the Council. It wasn't their lives that would be offered. "It's my call." His hand slipped down her throat and his fingers pressed lightly over the pulse that raced beneath his touch.

Yes, her heart still beat. She breathed. She wasn't dead, despite what humans thought. Purebloods were *born* as vampires. They simply stopped aging around their twenty-fifth year. Stopped aging and developed a lust for blood.

The others…those who'd been brought over by the bite, well, they *did* die, but only for a few moments. They came back, stronger than before, and their hearts beat again when they took their first breath of air as a vampire.

"So you're willingly offering yourself to me?" The wolf asked, voice darker than before.

The weight of his hand felt too heavy against her throat. Wolves were always so big, *too* big. In a second's time, their claws could emerge, and they could rip apart their enemies.

And when they went into a full shift…

We need their strength. "Once you help us to defeat the demons, I'll marry you." The wolves and vampires would be irrevocably bound.

Any supernatural that wanted a piece of them would find an alliance that was unbreakable. Unbeatable.

Jace laughed. The sound was sinister and strangely sexy. This time, Morgan couldn't stop her shiver, and she knew he felt it.

"Doesn't work that way." His head leaned toward her and his lips hovered over hers. "You want the demons taken out, then you give me what I want first."

What he wanted...

"Marry me, bond with me, and you'll have your own personal guard who'll tear apart anyone who comes near you."

She licked her lips. "It's...ah, not just about me." She wasn't doing this to save her own skin. "It's about all the vampires in my nest. They all need protection. Your pack has to give to all—"

"*You* are my concern." He shrugged. "But if they matter to you, then they can have pack protection. We'll take out the demons and leave a bloody trail to warn all others never to fuck with us again."

Yes, he was good at that kind of trail.

Over the years, the vampires had become, well, some said *too* civilized. They'd taken to drinking blood from handy little plastic bags. They married humans. They blended almost perfectly with society.

Because so many of them *wanted* to be human.

Morgan had wanted that, too. Then she saw how easily the humans died.

Now she wanted to be strong. A fighter.

The vampires were falling too quickly to the demon horde. The wolves—they were lasting longer. *Because they're stronger now.* If they were going to stop hell, then the vampires needed the wolves at their sides.

"Marry me..." Jace's whisper.

She knew she'd do anything, but before she could speak, a hard *thud* shook the wall. Morgan jerked. "What is—"

He wrapped his hands around her shoulders and lifted her up so that she had to stare straight into her eyes. "Demons followed you here tonight."

"No, that's not possible, I was careful, I—"

"Now my pack is tearing them apart."

If only. But, sadly, she'd discovered that it wasn't simple to kill a demon. You had to sever its head, and cleaving through demon flesh wasn't an easy task. While a demon's flesh *looked* like a human's, it was harder to penetrate than any armor she'd ever seen.

"Do I have your agreement? You will marry me right away?"

Why did she like the rumble of his voice so much? Morgan nodded.

Another thud shook the wall, and she was pretty sure she heard a scream.

Or two.

"Good." A growl. Then the wolf did something she hadn't expected. His mouth took hers.

Her lips had parted in surprise, and his tongue thrust inside her mouth.

He didn't taste like a vampire or a like a human. She had experience with those types of men. But Jace…

He tasted wild. Hot.

Her arms curled around his neck as she pulled him closer.

A growl worked in his throat when she sucked his tongue. Oh, yes, she liked that.

Vampires had the wrong image. Cold, stiff. Unfeeling. She'd never been like that. She'd always wanted. Needed.

Maybe he can give me what I want.

Her nipples were hard, stabbing against his chest, and her sex began to moisten. Wolves weren't easy lovers, or so the stories said. No quick tumble in the darkness for them.

Instead, sex that lasted for hours.

Hours.

The Council elder's face had been sad when he'd said, *"We hate for you to make this sacrifice…"*

It didn't feel like much of a sacrifice to her.

Just felt like white-hot lust.

Her fangs started to lengthen. *What will his blood taste like?*

She couldn't wait to find out.

His hands were on her ass now, holding her up and against the hard bulge of his arousal. No missing that fierce length of flesh. The wolf was big all over.

Yes.

Very slowly, and only after he tasted her once more, Jace lifted his head and lowered her to the ground. "Didn't expect that."

She could still taste him.

"Guess vampires can feel more than hate for the wolves."

Morgan pulled in a deep breath. "And I guess wolves can lust for the bloodsuckers they claim to despise."

He stared down at her, and she realized she didn't hear any muffled voices from the bar any longer. No more thuds. No screams.

His hand took hers and his palm felt red-hot against the mark on her flesh.

Wolves were so hot, when she'd known only the cold for so long.

"Come."

Do it. Go. Don't back down now. Just because she'd tasted the wolf and realized that controlling him might not be as easy as she'd planned, well, that didn't mean she could run away.

He opened the door. The smell of blood hit her. But it wasn't the normally sweet, tempting scent that called to her kind.

Rancid. Brimstone. Hell.

Demons.

Their bodies lay on the floor. Their heads had been severed, and their eyes — as red as the hell they'd escaped — stared straight up at her. Two demons down...

"How?" She breathed the word in surprise. The vamps had taken hours to kill demons, while the wolves had decapitated these two in mere minutes.

The wolf shifter that Jace had called Mike lifted his hand. His claws glinted. "We can slice through anything." His gaze seemed to bore into her. "*Anything.*" The unmistakable threat was in his eyes.

That wolf would be a problem.

She might just have to kill him soon.

Jace caught her hand and threaded his fingers through hers.

But the killing would have to wait. Because, ah, first, she'd have to marry her alpha wolf.

CHAPTER TWO

Morgan liked to bite. In fact, she was very good with her teeth.

But *being* bitten wasn't so much her thing.

She stood in the middle of Howling Moon, congealing demon blood getting way too close to her boots, and knew that she'd have to offer her neck.

The wolves surrounded her. Jace held her hand in a deceptively light grip.

"This is Morgan LaBeaux." Jace's voice boomed out and every wolf there stilled. When an alpha talked, you damn well listened.

Morgan's racing heartbeat filled her ears. He kept staring right at her as he said, "She's my mate."

"Oh, the fuck no!" The instant denial came from Mike. She'd expected that outburst.

What she hadn't expected —

Jace tore away from her and in an instant, his claws sank into that wolf's shoulder. "Oh, the fuck, yes," he snarled right back. "And if you can't accept her..." He yanked out his claws as Mike stumbled back.

Wolves are brutal. Another Council warning.

"If you can't accept her," Jace continued, "then get out of my pack."

Pain broke rough lines on Mike's face. "A vampire? You're tying to a bloodsucker—"

Now she wanted to claw him. The wolves kept acting like Jace was the one trading down. *Dude. Vampire princess.*

She toed the dead demon's body. The blood had reached her boots, and it wouldn't be coming out of the leather. "They'll destroy you."

Now it was her voice that captured everyone's attention.

Mike puffed out his bloody chest. "We did a good job of destroying them."

Yes, they had. And she was impressed, but she wasn't planning to show it. "You took out two..." Her gaze swept the room. "With twenty to two odds, I should hope you'd win the match."

Jace lifted a brow and watched her.

She braced her legs and tried to look all kick-ass. "What are your plans when there are two thousand of them...and still just twenty of you?"

"Did that bitch just say two thousand?"

"Two damn thousand?"

Shock coated the faces of the shifters. Even Mike looked nervous.

Jace didn't. He just kept watching her, and he kept his claws out.

"You're being hunted," she told them. "How many wolves have the demons taken out in the last few weeks?"

They didn't answer, but she saw the swift glances that passed between the pack members.

"They're also attacking us," she said. "For once, the vampires and the werewolves share an enemy." Now they were all focusing on her with narrowed eyes and tense faces. "If we don't take these bastards out, believe me, they *will* destroy us. They've got the numbers on their side. They have the power…"

"So what?" Mike demanded. "An alliance?" He fired a fierce stare at Jace. "Is this just some truce 'til we kick the ass of all —"

"It's a mating," Jace said, voice flat. "It's forever."

Until death. "A doorway opened between hell and earth, and the demons are slipping right through that door," Morgan said. More of the hell spawn came through each day.

"So close the damn door!" Mike snapped.

Jace's fingers stretched as if he were itching to plunge his claws back into the wolf. Maybe he was.

"We will," Jace said simply. "The wolves *and* the vampires will send them back and close the door."

They had to work together. In order for that doorway to shut, they'd both need to bleed.

Only she'd be the one giving up the most blood.

And Jace would be the one to face hell.

Murmurs swept through the bar. The wolves finally seemed to realize just how serious this night was. A vampire wasn't their prey. Instead, a vampire was becoming their alpha's mate.

Jace came to her side again. When his hands—still tipped with those deadly claws—rose to her throat, Morgan didn't flinch. He swept back her hair and his knuckles brushed over her skin.

The wolves closed in now, watching, and some—some were already shifting.

Mike swore and turned away. He stomped for the door.

"Don't be afraid," Jace's voice, right at her ear. She felt the whisper of his breath on her flesh.

"I'm not." Her own voice was just as soft as his.

His claws skated down her neck. "*Liar.*"

Wolf senses. Could he really smell her fear?

"Have you ever been bitten?" he asked.

So many eyes were on her. She'd known the bite would have to be in public. It was one of the pack rules. Claimings had to be public. Witnesses had to see the bite. Witnesses—just like in human marriage ceremonies.

Because that's what a marking was…marriage. When a male wolf bit his female in front of the pack, he claimed her.

I can do this.

It would just help if her knees weren't shaking.

She gave him the truth, "No." No one had ever bitten her.

"Good." Too much satisfaction purred in the one word.

"Don't forget," her voice was way too breathless. She wasn't actually looking forward to this, was she? "I get my turn later."

"I'm counting on it."

Oh, *damn.*

She tilted her head, arching her neck even as she closed her eyes. She wouldn't look at the others as he did this. She would just close her eyes and pretend that—

That I'm not giving my life to a werewolf.

His lips touched her skin first. She'd expected the bite. The sharp sting of teeth. Werewolves were supposed to be wild.

No better than animals. That's what the Council said, that's what—

His tongue licked her skin, and Morgan lost her breath. Her breasts tightened even as her body tensed.

She didn't open her eyes. *Don't want to see them.*

He sucked her skin, licked her, but didn't bite, not yet. His arms surrounded her, his body sheltered her, and he made her wait.

Worse, the bastard made her want.

Because her skin was too sensitive, his lips too wickedly skilled, and if a vampire had a sweet spot—okay, yes, they all did—it was the neck. Just a few licks there, and she was choking back a moan.

Then she felt the edge of his teeth on her skin.

"Do it," she told him, desperate.

"You accept me?"

Morgan nodded.

"Say it, Morgan, I need the words. You have to say—"

"I accept you!"

His teeth sank into her. Not her neck, but the curve of her shoulder. The pain was white-hot, pulsing. Then pleasure whipped through her. A wave of pleasure so intense that she cried out and opened her eyes.

And saw a giant, white wolf leaping right at her.

Barely a bride, and already, the groom's family was gunning for her.

Jace lifted his head at her cry and he roared, "Mike!" even as he shoved her back. Then her husband jumped into the air. His bones crunched, popped, and fur broke over his skin. The man vanished, and a giant black wolf attacked in mid-air.

Morgan touched her shoulder and felt the wet warmth of her blood. The skin ached, but she knew the flesh was already healing.

Vamp healing power.

The two wolves were a twisting, snarling mass. Claws flew, razor-sharp teeth snapped. Blood matted their fur, and their growls filled the air.

She lunged forward, but a hard hand wrapped around her arm.

"Easy, there, *cher*." The man's voice rolled with a Cajun accent she'd once heard during Mardi Gras in New Orleans. "Don't go gettin' between wolves. If Mike wants a challenge, then Jace will give him one…"

As she watched, the other wolves circled and howled. Jace tore into the white wolf. More blood. Her nose twitched at the smell.

Didn't they know better than to fill a room with blood when a vampire was around?

Her teeth began to burn as they stretched in her mouth. What would it be like? To have that fresh, wolf blood? Would it truly be as powerful as the Council said?

Jace went for the white wolf's throat. His powerful jaws caught the flesh, caught, held…

Mike sagged beneath him, the fight gone. Surrender.

Submission.

Jace tossed his head back. His howl filled the bar.

Then the black wolf turned and stared at her. His teeth were bloody. His eyes wild.

What have I done?

The Council was wrong. There was no way she'd ever be able to control him. The wolves were running around now, some human, some animal, and it was chaos.

Jace transformed as he approached. Fur melted. Bones shifted. By the time he reached for her, he was a man.

Even if his stare was still the wild gaze of the wolf. He came to her, caught her hand, and said, "Mine."

She knew that it was too late to run.

***

Mike raced away from the bar even as Jace's howl filled his ears.

Bastard. He'd hated that asshole for years and now Jace was pairing up with a vampire? Another reason to hate the SOB.

Mike had shifted, transforming in order to heal. Jace had sliced him too deep. Even now, the blood spilled down his neck.

"So sweet…"

The whisper had Mike slowing. His gaze swept the dark shadows. A row of broken buildings waited on the left. Empty. Faded.

His nostrils flared, and he scented…*bloodsucker*.

Mike slapped a hand over his throat, and he began to back away. Normally he wouldn't run from a vamp, but…but he'd already gotten his ass handed to him once tonight. "Stay away from me!" He shouted.

Laughter floated in the air.

"No…" The voice was closer now. "I saw you…I watched it all."

Mike spun around and came face-to-face with the vamp. Tall, as pale as the woman had been, but muscled.

And the vamp's fangs were out.

"You were going to kill the female, weren't you?"

Talk about being screwed. He should have known the bitch hadn't come in alone.

"No." He could be honest here. Maybe it would help his cause. "I was going to kill *him*."

More laughter, and then the vampire closed in. Mike didn't even have a chance to scream.

***

"This is...ah...your place?" Morgan paced in front of the fireplace. "It's not quite what I was expecting."

Jace pulled his gaze off her ass. The rush from the shift still fueled his body. No, not just from the shift. From her.

He had her taste now. Knew the feel of her body. Knew the sound of pleasure on her lips.

He wanted more.

"What did you expect?" His voice was rough. Always was. Like sandpaper when hers sounded like silk.

Morgan stopped her pacing. She slanted him a quick glance from beneath lowered lashes.

"A cage?" He tossed out.

Her small jaw tensed. "And I suppose you never once wondered if I slept in a coffin?"

He laughed. "No, princess, I know better." She just needed to stay out of sunlight because the light made her weak, almost human. Not because it set her skin on fire. That was just a Hollywood myth.

"And I know better, too." Her voice came even softer than before. She turned to stare at the heavy bookshelves that lined his walls. "But I did expect pin-up queens and at least one big screen TV."

Yeah, well, they were all on the other side of the house. Jace shrugged. Then he took off his t-shirt.

Her gazed immediately dipped to his chest. Her hand lifted and rubbed the curve of her shoulder, the tasty spot he'd sampled less than an hour before.

He'd be sampling a whole lot more of her soon.

The fucking princess. He'd asked for her because, hell, yeah, he knew the power that she wielded in her blood. If he got enough of that vampire blood in him, he'd be near invincible.

He wanted that power. Would need it if he was going to stop the demons. But there was...more.

He'd wanted her. Had, for a very, very long time. The lady didn't even know how long he'd been watching her.

"I remember the first time I saw you." He hadn't meant to say the words, but they broke from him. How many nights had his vampire princess haunted his dreams?

Her eyes widened. "Wh-what?" There it was again. That small stutter. The hesitation he hadn't expected from her. He'd thought that the years would have made her harder.

Perhaps they hadn't.

Or perhaps she was just playing him. Time would tell.

"You stopped aging ten years ago."

A slight inclination of her head. Fresh meat, or at least, that's what the pack would have called her.

Jace just thought of her as—

Mine.

"We've never met." Now her voice wasn't so hesitant, but her fingers were still curled over the mark he'd put on her flesh.

"No, but I've watched you." Before he'd taken over the pack, his job had been to monitor the vampires. To catalog their every move and report back to his alpha.

He'd watched and seen a blond beauty gaze up at the sun with tears in her eyes. Her twenty-fifth birthday. The day she'd finally changed.

Latham, the ex-alpha, had wanted the pureblood taken out. She was supposed to have been a message to the vamps. *We're taking over this town. Time for you to be our bitches.*

But Jace had seen her stare at that sun, and instead of hurting her, he'd torn his alpha apart.

Wolves couldn't really recognize their mates on sight. At least, they weren't supposed to recognize them.

Mine.

"Jace?" He liked the way she said his name, though he would prefer hearing her scream it in pleasure to whispering it so quietly. Later. "You didn't answer my question," she said with a lift of that stubborn chin.

He might as well put his cards on the table. In this devil's bargain, they only had each other. If he couldn't trust her...*then maybe I will be the one to kill her one day.*

"A few years back, I was your guard dog." He used the derogatory term deliberately.

A faint furrow appeared between her brows.

"For seven months, I watched you. Day and night." He'd even seen her drink her first batch of blood — and watched her vomit it out moments later.

She hadn't wanted to be a monster, but fate had different plans for her. And him.

Morgan's bedroom eyes widened. "When?"

"Right before your change." His gaze swept over her. "Right before—"

"Right before you took over the pack," she finished and her hand dropped.

Now he was the one surprised. "Did your research on me, did you?"

"Yes." Flat. "I know all about you. The lives you've taken — the vampires you've beheaded."

Because once, that had been his job. *Watch. Hunt. Kill.*

Until a vampiress had shed tears of blood at sunset.

Not that he'd exactly become Mr. Nice Guy since that night. He just hadn't killed *her*.

"You know, and still you're ready to fuck me."

She kept her chin up even as her hands clenched into fists at her sides. "We don't have to—to fuck for the bonding to take place. You drank from me, now I just need to drink from you."

Jace slowly shook his head as he stalked toward her. "You think you can drink from me, and *not* want sex?" He understood vampires so well. The reason most of them had stopped taking from live sources was because once they tasted blood—ah, fresh from the vein—the bloodlust tended to overwhelm them.

Her gaze held his. "I can control myself."

Interesting. His nostrils flared. She had control, but she was also aroused. From the idea of drinking his blood? Or just, from him?

He'd worried that a vampire female would be repulsed by him. Normally, they went for class.

Not for a beast that howled at the moon. But this princess, *his* princess, was something different. He'd known that for years. He'd just had to bide his time and wait for her.

"You might have control," he allowed, "but we wolves aren't exactly known for that."

"No." Again, not pulling her punches.

So he wouldn't either. "And I've wanted to fuck you for ten years."

Her lips parted, and she gave him a glimpse of those little fangs. "You—what?"

Why did he find her fangs sexy? "I don't care if drinking from me spikes your bloodlust. I don't care how rough you get." He wasn't worried about some bruises and scratches when pleasure waited. "I can handle anything you've got," he told her as his hand stroked down her arm. Such smooth, soft skin.

"Don't be so sure, wolf."

But he was. "So why are you doing this?" His hand deliberately brushed the side of her breast. *Want a taste.* "Why throw yourself to the wolves?"

"I'll be saving my people." Her lips firmed. "Isn't that enough?"

No.

Her lashes swept down but she didn't back away as she said, "I mean, that's why you're doing it, right? You're sacrificing yourself — mating to a bloodsucker — in order to save your pack."

He didn't speak, but Jace did begin undressing her.

"Wh-what are you—"

Her fast stutter almost made him smile. Would have, if he hadn't been so hard and hungry for her. He couldn't even draw in a breath without tasting her.

"It's time to finish this." They'd done the public ritual, and now they would bond.

He could feel a new power filling his body. He'd drank from her only once, and already the change was happening. Soon he'd be infinitely stronger, faster.

To stop the demons, he'd have to become more. So would she.

But first, they'd have to fuck.

Her hands caught his, stilling him.

He stared down at their bodies. She looked so breakable, but wasn't. Not even close.

So why the hell did he feel the need to be gentle with her?

"Don't worry," he told her. "I won't hurt you."

Her long lashes swept up, and she gazed at him. The gold in her eyes seemed even brighter. "Oh, wolf…" She sighed and then her lips curled in a smile that punched right into his gut. "You're the one who needs to worry about getting hurt."

Then her hands were on him, pushing back, and he realized Morgan was *very* strong.

The wolf inside growled.

Her fangs were out, and Jace knew what his lady was going to say even as her lips parted—

"It's my turn to bite."

CHAPTER THREE

They made it to the bedroom. Morgan had a fast impression of heavy furniture, thick curtains, and then—

Silk sheets. Black silk sheets.

The wolf had surprised her again.

She stared at him as the haze of need built within her. She wanted his blood. She needed it. And she wanted him. The lust for him wasn't unexpected. The guy was freaking sexy.

Jace was already naked. His chest flexed and rippled with muscles. His body was *perfect*. So strong. So dark. So...

Very aroused.

His cock stretched toward her, heavy and thick, and there was no doubt that he wanted her.

Not just a bloodsucker to him.

She ran her tongue over the edge of her fangs. "I need to confess—"

His gaze darkened.

"I, um, don't have a lot of experience at this." Most vampires she knew actually didn't.

He didn't move. But he did call, "Bullshit."

It must have been her boots. She'd thought they looked rather fuck-me. "Bloodlust and physical lust...they can combine too much. We don't, ah, drink from sources." They weren't supposed to, but the rules were changing.

"I know."

She felt hunted. The back of her knees hit the bed. "So I don't drink and — and —" *Fuck.*

"With me, you will."

His hands sank into her hair and tipped her head back. Then his lips took hers in a kiss that stole her breath even as it heated her blood. The wolf knew how to kiss. Oh, damn, did he. His tongue thrust inside her mouth, and Morgan found her arms rising and wrapping around his line-backer shoulders.

A kiss shouldn't sweep fire through her whole body, but his did.

Her shirt and bra were long gone. His hands slipped down and pushed away her skirt. It slipped over her boots and hit the floor. Then his fingers caught her panties and the rip of fabric filled her ears.

Morgan pulled back. *What am I doing?*

His glowing eyes stared down at her.

Her thighs hit the mattress, and she fell back onto the bed. She expected him to pounce on her, literally. Instead, he caught one foot and lifted it up, then slowly, inch by inch, Jace pulled off her leather boot.

His hands kneaded her flesh. Smoothed over her calf. Slipped up her thigh.

Morgan tensed even as her fangs burned.

His hand eased back, and he reached for the other boot.

She couldn't look away from him. Dark hair. Golden flesh. The boot came off, and his hand smoothed over her skin. He parted her thighs.

"So pretty…"

She was wet for him. Morgan wanted his blood so badly that she trembled and, even more, she wanted that hot, hard body of his against her. In her.

He licked his lips. "Who gets to taste first?"

Damn. She wasn't supposed to have sex with him. The Council had been adamant about that. Drink him, yes, take his power, give him hers, but sex?

Forbidden.

But the Council wasn't there, and for once, Morgan was going to take pleasure like other women did.

"I do," she said and reached for him.

His smile had her heartbeat kicking, but, to show him that she wasn't like the mortal women he'd probably known before, Morgan twisted and shoved him, forcing him onto his back on the bed. Then she climbed on top of him, spreading her legs so that the aroused length of his cock just brushed her sex.

More, please.

Her nails raked down his chest. Not enough to break the skin. No sense wasting blood.

His small nipples tightened beneath her touch. She leaned down and slid her tongue over the left nipple. He arched beneath her, and the head of his cock pushed against her core.

She lifted her head. "Not yet." Was that breathless, hungry voice really hers?

His hands were on her hips, holding her tight. So much power. She'd had a handful of lovers — all human — in her life. They'd felt warm and alive but Jace was something altogether different.

He wasn't just warm. He was a furnace, and the heat from his flesh warmed every inch of her.

"Don't play too long," came his warning to her.

A warning she ignored. She'd never played. Why not try now?

She kissed her way up his body. Morgan knew she should have felt hesitant, nervous, and moments before, she *had.* But now she just needed.

She licked his neck and felt the wild drumming of his pulse beneath her mouth.

A vampire's bite wasn't like a wolf's. There was no pain, there never was, not unless the vampire decided to play rough.

No pain, and, when done right…pleasure.

She really wanted to do this right for him.

His hands trailed up her body. Such big hands, with rough fingertips and a gentle touch. His hands curled around her breasts, and a moan slipped from her.

His name.

Her nipples were tight, and when his fingers pushed over the hungry peaks, she closed her eyes.

Her teeth pressed against his skin.

Her thighs shifted, spreading even more for him. She couldn't ever remember being this aroused for another.

Not about duty. Not about the vampire nest.

Right then, it was just about a man and a woman.

"Take me in," he whispered as his cock pushed up between her legs.

Her body resisted because the wolf was so big. The head of his cock stretched her, but it didn't hurt. It felt good, so good.

She pushed down, even as his hips thrust up, hard, *harder*.

Morgan took him all in and her teeth sank deep into his neck. His blood flowed on her tongue, and his blood was as addictive as his kiss. She drank him in, drank—

Jace growled, and the room spun. No, he spun, pushing her beneath him while never taking that thick cock from her body. And she didn't take her teeth from his neck. No, no, she wanted more of his blood.

More, Jace. More.

Images raced through her mind. A thousand flashes, like photos flying in a storm. They hit her, rolling through her mind as his memories became hers.

Bonding.

She took more of his blood. Licked his throat.

He thrust deep. Harder. His fingers pushed between her legs. Found the center of her need and stroked her.

The images vanished. The only thing that remained—Jace.

Her mouth eased from his throat. She swiped her tongue over her lips. Stared up at him.

His jaw was locked. His eyes glowed so brightly that it almost hurt to look into them. He'd obviously been waiting for her to look up, to see *him*.

"Now we finish," he promised and drove deep into her.

Her legs wrapped around his hips. Her nails sank into his arms. She arched against him, pushing as hard as she could. He thrust inside, filling her, every inch so stretched and full, and she loved it.

He withdrew, sliding nearly out of her eager sex, only to plunge back inside. Again. Again.

The headboard slammed into the wall. The bed slats gave way with a groan, and the mattress tumbled onto the floor.

He kept thrusting. She held on. Wanted more blood. Wanted more of *him.*

Pleasure had her sex clamping around him. The climax bore down on her, so close, so—

She bit him when she came.

He erupted inside of her, hot jets of semen that filled her.

And he held her tight. So tight that she wondered if he'd ever let her go.

Then she realized her hands were clamped around his shoulders. Her nails deep in his skin. Holding Jace just as tightly...

Because she didn't want to let *him* go.

***

Morgan dreamed of Jace's life that day. The images flew through her mind, one after the other.

A young Jace, had to be barely thirteen, running through the woods. Falling. Shifting. Screaming.

Changing.

Older, he strode into a vampire bar. When two vampires leapt at him, he struck out with his claws.

Blood covered the floor.

There was more blood. Always more. He hunted. He killed. A perfect weapon.

There were women. They passed in a flurry. Beds. Sex.

Jace. Aging. Growing.

Stronger, deadlier.

Not enough laughter in his life. Just death and violence.

Then...

Me.

Morgan saw herself in his memories, in the days that she already struggled to remember. Standing in the sunshine that last time, feeling normal. Human.

He'd watched her. Seen her cry. Not human tears, because then, she'd been beyond that.

Tears of blood. The sign that her change was at hand.

"Kill the bitch. Teach them that no vampire is beyond our reach."

An image of the pack's ex-alpha rolled through her mind. *"Do the job. Rip out her throat."*

Jace stalked toward her. She stood on her balcony, staring up at the night. His claws were out.

Then she looked down — at him.

There were no tears this time.

Jace turned away.

But the blood didn't stop. He'd gone back for the alpha. *"You can't take me, boy, you don't even know how strong I — "*

The alpha's blood had stained Jace's claws.

Morgan tried to shut out the memories. It was too much. She didn't want to see any more. No more death. It was all he knew.

Yet he hadn't killed her.

As the images kept pushing forward, she realized that Jace had visited her again. And again. She hadn't known it, but he'd been there so many times.

Not to kill.

To guard.

***

Jace watched her while she slept and wondered what memories she saw. He knew how the bite worked. Another reason the vamps had stopped drinking directly from humans was because they couldn't stand the memory overload.

When you drank from a live source, you saw memories.

What did the vampiress see?

He bent over the bed and wiped away the bloody tears that slid from her eyes. He'd always hated her tears.

You see me now, don't you? The dead had piled at his feet over the years. If he had one talent in this world, it was killing.

It would be a talent that aided them when the battle with the demons came.

But…what would Morgan think of him when she woke?

"I'm not a fucking monster." Liar, liar…and who'd know better than her? In his head now, always, there'd be no hiding from her.

She'd know it all and understand the obsession he carried. For her.

He eased away from the bed. He didn't want to look into her eyes with the memories between them. Not yet.

Jace spun away and left the room.

He hurried down the hall and shoved open the front door. The afternoon sunlight hit him, bright and hot, the way it always was in Miami. The buzz of insects bled from the nearby swamp, droning on and on. When he jumped down the steps, his first in command, Louis, pushed away from his truck.

Jace had heard the other wolf drive up. He'd just taken his time about heading out.

"We got trouble," Louis said, his Cajun accent rolling easily on the words. "No one seen any sign of Mike. Nothin' except his blood in an alley."

Jace's brows snapped up. "Look, that asshole is just sleeping it off someplace, he's—"

"That alley reeked of vamp, alpha." Louis shook his head. "Not your pretty little vamp. Didn't smell like sex and blood and flowers…"

Jace's teeth snapped together. But, fuck, yeah, that was how she smelled.

"More like hate, death, and...brimstone."

Brimstone? "You saying demons were there, too?"

Louis's shoulders rolled. "I'm sayin' we got us a missin' wolf. And blood and vamps where they damn sure don't need to be."

In wolf territory.

He glanced back at the house.

Gravel crunched beneath Louis's feet. "You gave that *cher* your blood?"

"I had to." It was part of the deal. The vamps wanted a power boost by taking wolf blood. "I gave her mine, and I took hers." Jace glanced down at his hands. With barely a thought, he had his claws springing out. "It worked just like we thought. Her blood in me..." The rush was still un-freaking-believable. "I can already feel the power."

"You gonna get more?"

"I'll get as much as I can take." His gaze held the other wolf's.

Louis nodded. "Will it be enough?"

"It has to—"

The world exploded. The blast tossed Jace into the air, and he slammed into the front of Louis's pickup.

It took him three seconds to realize it wasn't the world that had actually erupted. No, that giant ball of flames had come from his house.

Morgan.

The fire ripped up at the sky, twisting and turning.

Blood dripped down the side of Louis's face. "What the hell is—"

Jace ran for the house.

"Jace! No!" Louis's footsteps pounded after him.

He ran faster. *Morgan was in the house.* A vampire's skin couldn't stand the fire. She'd die—

He grabbed the door handle and shoved. The door collapsed beneath his hand. "*Morgan!*" He bellowed her name and rushed inside.

And he tripped over her. Morgan was on the floor, her arm stretched toward the door. Stretched fucking toward him.

He grabbed her and hoisted her into his arms. The flames crackled and flared around him, licking out at his skin. He ignored the burn. Morgan's head sagged against him, and her eyes didn't open.

Jace held her tight and leapt back through that broken doorway.

Smoke billowed out behind him.

She barely seemed to breathe. Ash and soot covered her, and Jace could see the angry red blisters that lined her perfect skin.

Hurt. On his watch.

Not ever again.

Windows shattered behind him, and Jace hunched his shoulders, curling his body in to protect her. Glass flew into the air, and shards sank into his flesh.

Rage grew within him with each step that he took away from the inferno.

Jace didn't ease his hold on Morgan, not until he'd settled behind Louis's truck. Then he carefully lowered her onto the ground. Her eyes still didn't open.

"Oh, hell…" Louis's drawl. "She's not…" The shifter's voice cracked. "The *cher* ain't alive, is she now?"

Jace put his hand over her heart and didn't feel it beat.

CHAPTER FOUR

Blood flowed into her mouth, hot and rich, and she drank greedily. The blood brought memories. *His* memories. Not of death and hell this time, but of a wild run through the woods. The thrill of the chase.

I'm hunting.

Morgan's eyes cracked open. She wondered why she *hurt*. Every part of her body burned and ached and—

Oh, yes, she burned because she'd been *on fire*.

Jace pulled his wrist away from her mouth. "Don't ever do that to me again, got it?"

She was on the ground. No, not on the ground, but sitting on Jace's lap. His blood was already sliding through her veins, healing her even in sunlight.

She wasn't naked anymore. Because she'd had to run through that fire naked. She'd woken in his room only because the fire licked at her skin. She'd leapt through the flames even as she screamed his name.

Now she wore his shirt. It smelled of smoke and him. Her teeth were still sharp, and she was *pissed.*

In a flash, she twisted around and pinned him against the ground. "What did you do?"

His twisted grin flashed. "Glad you're feeling better."

She felt rather like burned shit right then. "You tried to kill me." The bastard had left her to the flames.

That wiped the grin right off his face. "The hell I did."

But he hadn't been there. "You left me when you knew I was weak." Her hands dug into his wrists. She was aware of the other wolf shifter walking cautiously around her. Smart wolf, he wasn't coming too close, not yet. "You set me on *fire.*"

The Council had been right. She should have known better than to trust the alpha.

Not even married a full day and he was already trying to kill her.

Her teeth snapped together as she glared down at him. She'd actually started to trust the wolf. How stupid was she?

"I *saved* you," he threw at her and—and he wasn't fighting her. He was just staring at her, eyes too bright, and…bleeding. Cuts and blisters covered his skin. Blisters, as if he'd been in the fire.

Her head snapped up. An ugly green pickup blocked her view of the house, but she could hear the crackle of the flames and the stench of the smoke burned her nose.

"I was out here with Louis when the fire started." Jace's voice hummed with quiet fury. "Then I fucking raced in for you."

He'd...gone in there for her?

"I thought you were dead." So much rage underscored his words. "So I made you drink. I knew my blood could help heal you."

Not dead. But close.

She gazed at him. Her thighs hugged his hips just as they had last night. The memories were there, between them both.

"Uh, I hate to interrupt this would-be make-out scene..." The other wolf mumbled as he ran a hand over his face. "But I think we got us a real big problem." Tension had tightened the faint lines on his handsome face.

Morgan rose slowly. Her knees wanted to wobble but she forced herself to stand. A quick glance showed the blisters on her arms were almost gone.

Such powerful blood.

Jace rose and towered over her. He glanced back at his house, and she saw the muscle flex in his jaw. "Some asshole is going to pay." He pointed at the blond wolf. "Louis, get the pack." Then he was gone. Running back *toward* the fire.

No, really, just...*no.*

Morgan leapt after him. "Jace, stop!"

"Easy." The other guy — Louis — had his arms around her. She head-butted him and kept going after Jace. But Jace wasn't heading back into the flames. He raced around the house. Leaned toward the flames. Sniffed —

Got a scent.

He spun around and stared at her. His whole face seemed to just go blank.

"Something you need to tell me, princess?" He murmured, voice a silken threat.

The fire raged behind him. They were at the edge of the glades. No neighbors to see the flames and call 9-1-1.

His chest was bare. His eyes bright. *Sexy.*

Jace closed the distance between them and caught her hand. "Now's the time. If you've been holding back, tell me."

Holding back? Morgan shook her head.

His lips tightened. "So be it."

What? Her head throbbed. The sun was too bright. The flames too hot, and, even with Jace's blood, she was weak.

Almost human again.

Before she could speak, Jace had her. The guy moved in one of his quick lunges and caught her in his arms. The world spun, and she found herself hanging over his shoulder.

"Jace!" He ignored her yelp and marched for the truck.

Louis was already inside. Morgan slapped her hands against Jace's rather fine ass. He didn't stop marching. Didn't even pause.

"What are you doing?" Other than hauling her around like—

He yanked open the passenger door and tossed her into the truck. "The game just changed on us."

Her hair fell over her eyes. Morgan shoved it back and frowned at him. "This isn't a game."

"No."

The truck's motor snarled to life.

"You know whose scent I caught all around that house?"

Louis pulled out his phone and dialed quickly.

Morgan licked her lips. "Demon scent." It made sense. If they knew she'd agreed to team up with Jace, then they'd come after her. She just hadn't expected an attack so soon.

"Got a fire out on Mooreline Road," Louis said into his phone. "Send the trucks."

"Not demons." Jace spared a glance back at his burning house. "Not this time." His gaze came back to her. "You were almost burned alive by your own kind. It's the vamps who came— their stench was all around the house. They set the fucking place to blow with you inside it."

***

When a wolf stormed a vampire stronghold, he damn well stormed it.

Louis drove the pickup right through the fancy electronic gate at the vampire compound.

"Don't do this!" Morgan ordered Jace, grabbing his arm. "It's a mistake! They didn't attack me!"

Yeah, they had. And they'd pay.

The other wolves in his pack flooded in behind them.

Attacking in the daylight gave them the advantage, and Jace was more than ready to kick some vampire ass.

He jumped out of the truck and barely held back his howl of fury. She hadn't even seemed to be *breathing*. Oh, yeah, vamps were about to pay.

Morgan hopped out right behind him. Dogs were barking, snarling. Figured the vamps would keep Dobermans as their attack dogs.

Jace turned his head and snarled at the dog. "Bite me," he dared.

"He won't," Morgan said, voice soft and wan because she'd nearly *died*, "but if you don't stand down, I will."

Then his vampiress put herself between him and the entrance to the vampire pit.

Not a pit, really. More like a million dollar mansion. The vampires had to do everything with style.

"You're choosing the wrong side," he told her as his pack lined up behind him.

But she shook her head even as he heard the soft echo of an alarm from inside the mansion. The vamps were coming...

"They didn't do this."

"Their scents were *everywhere.*"

The door opened behind her. He'd expected human guards. Instead, the vampires filled the doorway. Three men. Forever young. Pale like Morgan, but with wide shoulders and hard jaws.

And eyes that burned with rage.

"What is the meaning of this, Morganna?" The first guy demanded, an old-school English accent dripping from the words.

"We've got a problem," she said, not glancing back. "He thinks you tried to kill me today."

Silence.

Morgan blinked and, this time, she did look back over her shoulder. "Tell him it's not true, Devon," she demanded. "Tell him you didn't—"

"Try to burn her to ash while she was still in my bed," Jace finished, his claws stretching. It would be so easy to kill that bastard. One stroke from his claws, and the vampire's head would hit the ground.

"We merely...tested," Devon said quietly as he shrugged. "It was necessary."

Morgan rocked on her heels, then spun around and caught the vamp bastard by his throat. "Run that by me again."

Devon blanched. "Ah, Morganna..."

"You *tested* me? With fire?"

He tried to talk, but no sound emerged from his lips.

"She's startin' to remind me of someone..." Louis murmured from beside Jace.

"Morgan?" Jace called out.

Her hold tightened on the vampire.

"I don't think he can speak," Louis shouted, probably in what he thought would be a helping way.

Morgan's hold eased a bit.

Oddly enough, the other two vampires didn't move to restrain her. Smart of them, because if they'd touched her, Jace would have ripped them apart.

They just waited. Watched. One even glared at Devon Shire, Council-fucking-extraordinaire-member.

Jace had come across Devon before. Almost killed him twice. *Third time will be the charm.*

"You drank his blood." Devon's voice held a distinct wheeze now. "We had to see...had to make sure it was making you stronger..."

"*So you set me on fire?*"

But Devon didn't back down. "If you're going to shut the doorway to hell, you have to be able to withstand the heat, Morganna. We have to test your skin, see how it's holding up against the flames—"

She punched him, a hard right cut that took the vampire down.

"Looks like your strength's improving, Morg," one of the other vampire's said, lips twitching.

Fuck this. "Kill them," Jace ordered.

Morgan whirled around, eyes wide. "Wh-what?"

The wolves were already shifting.

"Come." He held his hand to her. "No sense in you watching them get ripped apart."

The smiling vampire lunged forward then. A tall bloodsucker, with pale green eyes and a sloping scar that wrapped around his chin. One made, not born, or he wouldn't be sporting that scar.

The blond made the mistake of putting his body between Morgan and Jace. "We're not your prey," he snarled.

Morgan put her hand on his shoulder. "Paul…"

Fury pushed through Jace's body. There was something between them, he could see it. *Smell it.*

Morgan's blood, in the vampire. She'd *made* him.

Oh, the fuck, no.

His claws burst from his fingertips as he prepared to attack.

The wind whipped around them, blowing hot and hard. Wait, hot?

He glanced up at the sky and saw the creatures coming. Flying toward them. Fucking flying in daylight.

Demons.

"*They* are the ones we need to fight!" Devon screamed as he scrambled to his feet. "Not each other!"

This from the asshole who'd torched his place?

But then Devon surprised him. The guy grabbed Morgan and hauled her back toward the house. "You're not strong enough yet. We can't let them get you!"

Now the asshole was protecting her?

Jace's men spun around, snarling at the new threat. A threat that smelled of brimstone and death. The demons looked like humans, for the most part. Their faces appeared human, their bodies shaped like men. But they had claws that sprouted from their hands, claws even sharper than a wolf's. Big and strong, demons had eyes that blazed as red as hell and skin that was twisted and marked with scars that sliced across their flesh.

Demons could fly. Demons could control fire. And, most days, demons could kick ass.

Not today.

His gaze met Morgan's. A vampire in the sunlight. Even with his blood, how strong could she be?

He shoved back the one she'd called Paul. "Get inside."

Paul didn't move. "We fight, we don't flee, we—"

The demons hit the ground and came running. The wolves turned, holding their line, not attacking, not yet.

Not until Jace gave the word.

"I'm the one who gets to rip you apart," Jace promised. "Not them." Demons... "Now get Morgan *inside*."

"Jace!"

He didn't turn at her cry. He grabbed Louis, stopping his friend before he could change. The heavy metal door swung shut behind the vampires.

The demons were smiling, showing fangs as sharp as a vampire's.

"Guard the door," Jace ordered. "Nothing gets to her." *No one.*

Louis nodded.

"Send them back to hell," he told his men as his bones began to shift. The change didn't even hurt, not anymore. All he could think about now was the battle. "*In pieces.*"

The wolves attacked.

***

"They're fighting for us," Devon's voice trembled. "They're actually honoring the agreement."

Morgan paced. She'd quickly changed once she'd entered the compound. No longer overexposed in Jace's shirt, she now wore jeans, a t-shirt, and her boots. As she paced, the sounds of battle seemed to burn her ears. Howls. Screams. "We need to be out there!"

But Paul shook his head. "The demons came at us in the daylight. They knew we'd be weak." The sun would set soon, just not soon enough for them.

"They didn't know we'd have the wolves with us!" Devon was all but crowing. "The bastards can fight and kill each other off, and when night comes, we'll be stronger than them all."

She was tired of the Council leader's bullshit. Jace had fed her twice. He had to be weak from that loss, and now he was out there, fighting, while she stayed safe inside?

No.

"What if I'd died this morning?" She'd never forget waking to that blaze. The bastard must have planted one of his bombs. She knew he'd taken out other enemies that way over the years.

Am I an enemy?

"It was merely a test, Morganna. Merely—"

More howls from the wolves and screams from the demons. A demon's scream sounded like nails ripping down a chalkboard. *"What if I'd died?* Jace had to pull me from the fire. He could have left me there. I would have burned."

Devon just stared back at her with his soulless blue eyes. "Then we would have known the plan wasn't working."

The big plan. To mix the blood of a vampire and a werewolf. To create a being strong enough to shut the doorway to hell, a being who'd be able to survive the fires of hell long enough to make sure that doorway stayed closed. Forever.

A vampire couldn't do it on her own. Fire killed vamps too easily. At least, it had before. But today, the fire hadn't destroyed her. An inferno that *should* have killed her had only left her with blisters.

"You just need more blood from him," Devon said with a nod. "More blood, and you'll be strong enough for the job."

Paul had moved to peer through the series of spy holes located along the room's perimeter. "Or *he* will be."

Now Devon finally showed emotion. Confusion. "What?"

Paul whistled. "That wolf is cutting right through the demons. Slashing every last one. Never seen anything like this…"

She shoved him aside and stared through the spy hole. Her gaze locked on the wolf, a wolf that was bigger than he had been last night. The giant black beast turned around and Jace's bright stare flew past her as he snarled.

His teeth and claws were covered with blood.

"He's not supposed to be that big," Devon muttered. "I've seen him shift before, he's not —" Devon broke off as he caught her arm and jerked her toward him. "You let him drink from you."

Her shoulder seemed to burn, and she remembered his bite. "You know the rules of a werewolf mating. He *had* to drink."

But Devon started shaking his head. "I didn't realize…the bastard *knew!*" His hands wrapped around her shoulders, and he hauled Morgan off her feet. "Don't give him anymore blood." Spittle flew from his mouth.

"What? Look, you know you don't have to worry about me turning him. Werewolves *can't* become vampires."

The transformation from human to vampire was brutal. The victim had to be near death, a heartbeat away from the afterlife. The vampire had to drain her prey and then force him to drink her own blood.

Only…werewolves had never transformed. Vamps had tried to change a few of them, centuries before, but it hadn't worked. Their beasts were too strong to die. They couldn't transform.

Devon had told her that. He'd been the one to "experiment" on those unlucky wolves in the past.

Did Jace know? Did he realize that Devon had captured wolves over the centuries and sliced them apart to see how much pain they could take? To learn how fast they'd regenerate?

Know your enemy. One of Devon's favorite phrases.

Asshole.

He'd ruled the vampires in this area for too long. But now he wasn't the strongest vamp in the room.

I am.

Devon didn't even seem to see her as he said, "They can't become like us…" His gaze stared at the past. "Fucking animals…should have seen it…didn't think…" He spun around and his fist slammed into the wall. "They can become *more.*"

The screams stopped, but the howls didn't. They grew louder. Wilder.

The wolves had won. Vanquished the demons.

"More will come," Paul said and she knew he was right. The flood of demons wouldn't stop, not until that doorway was blocked.

Time to shut that door. If a demon was left alive, they could force him to show them the entrance to hell.

"You can't, Morg. You're not strong enough," Paul said. Ah, Paul, he knew her so well.

She glanced over at him. "Guess we'll see about that."

He flinched and there was no missing the worry on his face.

It had been three years since she'd turned him. He was the only human she'd ever turned. Sometimes, she wondered…did he wish that she'd just left him to die?

"You can't let him drink from you again!" Devon was still screeching as she marched away from him. "*Morganna!* Do you hear me? You can't?"

She threw a hard glance back at him. "You forget yourself, Devon. You can no longer tell me what I can or cannot do." She bared her teeth at him. "I'm not part of the vampire nest anymore."

His lips parted.

"I'm wolf." *So shove that down your throat and choke on it.*

"You don't understand. I didn't realize — he'll become *more!*"

She yanked open the door and the scent of hell hit her. "He already is." *And he's mine.*

Morgan strode into the sunlight. The big, black wolf stood in the middle of the carnage. When he saw her step out of the compound, his body tensed.

But the battle was over. His men were already shifting back to their human forms.

He began to shift as well.

And that was when the other two demons dropped from the sky behind him.

Demons...so tricky. So deceptive. They'd waited until he was weak. His attention divided.

Because of me.

"No!" She screamed even as they slashed at Jace. Their claws sank into his back.

She moved faster than she'd ever moved in her life. She grabbed the first demon and twisted his head. The snap barely slowed her down. She turned for the other hellspawn—

But Jace's men had already ripped him apart.

She spun back around. Jace stood before her, naked, body heaving, blood pouring from him. Fear tightened her throat. "Jace?"

His eyes were blind, not seeming to see her at all. She stared down at his chest. The demon's fist and claws had ripped right through him, back to front, and, oh, no, *please...*

The demon had cut through his heart.

CHAPTER FIVE

Morgan caught Jace before he fell. A scream ripped from her as she held him as tightly as she could.

And she knew what she had to do.

She'd found Paul like this. He'd been beaten, bleeding out, dying in a dirty alley all alone. He hadn't been able to speak because a knife had been stuck in his throat. His lips had trembled and he'd mouthed, *Help me.*

She had. A stranger, and she'd given him forever.

She'd damn well save the man she'd taken as husband.

She lowered Jace gently to the ground. The pack closed in around her, nearly blocking the light. Louis stood right beside her. She grabbed his hand before he could stop her. His claws were still out, and she sliced them down the length of her throat.

"*Cher, no, what —* "

Blood dripped down her neck and wet her shirt. She leaned over Jace. His eyes were open. On her. "Drink from me."

A slight flare of his pupils. She put her throat against his mouth. *"Drink."*

His lips parted. His tongue licked her skin. The edge of his teeth scraped over her neck.

Then he drank. Slowly at first. So slow.

After a tense moment, his hands rose and wrapped around her. He pulled her closer, held her tighter.

Tighter.

She felt his canines expand and push into her skin. Morgan held her body still. *He needs this.* His mouth worked on her flesh. Lips. Tongue. Teeth.

He took.

"Stop!"

Devon's scream. Over Jace's shoulder, she saw the Council leader trying to shove his way through the pack.

They shoved him back.

"Morgan, no! He'll destroy you! All of us!"

But Jace had saved them today. She closed her eyes. She'd begun to feel the heavy pull of the sunlight, like a weight upon her skin. Pressing against her.

Devon stopped screaming.

Her fast heartbeat slowed. Her breath sighed out of her.

Still Jace held her. So very tight.

He...he should have enough blood now. She brought her hands up and pushed against his chest.

He didn't stop. Fear tightened her stomach.

Then Jace swiped his tongue over her throat and his growled whisper reached her ears, *"More."*

She wondered just how much more he would take.

***

Devon stumbled away from the wolves. Fucking animals. Any minute now, they might rip into him.

He hadn't forgotten the alpha's order. The bastard had ordered his death as carelessly as he'd order dinner. *Kill them.*

When the alpha's strength came back, Devon had no doubt that he'd give the same order once more.

The way the alpha was gulping Morganna's blood, his strength would be back in seconds.

Should have realized...so blind...

He rushed through the compound, winding down deep into its hidden tunnels. Escape tunnels—because the vampires always had to be prepared.

He snaked through the tunnels, moving perfectly in the pitch blackness. To the left, to the right...

He punched in the combination to the door in front of him. The heavy lock opened with a hiss, and he hurried inside.

There wouldn't be time to waste. Kill or be killed.

Once Jace finished off all the demons, there would be no stopping that alpha. He'd want total control of the area.

And Devon wasn't about to bow down to an animal.

"Let me the fuck go!" The shout from his captive echoed in the lab.

His lab. His playroom.

Devon grabbed a scalpel from the table. Its edge gleamed so perfectly in the light. When he'd first started his experiments, Devon had always used his hands.

Then he'd realized the others thought he enjoyed the work too much.

Because I do.

So now he used the surgical instruments to make it look more...clinical.

Still the same. They bleed. I smile.

No one was in the lab but his latest specimen. If Morganna knew that he hadn't stopped the experiments...

Oh, well, the bitch couldn't stop him now. No one could.

He crossed to stand in front of the wolf. "You're going to be very useful to me, Mike." If Morganna's strength had increased with a few swallows of wolf's blood, just how strong would he become if he drained a whole wolf?

Strong enough to fight off the alpha. Strong enough to rule.

The wolf glared at Devon. "Go fuck yourself."

Devon sliced across the wolf's throat with his scalpel. Then he caught the flowing blood in a cup.

He wouldn't dirty his teeth on the wolf's flesh.

The wolf strained against his chains as his blood poured from his body.

Devon smiled.

***

Jace's men carried in the demon that Morgan had attacked as the wolves pushed inside the vampire stronghold. The guy's head was twisted and hung at a sagging angle. Not for long, though. A broken neck wouldn't kill a demon.

But when I take that neck from his body…

Dead demon.

Jace had never been inside the vampire mansion before. He'd stalked outside plenty of times. Come killing close, but never actually walked the hallowed halls. But, yeah, it was as high-priced as he'd figured. Fancy furniture. Marble tiles. Big, glittering chandeliers.

Money.

Class.

And...a blood fountain.

He turned away from the fountain and found Morgan staring at him. Even paler than before, but she still met his gaze. Her lips weren't red now. Instead, they were the lightest shade of pink, and the gold had faded from her eyes.

Took too much.

Her blood and the rush of power that came with it were addictive. He'd have to be more careful with her. Far more careful.

"How long?" Jace asked Louis.

Vampires lined one side of the room. Wolves the other. Jace stood in the middle. Morgan...she waited next to the vamp he'd been itching to slay. The one who touched her far too much. *Paul.*

"Ten minutes. Maybe five." Louis shrugged. "Could be sooner. You know they never stay out long."

Not much time, but... He strode forward and took Morgan's hand. When he touched her, he caught the deepening of her scent. Not with arousal.

Fear.

Took too much.

Louis had needed to pry her out of Jace's arms. He clenched his teeth as pain ripped through him.

If Louis hadn't stopped me... His breath rushed out.

Another debt I owe that wolf.

"We need to be alone." The blood had dried on her throat. Her wounds were closed already, but dark shadows lined her eyes.

"No, wolf," this came from the fool who would be her protector. "That's the last thing you need."

The wolves shifted, inching forward, and he could feel their aggression level spiking in the room.

Because his aggression level was damn well spiking. "Don't get between us again."

But the vampire stepped forward. "I'm not afraid of—"

"Death?" Jace finished silkily. "You sure about that? Because one fine dark night, in an alley that smelled of blood and vomit, you sure seemed afraid to me." Jace wasn't exactly sure how it had happened. Vampires were the only ones who were supposed to be able to drink memories.

But when he'd taken Morgan's blood moments before, he'd seen her life.

Seen her transform this one — Paul — even as she cried and whispered her apologies.

She hadn't wanted to make him into a monster, but she hadn't been able to let him die, not when he'd wanted to live.

"You *asshole* — " Paul lunged at Jace with bared fangs.

"Stop." Morgan's quiet voice. Her hand touched Paul's shoulder.

The vampire stilled instantly.

Morgan tilted her head back and met Jace's stare. "How do you know about that night?"

No point lying. Besides, he didn't want to lie. Not to her. "I drank your memories, princess."

Instant murmurs of disbelief came from the vampires. Paul shook his head. "No, no way, that *can't* happen. Plenty of humans have tasted our blood and seen *nothing*."

"I'm not human." Jace stated the obvious. "Those rules don't apply to me." And in their blood past, all those long centuries of hate that stood between the vampires and werewolves, well, his kind hadn't wanted to spend time tasting a vampire's blood. Ripping them apart. Beheading them.

Not sampling the blood supply.

"The game has changed now," he said as the vampires and wolves eyed each other. He didn't know if that was good or bad. Behind him, he heard the snap of bones.

Jace glanced back. That snap hadn't come from one of his own shifting. The demon's neck was popping back into place. *Not much longer.*

"Hold him," he ordered Louis. "Don't...start until I get back."

Torture would come. Anything, everything that he had to do in order to make the demon talk.

Then he glanced back at Morgan. "You need me," he told her.

"Why?" From Paul again. "Do you really think she *needs* someone to drain her dry?"

The bastard was begging for a beating. Begging. But...*Morgan cares for him.* "The way you did when she changed you? How many days did she sleep after that because you took too much? How many—"

"*Enough!*" Morgan's shout froze them all. She looked like a breeze would topple her then, but her voice packed a punch of undeniable fury. "*You.*" She jabbed her finger at Paul. "You were desperate, changing—you had to take my blood. I *offered* it to you."

Paul smirked. *Begging.*

"And you." She exhaled as she shook her head and focused on Jace. "What did you think I was going to do? Let you die in front of me?" Before he could answer, she ran a shaking hand over her neck. "You might be an alpha asshole, but you're mine, and I wasn't letting you go without a fight."

"And I won't let you go." Ever. His hand lifted and rubbed lightly over the marks he'd left on her flesh. "Now you need me...*let me help you.*"

Her tongue snaked out and licked over her lower lip. He knew she understood his meaning because her fangs started to grow.

"The battle's coming. You have to be strong." A strength she'd get from him. He eased back and offered his hand. "Come with me."

But she was shaking her head. "This isn't your place, wolf."

A stiffness filled his chest. Pain.

"It's mine." She grabbed his hand. "So *you* come with me." Then she led him away from the vampires and wolves. Led him up a spiral staircase and into a room without windows. A room that smelled of her.

Before the door closed, he had her in his arms.

Five minutes.

Not even that. Not now.

His lips took hers. Jace thrust his tongue inside her mouth. She kissed him back with no hesitation, even though the scent of fear still hovered on her skin.

He stroked her with his tongue, caressed with his lips, but the scent remained.

Jaw clenching, he lifted his head. "Stop."

Her lashes rose, and she blinked at him. "Why?"

"Because you fear me." He stalked away from her. It was either step away or pounce, and he wanted to show her that he could have restraint. *It won't last long.*

They were in an apartment of sorts. A leather couch. A TV. Bookshelves. Then toward the right...a bed. A big, four-poster.

Morgan, in that bed...

An image too tempting to resist. *Let the demon wait. The vamps and wolves could keep him...entertained.*

He reached for Morgan's hand. Entwined his fingers with hers and led her to the bed.

She sat down on the edge of the mattress and stared up at him. "I can't figure you out, wolf."

"You've tasted my life." Now he truly knew what that meant. "How can I possibly have secrets from you?" He lowered onto his knees and positioned his body between her spread legs. Then Jace tilted his head and offered his throat. "Drink." The ultimate pose of submission. For her, *only* her.

She'd nearly traded her life for his. *Louis, we'll name our first son after you — because you fucking saved my ass.*

If he'd gone too far, taken too much from her...

Her eyes seemed so wide as she gazed at him.

"Don't fear me," he'd meant the words as a plea but they came out sounding like an order. Dammit. He cleared his throat. "It won't happen again. I give you my word it—"

"You were already pulling back before Louis dislocated your shoulders."

He blinked.

"You kept your control. And the blood—it was freely given."

She wasn't drinking from him. Why the hell not?

Her hand slid down his chest. Pressed against his heart. After the shift and the fury, the wolves had dressed in their back up jeans, but most hadn't bothered with shirts. Her touch seemed to burn right through his flesh.

She stared down at her hand. At his chest. "What separates the man from the beast?" Morgan asked softly.

He forced his jaw to unlock. "There is no separation."

Her hand dipped lower. Found the snap of his jeans. "When you're a wolf," her voice grew huskier, "do you still have the mind of a man? Some stories say no. Others say yes."

The zipper hissed down. "It's...both." Man and beast.

Her fingers curled around his aroused flesh. "How do you see me then? As prey?"

"No." The wolf had only wanted to protect her. As did the man.

Her thumb slid over the head of his arousal. "As what?" Her eyes held his.

"As everything." Because that was what she'd become. Had it started that long ago night? Started with bloody tears and culminated when he'd taken her flesh?

Didn't matter. To him, she was...all. *Everything.*

"Good answer," she whispered as she leaned forward. "Very, very good." Her fangs sank into him—not in his throat, but at the curve of his shoulder.

The exact place he'd marked her for their wolf claiming. She was—she was *claiming* him.

Pleasure exploded through Jace at her bite. White-hot, pulsing. Inside, his wolf howled even as Jace wrapped his arms around Morgan and held tight.

They tumbled back on the bed. Her mouth stayed on him. He shoved off her jeans. She hadn't bothered with underwear. Good. That made things so much easier.

Her tongue swiped over the small wound she'd made on his flesh. He shuddered against her. "Oh, damn..." His head rose, and he stared down at her. She was the most beautiful thing he'd ever seen in his life.

No way would he be heading into hell without having her once more.

Jace thrust into her in one long, hard drive. Her gasp filled his ears, made him all the wilder, as her legs wrapped around him. Morgan arched her body and met him, thrust for thrust. Faster, faster.

Their eyes held. Their breaths heaved out.

Her body was tight and slick, and Jace's thin control slipped away with every sensual move of her body.

He took her mouth even as he took her body.

Nothing was as good as this.

Her sex clenched around him when she came, and he felt the ripples of her release all along the length of his cock. Still he thrust. Deeper. As far as he could go—

"My turn," Morgan whispered.

In the next instant, Jace was on his back, and she rose above him. Then she rode him, her movements as wild as his, and he knew, he *knew* he'd never find anyone else like her.

He heaved up and took her breast in his mouth. The nipple was pink and sweet, and he scored her flesh with his teeth.

They both liked to bite.

This time, when she came, he erupted with her. Pleasure had him going nearly blind. He held onto her as tightly as he could.

The drumming of his heartbeat filled his ears. Morgan gasped his name, and he was pretty sure he'd shouted hers.

The pleasure faded slowly. The ravenous need met, they stared at each other.

Jace realized this moment was important, but damned if he knew what he should say to her.

Morgan didn't climb off him. She stayed there, and her pale skin seemed to shine. From the pleasure? His blood?

"If we keep this up," she finally said as her hands slid over his chest. "You could get me pregnant."

That was the plan. Or it had been. To have a child with a vampire's immortality and a wolf's brutal strength. A child to rule them all.

But now…

Was that ever really the true plan? Or just an excuse he'd made to have her?

"Could you love a child that was part vampire?"

I already love her mother. I have for years. Instead of answering her, he asked, "Could you ever love an animal?"

She blinked. Now her fingers rose and traced just under his jaw. "I don't see an animal."

The woman could break him.

Fuck, how had this become confession time? "Hell's waiting." As much as he wanted to ignore the devil at the door, he couldn't. Slowly, he eased away from her body. He rose, snagged his jeans, and dressed. His eyes couldn't seem to stay off her.

She climbed from the bed. Didn't dress, but did grab his arm. "I'm not letting you go in alone."

His body iced. "That wasn't the deal." He knew. He'd been the one to go to the Council and lay out the scheme. "I'm the one who goes in, who closes that bitch from the inside. You were the one who was supposed to—"

But she gave a sad shake of her head, interrupting him, and confessed, "I was the one who was supposed to betray you and make sure that the doorway closed with you trapped inside."

CHAPTER SIX

Sonofabitch. He'd wondered...and had known that the vampires gave in too easily to his demands. "Let me guess—Devon's plan?"

"Devon hates wolves." A faint shrug lifted her shoulders. "He told the others I would go in as an assassin. Fool you, take your blood, and get strong enough to close the door."

His claws were out. "So why are you confessing to me? Seems like one fine plan." And he'd been such a blind fool. Wanting her, needing her so much, and she would have just—

"Because it was never *my* plan." Her gaze locked on him. "But maybe those memories haven't come to you yet."

What? "I only saw you change Paul." He'd seen it, like a living nightmare in his head. Her, running into that alley. Finding the bloody mess that was Paul, with stab wounds all over his body and a knife shoved into his throat.

He'd wanted to live...

"When we find that doorway," she told him, voice calm, "I am going in with you—and we're both coming out. That's the new deal."

He swallowed. "Why?"

"Because I won't let you face hell alone." Now her expression changed. Softened. "And if I need to, I'll haul your ass out myself. I just found you, wolf, and I'm not about to lose you."

His fingers slid under the thick weight of her hair as he tilted her head back. "You won't." He kissed her. Long, hard, hot. Kissed her and wanted her again.

Soon…*soon* he'd have her forever.

If he managed to survive the night.

***

The vamps and the wolves hadn't killed each other.

Morgan thought that was a good sign. Well, mostly good.

When she and Jace re-entered the great room, the wolves were still lined up on the left, and the vamps were glaring on the right. The vamps seemed a bit cockier now, probably because they were gaining strength from the setting sun.

Two of the wolves held the now conscious demon. The guy's face was broken and bloody, so it looked like the wolves had been enjoying some play time.

Louis raised a brow. "All better now?"

Jace growled at him.

But, actually, yes, she was better. One hundred percent better. Power seemed to pulse in her veins. If this rush would come to her each time that she and Jace exchanged blood, then she'd make sure they exchanged every day for the rest of her life.

Since she planned to spend all of her days and nights with him, an exchange wouldn't be a hardship at all.

Her blood would enable him to live longer. Human mates who sipped from their vampire lovers could stay young and strong as long as they had that blood supply.

She'd make sure Jace fed well and often.

"You're feeding a dog?" The demon spat blood on the ground at Jace's feet. "Vampire, don't you know better than to—"

Jace lunged and grabbed the demon around his throat. "I'm going to slice you open."

The demon just laughed. "I've been in *hell*, asshole. You can't do anything to me that hasn't already been done."

And Morgan hesitated. The demon had a point.

"We'll see." Jace didn't seem worried. "Once I slice off your hands and crack open your rib cage, we'll find out if you feel like talking then."

But the demon shook his head. "Been there, *done* that. Why do you think we're all coming out? This world..." His red eyes flew around the room. "It's *life*. We're coming, and we're taking it over, and you can't stop us."

"We'll shut your damn door," Jace promised, "and you'll stay in your cage."

More laughter. "Not if you can't find it."

"You'll talk," Jace promised. Then he glanced back at Morgan. "You don't...want to see this." But she read his eyes and understood. *Don't watch me do this.*

He would torture. He would push and push and push...because he wanted to save her. Save his people.

But sometimes, there was just too much darkness, too much of a price, to be paid for some actions.

"There's another way." A better way because her gut told her that the demon wasn't bullshitting. He wouldn't break. *What can we do that hell hasn't done?*

Jace stilled.

Morgan spared a swift glance for the vampires. Men. Women. Their gazes were determined, their bodies tense. They understood what she meant. They were ready. She licked her lips and offered, "We can drink from him."

The demon's bellow shook the mansion, and she knew that they had the bastard.

You won't talk. Fine. "We don't need you to talk," she said as she crept closer to him. "We just need you to bleed."

Time to sample the demon's memories.

Jace blocked her path. "This is a shitty plan."

She smiled at him. "It's a plan that will work. You know we pull memories with the bite."

"Yeah, but just what else will happen when you bite him? You ever had demon blood?"

No. "Never had the pleasure," she said and saw the demon tense.

"It could be poison. It could fry you from the inside out. It could—"

"I'd never had werewolf blood until I tasted you."

That stopped him. Only for a moment. "Yeah, princess, but we all know that once you go wolf, you don't go back."

And there, when she shouldn't have, when it was the wrong time and the wrong place, she laughed.

Jace froze. Then he squeezed his eyes shut. "Don't do that."

"Do what?" What was her wolf talking about now?

His eyes opened and a muscle flexed along his jaw. "You aren't tasting him." He pointed to the vamps behind them. "One of those assholes can do it. They can *all* do it. But not you." He pulled her close. "I don't want you having memories of hell."

He still didn't get it. "I don't need you to protect me." She motioned to the vampires. They lined up. All of them ready.

"Because they've got your back?" Anger roughed his voice.

"No, because I'm a fucking vampire princess." She bared her fangs. "And I'm riding high on my wolf's blood." Time for ass kicking. She pushed past Jace and grabbed the demon, wrenching him away from the wolves. "Remember me? I'm the vamp bitch who broke your neck."

His red eyes bulged as she promised, "I'm also the one who's going to drain you dry."

Louis snapped his fingers together. "Now I know who she reminds me of..." His gaze flew to Jace. "*You.*"

Jace snarled.

"Come ahead, bitch," the demon dared. "You think you're strong? My blood will burn you from the inside out."

"Promises, promises," she whispered and moved as fast as Jace had, a blur. She grabbed the demon's head and yanked it back. "Bleed for me."

She sank her teeth into him.

His blood filled her mouth. Warm. Not burning. But bitter. So bitter. She drank and took the memories. Fire. Hell. Screams that never ended.

"Morgan." Jace's hands settled on her back.

She kept drinking.

A white light entered hell. Small. Such a narrow opening. A man's voice called. Chanting. Serving up blood sacrifices. Trading lives because he wanted power.

"Stop!" The demon bellowed.

She drank more.

More.

The doorway opened. She saw the bastard who'd unlocked that door. Fucking asshole.

Betrayal.

The door opened in her mind, and fire raced out, burning, *burning…*

Morgan jerked away, screaming, as smoke rose from her mouth.

The demon laughed. "Told you, b-bitch…you'll burn…"

She could feel the blisters in her throat. But…but she was already healing.

Jace's blood.

She blew the smoke into the demon's face. "Time for you to go back home."

He flinched.

"Tell me you know where the doorway is," Jace growled the words behind her.

She held the demon's red stare a moment longer, long enough to see the fear flare in his eyes, then she faced Jace. "I know." But first she had another matter to take care of.

A little matter of a blood betrayal.

"Good." Jace pulled her away. "Then it's time to kill the bastard."

The demon screamed in fury and surged against the wolves who'd grabbed him.

Morgan slipped back a few steps. She caught Paul's stare and inclined her head toward the door.

The demon's screams rose.

She swallowed back the taste of ash. "Where's Devon?" She whispered to Paul.

Betrayal. She should have seen this coming. He'd always been such a power hungry asshole.

He hadn't been testing her with that fire. He'd wanted to kill her. So she wouldn't find out what he'd done.

You nearly killed us all.

Paul's eyes narrowed. "What did you see?"

"Devon killing humans." Not just killing. Torturing. Sacrificing. "He's the one who opened the doorway." It made sense, but she'd been too blind to see it before. Devon was over five hundred years old. He would know all the ancient legends and spells. He would know how to raise demons, how to open a doorway.

And to get power, he'd done it.

Only the demons he'd let out hadn't exactly been keen on obeying him.

You can't cage some beasts.

"Bastard." Paul's hands fisted. The demon wasn't screaming anymore. *Out of time.* "I haven't seen him since the wolves came inside."

"Because he's running." Dammit. "This is our mess to clean up." Not for the wolves. Vampire business. "Get the others. Hunt him." The order she'd never thought to give came from her as Morgan said, "Kill him."

Paul nodded. He always followed her orders. Always.

Morgan rushed away from him, already heading to the winding tunnels that led beneath the house. Before she faced hell, she'd take care of her own nightmare.

And she'd take full control of her vampire nest.

Morgan raced down the stairs. The others would come soon, spreading out. Searching.

Rage fueled her blood. So many vampires had died at the hands of the demons. The demons hunted in heavy packs. Swooping in, preying when the vamps were weak—*ripping us apart.*

They'd tried to stop them for months. And Devon, he'd been the asshole to bring those monsters into the world.

She twisted to the left. Snaked down the tunnel to the right.

The scent of blood hit her. Fresh blood.

Dammit, what had he done now?

A heavy metal door waited in front of her, open by a few precious inches. Open just enough to let the scent of blood spill out.

"Devon!" She called out as she shoved at the door. "What are you—"

Inside, a pool of blood soaked the floor. And in the middle of that pool...the broken body of the werewolf who'd attacked Jace at Howling Moon.

Footsteps thudded behind her. "Morgan!"

Jace's rumbling voice. She swallowed and glanced around the room. Blood-stained footprints led to the left, to an escape tunnel. One that opened in the heart of the swamp.

"Fuck!" Jace's shoulder brushed hers.

Paul came in behind him and scanned the room. Disgust tightened his face. "Looks like Devon was still *experimenting.*"

Right below them. Right damn below them. The other Council members had forbidden his work long ago. But the bastard must have liked his blood and pain too much.

Jace's nostrils flared. "He fucking slaughtered a wolf." And that's what it was—a slaughter. The wolf's flesh was a pale white, and Morgan knew that Devon had drained Mike's blood. A fresh kill. While they'd been upstairs, this wolf had been dying.

Jace's dark eyes locked on her.

She swallowed back the bile that rose in her throat. "Jace, I-I didn't know." Like that would make it better. She should have known. Her nest. Her responsibility. It was all...*on me.* "Look, I was coming to kill Devon, okay? He's the one who opened the doorway for the demons. When I drank that demon's blood, I saw him!"

Jace stared at the footprints, following them with his eyes. His shoulders were tense, and she could nearly feel the fury roiling from him. "The vampires summoned the demons." Jace's claws burst out. "The vampires have been capturing wolves...what other little secrets haven't you told me, *mate?*"

Oh, this wasn't going to be good.

"Jace, let me explain, I—"

"Too late." He grabbed her and put his claws at her throat. "*Too late, princess.*"

Morgan knew she was staring at death.

"I want every single one of you bloodsucking assholes to get in that cage." His head jerked toward the left. Toward the heavily barred cell that Devon had used to house vampire prisoners over the years.

Those bars were reinforced. Able to hold demons, wolves, and, yes, even vamps.

We won't be able to get out.

"Move," he ordered, "or I slice open her throat."

Her blood chilled at that threat.

Paul raised his chin. "You wouldn't."

Jace held her gaze. His stare seemed so cold. So...empty. *Would he?* "Get in the cell, Paul," she told him quietly.

Jace's jaw tensed.

Footsteps shuffled and snarls filled the air as the vamps went into their prison.

"They're in!" Louis called out.

Jace didn't let her go. "What are you going to do?" she asked. "I'm the one who knows where the doorway is. You need me to—"

"Devon knows where the doorway is. I bet that bastard is running there right now. How did you put it? *High on wolf blood.* He'll think he's fucking invincible, and he'll go back."

Maybe. Maybe not.

"Either way, I've got his scent." Jace brought his head close to hers and those wicked claws didn't move from her flesh. "I'm going to track him down and rip him apart."

Because Devon had killed a wolf.

"He *risked* you. Tried to kill you." His claws fell away. "The vamp will burn by dawn."

Wha—

Jace lifted her up, moved too fast—damn him—and put her in the cell. Then he swung the door shut and locked her inside.

She grabbed the bars. "You can't leave us like this."

His brows rose. "Watch me." He paused, staring down at Mike's lifeless form. "Take care of him," he ordered two of his men, and they immediately bent to pick up the body.

Then Jace followed the bloody trail of footprints.

"Jace! Dammit, I wasn't going to betray you."

He didn't stop, but she caught his growled, "I know."

What? "Then why are you doing this? *Why?*"

One-by-one, the wolves exited the containment area. Jace was the last to leave. His broad shoulders scraped the arching sides of the doorway. "I'll be back, Morgan."

Her breath heaved in her chest.

"We're not ending." He spared her a glittering stare. "I'm not risking you, and I'm damn sure not taking the chance that the fire will get to you."

"Jace—"

But he was gone, and Morgan was trapped with an angry cell of vampires.

Her knuckles whitened around the bars. Alpha asshole. He thought he could go out and take all the risks? While she what—stayed there and worried about him?

She wasn't the kind of girl who stayed behind. Mostly because she wasn't a girl.

"I knew he wouldn't hurt you." Paul's cocky voice.

She'd known it, too. His claws had trembled and never so much as nicked her flesh.

"We really going to let those wolves get all the glory?" He continued. "Because I've been wanting to give Devon a beating since I turned."

She pulled at the bars. Yes, they'd been reinforced, and normally, she'd never be able to break them.

High on wolf blood.

The bars began to bend.

"Don't worry," she told Paul and the others. "Jace isn't getting away from me." And he sure wasn't going into hell without her being there to pull her wolf right back out of the fire.

CHAPTER SEVEN

Jace and his pack chased Devon into the center of the Glades. The vamp had escaped by car, but instead of going back into the city, the guy had headed down the long, winding roads that led deeper into the growing darkness.

When the road ended, they found his car. Lights on. Door open.

Jace stared out at the night. The insects had stopped chirping when the wolves approached. They knew when danger stalked.

He inhaled, catching all the scents. Those that belonged, those that didn't.

Blood. Brimstone.

Fuck.

"Your vamp's gonna be real pissed at you once she gets out of that cage," Louis warned him.

Tell me something I don't know. But better her alive and pissed than dead and burned to ash.

He caught the whisper of sound in the air. His head tilted back as he stared at the rising moon. He could see the shapes before the blood moon. So many.

Too many.

Outnumbered. The demons were coming.

"*Shift!*" They'd have to change quickly. "Take their heads—take out as many of them as you can."

Then he leapt forward. The demons were coming because they were close to the doorway. Fuck that. Jace was slamming that door. Devon had run right back to this hole, and now Jace would kill him and stop the demons.

Endgame.

He shoved through the brush as the howls behind him filled the night.

***

Morgan had seen the doorway, the great gaping hole in the middle of the blackened earth. Devon had opened the door to hell—opened it on vampire land, and she hadn't even realized it.

The vamps spread out when they arrived at the battle. The snarls and growls of the wolves blended with the vicious cries of the demons. Blood bathed the ground.

"Don't get any of their blood in you," she warned, still tasting ash. "And make sure you cover the wolves."

Because the dead were already on the ground, and she didn't want to lose anyone else.

Demons flew from the air at her. "Go!" She shouted to the vampires.

She lifted her gun. The vamps had taken the time to load up before they'd gone hunting. She aimed. Fired. The closest demon hit the ground. A wolf jumped on him and bit into his neck.

More shots fired. The vamps knew what to do. Take the demons down. Make them weak. Let the wolves finish the kill.

She fired as she ran through the heaving bodies. No sense calling for Jace. She didn't see him there. Didn't see Devon either.

The twist in her gut told her where she'd find them both.

Deeper, deeper into the dark she went.

Her enhanced vision allowed her to see easily as she leapt over fallen trees and darted into the thick brush.

The crackle and hiss of fire reached her ears. *So close.*

The grass disappeared. The ground hardened beneath her feet.

Then she saw the broken skeletons. The remains of the sacrifices.

So many. Far more than she'd ever imagined. Hundreds of skulls and spines. Broken bones tossed aside like garbage. She stared at the stark white graveyard as rage filled her.

Devon.

She leapt over the bones. There — *there.* A sunken, sloping entrance on the ground. Smoke trickled from the thick hole and…she could hear the faintest echo of screams emanating from within the pit.

"You always did let emotion rule you," came Devon's voice from the darkness.

Morgan spun around, and took a few quick steps away from the pit. "You did this."

He shrugged.

"They've been attacking *us,* Devon! Killing us! You were the Council leader, you had—"

"Fuck the Council." He smiled, showing off his bloody fangs. "And fuck you."

Her hands fisted.

"Vampires were always so busy hiding. Oh, no, mustn't let the humans know we're here." He smirked at her. "Wrong. It's time for them to know. Time for us to show the humans that their only purpose is to feed us. They're prey. We're fucking gods."

She could only shake her head. "You bargained with the devil, you opened a doorway because—"

"Because I wanted a war. Because the vampires needed to learn…it's kill or be killed. We weren't meant to hide. We're meant to dominate."

Bastard. "And so you sent the demons after your own kind? How is that us dominating?"

"I sent the demons after the *weak*. Those vampires who can't survive don't belong in this world." His lips still twisted in that sick grin as he said, "And it's not like I can't make *more* of our kind."

More like him? No way. "You won't be changing anyone. You won't be killing anyone else." Where was Jace? "This ends tonight."

He laughed. "Funny. That's exactly what your wolf said…"

A fist squeezed her heart.

"Right before I kicked his ass into hell."

The screams behind her seemed louder. Like more demons were fighting to get out.

"Sounds like they're enjoying their new meal." His fangs flashed in the dark. "That's how it works, you see. For them to come out, I offer a trade. A life."

That's why there were so many bones. A skeleton for each demon he'd brought forth.

"They devour the flesh, then toss out the parts that are too hard."

Not Jace. He wasn't in that pit. "We're closing that hole."

Devon took a step toward her. "You don't have that kind of power. You think you're so fucking special." Another step. "Just because you were born pureblood. You always thought you were better than me."

"No, I didn't." *But I do now. I'm not a psychotic asshole, so yes, that makes me better.*

"Do you know why I wanted you to marry the wolf?"

Well, saving the vamp nest obviously wasn't the reason. Morgan held her ground. Hell waited behind her, and this bastard caged her in front.

"I needed you to get close to him," Devon said. "I needed you to take his blood…because I wanted to give the demons a special tribute." He inclined his head. "You see, now that they've been killing, they're developed a taste for wolf blood."

"They're not taking his blood!"

"But in order to close the deal with them, I had to prove how much I'd be willing to sacrifice." His eyes narrowed. "With demons, it's all about the sacrifice. You have to offer them something, or the lazy assholes won't do a thing."

"You've offered them humans—"

"Because I'm fucking tired of hiding in the shadows. The vampires wouldn't take control, they were too scared of humans finding out the truth. But my demons— *they're not afraid of anything."*

The screams from the pit almost drowned out his words. "What are you sacrificing?" Because, shit, this was a trap. For the wolves. For Jace. For—

"*You.*"

Then he lunged at her.

But Morgan was ready. She grabbed his arms, twisted, and tossed the traitor right over her shoulder. He hit the ground just feet away from the pit, and smoke billowed out in a heavy burst.

He flew back to his feet. Smiled. "This will be fun." He licked his lips, tasting the blood that stained his mouth. "You're the only pureblood around here. You're the best sacrifice I can give them. I bet you'll be worth ten demons…"

He'd lost it. "And I bet it will hurt when you fall into hell."

That wiped the smile off his face. "Your wolf sure screamed when the demons took him."

Dammit, that was the second time he'd said—her gaze darted to the pit. "*Jace!*"

Devon slammed into her, and they hit the earth. "Bitch, I've got wolf blood in me. More than you. I drained that mutt."

And he'd left Mike's broken body behind. Another casualty.

Morgan kicked up, slamming her knee into his balls. He jerked back. "You've got wolf blood," she said, "but now you also have balls in your throat."

She jumped to her feet. *"Jace!"* Her scream broke through the night. He couldn't be in that pit, he couldn't…

Devon's arms wrapped around her from behind. He squeezed so tight she lost her breath and her ribs burned…burned.

Snap.

Pain beat through her as her ribs broke.

"So tired of you…" Devon lifted her and carried her toward the pit. "Fucking a wolf…blending with humans…crying when you lost the light…"

She slammed her head back and heard the sweet crunch of bones when she broke his nose. Morgan clawed at his arms, slicing open his flesh as she fought him. His blood littered the ground as he took her to the pit.

"Let her go!"

Jace. His roar. Relief had her feeling light-headed. Or maybe that dizziness was from the pain.

Jace leapt forward. He was naked and blood poured from a gash on his cheek. His eyes glowed as he raised his claws and ran toward them.

Devon had her nearly over the pit. This was what she'd planned. To enter hell. To close the door from the inside out.

Only…well, in the original plan, *Jace* had been the one to go through the doorway. She was supposed to stay back and then pull him out.

I won't sacrifice him.

The rules had indeed changed. Jace didn't realize it. She did. If demons were all about sacrifice, then she'd give them a sacrifice all right.

But she wouldn't give them Jace.

"Watch her burn, wolf!" Devon shouted. *"Watch. Her. Burn!"*

Morgan stopped fighting. Instead of slicing her nails against Devon, she twisted her hands and locked tight to him. Her gaze met Jace's. He yelled her name.

"Bring me back," she whispered. Then Morgan heaved toward the pit, and she yanked Devon with her.

He tried to wrench back his arms, but she wouldn't let go. His yells filled her ears as he fought and twisted, but Morgan *wouldn't let go.*

No more dead humans. No more tortured wolves. This was it.

They fell into the pit, and the screams from the demons drowned out her voice as she told them, "I've got a sacrifice for you, assholes…"

The fire burned, blasting at her skin and she refused to cry out.

Even when the demons reached for her.

***

Jace's heart stopped when Morgan jumped into that fiery pit. "No!"

Not her. She wasn't supposed to go in. *Not. Her.*

He flew forward, and his body slammed into the ground even as his arms snaked into that hole in a desperate bid to grab her.

He'd moved fast, faster than he'd ever moved in his life, and when he shoved his hands into that hot furnace, he touched...

Flames.

The fire lanced his skin, but he didn't let go. He could feel a body in the middle of that wild heat. He could smell the acrid scent of burning flesh.

Morgan.

He didn't let go. He pulled even as he felt another force tugging his prize back down.

"No! You can't have her!" He yelled as the fire licked him.

His upper body fell into the pit as he struggled.

"*Fuck, Jace!*" Louis's yell from behind him. Then suddenly Jace felt other hands on his body, trying to haul him back.

But he wasn't going back without Morgan. "Keep him!" He roared the words in the fire. "Choke on him — but give her to me!"

A breath of flames blew against him and blisters immediately covered his flesh.

"*Give her to me!*" He bellowed.

"*Pull him up!*" Louis snarled at the same instant. "Get him out of there, *now!*"

They yanked him back, but he didn't let go of the fiery prize he held. *Be Morgan. Be…*

He broke from the pit and fire raced along his body. Louis shoved at him and Jace fell to the ground. He rolled, battling the flames on him and — *on her*.

Sweet fuck, he'd pulled her out.

The others immediately joined him and battled the flames that covered her flesh. Red, swollen, every inch of her body had felt the kiss of the fire.

Should have been me.

Her eyes weren't open. "Morgan?" Now, he was afraid to touch her. He didn't want to hurt her, and he knew his touch would. She was injured so badly, even a breath on her skin would hurt.

His touch would pain her, but his blood wouldn't. Jace lifted his hand to his mouth and bit his wrist. He tore with his teeth and put his hand over her mouth. "Princess, *please…*"

The blood trickled into her mouth. Her lips moved the faintest bit against his skin.

"*Take more.*" She could take everything if she needed it.

"Alpha." Louis's quiet voice had his head lifting. His friend stared at him with a tense face. "You're weak, too. Let me help you."

Jace shook his head. "No, she's—"

"I know she's yours, but she's also pack." Louis offered his bleeding wrist. "If the blood of one wolf makes her strong, how fast do you think she'll heal when she drinks from six?"

And the others who'd survived the battle crowded behind him. All had their wrists open.

All were ready to sacrifice for the vampire who'd seen hell.

As she fed from him, her lips like a whisper on his skin, Jace's gaze tracked back to the pit. Only the entrance wasn't there any longer. Dirt had filled in, totally blocking the gaping hole. The ground was blackened, cracked, but no smoke drifted into the air.

The doorway was closed.

He leaned close to her. "You did it," he whispered. Her vampires were safe. The battle was over.

Now, his princess just had to survive.

CHAPTER EIGHT

The vampiress walked into the werewolf bar as if she owned the place. Since she was mated to the alpha, Jace figured that, well, she pretty much did.

Her skin was pale and perfect, not even a blister left from the fire that had nearly stolen her from him. Her lips were red, full, and he'd soon feel them beneath his mouth.

She was wearing a new pair of fuck-me boots that showed off the long length of her legs.

And her eyes — they were on him.

When the others became aware of her, they stopped talking. Heads swiveled toward her. Toward him. The bar waited.

He didn't move. Jace wanted to jump up, run to her, *grab* her, but he was also enjoying the sexy picture she made as she crossed the bar.

Morgan smiled at him, flashing fangs. "The Miami Vampire Council would like to officially extend its appreciation to you," she said, her voice clear and her eyes bright. "And if there is anything that the Council can do for the pack…"

She stopped just a foot away from him. "You have only to ask," Morgan finished, her voice softer.

She'd spent two days healing. Even with all the wolf blood, she'd had to battle to stay alive. He'd been by her side, determined to keep death away.

He'd succeeded.

When she'd woken, the vampires had made her the head of their Council. He knew she'd weeded out the vamps who'd been secretly working with Devon. The bastard hadn't been implementing his plan alone.

She'd cut the head off the snake when she sent Devon to hell, and now Jace knew that she'd cut up the body, too.

Still, he didn't touch her, not yet. "Glad the *Council* approves," he said, his own voice mild.

Understanding flared in her eyes. She lifted her hand and put her palm against his chest. "And you have my personal gratitude..." Her lips curved. "For pulling my ass out of hell."

He caught her hand. Pressed it harder against his chest. "Leaving you there wasn't exactly an option for me."

Jace saw the delicate movement of her throat as she swallowed.

"What was it like?" Louis called out. "What did you see, *cher*?"

She glanced back at him. "It was damn hot."

Some of the wolves laughed.

"As for what I saw..." Morgan shook her head. "Some things are better not said."

When she turned back to him, memories were in her eyes. While her body might have healed, Jace knew she'd carry the scars inside. Some memories couldn't be forgotten.

"Is the gateway closed for good?" Because he didn't want any more demons coming after her.

"Yes." He still held her hand. She didn't pull away. She inched closer as she said, "It closed when the demons killed Devon. *He* was the sacrifice I gave to them. He opened the pit, so it only seemed fitting that he close it."

Jace waited. He knew there was more.

"I made a deal while I burned." Her lashes lowered as she stared at their hands. His dark, hers so light. After a moment, she glanced back up at him. "I told those demon assholes that if they accepted Devon and shut the door, I wouldn't send my wolf down to tear hell apart."

And he would have. If they'd kept her...

"When you yanked me out of their hands, they realized I was serious. You were ready for hell. But hell wasn't ready for you." Her hand fisted beneath his. "Besides, I don't think the guy in charge down there really liked for his demons to escape."

No, Jace bet he hadn't been eager to lose those bastards. "So it's over," he said.

"No." Now her body brushed against his. "The demons are gone, but things are far from *over*." Her head tilted back. Her lips were inches from his. "In fact, I think you promised me that things would just be getting started…"

They would be.

"You locked me in a cage," she told him, a faint frown pulling between her eyes.

He brought his hands up to curl around her shoulders. "But I also pulled you out of hell. Makes us even, doesn't it?"

Her soft laughter put an ache in his chest.

"I don't know," she told him, "I think that might put you ahead."

His lips took hers because his control broke. The kiss was too rough, too wild, but that was his way.

And she kissed him back just as wildly and with just as much desperate need.

He lifted his mouth from hers long enough to growl, "There's no score between mates. You don't owe me anything." He wanted her out of the bar and naked beneath him.

"I owe you forever," she told him as she rose onto her toes and kissed him again. "And that's what I'm giving you."

Forever with his vampiress…it was the only thing he wanted.

"You're mine, wolf," she told him. "And I'm not letting you go."

Enough. He grabbed her and hoisted her high into his arms. The pack shouted and laughed as he passed them, but he didn't slow down. He wanted her alone.

Wanted *in* her.

Jace took her upstairs. Since his house had burned, he'd taken over Howling Moon. The apartment above the bar had a bed, and that was all he needed.

He kicked the door shut behind them and lowered her in front of him.

Morgan smiled at him. "When are you going to say that you love me?"

He blinked. "But...you already know." She had to know.

"A woman still likes to hear the words."

He yanked off his shirt and kicked off his boots. Then he reached for her. If she needed the words, he'd damn well give them to her. He'd give her anything. "I love you."

Her fangs glinted. "And I love you, wolf."

Enemies no more. Lovers.

Mates.

Forever.

They'd told the devil to screw off, and now they had eternity waiting.

Sometimes, it was good to be an alpha wolf...

Very fucking good.

BOUND IN DARKNESS

PROLOGUE

"I know what you are."

Cade Thain carefully put his whiskey glass down and glanced up at the woman before him. "And what's that?" His hands flattened on the old, wooden table.

She sat down and leaned toward him. Her hair was blonde, her skin a sun-kissed gold. And her eyes—they were the coldest blue he'd ever seen in his life. "You're a werewolf."

He laughed, the sound deep and loud.

Her jaw tightened. "And you're an assassin."

Cade kept the smile on his face. "Lady, you're crazy."

"No, I'm not." A thread of anger—no, that thread was far closer to fury—rumbled beneath her words. "I'm here to hire you."

Cade glanced to the left. To the right. In this pit of hell that passed for a bar in some hole-in-the-wall Oregon town, no one was paying any attention to anyone. Or anything. "You've got the wrong man," he said slowly.

Her gaze searched his face. "Not too many men have scars like yours." And that icy stare had locked on the scar that slipped from his right eyebrow all the way down to his jaw. Another scar sliced around his neck. There were more, so many more, hidden beneath his clothes. "Cut you with silver, didn't they?" she asked softly. "When you were so young that you could barely heal."

Fuck, yeah, they had. His back was covered with long, twisting scars. Wounds administered by sick pricks that Cade had personally sent to burn. Cade had been fourteen when he made those kills.

His first, not his last.

"Werewolf…" She breathed the title. "I've got a vamp for you to slay."

Now the lady had his full attention. He dropped the act and focused totally on her.

Vampires had been the ones to torture him. To destroy his family. His pack. They'd introduced him to hell.

Made him into the monster that he was today.

She leaned closer. Her scent—already too strong for someone with his enhanced senses—surrounded him. A bitter scent, heavy with incense. *A witch.* The scent of their spells always clung to them.

His would-be-client told him, "The vamp's name is Allison Gray, and she'll be such easy prey, especially for someone like you."

Her fingers slid over to touch his hands. His claws weren't out—not yet. *Not yet.* "Why do you want the vamp dead?" Cade demanded to know

Hell, vamps were *already* dead. They only kept living by draining their prey. Feeding on them.

Like they fed on me.

Parasites.

"She's a pureblood."

Shit. Now the witch was talking some serious power. Most vampires were made the old-fashioned way—they were humans who were bit, drained, and brought back as vampires. But a pureblood? Purebloods were extra strong because they were *born* as vampires.

Lucky for the rest of the world, most purebloods were rare. Otherwise, hell would be calling on earth every damn night.

But killing a pureblood? "That'll cost you extra," he warned.

Her smile didn't make her eyes appear any warmer. Beautiful, but the witch was stone cold. "I'll pay you one hundred thousand dollars."

Paranormal hits were never cheap—or easy. "Make it two."

Her eyes narrowed.

He offered her his own, cold smile. "And I'll want the cash up front, before I take my prey."

The witch hesitated.

"You can always go find someone else." Total bullshit. There weren't any other werewolves in this part of the U.S. And when it came to vamp killin', no one got the job done better than a wolf.

The witch would know that.

She nodded. "Done." Then she eased back, licking her lips. "But you have to do it fast, before the next full moon."

Five days away. Werewolves always knew exactly when the next full moon would rise. They were at their strongest when the full moon hung in the sky.

Her fingers drummed on the table. "And you have to make it *hurt*."

Killing a vamp? Torturing her? Cade shrugged. For two hundred grand... "Done."

His conscience had died long ago. He'd left it, broken and bloody, in that pit where the vamps had tortured him.

Besides, it wasn't like he was slaughtering the innocent. The world would be a far better place with one less bloodsucker on the streets.

He reached for his whiskey. Barely felt the burn as the liquid slid down his throat.

One more down…thousands to go.

CHAPTER ONE

She was being hunted.

Allison Gray had felt the unseen eyes on her for days. Ever since she'd left Alliance, Nebraska, and begun this crazy journey.

Ever since she'd started to change.

Her hands fisted as she slid through the crowd inside Blood Bath. Blood Bath? Jeez, just what kind of name was that for a bar? Nestled near the Cascade Mountains, the bar was like the rest of the small town—pretty damn scary.

Allison found what she hoped was a private corner. One hidden by shadows. She'd never expected this town—not here. The tiny spot of Lost, Oregon, was filled with folks who looked like they could—*and would*—kill at the drop of a hat. She'd been told that she had to journey to this town. That she'd find the answers to all her questions here.

Her breath eased slowly from her lungs as her gaze swept around the bar. As always these days, she was aware of the strange ache in her gut. Hunger, one that just couldn't be satisfied with food. No matter how much she ate, she stayed hungry.

And her senses — they were in freaking overdrive. So many scents burned her nose. Alcohol. Cigarettes. Cheap perfume. Sex. Blood.

Her nostrils flared.

Blood shouldn't smell good. But, lately…the scent had started to —

"Well, hello, pretty lady…"

She didn't start in surprise. She'd known the big biker was heading her way. The guy with tribal tattoos that covered his arms and shaved head. A dozen piercings penetrated his face. And…the guy had blood under his fingernails.

She was betting that blood wasn't his.

"You all alone tonight?" he asked as he closed in on her.

Allison kept her chin up. Elsa, the witch who'd found her, had promised that Allison would find a guide in this bar. A protector who would help her on the rest of her journey. Elsa had said that her guide would come to Allison immediately. The witch had also told her that he'd be the strongest guy in the bar.

Allison could sure use some strength to help her out. Especially since she didn't have any of her own to speak of at that moment.

She licked her lips and studied the guy before her. *Big, check.* Definitely strong, but…

But he scared her. His eyes were hot, almost feral as they slid over her body.

Allison realized she should say something. "Uh...I'm...waiting for someone."

"Don't have to wait no longer." He reached for her hand. Pulled her up against him. Allison was barely five foot three, and this guy towered over her. "I'm right here, baby."

Laughter followed that comment. The guy had friends in this place—a lot of them by the looks of things. And they were all watching her now.

Why weren't there more women in the bar? Allison counted two in the whole place. Her and a chick who was—*leaving*.

Okay, that wasn't good.

She put her hands on the biker's chest. "Are you...are you my guide?"

He laughed, a hard burst of sound that grated in her ears. "Oh, yeah, baby, I'll guide you all right." His hands dropped to her ass. "I'll guide you all night long."

Crap. This guy wasn't *him*.

The biker was pulling her even tighter against him now, and she was trying to get away but she wasn't strong enough.

Story of my life.

She hadn't been strong enough to save her family. Hadn't been strong enough to stop the death.

Not strong enough to—

"Let her go."

The voice was low, but it cut sharper than a knife, and the hard order pierced through the laughter in the room.

Because she was staring up at the brick wall of a biker's face—a face that looked like it had actually hit a few brick walls over the years—she saw the fleeting expression of fear that whispered over his features.

"Thain." The hands holding her eased as her captor bit out the name.

Allison hadn't even seen the new guy yet, but if he was scary enough to make the biker tremble...

Trouble.

"She's mine, Griggs." Lethal words accompanied by the hard thud of footsteps as the Thain guy stalked closer. "So I'll say it again, but only once more...*let her the fuck go.*"

No one seemed to be breathing in the bar. No one-including her. Allison's lungs burned, but in that moment, she was too afraid to move at all. Griggs slowly, *very* slowly, released his hold on her. "Wasn't gonna hurt her. Just gonna give the pretty lady some fun."

She bet they had different ideas of *fun*.

"Allison." Now that hard, dark voice of Thain's was saying her name. If he knew her name…he had to be her guide. No one else should know her in that place. "Come here."

She eased around the biker, took a step, and froze.

Because Griggs looked a hell of a lot more safe and welcoming than Thain did.

He was big, probably taller than Griggs, and far more muscled. His shoulders just…stretched. Allison swallowed. His muscles had the black t-shirt he wore pulling taut over his chest and arms.

His eyes were dark green and burning with intensity. A thick scar slid from the top of his right eyebrow all the way down to the underside of his square jaw. The scar just made him look…

Scary. Extremely scary. No—actually, it was the eyes that did that. Eyes that promised hell would be coming.

"Don't know if she wants to go with you," Griggs said. His hand came up to clasp her shoulder. "You can always stay with me, pretty lady."

Allison sucked in a deep breath and stepped toward Thain. Her gaze slid over his face once more. This time, it was his mouth that caught her stare.

She took another step. The biker's hand fell away.

Thain's lips, strangely both cruel and sensual, were parted a bit to reveal the edges of his white teeth.

Her gaze lifted again. His hair, a shade darker than her own locks, was thick, heavy, brushing back from the strong lines of his face.

"Touch her again," Thain warned, "and you'll lose the hand."

Everyone backed up a few feet.

Even Griggs. She heard the fast scuttle of his feet.

She was almost close enough to take Thain's offered hand now. Almost.

Allison saw Thain's nostrils flare. His eyes narrowed and swept over her. When he glanced back up, there was no mistaking the fury in his stare.

His hand began to lower.

No.

Allison grabbed his hand and held tight. "I've been waiting for you," she said.

A muscle jerked in his jaw. Then he pulled her forward. His scent — a little wild and with the richness of the forest clinging to him — wrapped around her. Allison stared up at him and tried not to show her fear.

She wasn't supposed to be afraid anymore. This was the man Elsa had told her about. The man who would end her nightmare.

She just had to trust him.

"Let's get out of here," Allison whispered. They could leave. Go someplace safe. Then maybe she could finally stop feeling like death stalked her every minute.

This man...*he* could stop death. To her, he looked like he was strong enough to stop anyone and anything.

His arm wrapped around her shoulders. He led her from that godforsaken bar and out into the still night with the moon that hung high in the sky.

Her heart raced so fast, she could feel it thudding in her chest.

He paused and glanced down at her. "You're afraid of me." His voice was still a deep rumble.

Allison managed a nod. Despite her efforts, she couldn't help it. She couldn't—

"Good," he told her as he pushed them into a dark alley.

Whoa, wait—*good?*

In the next instant, he had her shoved against the alley's wall. "You should be scared." His face came toward hers. Dangerous and threatening in the faint moonlight. "You should be damn well *terrified.*"

Allison's body shook.

"You're being hunted," he told her, "stalked. There are people who want you dead."

"I...I know." Some had wanted her dead for years.

He leaned in closer. Odd. His teeth seemed sharper than before. "And you just blindly walk off with me? How the hell do you know I'm not one of the assholes who wants to kill you?"

She didn't know that. But she wasn't stupid. Or crazy.

Allison slipped her concealed knife up to press against his heart.

Okay, maybe she was a *little* crazy. "If you're the guide that the witch sent to collect me, then you'll be able to tell me her name."

She drew in a breath and could almost taste him because he was so close.

Actually she *wanted* to taste him. What in the hell was up with that?

Allison pressed her knife harder against his chest. Not hard enough to break the skin, but hard enough to show that she meant business. "Tell me her name." So she could trust him. So she wouldn't have to be alone any more. "*Tell me.*"

He glanced down at the knife. A faint furrow pulled between his brows as if he were trying to figure out a puzzle.

"Elsa," he breathed the witch's name slowly. "Elsa sent me to you."

Her heartbeat began to slow. Her knife slid away from his heart. "Then it is you." Big, scary, tough — yes, she'd take him, please. He'd keep her safe. "You're the one who has been sent—"

He ripped the knife from her hand. Tossed it to the ground. And in the next second, his hand was at her throat. Only...something was wrong. Something sharp had burst from his fingertips.

Claws?

He had *claws* at her throat. Why would—

"I'm the one she sent," he growled. "I'm the one who's here to—"

A shout broke the night. Not so much a shout, but more a bellow that was her name.

The watcher. She'd only been in town a few hours. Had he already caught up to her?

Thain's head whipped to the right. His nostrils twitched. "Vampire." He said the word like a curse.

Because it was.

Most thought vampires weren't real. Just stories to tell in order to frighten children.

She'd been a scared child once. She'd seen the vampire that came into her house. That fed on her family.

Not just a story.

"We have to get out of here," she whispered. "*Now.*"

Thain glanced back at her, frowning.

Why wasn't he moving? Did the guy want to get eaten by vampires? That wasn't exactly the best way to go.

He stepped back. Well, that was something. Movement. Then Thain shook his head and stared at her like she was some kind of mental case. Yeah, she'd seen that look before. After her parents were killed, she'd tried telling the cops about the vampires. Only the cops hadn't believed her. They'd just given her the *look* that said she was insane. The same look Thain was giving her now.

So not time for this.

"*Allison!*" That roar again. Closer this time. Coming too near.

A growl rumbled in Thain's chest.

Uh, okay.

Then he caught her hand and they started to run. Not away from that yell. Oh, sweet baby Jesus, they were running *toward* it.

Allison dug in her heels. "We can't! Stop!"

But it was too late. The blond vampire had rounded the corner. He rushed at them with fangs bared.

Thain leapt forward and drove his claws — yes, definitely claws, *very* definitely — right into the vampire's throat.

Using those claws, Thain lifted the vampire up and tossed him back through the air. A good ten feet through the air.

Allison realized her jaw was hanging open.

The vampire thudded into the side of the alley. Blood gushed from his throat as he shoved his hands up to cover the wounds. He tried to speak, but only a gurgle slipped from his lips.

A gurgle, and more blood.

Thain lunged for him again, but vampires were fast—so fast.

The vampire leapt up and raced away.

For an instant, she thought that Thain would give chase. Instead, he turned to her, breath heaving, claws still out.

His green eyes were glowing.

"What are you?" Allison whispered.

He smiled. His canines had lengthened to razor sharp points.

"Scared?" he mocked. She couldn't even hear the vampire's footsteps anymore. He'd run too far, too quickly.

Allison shook her head and hurried to Thain's side. She knew there was a whole lot more to this world than met the eye. Vamps were real, and she'd heard stories of other monsters lurking in the dark.

Right then, she didn't really care *what* Cade was…all that mattered was that he'd just rescued her ass from the vamp. Laughing, she threw her arms around him. "Thank you!" He could do it. He could keep her safe. Elsa had been right. This man—*he* was the one she needed.

The one man who could help her.

Thain stiffened in her arms. His whole body felt rock-hard. She glanced up and stared into eyes that were too bright.

Slowly, his arms closed around her. His head lowered toward hers.

She actually thought her hero might kiss her. Even wilder, in that instant, she *wanted* him to put his mouth on hers.

Sensual and cruel...how would he kiss?

But Thain pulled back. He took her hand and led her through the alley and to a motorcycle that waited in the shadows. He climbed onto the back of the bike and glanced over at her. "If you come with me, there'll be no going back."

Allison slid on the bike behind him. Her thighs hugged his even as her arms curled around him. "I have nothing to go back to."

Only death. But Thain...he offered her life.

The motorcycle's engine snarled, and they raced forward into the darkness.

***

Elsa LaSpene crept slowly through the night. She didn't head into the bar. No point. Her prey would be long gone by now.

She closed her eyes and inhaled. The sweet scent of blood had her smiling.

Fresh blood.

She slid deeper into the alley. There. Against the wall. The dark stain of blood could be seen in the moonlight. Her fingers lifted and touched that perfect wetness.

So fresh.

The little pureblood hadn't lasted long. Not long at all. Not once the wolf had gotten his hands on her.

He'd taken Allison from the alley, just as he'd promised. Taken her, but blood had already been spilled.

The wolf had started his fun early.

"You'd better make it hurt," Elsa whispered as she tilted her head back and gazed up at the moon. *"Make it hurt."*

CHAPTER TWO

Fuck. Fuck. Fuck.
Cade drove the motorcycle deep into the forest. Allison held on tight behind him. Her body was soft, warm.
Human.
That witch had lied to him. Set him up. Dammit. He hadn't signed on for killing a human.
Not one that smelled like roses and looked like the sweetest sin he'd ever seen.
Not her.
The motorcycle roared as he pushed it faster. Faster.
Soon the trees thinned, and he saw the stark outline of his cabin. Small, but made with heavy wood that could stand against the rough winters, he'd thought the cabin would be the perfect place to hold the vampire.
To kill her?
His fingers clenched around the handlebars. Cade turned off the motorcycle and shoved down the kickstand. He didn't speak at first because the

rage choked back any words that he wanted to say.

"Thanks for getting us out of there," she said, and, hell, even her voice was sexy. Smooth and soft, with a slightly husky edge that made him think of tangled sheets and warm flesh. "Thain, I—"

He turned toward her. "Cade."

She blinked her wide, fuck-me bedroom eyes at him. "What?"

His enhanced vision let him see her perfectly in the dark. So he could easily read her confusion. "The name's Cade. Cade Thain."

And why was he even talking to her? She should have been dead by now.

But…

But he was rising off the bike, taking her arm and leading her toward the cabin like they were on some kind of damn date. And she came right with him. Her steps double-timed it to keep up with his, and her long, dark hair brushed his arm as they walked.

Lamb to the slaughter.

He shoved open the door. She slipped right over the threshold, never even hesitating. Just blindly walking in. Trusting him.

That trust pissed him off.

Slamming the door behind him, Cade pounced. In less than a second's time, he had her body pinned to the nearest wall. He had his hands on her — *damn, she's soft* — and his fangs were ready to rip and tear.

Only…he wasn't ripping anything.

She gazed up at him. The light from the hallway spilled onto them, and he saw the faint ring of gold that circled her pupils. That gold around her eyes was one sign that marked her as a vampire pureblood.

He caught her left hand. Yanked it up.

"Cade!" Allison yelped. "What are you—"

The mark was there. A blood-red rose, nestled in her palm. A real particular birthmark.

Pureblood.

Fuck.

"You're not human," he told her. Unfortunate — for her.

Her eyes widened even more. "Uh, yes, I am." She jerked against his hold. He just lifted a brow and kept right on holding her.

"Who sent you to that bar tonight?" Cade asked her, but he already knew the answer.

"The same witch who sent you." Allison huffed out a breath. "M-my friend, Elsa. She told me you would be there — that you'd guide me to safety and—"

He started laughing. "You don't have any clue, do you?" No wonder the witch had been so certain.

Allison stared up at him, the long tangle of her hair sliding over her shoulders. Her skin was pale—so pale, just like that of most vamps, but her body was warm. She was small and curved just the way he normally liked women to be—with pert breasts, flaring hips, and an ass that could make a man beg.

And her face...*beautiful*. Not that he'd had a whole lot of beauty in his life, but he knew it when he saw it.

He saw it then in the high sweep of her cheekbones. The soft slide of her nose. The heavy lashes that covered her eyes—and in the delicate chin that angled up in the air.

Allison Gray was a beautiful woman.

A beautiful, soon-to-be dead woman.

Hell. He could feel Allison's heart racing against him. She was afraid again. That should have been a good thing.

Why did her fear piss him off? It angered him just as much as her blind trust. The scent of her growing fear seemed to burn his nose.

"Vampires are chasing me," she told him. He'd pushed her hands back against the wooden wall. "That guy in the alley—he's been after me for months."

Yeah, Cade bet he had.

"They want me dead."

*Un*dead.

"Elsa said you'd help me." Her lips trembled. Wide, full lips. Flushed dark red. Plump. Those lips were so close to his.

The beast within began to snarl. "She lied." Blunt. Brutal.

Best to go ahead and tell her. Best for her to know…

Her tongue swiped out and licked a slick trail over her bottom lip. "Wh-what?"

Take. The beast inside roared. Cade brought his mouth closer to hers. What would it hurt? Just one little taste…

Her eyes were so very blue as they stared up at his. Not cold like the witch's had been, but filled with a tangle of emotion.

Her lashes began to lower.

His lips pressed lightly over hers. Allison didn't fight. Didn't try to turn her head away.

Her breath whispered out, and he pulled that soft gasp into his own lungs, taking her taste with that breath.

Sweet.

He'd take more.

He kissed her again. Harder. Deeper. Her lips parted and…and she let him in. His tongue thrust past her lips and into the warm cavern of her mouth. His body pushed against hers, so close he could feel the tight tips of her nipples and the wild beat of her heart.

Innocence and sin. One woman shouldn't taste like both.

She did.

Allison met him, kissing him with a wild, hot need as a moan built in her throat. Kissing him…because the woman thought she was safe with him.

That he was some promised protector.

His claws began to stretch.

He let his fangs rake over her lower lip.

Allison froze in his arms.

Time for her to understand exactly what was happening. Cade lifted his head. Gazed into her eyes. "I'm not here to keep you safe." His words were growled, the snarl of a beast.

Her gaze slid from his, searching the darkness of the cabin that waited to the left, then to the right.

"No one followed us out here." She'd come so willingly. She could have screamed back at that bar. Asked for help. Begged for help.

Maybe Griggs would have fought for her.

Perhaps some other dumb asshole would have played white knight.

Slowly, he released her wrists, but he didn't step back. "There's no one to hear you scream out here, sweetheart."

Allison flinched. "Wh-why would I scream?"

He brought up his hand and let his claws slide down her cheek. She needed to stop seeing him as some kind of damn hero and see him for what he really was.

"Your Elsa didn't send you to me for protection." He paused. Watched because he knew the horror would come. "She paid me to kill you."

And since Allison looked so incredibly delicate, so innocent and *human*, he wasn't expecting the blade of her knife to shove into his chest.

He glanced down, stunned, and realized that when they'd been in that alley, she'd stopped to retrieve her weapon. He'd been fighting the vamp, and she—

His blood dripped down his chest, and Allison shoved him back with very *un*-human strength. He flew back and crashed into the opposite wall. She gazed at him with desperate eyes, stunned, scared, then she rushed for the door.

The screen door slammed behind her as she fled into the night.

Taking his time, Cade rose to his feet. The knife had missed his heart by a good three inches. And it wasn't even silver.

Amateur hour.

He yanked out the blade. Stared at the bloody metal, then broke it with his tightened fist.

She was running from him now. Running fast into that dark night. Pity. She wouldn't realize just how much he enjoyed the hunt.

The beast always liked to chase prey.

Cade let the change sweep over him, brutal, hard, as his bones popped and broke, reshaped and elongated. Fur sprang along his skin, and when he opened his mouth to cry out to her, a howl filled the night.

Time to hunt.

***

When Allison heard the long, angry howl, she glanced back even though all her instincts screamed...*Keep going. Hurry.*

Her savior was her executioner. Allison stumbled away, plunging for the thick shelter of the trees. If she'd known how to hot-wire the motorcycle she would have jumped on it and fled, but, dammit, she didn't have that skill set.

Her side heaved as she raced through the woods. Her legs burned, but she pushed herself as fast as she could go. There was no safe place for her anymore. No one to trust. Even Elsa had sold her out.

Elsa...the woman who'd come to Allison when she'd stood, crying, over her parents graves in that cold cemetery. Elsa had promised friendship.

But tried to give death.
Lying witch.

Another howl shook the night and she whipped around, following that sound.

Oh, hell. A big, black beast of a wolf charged after her. Too big, freaking *huge*. And he was running too swiftly.

She lurched to the right, tripped over a fallen log, and hurtled down the hill, spinning again and again and slamming into the earth with each painful turn.

When her body finally stopped hurtling, she was face-down on the ground. Every part of her hurt and…

"Allison."

Her head jerked up. Elsa stood there. Lying, scheming Elsa. Smiling.

"Guess the werewolf has already started his fun…"

Werewolf. Then she heard it—the thunder of the wolf's approach as he raced down after her.

"He's going to rip you apart." Elsa stood near two twisted, gnarled trees. "And I can't wait to watch."

Allison made it to her feet. Nothing felt too broken. Maybe. But she was trapped between a witch and a wolf. *A freaking werewolf.* She'd heard plenty of stories about the werewolves. Dangerous, more animals than men. And she had to fight one of those beasts? Without a weapon? "You were supposed to help me!" Screw this. She wasn't standing around to—

Elsa lunged at her. Grabbed her and held on tight. Elsa's nails sliced into Allison's arms. "You think you'll take my power? My life? You won't," she gritted, spittle flying. "You won't take a damn thing from me." Her nails dug deeper. "But I'll take *everything* that you are."

The wolf snarled, and Allison actually felt the hot stir of his breath behind her.

Elsa twisted her around and shoved Allison back toward the wolf. "Rip the vamp's throat out."

"*I'm not a vampire!*" Couldn't the chick *see* that?

And could the wolf even understand her now?

Her breath heaved as she stared at him—at green eyes she'd never be able to forget. No wonder Cade's teeth had looked so sharp. His teeth, his claws…

All the better to freaking kill me with.

"Rip her apart!" Elsa shouted the words with feverish excitement. "*Rip. Her. Apart.*"

Allison didn't move.

The wolf stalked closer. She'd stabbed him. Shoved him—and the guy had hurtled pretty far when she'd hit him back at the cabin. Maybe she could hold him off. Hold them *both* off, just long enough to—

The wolf leapt forward.

Allison screamed. She couldn't help it. She wasn't brave and super kick ass, and she didn't want to die, she didn't want—

The wolf pushed her behind his body and faced off against the witch. He'd shoved her back with his powerful paws, and Allison found herself on the ground again.

The wolf was so big that she could barely see around him, and she rose quickly to her knees in order to get a better view.

The witch wasn't smiling any longer. "What in the hell are you doing?" Elsa screeched.

The wolf glanced back at Allison. His green eyes—glowing, so wild—seemed to see right through her.

Bones began to snap then. To break, to crunch. The sounds were horrific, and Allison wanted to turn away, but she couldn't.

Watch him. Her legs trembled as she stood.

Fur melted from the wolf's body. Golden flesh and toned muscles appeared. Naked male. Powerful. Primal.

He rose to his feet, still making sure to keep his body between her and the witch.

"She's not a vampire yet." His voice was rougher, harder than before.

Allison bit her lip to keep from speaking. He *knew* about her infection?

"It doesn't fucking matter!" Elsa snapped back at him. "Kill her!"

Two against one. Bad odds. Especially when one of those two was a werewolf.

Her mouth had gone desert dry. Her nails dug into her palms, and her body locked as she waited for Cade's next move.

He spared her a glittering glance over his shoulder. *Please.* She didn't speak the word, but she sure thought it and knew the plea had to be reflected in her eyes. *Don't kill me.*

Did his head incline? Did she imagine it?

"Kill her!" Elsa yelled.

"No." Cade's response. Low but fierce.

And Allison didn't know who was more shocked.

The wind began to whip around them in heavy bursts that caught Allison's hair and lifted it into the air.

"I *paid* you!" Elsa thundered at him. "We had a deal."

"You paid me to kill a vampire." The guy was naked and still damn dangerous. "Right now, she's just a lost human."

She was a scared-as-hell human who had a bit of hope stirring in her chest.

When she craned her neck, Allison caught sight of the red-faced witch. "She'll change!" Elsa's hands were fisted on her hips. "Just a few more days, and she'll be—"

"Then I'll see about killing her," he said with a shrug.

And that simply, her hope faded.

Elsa lunged forward, coming at Allison with a scream. But Cade caught her and tossed her back. "You're not touching her," he growled.

Allison shivered at the threat lacing those words.

"If you won't do it—" Elsa began.

Now Cade was the one to laugh. "You *can't* kill her. If you could've done the job, you never would have come crawling to me."

Uh, why couldn't the witch kill her?

"So get the fuck out of here, witch, and I damn well better not see you again." He lifted his hand, and claws had broken through his fingertips. "If I do, you may just be the one to die."

Allison backed up a step and a stick snapped beneath her feet. But the wolf and the witch didn't glance her way.

"You'll pay for this," Elsa promised.

Cade just shrugged again, clearly not worried. What did it take to worry a werewolf? Not threats from a witch, obviously…

"She'll turn on you. The minute the hunger strikes her, she'll feed on you…*just like the others.*" A heavy pause. "But maybe you like that. Maybe you like just being fucking food for the vamps!"

Elsa yanked away from him, chest heaving. "You've made the wrong enemy." Her blonde hair rose in the thrashing wind. "Soon enough, you'll both die."

The wind whipped in an even wilder frenzy. Allison struggled to stand and —

And Cade had her. He pulled her tight against his chest as the wind seemed to scream and rake her flesh. He held her close, his warm body a solid anchor against the fury.

Then, in the next instant, there was only —

Silence.

His fingers curled around her chin and forced her head up. Allison stared into his eyes, not knowing what to say. Because the werewolf she was looking at just might be her savior…or he could be her worst nightmare.

CHAPTER THREE

"You're...not going to kill me?" Allison asked softly from her position in front of the fireplace.

Cade buttoned the jeans he'd donned and headed toward her. Her scent pulled him in—no one should smell like that.

Good enough to fucking eat.

Her gaze darted to his face, then dropped to his chest. Her lips parted when she saw his scars.

He'd be willing to bet she didn't have a single scar on that soft, silken body.

She glanced away, too fast, and his jaw locked. The woman had better start getting used to the way he looked. If she wanted to keep living, he was her only shot at survival.

Why? What the hell am I doing?

Helping her hadn't been the plan...had it?

She looked at him again, locking those fuck-me blue eyes on his.

The wolf within started to growl.

"Why are you making that sound?"

So maybe the man was growling, too. Vamps weren't the only ones who liked to use their teeth. Right then, he was real tempted to bite.

He could start on her shoulder. That delicate spot where neck and shoulder met. He could mark her and—

"S-stop staring at me like that." She hunched her shoulders and pulled up her blanket. "Either you're gonna kill me or you're not."

Those weren't the only choices he had. What about fucking? Where did that fall on her little to-do-list?

"I can leave, you know. Go out that door, and you won't ever have to see me again."

She didn't get it. Cade lunged forward, grabbed her arms, and lifted her up against him. The blanket fell to the floor. Her lips parted as she sucked in a startled breath. "Without me," he told her flatly, "you *are* dead. You've been marked for death by a witch."

Her eyes caught his—trapped him. Fuck. A woman's eyes shouldn't make a guy feel like she was stealing his soul with just a glance.

He forced his hands to ease their too tight grip on her. "Since I didn't kill you, you can bet that she'll just send someone else to finish the job."

"*Why?*"

"Because vamps aren't exactly loved, sweetheart. Humans and supernaturals, hell, we all want to stake them."

She shook her head and her hair brushed over his arms. "I-I got infected and—"

At that, he laughed and stepped back, freeing her. "Is that what you think happened?"

Allison nodded quickly. "When I was a kid...vampires killed my parents. They tried to kill me—when they bit me, th-they must have infected me—"

Had Elsa told her this BS?

"If we can just find me a cure..." Allison continued, voice desperate, "I'll be okay. Whatever's happening...it can stop. It stopped for years. Nothing happened to me until just a few weeks ago—"

She had no clue. "You're not infected." The vamps who'd attacked her had no doubt realized the truth about Allison with one bite. They would have tasted the power in her blood. "You're a pureblood."

Allison blinked. "I'm a what?"

"A human who is born to the call of blood. You don't have to get a blood exchange in order to change. You're one of the rare few who will change on your own."

She shook her head at him again. Right. Why believe what he had to say? Figured. He exhaled on a rough sigh. "That family of yours that died,

I'm betting they weren't your *real* family, were they?"

"They sure as hell were!"

Ah, now she was showing some bite.

He cocked his head as he studied her. "Easy. I meant, they weren't your *blood* family, right?" No way two humans could have created her. That wasn't the way purebloods were made.

Her jaw tightened. "I don't have any clue who my birth parents were, okay? All I know is they dumped me on the steps of a hospital and never looked back."

"To leave a pureblood behind, they probably *couldn't* look back."

A furrow appeared between her brows. *No clue.* He tried to explain by saying, "Purebloods are rare. Only newly turned vamps can have kids, and they don't just toss 'em out." No matter what else you could say about the vamps, they protected their own. "Your parents…"

She watched him with troubled, lost eyes, not speaking.

Cade exhaled. "I'm guessing they were being hunted, and if they never came back for you that means…"

They died.

Her lashes lowered, and he knew she understood. Her throat worked as she swallowed, and, still not looking back at him, she said, "I-I can't be…"

Deal with it. Life sucks, sweetheart. It's a lesson we all learn. "You are. In just a few days, you'll be kissing your human life good-bye." Then what was he supposed to do? Stake her? Cut off that pretty head?

No.

Her cheeks grew even paler.

But it was best that she go ahead and understand this now. An infection? Not for her. "You're gonna change. By the time the full moon rises, you'll be a vampire."

"I can stop it! Elsa said there was a cure, I can—"

"There is no stopping it for you. Elsa just set you up to die."

She flinched at his words. Right. The truth could hurt, huh? Better to shatter all her illusions now. "There's no cure. There's not a damn thing you can do to stop the change."

Her body trembled.

"You *will* be a vampire." His hand lifted, and traced the thick scar that circled his neck. A scar that he'd received when he'd been too young to readily pull forth the full wolf within. "And then…"

"Then?" Allison whispered.

"Then you'll go for the throat of any asshole dumb enough to get near you."

"You—you…*hate* vampires." Her eyes had fallen to the hand that slid across his scar.

He stared at her, caught by her words. "Yeah, I fucking do." Fury broke beneath the words. He hated those parasites and wanted them all in the ground—so why was he standing there, talking to her, *wanting* her?

Offering to protect her?

Cade spun away. "Stay the night. You'll be safe here." He'd know if anyone tried to sneak onto his land.

"Thank you." Her whisper followed him.

Cade glanced back. She'd wrapped her arms around her stomach. She stared after him, looking lost.

Fuck.

"Don't thank me," he growled. *Don't thank me because you don't know what I'm going to do yet. You don't know what I want.*

Soon enough, she would.

***

It was the same nightmare she always had. Allison *knew* it was a nightmare, but she still couldn't wake up. Her parents were dead around her, their blood staining the white carpet a dark red. Her neck hurt, and she could feel the wetness sliding down her skin.

Her blood.

"We'll be seeing you again..." The vampire told her, smiling with a flash of his blood-stained

teeth. "Grow up for us, get strong...*we'll be seeing you again.*"

Because she was one of them. *Just like them.* She'd kill, torture, listen to her prey scream—

"*Wake up, Allison.*" Hands were wrapped around her arms, shaking her not-so-gently. "Dammit, wake up!"

Her eyes flew open, and she found Cade crouched over her. She almost screamed again.

Just in time, she managed to stop herself. "I— is something wrong?" Her heart thudded in her chest and her voice came out far too husky.

She was in the bed. His bed. He'd taken the couch and offered his room to her.

A nice gesture for a killer.

"You were screaming."

And now she was awake, in bed, mostly naked, with a bare-chested werewolf crouching over her. "Bad dream," she managed.

Cade grunted. Was that supposed to be a sympathy sound? He started to pull away.

She grabbed his hand.

They both froze then. Suddenly, the air seemed very, very thick. And he seemed even...bigger than before.

"You want to let me go," he said the words softly, but she heard the order in them.

She didn't let him go. "You're not the hard-ass you want me to believe you are." Hard-ass killers didn't comfort you when you had a nightmare. Hard-ass killers didn't give you their beds. They didn't—

One second. That was all it took. He had her flat on her back as his body crushed hers into the mattress. His lips were on hers, not soft and gentle—wild, hard, rough.

He didn't kiss like a new lover. He kissed like a man taking what he wanted.

Me.

She couldn't pull away. His hold was too strong. But—

But she didn't want to pull away. Allison let her lips part even more, and she kissed him back, loving the hot surge that heated her veins. She'd been alone and afraid for so long and now—*I want him.*

His mouth jerked away from hers. "What the hell are you doing?"

She licked her lips. Tasted him. *Wild.* "Kissing you?" Sure, she might not be the most experienced chick in the world but she did have some skills.

"Why?"

Uh, shouldn't that be—

"Do you like to play with fire? I want you..." His voice had roughened, deepened so that it sounded like the rumble from a beast, "and werewolves aren't exactly known for their control."

Her hand rose and traced one of the twisting scars that crossed his chest.

Cade's muscles stiffened at her touch. "You *don't* want to—" His words broke off as his head jerked to the right. She saw the slight flaring of his nostrils as he scented the air.

"Cade?"

He didn't look at her. Just stared toward the dark window. "Company."

Cade leapt out of the bed and raced for the door. Allison grabbed for her clothes and yanked them on as she stumbled after him.

Then she heard the growl of motors approaching. At least two. Oh, crap, this wasn't good.

She grabbed Cade's arm. "Wait!"

He spun to face her.

"You don't know what's out there—"

"Two trucks. Seven dumbass humans. I can smell 'em." He inhaled and offered a grim smile. "And those humans are about to get an ass beating."

Okay, so he *did* know.

Cade stalked outside. He was still bare-chested, and the guy didn't even look for a weapon to take with him. She didn't know much about werewolves, but no way were they indestructible.

Allison rushed after him, yanking down her shirt. The trucks had just braked to a halt, and dirt danced in the air around them.

Cade stopped on the small porch, braced his legs apart and kept his arms loose at his sides. "Griggs!" He called out. "You dumb bastard, you don't want to get in this battle."

Griggs? The guy from Blood Bath? Like she'd be forgetting him anytime soon.

The truck door opened, and sure enough, Griggs poked his shaved head out. "For enough money, I'd gut my own mother."

Lovely.

The men climbed out of the trucks. Cade had been right about their "company" after all.

"The money's *real* good," Griggs continued as he began to edge toward them. Oh, damn, was that a wooden stake in his hand? "Too good to pass up. Not my fault if you went all pussy weak."

A quick glance showed her that Cade's claws were coming out.

"What?" Griggs demanded. "Did you decide to spend some time screwing the target? I mean, she's hot, but not worth the—"

Cade lunged forward, and when he moved, in that instant, Allison saw the flash of metal. A gun. The jerkoff sidling up behind Griggs had a gun that he was aiming at Cade.

Had Cade even seen the weapon?

She screamed a warning and leapt toward Cade. Leapt—and moved faster than she'd ever moved in her life. Faster than a human *could* ever move. Her body slammed into his, and she knocked Cade out of the way even as she felt a fierce burn lance her skin.

She hit the ground, stunned, and realized that her side was still burning. Allison glanced down and in the growing dawn light, she saw the blood seeping through her shirt.

"Fucking *wrong* move," Cade snarled.

Her head lifted, and she saw him charge for the gunman. One twist, and he'd broken the man's wrist. Cade grabbed the gun, and fired two quick shots at the two men coming from the second truck. They fell, screaming.

I know the feeling, assholes. Allison pushed her hand against the wound as she tried to stop the flow of blood.

Griggs just kept standing there with the stake clutched in his fist.

"You're a fool," Cade snarled the words at Griggs. He tossed the shooter against a tree. The guy moaned and fell to the ground. "You come out here, and you think a bullet's gonna stop me?"

Griggs backed up a few steps.

Cade stalked after him. "Because you know about the supernaturals, you think that makes you some kind of bad ass slaying machine?"

Allison managed to get to her feet. She only swayed a little, and the blood was slowing, wasn't it?

She blinked, and Cade had Griggs pinned against the truck. All of the men Griggs had brought with him were on the ground, moaning in pain.

Cade's fingers, no, his *claws*, were at Griggs's throat. "Come after me again," Cade warned, "you're dead. So much as *look* at Allison wrong…and *you're dead.*"

Oh. Allison swallowed. He was protecting her again. If he didn't watch it, she'd definitely start to think he had a soft spot hidden beneath those claws and fur.

"I'll rip you open," Cade continued, voice grim, "and cut your heart right out of your chest while you scream and beg for me to stop."

Maybe not such a soft spot.

"Now get the fuck out of here," he ordered. "And make sure every hunter in the area knows…*stay away from what's mine.*"

Wait—hold up—did she qualify as his?

Cade stepped back from Griggs. Griggs hauled ass for his truck and his men, wounded, bleeding—*their blood smelled sweet*—limped after him.

The trucks roared away, fish-tailing it through the woods.

Slowly, Cade turned to face her. "Why?"

She lifted her hand and saw the blood on her fingertips. "Because you couldn't die for me."

He stalked toward her. "I wouldn't have."

Well, that seemed harsh. She'd saved his butt. Didn't that count for anything in his mind?

His nostrils flared. "Wolves like the scent of blood."

So did vampires.

He was almost upon her now, and she could see the sharp edge of his canines. "It usually makes us want to attack," he said in that lethal voice of his.

Allison barely managed to swallow the lump in her throat as she looked up at him. *Don't attack. Down, wolf. Down.*

He'd said his control wasn't that good. She sure didn't want him losing control right then.

His hands flew out and grabbed the edge of her t-shirt. He yanked the bloody fabric, ripping it. His breath hissed out. Or was that hers?

"The bullet's still in you."

Her knees almost buckled at that.

"It's still in you..." His green gaze measured her, and he said, "and you're on your feet."

So she was. "I wanted to...help you."

He just stared at her for a moment. His gaze searched hers. For what, she didn't know. Then he shook his head. "Let me help you now." And he picked her up, lifting her easily into his arms.

Maybe it was stupid, but she felt…safe…in those strong arms.

"This is gonna hurt," he warned her as he carried her back inside the cabin. "But you can't heal until that bullet comes out."

Her head rested against his shoulder. It seemed natural to put her head against him. To let her body soften against the hard strength of his chest.

She took a deep breath and tried to ignore the pain lancing up her side. "You said…blood usually makes you want to attack." *Please, no attacks for the next, oh, hour or so.* Not until she was back to better fighting form.

He slammed the door behind them and headed for the bedroom.

She wasn't letting this one go. "Wh-what does my blood make you want to do?"

Cade lowered her onto the bed. He ripped away the rest of her shirt, leaving her clad in her black bra. His fingers slid up her side, a gentle touch that she hadn't expected. A caress? That soft touch was *almost* enough to make Allison forget her question. *Almost.*

But having a werewolf so close to her when she was weak and bleeding…*Focus.* "Cade?" Allison breathed his name. What if the scent was too strong? What if his beast took control?

He looked up at her, and his green eyes were glowing with the power of the wolf.

Chill bumps rose on her arms.

"Your blood…the scent…" His jaw clenched, and he gritted, "It makes me want to kill."

Not good.

"It makes me want to tear apart those bastards—to make damn sure that they can't ever hurt you again."

Her lips parted but Allison realized she didn't know what to say.

"Now scream if you have to," and his sharpened claws hovered over her wound, "because this is gonna hurt like a bitch."

CHAPTER FOUR

She screamed.

The sound pierced right through him. The wolf howled inside of Cade, but his fingers were rock steady as he drove his claws into her wound.

His left hand pressed against her stomach, holding her in place on the bed, while his right hand dug into the torn flesh.

Tears leaked from the corners of her eyes, but after that first scream, she didn't make a sound. He glanced at her, only for a moment, and saw that Allison was biting her bottom lip to hold back her cries.

Should have killed them.

Why the hell hadn't he?

Because you didn't want her to think you were a monster.

He found the bullet. Held tight to it and felt the burn on his flesh. Smoke rose from his fingertips and drifted from her body.

"C-Cade?" Her voice was soft and scared. "What's happening?"

He pulled out the bullet. The flesh on his fingers was bright red and already blistering. He tossed the bullet onto the nightstand. "They used silver."

Should have killed them.

Those bastards hadn't just been after Allison. Elsa had sent the humans to take *him* out.

Allison's wound began to close, right before his eyes.

"It feels...strange," she whispered. "Tingling..."

Because the flesh was mending. She was so close to the change now, so close to becoming fully vampire, that her body had already prepared for the shift.

Vamps could heal from nearly any wound. Because they were such fast healers, they were often damn hard to kill.

There were only three ways to kill a vampire—fire, beheading, or a stake to the heart.

No wonder Elsa hadn't come after Allison on her own. The witch literally wasn't strong enough to kill her.

But I am. A werewolf's claws were the perfect weapon to behead a vamp.

He realized that his fingers were caressing her stomach. Sliding lightly over the flesh. His gaze lifted, met hers.

Want her.

"You...protected me." Who'd ever done that before? And why the hell had *she* done it? He'd told her that he'd been sent to kill her, and the woman had still gone ahead and taken a bullet for him.

Why?

Allison stared back at him.

Fuck. He rose. Left the room.

"Cade?" Allison called after him. He liked it when she said his name. Liked it when she touched him. When her scent surrounded him. "Don't leave," she said, the words quiet, but he heard them perfectly.

His chest ached. "I'm not." He went back into the room with a wet cloth held in his hands. She was sitting up now, and her breasts pushed against the cups of her bra. Damn fine breasts.

Cade's cock shoved against the front of his jeans, but he yanked back the lust.

For now.

Carefully, he put the wet cloth over her side and washed the blood off her skin. Creamy, smooth skin. The wound was all but gone. Vamps and their amped up healing powers. She'd have no scar to bear, not like him.

Scars covered far too much of him.

He glanced up and found Allison staring at the scar that sliced down his cheek and curled under his jaw. Cade's back teeth clenched.

Then she lifted her hand and touched the rough skin. "What happened to you?"

Sympathy. Pity. He didn't want either from her. He tossed the cloth onto the nightstand. It covered the bullet. "Nothing I couldn't handle."

He expected her to drop her hand. She didn't. Just kept right on touching him, and the lust that he'd tried to hold back grew stronger with every second that passed.

Her heady scent filled his nose. Her body was so close, waiting for him. And she was touching him. Stroking his cheek. Staring up at him with those big, blue eyes.

She knew how dangerous he was. The lady should be hauling ass away from him.

Not—

"Tell me." Her words were husky, whispered, and they slid right over his flesh better than any silken stroke.

Fine. Not like it was some deep, dark secret. His story had been talked about in bars. Whispered in the woods. "When I was fourteen, vamps attacked my pack."

Her hand stilled on his cheek. Her eyes didn't look away from his.

"I was too young to shift, but too damn big to be seen as anything other than a threat that they had to eliminate." He'd always been big. But being big didn't matter when you were up against a vampire's enhanced strength.

"Before they got around to that eliminating..." He exhaled and remembered the scent of burning flesh. "They thought it would be fun to torture me."

He saw the delicate movement of her throat as she swallowed. "Your face."

Cade couldn't help it. He laughed at that. Then he rose and made sure the light fell on his body. There would be no shadows to hide him any longer. He hadn't taken the time to put his shirt back on before heading out to face Griggs and his gang. No shirt to cover him. No darkness to cloak the old wounds. "Sweetheart, my face was just the start."

He turned around, real slow, making sure she had time to see all the marks that twisted his flesh.

Nothing nice or neat about him. The vamps had used silver knifes to peel away his skin. Then they'd used liquid silver to burn his muscles. To burn and burn until agony had been all he'd known.

He kept his back to her and stared straight ahead at the wall. The vampires had been laughing as he screamed.

"But I stopped them," he said, still remembering. Still seeing. "I got out of the chains." Out of the silver that had held his wrists so tightly. "At the first light of dawn, when they were weak and I was strong, I got out, and I killed every one of those fucking bloodsuckers." With the claws that had finally sprang from his fingers. The pain, the fury — something had brought on the change in him. The wolf had burst to the surface that blood-soaked day, and his claws had ripped into his prey.

"But it was too late for the others in my pack," he said. Far too late. "Everyone else was dead." Tossed aside. Broken.

He'd never joined another pack. What was the point? To grow close to them, to care, only to wind up one day watching them all die in another attack?

He didn't need anyone else. Didn't want anyone else. It was far better to be alone.

When Cade felt the light touch on his back, he stiffened. Not fingers on his skin — the touch was too soft. That was—

Allison was kissing his back. Kissing the marks left by torture almost twenty years ago.

He spun around and caught her shoulders. *"Don't."*

She didn't look afraid. She should. The wolf was far too close to breaking free. "Why not?" she asked him, staring into his eyes and he found he couldn't look away. "You took care of me…why can't I take care of you?"

"Because I don't want your damn pity!" His words weren't loud. Lethally soft.

"Pity isn't what I want to give you." Then she pulled from his hold, far too easily.

Barely human now. The vampire transformation was so close. Did she realize it?

Allison straightened her shoulders, and then she reached behind her back. He heard a soft snick and her bra slipped to the floor.

"I know what's happening to me."

Shit, were those tears in her eyes?

"I can feel the change. I mean, I just instantly healed from a freaking *bullet wound.* I know, okay? I *know* what I'm becoming."

Some would say that she was becoming a monster.

Just like him.

"I know what I'm becoming, but I don't know what will happen to me when—" She broke off and shook her head. Her breasts pointed up toward him, the nipples tight and hard and a pretty pink.

Want to taste.

His cock was so hard that it hurt. He wanted *in* her.

"I don't care what's going to happen tomorrow. I just care about right now." Her hands dropped to the front of her jeans. They were undone. *He'd* undone them in his frenzy to repair her wound. "Right now, I want you."

That was all he needed to hear. Before she could say anything else, before he could think of a reason why this was wrong, Cade had her flat on the bed. His body trapped hers, and his mouth tasted one sweet breast. And it was sweet. Sweet and tight and perfect in his mouth.

Perfect.

Her hands slid over his back. He didn't tense when she touched his scars. Didn't try to pull her hands away from the marks he'd always carry.

He just sucked her breast harder. Lapped at her nipple. One, then the other. His hands shoved down her jeans and yanked her panties away.

She wanted him.

He didn't know how the hell he'd gotten that miracle, but he wasn't about to turn her away.

In that moment, there wasn't a single force on earth that would have made him leave her.

***

"You want him dead, witch?" Griggs swiped the blood from his nose as he glared at Elsa. "Kill him your own damn self. We're not goin' back. Not facin' that fuckin' freak again."

Elsa glared at him and his worthless bunch of humans. These were supposed to be hunters? More like whipped puppies. "One man," she snapped. Her hands flattened on the table. Her mirror, the scrying mirror she'd used since her eighteenth birthday, gleamed upon the table's surface. "You let one man defeat all of you?"

"Not a man." Griggs spat blood on the floor. "Werewolf."

"Werewolves can die." Everyone and everything could die.

"You're on your own." Griggs turned away.

Her hands fisted. "I'll double the money!" She was running out of time…and options. Vampires were closing in. They were already in the city. It wouldn't be much longer before they found Allison.

Griggs hesitated. Greedy bastard. Sometimes, humans could be so predictable. Elsa started to smile.

"That guard dog she's got…" Griggs glanced back over his shoulder and shook his head. "If we go back, he'll kill us all."

She could almost smell his fear. Rancid.

"You're on your *fucking own*." He stormed out, taking his men with him. Their thudding footsteps blended with the wild racing of her heart.

No, no, this couldn't be happening. Not to her.

Elsa grabbed her knife. One quick slice over her arm and she had blood dropping onto her mirror. With her index finger, she slid the blood over the mirror's surface as she chanted.

The image came to her, not slow and blurry, but fast and crisp.

Her future hadn't changed.

The full moon hung in the air. Allison stood over her, with her vampire teeth bared. Allison's eyes were wild, and blood dripped down her chin.

Elsa stared at the image. *No change.* Allison would still kill her in just a few days' time. When she changed, when she became fully vampire, Allison *would* come after her.

"I'll kill you first," Elsa whispered. That's why she'd first sought out Allison. Because of the death vision. She *would* change that vision.

She had to.

Elsa wasn't planning on dying for some vampire bitch. Allison would be the one to die. She'd be the one to bleed and beg and scream and *die.*

"Not me," Elsa said as she reached for the knife again.

She just had to find a way to hit the vampire's weakness. Everyone had a weakness, even a pureblood vampire.

You're the one who'll die.

CHAPTER FIVE

Allison's breath heaved out as she stared up at Cade. His arms were on either side of her body, his hands pushing down into the mattress as he caged her in place.

Lust and stark need etched hard lines onto his face, and his broad shoulders seemed to block out the light around them.

She was naked beneath him. Naked…and she could see the sharp edge of his teeth.

And the glow of the beast that lit his eyes.

Maybe she should have been afraid then.

But her head lifted and she met him in a hot, open-mouthed kiss. Her tongue slipped inside his mouth and tasted him. The werewolf's power wasn't scaring her.

It was turning her on.

Her hand fisted in his hair as she pulled him closer. Allison had enjoyed a handful of lovers in her life. The first few had been fumbling, the others more skilled.

Yet right then, she couldn't remember any of their names. Couldn't pull up their faces.

Only Cade.

She sucked on his lower lip. Heard his growl and felt her body tense in anticipation.

This wasn't going to be some gentle ride. No sweet release.

Good. She wanted fire and passion. Wild pleasure.

Him.

Her lips slipped from his, and Allison kissed her way down his neck. His pulse raced beneath her lips, thudding in time with his heartbeat.

Blood.

She licked him. Bit lightly.

Blood.

Allison turned her head away, squeezing her eyes shut as she fought the dark impulse to drink from him. That wasn't what she wanted. She wanted—

The bed shifted as he moved, sliding down her body. His fingers were rough, strong, as he pushed her thighs apart. Then those fingers were sliding up, stroking right over the core of her need, and a gasp broke from Allison's lips.

"Look at me," his growl.

Slowly, her eyes opened and her head turned toward him.

"What do you see..." His fingers pushed inside her. Stretched her. Thrust and made her want more. "When you look at me?"

She saw the man she wanted.

"Monster?" His fingers withdrew. Thrust deeper. Her hips lifted helplessly against him as she arched off the bed. "Or man?"

Allison licked her lips. "Man." But what did he see? When he looked at her what—

"And I see the most fucking beautiful woman I've ever met." He pulled his hand back. Yanked open his jeans and positioned his cock at the entrance of her body. "*Beautiful.*"

He made her feel that way.

"I'm safe," he told her, voice rough and deep as he fought to hold his desire in check, and his gaze seemed to burn even brighter. "Werewolves can't carry any diseases. Neither can vamps."

She already knew that, just as she knew pregnancy wasn't a risk for her, not then. Could a vampire and a werewolf even have a baby together?

Cade waited at the entrance of her body. She felt the broad shaft of his cock and she wanted him inside but…

"No fear," he told her.

Allison shook her head. She didn't fear him. Right then, she just wanted him. "Now, Cade. *Now.*"

Her wolf smiled and drove into her. He filled her, so full and thick, and Allison realized that she'd forgotten to breathe. He stilled for a moment, letting her adjust, and when she tightened around him, wanting *more,* Cade withdrew—then thrust in again, *harder.*

Her nails dug into his shoulders. She wanted hard. Wild. *Him.*

Each slide of his flesh sent need twisting through her. Her sex was so sensitive, stretched, eager.

Pleasure beckoned just out of reach.

The bed squeaked in time with their rhythm. Thrust. Withdraw. Thrust. Stronger each time. Deeper. Wilder.

Allison laughed. It just felt good. *He* felt good. Her nails dug deeper. Her legs wrapped around him, pulling him closer.

Cade's mouth was on her neck. No, not her neck, but right at the curve of her shoulder. She could feel the edge of his teeth.

Maybe she wasn't the only one who liked to bite.

And…and she liked the feel of his teeth. Allison tilted her head back and pushed harder against him.

Harder.

The climax hit her, slamming right through her body so that her breath choked out and pleasure rocked her. Not gentle. Not easy. So fierce that the room dimmed. Aftershocks trembled through her sex as ripples of release tightened her around him.

And Cade came. She felt the hot release inside of her even as his teeth nipped at her shoulder. He shuddered and his hands held her so tight.

As if he'd never let go.

His heartbeat raced. She could feel it against her. Drumming far faster than hers ever could. He was so warm around her. Warm and strong and solid.

In his arms, she was safe. Nothing could hurt her. No one.

Not while she was in his arms.

He pressed a soft kiss to her shoulder and lifted his body as he stared down at her.

She didn't want the moment to end. Not yet. Allison didn't want to talk. Didn't want to worry about what or who would be coming for them next.

Right then, she just wanted to pretend that the rest of the world didn't matter. Just a man and woman — that's all they were.

No monsters.

No darkness.

Just a man.

She pressed a kiss to his chest.

And a woman.

Cade began to thrust again.

***

She was gone. Cade knew he was alone even before his eyes opened. The bed felt cold. Allison's scent was weak, barely hanging in the air.

She was gone.

Growling, he jerked up in bed. The woman never should have been able to give him the slip. If he hadn't spent half the day screwing her until he fell into an exhausted sleep, she damn well *wouldn't* have gotten away.

He leapt from the bed. Didn't she know how dangerous it was out there?

She needed him.

And he…fuck it, he wasn't letting her get away from him. He grabbed his jeans, yanked them on, and followed the faint trail of her scent in the air. *Roses.*

He threw open the screen door, and it banged against the side of the cabin. She hadn't taken the motorcycle. That was something. But then, he'd taken the liberty of hiding the keys.

His head turned slowly, and he stared at the thick line of trees. At the mountains that waited.

She'd gone off alone. Fuck.

Didn't she realize? There was no place that she could go — no place that he wouldn't follow.

He'd had one taste, and he wasn't about to let his little pureblood go.

***

Elsa stood in the clearing, smiling. Her mirror had shown her just what she needed to see — Allison, running. Allison, scared and desperate.

The fool didn't fully understand what was happening to her body. She didn't know about vampire weaknesses.

She was about to find out. And a vampire running in the day…she might as well be human. Elsa could take out a human any day of the week. She'd been wrong to think that Allison was too powerful for her to handle alone. She could destroy the pureblood vamp. She *would*.

Elsa lifted her arms and called forth her magic. The spell of fire was always the first mastered by her kind. The first, and the most powerful.

The flames began to spread to the trees around her. The fire leapt from branch to branch, jumping through the forest. Soon, the fire would sweep out into a giant circle that would surround the fleeing vamp-to-be.

Surround Allison and trap her. The fire would close in. Slowly. *Slowly*.

The wolf had done his job after all. He'd lured Allison from the protection of the city. Got her into the wilderness where she was helpless. And soon…

Soon the fire would take her.

Elsa would make sure she stayed close enough to hear the bitch's screams.

***

The scent of smoke reached her, thick, cloying, and Allison froze. Her heart thudded wildly in her chest, pounding hard enough to shake her.

She turned slowly. The smoke…it was coming from the right. Allison could see the dark streak of gray in the sky. A forest fire? Hell, that couldn't be—

Flames crackled. But that crackling came from behind her, to the left.

Her gaze jerked toward the sound.

More smoke. More fire. And that blaze looked like it was racing right toward her.

No…no…

"Allison!" The roar was her name. A roar loud enough to push across the crackling fire. "Allison!"

Cade was coming for her.

She spun around, seeing only smoke and fire now. So much. Too thick. She began to cough. This…wasn't right. The afternoon had been fine moments before. Clear. Calm. *She'd* been the one running wild and—

"Allison!"

She choked, but managed to cry out… "Cade!" And, oh, damn, was that fire racing toward her?

She jumped back, barely avoiding a wild surge of heat. The fire was so close now. It seemed to be heading right for her.

Because it was. Understanding was like ice in her veins.

Freaking witch.

There wasn't anywhere to run. The flames were all around her. No, not just around her.

Allison screamed when fire licked its way up her arms. She dropped to the ground, rolling and slapping at the flames. But more flames just came, burning her, *burning...*

"I've got you."

She was still screaming so she barely heard the words. He had to tell her three times, then Allison managed to glance up.

Cade was there, pulling her against his chest. And it hurt. She hurt. Deep blisters covered her skin, and the smell of burnt flesh — her flesh — had her stomach rolling.

"Hold on," he told her as he rose, tucking her body close against his. The movement hurt, but she locked her teeth to hold back the cry.

A wall of fire blocked them. There was nowhere to go. No —

He bent his head over hers. Curved his body so that he was covering her, and he leapt right through the flames.

Allison heard the rush of the fire—a wild *whoosh* of sound—and the burning breath of the flames blew over her body.

Then they both hit the ground. They fell in a tangle of limbs, spinning, rolling, falling down a hill. Faster, faster.

She didn't feel the bumps. Didn't feel the bruises. But when they fell into the too-chilled water of a lake, oh, sweet hell, yes, she felt that.

And she just sank beneath that cold water. Her eyes wanted to sag closed. Why was that so wrong? She'd rest a few moments in the sweet cold, then everything would be fine.

Something grabbed her. Her eyes flew open. Through the murky water, she could just make out Cade's form. He looked furious, his eyes glowing. His hands wrapped around her shoulders, and he pulled her toward him. A powerful kick from his legs sent them shooting toward the surface. Allison couldn't get her own legs to move and was grateful for her wolf's strength.

And it was only when they broke the surface and when his gasps for breath filled her ears that Allison realized…

I'm not breathing.

CHAPTER SIX

Fuck, fuck, *fuck no.*

Allison's eyes were wide open. Staring straight at him, but the woman wasn't *seeing* him. She wasn't breathing. Her body was ice cold.

A shudder shook his frame as Cade lowered her to the ground. "Come on, sweetheart," he muttered as he pushed back her wet hair and ran his fingers over her face. "Breathe for me."

Blisters and deep burns covered her forearms and hands. Her legs had fallen victim to the fire— he'd seen the wounds.

So much pain.

Too much.

She wasn't breathing.

He wasn't letting her go like this. *Not like this.*

He put his mouth to hers. Damn she was cold. Her lips were like ice against his.

Cade blew into her mouth. *Take my breath, sweetheart. Take it.*

Nothing.

He gave her his breath again. *Come on, Allison. Don't leave me.*

He pushed air into her mouth once more.

And she jerked beneath him. His head lifted and he stared down at her, desperate, wild.

She'd coughed up water and seemed to be breathing now. Her eyes actually *saw* him. But she was still so icy. So pale.

And hurting so much.

His canines had stretched when he'd first caught the scent of smoke. The wolf within had known that danger stalked Allison. His claws had come out, his teeth had prepared to rip and tear—he'd been ready to do anything in order to protect her.

Anything.

He lifted his hand and slashed his wrist with his teeth.

"C-Cade?" Her voice was a broken whisper. "Why…don't hurt…"

He put his wrist to her mouth. "Drink." Because if she didn't, he could still lose her.

Allison shook her head. "N-no." Her body shook, trembling hard, and he knew shock when he saw it.

Fire was a particular bitch for vampires. They burned far faster than humans. Faster than any of the other paranormals.

But you knew that, didn't you, Elsa? He had to deal with that witch. Payback.

After he made sure Allison wasn't checking out on him. "Take it," he ordered, staring into her eyes. The gold was almost gone now, never a good sign with a pureblood vamp. It meant her body was too depleted.

But she turned her head away. "I...can't. I don't want to be..."

A vampire.

Screw it. "No changing what we are." He knew the scent of his blood had to be driving her crazy. He'd seen her nostrils flare. Oh, yeah, she liked that scent. "So either drink or die."

Her head slowly turned back toward him. He could see the fear in her gaze. And the desperation.

He could also see that just beneath her too-pale lips, her fangs were growing.

With every second that passed, Allison lost her mortal self. Before his eyes, she was becoming more.

Vampires are the enemy. That had been his line for years. *Parasites. Good only for killing.*

Slowly, her mouth pressed against his wrist.

The only good vamp...

She didn't look like a parasite.

Is a staked vampire.

Her tongue slipped out and licked the blood. Her eyes were open, on his. At the first taste of his blood, he heard the sharp inhale of her breath.

She likes it.

She licked up another drop of blood.

Her eyes were still on his.

But…

A tear streaked down her cheek. Not a blood tear, and usually those were the only tears a vampire could shed. Allison still shed human tears as she took his blood.

"More," he whispered because she hadn't taken enough blood to heal her wounds. Not even close.

Her mouth pressed harder against him and when he felt the scrape of her teeth, Cade expected the memories to slam into him. Another bite, another time.

Torture.

Screams.

Hell.

But…but he only saw her. Saw the gold come back into her eyes. Saw the wounds begin to fade from her body. He didn't feel like prey.

Her mouth on him—damn, it felt *good*.

No pain. A pleasure he'd never expected to feel from a vampire's bite.

Fuck. He was getting turned on while a vampire fed from him.

Her teeth sank into his wrist. She sucked harder and damn if his cock didn't swell even more.

The rush of pleasure had his breath panting out. This wasn't just about saving her any longer. Now he was the one who wanted more.

Cade hadn't gotten enough of Allison when he'd had her in that bed beneath him. Maybe he'd never get enough.

His hand tunneled in her hair. Not to force her away from his wrist, but to hold her against him. To make her take more.

When she licked him again, it was like a shot of pleasure right to his cock.

Want.

But not there. He forced his head to lift, and he gazed at the smoke billowing above them. That witch was out there, she could come at them anytime, she could—

"Cade." Allison's voice wasn't weak now. He glanced back at her. She'd pushed against him, let go of his wrist, but she stared at him with hunger in her eyes.

Not hunger for blood.

Lust.

For vampires, those two needs could intertwine so easily. That was why some vamps and their fancy-ass vamp councils had started to spread the PR in the paranormal world about their kind not taking directly from living prey.

Like he bought that bullshit.

Her tongue swiped over her lips. Dark red lips. The burns were already gone from her body. The woman was gonna make one dangerously powerful vampire.

No, not make. She already *was* powerful.

Her hand rose. Touched his lips. "I want you."

And he wanted to be buried in her as deep as his cock could go.

But first… "We need to get out of here." Because he could hear sirens coming. Like anyone could ignore a blaze this size. The humans would rush in and fight the flames. Their trucks were already so close that his ears picked up the hard growl of the approaching engines.

If he let Allison stay there, the witch could try again with her fire and fury. The humans could get caught in the cross-fire.

He gazed down at Allison. Her dark hair was wet around her, and her clothes clung tightly to her body. A body he'd learned so well with his hands and mouth.

A body he'd know again.

"Come on…" He pulled Allison to her feet. Watched her carefully. After her first feeding, he wasn't sure what to expect. Her standing there, looking increasingly lost…that wasn't it.

He pulled her close. "I've got a back-up motorcycle stashed close by. Don't worry." His lips pressed a quick kiss to her temple.

And he froze.

Shit. *Shit.* What was happening to him? How could he care so much about what might happen to a vampire? About how she might be *feeling* for fuck's sake?

His back teeth clenched.

Screw it. He kept a tight grip on her arm and raced for the hidden motorcycle. He jumped on the bike, and she climbed on behind him, sliding close and putting those never-ending legs of hers alongside his. When the engine roared to life, they leapt forward, driving fast and hard through the woods. With every minute that passed, Cade realized just how dangerous Allison truly was to him.

Dangerous…because she could make him *care.*

Sonofabitch.

***

Something was wrong with her. Very, very wrong.

It wasn't just the drinking blood bit. Oh, hell, she'd actually done that. The blood should have revolted her.

Instead…

It had tasted better than any champagne she'd ever had.

Cade's blood had been so good, and it had made her *hungry.*

For him.

She ached. Her nipples hurt, wanting his touch so badly, and with every vibration of that motorcycle…

Cade.

Allison wanted to scream with the frustrated need building so wildly inside of her. This wasn't normal. This wasn't right.

And her fangs hadn't gone away.

Her fangs were out and her fingernails had sharpened up like mini-claws.

Cade parked the motorcycle in front of what looked like your average no-tell-motel. She followed him quickly to the front desk, wondering about the fierce looks he kept sending her.

Did he realize that she was barely keeping it together? That she was seriously considering throwing the guy down on the ground and jumping him?

What is wrong with me?

She'd never been like this.

The balding guy behind the counter didn't even give them a second glance. So what if she was still wet and her clothes were mostly burned? He just scooped up Cade's money and tossed them a key. About thirty seconds later, they were entering room number 16, and Allison was trying hard to hold onto her control.

The door clicked shut behind them.

Want.

The whisper in her mind didn't even seem to be her own. It felt too strong. Too dark.

Her eyes squeezed shut. "This isn't me."

The floor creaked as Cade stalked closer. "It's who you're gonna be."

"Don't." The word was a snarl, but this was wrong. Her claws, her teeth — she could *hurt* him. If he touched her, Allison's control would shatter.

Can't hurt him.

But she had to get herself under control. Had to quench the fire that was building —

Her eyes flew open. Without glancing at Cade, Allison lunged across the room. She rushed into the miniscule bathroom and yanked on the shower's cold water. That was what she needed. A good, cold shower and everything would be fine again. She'd cool down. Pretend she was back to normal and *everything would be fine.*

Her burnt clothes hit the ground. Naked, she stepped into the shower. The water hit her, hard and stinging and —

Cade's hands wrapped around her shoulders. He turned her around as that pounding water slid over her flesh.

He'd shed his clothes and he stood before her, naked. He stepped into the shower.

Fighting herself, she backed up. Allison could feel her control splintering and she knew, right then, she *knew* that she was becoming someone else.

Something else.

In an instant, she grabbed Cade and pushed him back against the rough tiled wall. "Don't."

She barely managed to speak. "I can *hurt* you." Her words were close to an animal's growl.

But her werewolf laughed. "Ah, sweetheart, trust me on this...I can handle you."

He broke her hold. Took her mouth in a kiss that made her sex clench and her knees tremble and suddenly *she* was the one with her back pressed against that tile.

He'd reversed their positions so fast she barely had time to blink. Her back was against the tile. He'd lifted her up effortlessly, and he held her in his rock-hard embrace.

His mouth was on her throat. Licking her, sucking her flesh.

His cock pushed at the entrance of her body. *In.*

His teeth scored her flesh and she shuddered in hungry arousal. "Cade!"

The water pounded down on them. He drove into her. She gasped as he filled her, stretching her body, only to withdraw seconds later and thrust in deeper, harder than before.

Again and again.

Her legs wrapped around his hips. Her hands slid over his slick flesh. The water didn't seem so cold anymore. Not when he was burning hot against her.

Allison's teeth began to burn, stretching and sharpening in her mouth. She wanted to bite him. To taste that delicious blood once more.

She clamped her lips together and arched her hips against him.

No, no she *could* be just a woman. She could —

He pulled back a bit, kept her pinned. Then took her breast in his mouth. Her nipples were so sensitive that the rough lick of his tongue had her moaning.

Her nails raked over his skin. He growled, and she caught the scent of blood.

Her eyes widened in horror when Allison realized that she'd scratched open his skin.

Cade's head lifted. His thrusts stilled as his cock filled her. Her sex clamped around him, sensitive, eager for the pleasure that would come. His gaze held hers, and she wondered if he'd pull away.

"Go ahead," he told her, voice deep, dark, and rumbling, "bite me." A dare.

Then he withdrew…drove deep.

She bit him. On his neck this time. Hesitant at first because she didn't really know what the hell she was doing, but her sharpened canines figured it out fast. They sank right through flesh and his blood slid onto her tongue.

She came at that first taste, her body shuddering with the blasts of pleasure that had her holding him as tightly as she could.

But Cade wasn't done with her. Not yet. He kept thrusting. Stronger, wilder, and the feel of his cock sliding in and out of her sex had pleasure sweeping through her again.

Allison licked gently over the small wound she'd made on his neck. Shame lurked inside of her, but she wouldn't feel it, not then. Then she only wanted the pleasure and *him*.

Her gaze met Cade's.

"My turn."

Allison's lips parted. "What—"

He carried her out of the shower. Not withdrawing from her, but filling her as he strode back to the bed. They fell on the mattress, both soaking wet, and rolled in a tangle of limbs. Cade rose above her, and there was no mistaking the hungry lust burning in his gaze. "You're not the only one who likes to bite."

Her own eyes widened even as she reached for him.

His mouth closed over her flesh, right there, where the curve of her shoulder met her neck. She didn't know what she expected but—

His teeth pressed into her flesh, and the Allison that she was becoming—the woman who tasted blood and climaxed—her breath whispered out in anticipation.

Cade bit her. Not to drink, not like she'd done before with him. This seemed…different. More of a marking.

Claiming?

Then she stopped worrying about bites and differences and just enjoyed the feel of his cock within her.

This time, when she came, he was right with her. Growling out his pleasure and holding her even tighter than she'd held him.

In that one moment, she didn't care about what she was becoming.

She didn't really give a damn about anything else but him.

***

Elsa stared into her dark mirror. It wasn't showing her anything now. No past. No present. Nothing.

Her hand slammed into the glass surface. It cracked beneath her palm, tiny, spider-web like cracks that rippled across the surface.

Allison wasn't dead. Because of that asshole wolf. He'd given her shelter. He'd protected her. Gotten her ass out of the fire.

He should have been the one to kill Allison. Not to keep her alive. What use was an assassin if he couldn't fucking kill anyone?

She lifted her hand, not caring about the drops of blood that flew from the scratches on her palm. All the supernaturals in the area knew just what Cade Thain was. They knew how much he hated vampires.

But, now, unless she missed her guess, he was fucking one. Why else would he keep Allison alive?

Why else?

A loud crash sounded behind her. Elsa didn't move. She just kept staring into her broken mirror. Footsteps pounded up the staircase

"Where is she?"

So the vampire had finally found her home. He must be mighty pissed if he'd come out hunting in the daytime. He could have waited. Dusk was only an hour away.

Elsa didn't answer him. She didn't want to look away from her mirror. She didn't—

A snarl hung in the air, and, in the next moment, *she* hung in the air, held up by the vampire's grip on her throat. The big, blond vampire shook her like she was a rag doll and if he hadn't been choking her, Elsa would have laughed right in his face.

"Where is she?" he demanded.

Elsa knew this vampire. Charles Crawford. A vamp who'd been walking the earth for over two hundred years.

A vamp who'd been tracking Allison for weeks.

He knew what she was. Vampires could always sense when a pureblood turning was at hand. And Allison had been right there in the city with the guy just nights before. No wonder he'd almost caught her in that alley.

Would have caught her, if Cade hadn't plunged his claws into Crawford's throat. Yes, her mirror had shown her that truth, too late. It hadn't been Allison's blood dripping from that alley's walls the first night. Cade had attacked Crawford.

She smiled.

Crawford's eyes narrowed. "What have you done?"

His hold eased, just enough for her to speak. "N-not me." Her smile widened even more. "*Werewolf.*"

"That bastard? He still has her?"

"Gonna…kill her." And the perfect plan hit her. "Unless…" Her breath heaved out as she studied the vamp. Maybe he could get the job done for her.

Wouldn't that be fitting?

"Unless what?" he snapped. Poor vampire. With the werewolf hiding Allison in the woods, he wouldn't have been able to catch her scent anymore.

And he'd be wanting to find the lost pureblood very badly. Purebloods were the favored in the vamp clans.

Elsa tried to appear careless as she said, "He'll kill her…Unless you can kill him first."

Now that bit had Crawford stepping back. "Tell me where the wolf is, and he's dead."

Elsa rubbed her throat and glanced back at her broken mirror. She saw nothing, because there was nothing left to see.

The end was coming.

It won't be my end. It won't. Crawford could take out the werewolf, and she *would* find a way to kill the pureblood.

"Don't worry," she told the vampire. "You won't have to wait long." Not long at all. "When night falls, he'll come here. To you."

She didn't need her mirror to know that. Cade wouldn't wait for her to attack again. She'd studied him. Learned his habits before she approached her would-be killer. No, he wouldn't sit back and wait for another attack. He'd come after her.

And find a vampire waiting to kill him.

CHAPTER SEVEN

Vampires tore into her flesh. They cut her with gleaming silver blades, and they licked her blood from the edges of their knives. They laughed when she screamed.

And they tortured her even more.

They chained her and poured liquid silver onto her back, just so they could hear her screams.

And Allison did scream. Over and over as her flesh burned away.

She looked up, staring straight at the bastards who loved her pain, and something broke inside of her. Broke, even as the chains holding her arms broke free, and she lunged forward with a strength born of fury. One swipe, and she cut the head off the nearest vampire. She drove her claws into the throat of another. And as they fell, this time, she was the one who laughed.

"Allison!" Hard hands grabbed her, shook her.

Her eyes flew open, and Allison found herself out of that dank pit. The peeling walls of the hotel room surrounded her. She was on the bed. With Cade.

The man seemed to always be saving her from nightmares. But then, it wasn't like she was the sweet dream type.

Always nightmares.

Sweat covered her, and she could still smell the scent of her own burning flesh.

Only, it hadn't been her flesh that burned. Not really. Her trembling fingers lifted and touched the rough scars that marked Cade's face.

His pupils widened when she touched him. His hold on her gentled, but he didn't let her go.

Why not? Her hand fell away. How could he stand to have her near him? Those other vampires had tortured him for hours, days, and they'd drank his blood.

Just like she had.

"I'm sorry." Her stark whisper.

Cade frowned down at her but there wasn't surprise on his face. Just a kind of angry understanding. "The blood," he said. "Fuck, how did I forget that? Vamps don't just take blood, they take memories, too."

Allison flinched. "I-I didn't—" What? What was she supposed to say? That she hadn't meant to steal his memories? That she hadn't meant to drink his blood?

She *had* meant to do it.

Allison realized she was still naked. It hadn't mattered before, not when she'd wanted the press of his flesh against her more than she'd wanted anything else. But at that moment, she felt…lost.

She pulled free of him and yanked the sheet up to cover her breasts. Taking a breath, she asked the question that she feared, "Am I even human any longer?" She didn't feel weak. In fact, her body seemed incredibly strong right then. No blisters, no wounds. Only healed flesh.

Her heart was still beating. She still breathed. But she'd taken blood. Grown fangs. Her own version of claws.

"You were never human."

His words hurt as much as a slap would have.

Allison jumped from the bed, dragging the sheet with her.

"You were born a vampire, it just took a little while for the DNA to kick-in." His voice followed her, cold, no emotion. There'd been plenty of heat in the daytime hours. But with night, all of that seemed to have vanished. "It usually takes about twenty-five years of life, maybe a few years more, before the vamp side takes over for a pureblood."

"Why?" She needed to learn all that she could. No more denying. No more hiding.

Deal with this.

"Because the vamp genes freeze the body at its peak. They keep you strong and young, forever."

"Forever…" Or as long as she kept drinking blood. As long as she didn't lose her head or get staked.

Or die in a fire set by a sadistic witch.

"You'll keep breathing," he told her, and she glanced back to see him pulling up his jeans. *Sexy.* "Your heart won't stop. That only happens to the turned humans, and only for a little while. You were born this way…you'll stay this way."

She felt something wet on her cheek. Allison swiped the back of her hand over her face, and when she looked down, blood stained her fingers.

Humans didn't cry tears of blood.

"Wh-what about you?" She hated to ask, but she *had* bitten him, and he'd bitten her. What if she'd…changed him?

What if he turned into the one thing he hated more than anything else?

His eyes narrowed. "What about me?"

"Will you become…like me? Because I swear, I never meant—"

He laughed then, and some of the tension eased from his face. "I won't turn into a vampire, no matter how many times I'm bitten."

Her shoulders sagged.

"It doesn't work that way for my kind. We can't change but..." Now he rubbed his chin. "I have heard a story about another werewolf down in Florida..."

"What story?"

He buttoned and zipped up his jeans. "Seemed he married a pureblood vampire and by drinking her blood, the guy made himself even stronger."

Her heartbeat kicked up. Last night, she'd been only thinking about him and pleasure. But just what had Cade been planning? "Is that why you bit me?" Anger began to simmer in her gut.

Where the hell were her clothes?

Oh, yeah, right. Pretty much burned to bits. So she'd keep having this awkward conversation wrapped in a sheet.

He stalked toward her. Didn't touch her. Just came close enough that she could feel the hot warmth of his flesh. "I wasn't trying to get a power boost last night."

"No?" Crap. She sounded way too hopeful. She could play this semi-cool. "Then what were you doing?"

His jaw clenched. "Claiming you."

Um...

"I'm taking care of this witch," he told her, "I'm gonna make sure that she never comes after you again, and then..." His hand lifted. Brushed over her cheek. "Then you and I—we're gonna work this thing out between us."

"This thing?" The guy didn't exactly have a golden way with words.

He pressed a kiss to her lips. An open-mouthed-I-want-more kiss. "You want me. I'm fucking burning alive with need for you."

Okay, better. Her lips curled. A girl liked to hear some occasional sweet—or hot—things from the guy who'd fought his way past her defenses.

And into her heart?

Don't go there. Not now. Focus.

"So let's take her out," Allison said and this time, she was the one to kiss him. Her kiss lasted longer. "Because I'm tired of looking over my shoulder." She wanted to look ahead, instead.

To a future? A few days ago, Allison would never have thought that possible. But now...

What if she could have a future, with Cade?

That was sure as hell something worth fighting for.

But first...Allison caught the hand that he'd put to her cheek. She entwined her fingers with his. Stared deeply into his eyes. "I won't ever let another vampire hurt you." She *needed* to say this. To make him understand.

She wasn't like the others. No matter what happened, she wouldn't become like them.

And they'd damn well never attack him with silver again on her watch.

"So tough." His smile had her heart jumping in her chest. "I think I'm rubbing off on you."

"Maybe you are." Or maybe the vamp in her was just developing her own killer instincts.

Kill to protect what was hers? Yes, she would. Because she was definitely starting to think of Cade as hers.

"Let's find me some clothes," Allison said. There had to be some kind of store around there somewhere, right? "Then we'll hunt the bitch." And part of her nightmare would end.

Then she could deal with what was becoming, *had become.*

A monster who wasn't afraid to kill.

***

Tracking the witch wasn't hard. Once they made it back to town, Cade made short work of finding Elsa's scent trail. Actually, finding her scent was a little *too* easy. Elsa should have covered her tracks better.

He stared up at the old Victorian house near the edge of town. Lights glowed through the windows, firing out through the stained glass on the second floor.

He'd followed the scent of ash and power all the way back to this place. Elsa waited inside. But the witch wasn't alone.

The scent of blood was far too strong.

Vampires.

His wolf pushed to break free.

Allison's hand pressed against his shoulder. "What is it?"

He didn't look away from the house. He'd wanted Allison with him because he'd been afraid Elsa would trick them and attack again. Leaving Allison behind to be a sitting duck hadn't been his fucking plan.

But leading her straight into a nest of vampires wasn't an option, either.

He inhaled, catching all the scents and said, "There are four vamps in there with her." The scent of those vamps was so strong that it nearly overpowered everything else.

He caught the ragged sigh of her breath.

"Don't worry, sweetheart, they won't be a problem for long." Not once he ripped their heads right off their bodies.

Her nails dug through his shirt and into his flesh. "You can't take them all on."

The wolf was clawing to the surface now, determined to be free. "Watch me."

She didn't let go. Her hold just tightened more. "I don't want you dying for me!"

He could think of worse things to die for but… "I won't be dying tonight." No matter what Elsa had planned, "And neither will you." Then, because he had to taste her, just once more, Cade pulled her close. His lips took hers in a hot, deep kiss, and he knew he'd carry her taste with him when he faced the enemies who waited.

The only good vamp is a staked vamp.

Not his motto anymore. But those bastards who'd sided with Elsa? They were begging for death.

He pushed Allison back. The change took him then, hard, brutal, as bones broke and reshaped. He fell to the ground, body contorting, and fur burst along his flesh.

At fourteen, his first change had been a burning agony. Now, he hardly felt the pain at all.

In moments, a wolf stalked the ground, heading toward the house. Allison stayed behind him, following close. He could go in quiet, try to surprise the vamps or—

Or he could just tear them apart.

Cade leapt for the door. His powerful claws slammed into the wood and sent the door crashing inward. Before it had even slammed to the floor, Cade jumped away and swiped out at the vamps who rushed toward him.

One slash across the chest to the dark-haired jerk who attacked with fangs bared. Even as the guy screamed and stumbled back, Cade drove his claws into the chest of the vampire on the right. The red-head's eyes widened as the claws jerked inside of him, and the scent of the vampire's fear filled Cade's nose.

Kill. Destroy.

"*Don't hurt the girl!*" The vampire's bellow seemed to shake the whole house. Cade dropped his prey and saw that a big, blond vampire was rushing down the stairs, with another vamp right on his tail.

Their fangs were out, bloodlust glowing in their eyes but—

A gunshot thundered and a bullet thudded into his flesh. From the red-hot burn, Cade knew he'd taken a silver hit. His head jerked toward the top of the stairs. Elsa smiled at him even as she lifted her weapon once more.

Now he knew where Griggs had picked up his silver bullet ammo. Figured.

Allison screamed even as Cade's wolf form tore up the stairs. He slashed out and knocked the vampires out of his way. But those vamps, they weren't going down easy. The blond shoved a knife into Cade's back.

More fucking silver.

His body burned.

"*No!*" Allison's shout. "Get away from him!"

He felt the vampire jump in surprise. That shift of focus, that second's hesitation, was all that Cade needed. His head twisted, and he sank his fangs into the vampire's neck.

Another bullet thudded into him. Elsa's laughter grated in his ears.

Won't stop. Kill.

Then Allison was there. She punched at the vampires. Swiped with her own claws. *"Let him go!"*

The vampires didn't fight her. They fell back—one actually fell off the stairs, and Cade raced toward the witch. She was still smiling, still holding up her gun—

"Cade, no!" Allison's steps pounded after him.

The witch's finger tightened around the trigger.

His hind legs shoved down, then pushed him high into the air as he launched toward her. The bullet fired, scraped right by his left ear, and he slammed into the witch.

His claws sank into her flesh.

She didn't scream. Just kept laughing.

"Cade, watch out!" Allison's yell.

But the warning came too late. He'd been too focused on the witch. On the vampires. Their scents had been so strong that he hadn't noticed—

A knife plunged into his back. The pain had a howl of fury and agony breaking from him. He rolled, swiping with his claws, and Griggs—*fucking bastard Griggs*—fell to the ground, dead.

But Cade fell, too. He couldn't get up. His legs had gone numb, and the shift swept over him again in an uncontrolled rush.

Too much silver. Too much blood.

He tried to find Allison. Saw her being held by the blond vampire. She was struggling in his arms and red tears leaked down her cheeks.

She thinks I'm dying.

Maybe he was.

He still couldn't get up.

Griggs would *never* get up.

"Greedy bastard...for the right money, Griggs would always do anything." Elsa, dripping blood, eased down beside Cade. She had a mirror cradled in her hands, a cracked, blackened mirror. "I knew he'd come back...he just wanted you to be weak enough first. Likes to attack when...his prey is weak."

Too bad for the bastard...Griggs hadn't waited long enough. Cade had made sure that prick went to hell first.

"Get away from him!" Allison yelled.

Elsa didn't look her way. She leaned closer to Cade. He still couldn't move. That fucking knife lodged right in the middle of his back. Griggs had driven it in deep, all the way to the bone, and when Cade had spun to kill the human—

I just drove it in deeper. When his back had hit the floor, the hilt had broken off, and the silver blade was lodged deep within him.

"What did you think would happen?" Elsa whispered as she clutched her mirror. "That you'd save her? That you'd get to keep her?"

Forever. He'd wanted a chance, a shot at—

"She would've stayed young for centuries, and you would have wasted away." She held up the mirror to him. "See what would have been — *see it!*"

Cade stared into the mirror. He saw the future that had waited for him and bellowed in maddened fury.

CHAPTER EIGHT

That bitch wasn't killing Cade. Allison jerked, twisted like a snake, and drove her claws—*not nearly as fierce as Cade's*—into the blond vampire's stomach.

He barely grunted. His eyes, too blue and bright, glittered down at her. "Don't worry, we'll keep you safe."

Screw that. Like she believed a word he said.

Gritting her teeth, she pulled back her fist and slammed it right into his chest.

She heard something break. Luckily, it wasn't her hand.

The vamp's eyes widened. "Pureblood," he whispered as he fell back a step.

That step was all she needed. "You aren't killing Cade!" She'd promised that vampires wouldn't hurt him again, and now he was up there, not moving.

Dying?

No.

"Cade!" She spun away and jumped up half the stairs.

But the blond vampire moved faster than her. He blocked her path in an instant. "I'm like you. Born to the blood, I can help you...show you..."

The witch was next to Cade. Her werewolf was shouting, but his body wasn't moving. Dammit. "I don't want you to show me anything! I don't want anything—just *Cade!*"

Surprise slackened the vampire's face. "He was...hurting you...holding you captive..."

She slammed her body into his. The vampire crashed into the wooden railing. "He was keeping me safe." The wood began to splinter. "From all the murdering vamps who wanted me dead."

The wood gave way.

The vampire didn't try to fight the fall. He just plummeted to the hard floor below.

Allison grabbed a chunk of broken wood from the stairs. She rushed up toward Cade and the witch. "Get your ass away from him!"

Elsa turned around, her eyes were wide, and, oh, yeah, Allison saw the fear flash in her gaze. "You want to take me out so badly?" Allison snarled. "Then here's your chance!"

But Elsa backed away. She dropped a mirror, and the heavy chunks of glass shattered at her feet.

"Better save him..." Elsa told her as she edged back. "With that silver lodged in his spine, he could be dead in seconds."

Allison froze, the wood gripped tightly in her hand.

Elsa was still backing away. Going for another weapon? Preparing for another spell attack?

"Unless he doesn't really matter to you…" Elsa threw out, taunting her. "Unless you *want* to watch him die."

Cade was trying to crawl toward the witch. His legs weren't working—because of the silver in his spine.

She wouldn't leave her wolf helpless.

Never.

Allison rushed to his side. The wood dropped from her hands as she reached for his back.

"I thought so…" The witch's nearly purring voice said. "I knew your weakness."

A rush of wind filled that second-story room. Allison caught the sharp edge of the silver and ignored the pain when it sliced her flesh. "It's okay," she whispered to Cade. "I've got you. You're going to be—"

The wind rushed harder, beating on her like hands, and a wooden stake burst through her chest.

Allison didn't let go of that broken knife. She glanced down and saw the bloody edges of the wood. The same wood she'd brought up to use as *her* weapon.

That rushing wind, it had been Elsa, using one of her spells…she'd moved faster than Allison could see. The witch had come up behind her and—

"Got your heart, bitch," Elsa told her.

Allison yanked out the silver blade. She heard Cade's fast inhale. *He'll be okay now.* "No…" She managed to tell the witch even as every breath sent pain pulsing through her chest. "You didn't."

The makeshift stake had gone from her back all the way through the front of her chest, but the witch had shitty aim. She'd missed Allison's heart.

Allison rose to her feet, swayed, but managed to stay upright.

Elsa scrambled back. "No, *no!*"

A stained glass window waited behind her, one designed to show the beauty of a blooming red rose. But with the moonlight spilling through that glass, it appeared as if the witch were surrounded by blood.

She would be, soon enough.

Allison stalked slowly toward her. Every move *hurt,* but she wasn't giving up. Wasn't stopping. Her hands, already bloody, caught the edge of that stake. Slowly, inch by inch, she pulled it out. Then she held her weapon gripped tightly in her fist.

"Why?" Allison asked because she had to know. "Why did you… come after me?" Her fangs were fully extended, and she wanted to tear Elsa's throat wide open. *I've become the monster…and I don't give a damn.* Not then. Then, she wanted the strength that being a vampire gave her. "I never…never would have…"

"You were going to kill me!" Elsa screamed, backing away even more. Her elbows bumped into the big, stained glass window. "I saw it!"

Allison shook her head. That small move had the room spinning. Blood soaked her clothes.

"I tried to change it…" Elsa glanced around the room with bright, almost feverish eyes. "I *have* to change it." Then she glanced over her shoulder, back through the stained glass, and the witch started to laugh. "The moon's not full…it's not time yet! You can't kill me!"

Watch me. Full moon or no full moon, Elsa was dying. Allison wasn't gonna give the witch another chance to attack.

Behind her, Allison heard bones snapping and popping. Cade. Shifting. Healing. Her breath eased out slowly. *He'll be all right.*

Elsa wouldn't be. "I am going to kill you," Allison told her quietly, hands fisting. "You won't get out of this house alive tonight." She wouldn't give Elsa a chance to come at her again or to come at Cade.

"I had to save myself!" Elsa's face flushed bright red as they faced off. "The mirror—I saw what you'd do! I saw—"

Screw the mirror. "*You* made this happen. *You* started it all. But I'll end it." Then, using every bit of strength that she had left—which wasn't a hell of a lot—Allison jumped forward, diving right for Elsa. She shoved the stake at Elsa's chest. "My turn." The stake sank into Elsa's flesh. Then Allison grabbed the witch, and she shoved her back into that stained glass window as hard as she could.

The glass shattered, raining down to the ground, and as Elsa fell, Allison yanked her hands back.

But the witch didn't let her go. Elsa's hands had clamped around her, and Allison was too weak then to break free. She'd used her last bit of strength in the attack and—

Elsa pulled her through that broken glass. The shards sliced into Allison's skin. They fell, glass covering them, surrounding them, and the wind whipped past Allison's body.

Then they hit the ground.

***

When Allison went through that window, Cade leapt after her. He'd just shifted back to human form, and he rushed for the window as quickly as he could, bellowing her name.

Not fast enough.

So when the witch pulled her through, Cade followed them right down to the ground below. Their bodies hit the earth with a sickening thud, and he leapt down just behind them, his knees barely buckling when he landed on his feet.

Glass littered the ground. Blood stained the earth. "Allison?"

She was face-down, half on top of the witch. His heart froze in his chest. He stepped closer. "Allison?"

At his voice, her head rose slightly, and his heart started to race in his chest. He could see the blood on her cheek. The scratches. She pushed up slowly as she stared down at the still form of Elsa.

The witch hadn't survived the fall. Maybe it was the stake in her chest that had killed her. Or the twisted angle of her neck. Either way, Elsa wouldn't be hurting them or anyone else ever again.

He reached for Allison and lifted her gently into his arms. He noticed that, hell, yes, dammit, his hands were shaking. *Fear.* "Don't ever fucking do that to me again." He'd seen the stake go into *her* chest. Had thought for one lost, desperate moment that she'd been dying.

Won't lose her.

He pulled her closer. Held her tight. He'd seen what waited in the mirror. What the future held for him and—

"Werewolf."

And the fucking vampires were back. Could no one just leave them the hell alone?

Snarling, Cade pushed Allison behind him. He'd deal with these jackasses and then get her some place safe. Warm.

Then he'd make love to her all night long. Until he forgot what it was like to fear that death could steal her from him while he was helpless to do anything but just watch her die.

One leap forward, and Cade had his claws at the big, blond vampire's throat. Cade knew the lead asshole when he saw him. "Ready to lose that head?" One swipe, just one, and he'd be rid of the bastard.

"I'm not here…" The vampire didn't seem particularly afraid. Obviously a dumbass. "To hurt her…or you."

Bullshit.

"Elsa said…" The vampire swallowed and Cade sliced his throat, a small, warning slice. More would come. "She said you were the threat…that you were sent to kill Allison."

Plans had fucking changed. Everything had changed for him from that first moment in the alley, when he'd looked into bright blue eyes and realized that he still had part of his soul left.

A soul and a heart. He should have killed her, but Cade had only come alive when he met her.

Allison slid her small hand over his shoulder. Cade forced himself to take a breath. The urge to strike was so strong that he trembled but...

But the vampire wasn't making any move to attack.

"You got your Intel wrong," Cade snapped. Okay, fuck, he had been hired to kill Allison, but that plan had changed day one. He'd become the man who'd stand between her and any threat that might be out there.

Kill her? Hell, no. He wouldn't even so much as bruise her skin. Right then, all he wanted to do was take her away, give her his blood, let her heal—

Then make love to her until he stopped being afraid that she'd slip away from him.

Death, you can't have her. So fuck off.

"No one takes her from me," he said, the words a vow. He hadn't found her just to lose her. Wouldn't happen. If he had to behead this vamp to prove it...

He was ready to slice.

"I mean her no harm." Blood dripped down the vampire's throat. "I thought...that night in the alley, I thought you were the threat."

"He wasn't," Allison said as her fingers pressed against Cade's shoulder.

Her voice was weak. *She needs blood.* His blood. But as much as he wanted to turn and scoop her into his arms, he didn't move. Not yet.

Cade kept his hold on his prey.

The only good vamp…

"I have no quarrel with you, werewolf," the vampire told him. The guy's cronies had come outside, but they stood just in front of the house, wisely deciding not to interrupt right then.

Smart. They might keep their heads.

"I know who you are," the guy went on. "And I know what you did to that nest in Oregon who made the mistake of fucking with your pack."

The rage built within Cade.

"If you hadn't killed them," he added, "then my team would have. We don't tolerate rogue groups, and we sure as hell don't make a habit of torturing children."

The guy looked sincere.

But vampires could lie.

As easily as witches. Werewolves.

Humans.

All were good. Bad. None were perfect.

Allison stroked Cade's shoulder. "You might know us, but who the hell are you?" She wanted to know.

Cade risked a glance her way. Bruised, bloody…so beautiful. The dumbass vampire probably thought so, too.

"Charles Crawford. I'm on the Northwestern Vampire Council."

Big deal. Vamps and their councils. He knew all about them. The councils were *supposed* to keep the vamps in check. Stop them from killing humans.

Keep 'em on a leash.

From what he'd seen, those fancy councils did jack and shit.

Crawford glanced at Allison. "I was sent to protect you."

"Then you arrived a bit late to the party, buddy," Cade drawled. "Very late."

Crawford's jaw clenched. After a moment he said, "I vow that I won't hurt her," the vampire said, "or you."

He'd like to see the fool try.

"Truce?" The vampire asked.

Oh, that grated and —

Allison swayed beside him. Cade lunged for her and caught Allison just before she would have fallen. Her skin was ice cold.

Her eyes were closing.

"No, sweetheart, don't you even *think* of leaving me." He held her gently, like the fucking precious thing that she was. He cradled her head and pushed her toward his throat. "Drink, Allison." *Take everything you need.*

Because he wasn't letting her go.

CHAPTER NINE

A gasp came from a few of the assembled vamps when Cade offered his neck to her. Yeah, he got it—werewolves didn't usually offer themselves up as food to a vamp. He sure as hell wouldn't to anyone but her.

He felt the press of her small fangs against his skin, a quick slice that was too fast for pain, then a surge of pleasure hit him as she began to gently suck on his neck.

He held her tighter and lifted her easily in his arms. As she drank from him, he faced the vampires.

Crawford watched him with blood still dripping down his own neck. Mild curiosity lit the vampire's eyes. "So…it's like that."

"She's mine." And he was hers. Forever.

Crawford inclined his head. "Do you know…" He seemed to hesitate, but then he asked bluntly, "Have you taken her blood?"

Same old song and dance. "We both know werewolves can't become vampires, so don't worry, I'm not about to turn." He tensed when

Allison's tongue licked over his skin. What he wouldn't give to be alone with her then.

"You won't turn…" Now Crawford's eyes had narrowed. Filled with speculation. "You'll just become…more."

He already knew that. He'd seen his future in the mirror.

Allison's tongue swiped over his neck once more. "I'm okay," she whispered. "You can put me down now."

He rather liked her where she was.

"There's another vampire and werewolf pairing, down South." Crawford motioned to his men, and the others began to walk away, back into the darkness that surrounded the old home. "He's become more, too."

"More?" Allison asked, voice stronger.

"Your blood will make him stronger," Crawford told her. "As long as he has you, he'll always be stronger, faster…"

Immortal.

Cade had seen all of this in the mirror. Elsa had thought that he'd see his death. That he'd see his body withering away over time while Allison stayed young forever.

He hadn't seen that. He'd seen them. Laughing. Loving.

His life didn't have to be a walking nightmare. With her, it could be more.

With her, *he* was already more.

But even if his power had faded, even if they'd only been offered a few years, he would have taken those years.

Taken them and counted himself damn lucky.

"Maybe our kind can help each other…" Crawford murmured with a slight nod of his head. "Maybe." He stepped back. "I'll send a team to…clean up this area."

Nice code for body clean-up.

"And if you two should ever need me, I'll be close."

"Not too close," Cade warned him, the power of the wolf rolling in his voice. "I'd hate to behead you…on accident."

The vampire nodded at the warning, but his eyes were on Allison when he said, "Despite what you may think, we're not all evil. I can help you."

Cade's back teeth clenched.

Crawford laughed. "I said *help*, wolf, not screw. I'm really not that eager to feel your claws at my throat again."

Cade lowered his head close to Allison's cheek. The scent of roses filled his nostrils and soothed the beast within.

Before her, he would never have stood there, *talking* to the male vampire. Slashing and fighting? *Hell, yes.*

But now…

Crawford backed away.

Perhaps there could be more between vampires and werewolves. Maybe it didn't have to just be about centuries of fury and rage and pain.

Allison looked up at him.

Maybe, just maybe, it could be about something so much better.

***

Allison gazed into Cade's eyes as he thrust deep into her. A moan slipped from her even as her hands flattened on his chest.

She was above him, both her knees digging into the mattress on either side of his body.

She'd healed. They'd survived.

No more running. No more fear.

Just…

His cock slid along her sensitive flesh.

Pleasure.

His hands were on her hips. Holding her tight. Lifting her up, down, and she moved with him. Not too fast. Not too hard.

This wasn't like the times before. The wild fury was gone.

Oh, the lust was still there, burning as hot as before but…

Allison leaned forward and kissed him. Her lips, open, eager, feathered over his. Her tongue pushed into his mouth.

He growled, and she knew that he liked her taste, but he didn't thrust harder. Just kept up that perfect driving pace. Smooth, slow, so deep.

When the climax hit her, the release sent a wave of pleasure rolling through her whole body. Cade came with her, surging deep into her core.

And he held her close.

Just as she held him.

Her head lowered to his chest. Her ear pressed against him, and his heart raced so quickly, almost shaking her with its strength.

"It's over," she whispered.

His heartbeat jumped. Then he stiffened. "What?" His hands caught her shoulders, and he lifted her up. "You're…going with the vampires? Allison, you don't have to, I—"

She shook her head. The flash of pure panic in his eyes made her feel braver. "I meant that we didn't have to worry about Elsa anymore." Though the witch's final moments would haunt her dreams—nightmares—for months to come. Dammit, Elsa should never have looked into that mirror. There were some things that folks weren't meant to know.

If Elsa had never glanced in that mirror, would the witch have ever come after her? Would their paths have ever even crossed?

Or, just by looking into that dark glass, had Elsa started the whole chain of events that had led to her own death?

Don't think about her. Not now.

Allison's fingers trailed over Cade's muscled chest. He was still inside her, growing bigger and stronger by the moment, and this—*he*—was what she wanted.

"I know...things won't be easy." She'd managed to take his blood without a problem, but the thought of drinking from anyone else had her shuddering. Adjusting to vamp life wouldn't be a quick, over-night process.

No more real food? No chocolate? No drinks? Only blood.

Her breath sighed out. "Maybe being with me, the way I am now," *not human, not anymore,* "that might not be what you want." No kids. No white picket fence.

"You're exactly what I want."

Oh, that sounded so good. Her lips started to curl. "And you're the only man I want." Through blood and death, darkness and fire—just him.

His hand lifted and threaded through her dark hair. "We'll take it as slow as you want. We've got nothing but time."

Not death.

She nodded and for the first time in weeks, her heart felt lighter.

"I'll keep you safe and give you nights filled with pleasure," he told her, his eyes beginning to show the light of the wolf. "And I'll stay by your side as long as you want me."

Then he'd stay with her forever because she'd always want her wolf.

Want him. Need him. Love him?

Yes.

But could he love a vampire? She was afraid to ask. Allison didn't want—

"When I look at you," Cade told her, "I see every fucking dream I've ever had. You make me want to be better, for you."

She lost her breath.

"Hell, I'm far from perfect, we both know that. And you could damn well do better—"

There was no one better. Stronger.

"But let me show you that I *can* love you."

Her heart broke a little then.

"I can be the man you need."

Allison shook her head. "You already are." Maybe he wasn't perfect. She didn't want perfect. *She* wasn't perfect. Far from it.

Perfect was boring.

Instead of some pristine prince charming, she'd much rather have her big, bad wolf.

They'd make their own happy ending, one that would last forever.

Forever with blood, monsters, and more than a bit of hot sex.

What vampire could ask for more?

Allison smiled and bent to kiss her wolf again.

Forever.

BOUND IN SIN

CHAPTER ONE

Some bodies just wouldn't stay buried–no matter how much dirt you shoved on top of them. Those bodies…they just kept digging out of their graves.

And chasing a girl until she was so damn tired of running. So tired that she'd consider trading her own soul, just for a few moments of safety.

Paige Sloan stared up at the high stone walls of the werewolf compound. It had been ten years since she'd last been inside of those thick walls. Only she hadn't been looking for protection back then. She'd been looking for love.

Will he even remember me?

Paige stood there, trembling from the cold– she *hated* the bone-numbing cold of Alaska–and then she heard footsteps coming her way. Strong. Determined. She sucked in a deep breath and straightened her shoulders. *Showtime*. She just had to play this bit right and get past the guards. Paige lifted her arms into the air. "I'm not carrying a weapon!" Better to just go ahead and get that part out early.

Werewolves could be too unpredictable. She didn't want them attacking first, then trying to get answers from her cold, lifeless body later.

The gate opened with a screech. Two men came rushing out. They weren't carrying weapons. Then again, they didn't need to carry extra firepower. If they wanted, she knew those two men could shift into powerful wolves in an instant.

Most humans didn't realize the truth about the world that surrounded them. Humans thought monsters were make-believe. Just stories to scare children in the darkness of the night.

If only.

Paige knew monsters were real. They were the nightmares that walked the earth.

"*Vampire...*" One of the men snarled the accusation at her, and just that quickly, his claws burst from his fingertips.

Under the moonlight, she saw his nostrils flare and knew the guy had caught the scent that revealed her for exactly what she was.

A monster. A vampire.

"You want to die, vamp?" The other guard demanded. He was the taller of the two, with close-cropped, dark hair, and huge, hulking shoulders. "Is that why you're here?"

Well, they weren't trying to rip her open yet, so that was a good sign. Paige cleared her throat and kept her hands up. "Technically, I've already died." That was how she'd become a vamp and–

The smaller werewolf lunged at her. Smaller, but still wicked strong. He wrapped his claws around her neck and snapped, "You're about to die again." His dark eyes promised a world of pain.

She could do without that promise. *Been there, done that. Not really interested in that scene again, thanks.*

Paige didn't fight his hold, not yet. If things got desperate, then she'd be the one delivering the pain. But first… "Drake…" She whispered the name that had haunted her memories and a small, icy cloud appeared before her mouth. She ignored the cold and focused on what mattered right then. She needed these wolves…and their new alpha. "Drake Wyler."

The werewolf holding her leaned in even closer. She could see that his blond hair was long, brushing his shoulders, and his face was all hard angles and lines. "What do you want with the alpha?"

This was the part that would be tricky. Slowly, because she didn't want to set the guys off, Paige lifted the long necklace that had fallen to rest between her breasts. She saw the blond werewolf's eyes widen as he stared at the necklace. Stared at it–then hurriedly jumped the hell away from her.

That was right. No other werewolves were supposed to *touch* her, not when... "I belong to him," Paige said simply.

And in an instant, those werewolves started tripping over themselves as they hurried to open the gate for her. Sure, they might hate her kind, but as long as she had their alpha's protection, they couldn't touch her.

Well, not if they wanted to keep living.

Paige stared into that wolf compound. Dark. Dangerous. But, hopefully, not as deadly as what waited behind her.

And if she could just get the alpha to overlook that little matter of her vanishing for ten years...

Then maybe she'd have a chance of surviving the coming days and nights.

Maybe.

Maybe not.

The werewolves took her into the heart of the compound. Right inside the big, three-story house with heavy stone walls that stood starkly against the night.

They walked into the foyer, and the tap of her boots seemed to echo on the marble floor. *Marble.* The wolves were kicking things up a notch. Normally, the vamps were the ones who liked to throw around their money.

She glanced down at her scuffed boots. *Not that I ever had money to toss at anyone or anything.*

But it looked like Drake had plenty of money now. And one big, fancy house. This place wasn't where she belonged, and soon enough, she'd be leaving. After she took care of a little business.

"This way." The werewolf on her right–the blond one who'd wrapped his claws around her neck moments before–was pointing to the stairs.

She nodded quickly and followed him up those winding stairs. Then they hurried down a hallway. Turned around a corner. As they headed down that quiet hallway, Paige got a really, really bad feeling in the pit of her stomach. "Are you taking me to Drake's office?"

The werewolf beside her, the dark-haired one, just grunted.

That bad feeling got worse. This looked like private quarters to her. Like they were taking her–

A door jerked open to her left. And then, right there, bigger and even sexier than she remembered, with wide shoulders that brushed the edges of the doorframe, a muscled and *bare* chest, a wild curl of black hair, and eyes that blazed golden fire…right there stood the werewolf alpha, Drake Wyler.

The man she'd loved and lost before.

The man she needed now.

But at that moment, he stared at her with so much fury she almost felt the heat of his glittering gaze burn her skin.

"*Paige.*" Her name was a growl of rage. Okay, so coming here hadn't been the best idea but–

His nostrils flared.

Hell. Her whole body tensed. With werewolves, their sense of smell was so strong that it only took one whiff to realize… "*Vampire.*" The word was a curse.

She didn't flinch. Well, perhaps she did. When he'd known her before, his voice had always been softened with need, with love.

Not hardened with deadly rage.

He grabbed her, not with his claws out, like the other werewolf had, but Drake wrapped his hands around her shoulders and pulled her over the threshold of the room–and into his arms.

Then he kissed her. His lips pressed down on hers, and because she'd wanted him, for so long, Paige kissed him back. Her mouth opened beneath his. Her tongue met his, and the desire that only Drake seemed to be able to stir burned through her.

Her heart raced. Her hips arched toward him even as her nipples tightened against his chest. One kiss…and she craved. It was the way it had always been with them. She'd never wanted anything more than she wanted him.

And she'd never been meant to have anything less.

His tongue slid over her lower lip. Stroked into her mouth. Her wolf had become an even better kisser over the years. Seducing, taking, and making her want so much more. Making her–

Drake's head lifted. He stared down at her– with that strong, chiseled face that often slipped into her dreams, a face that had a few more fine lines now, but the same square jaw, the same high cheekbones, and the same sensual but slightly cruel lips. His eyes blazed so brightly, and she could see the same raw lust she felt reflected in his stare.

The years hadn't changed the way he felt. He still needed, just as much as she did. He still–

"Guess that means she is yours..." The blond werewolf behind them muttered. "A vampire...with a werewolf, how twisted is–"

Drake pushed Paige away and grabbed the wolf in one fast, brutal move. "I saw your claw marks on her throat."

Paige lifted her hand and touched the skin. She felt the light wetness of her own blood. Huh. She hadn't even noticed the sting. After all she'd experienced in the last ten years, what did a few scratches matter?

"You don't *ever* touch her." Drake tossed the guy down the hallway. The smaller werewolf's head thudded into a wall. "You come at her with your claws again, Michael, and I'll rip you open."

Ah, all right, so Drake thought that the scratches mattered. She hadn't remembered him being quite so blood-thirsty.

He swung back toward her. The lust and fury were still battling in his eyes. This wasn't the man she'd fallen for all those years ago. The guy staring back at her–he was a primal wolf.

"Make sure no one disturbs me," Drake ordered and he stalked back toward her. She should speak. Say something. She hadn't said a word to the guy yet. Maybe she should start with something like…*Hi, there, long time, no see. You might wonder why I disappeared without a word. I've got a really good story to tell you.*

More like a nightmare tale. A nightmare that she'd just brought to his door.

And the door closed behind him with a soft click. Her gaze flew around the room. She'd been right. This was definitely a bedroom. Complete with one huge, rumpled bed. But at least it looked like Drake had been sleeping alone. If there'd been a she-wolf in there with him, Paige might have just let her own claws out.

When he touched her, she jumped. Paige wanted to hide her fear, but being a werewolf, he could probably smell the scent on her. Werewolves had such damn superior senses. Better than anyone or anything else in the world.

His fingers brushed over the curve of her breasts. The guy had to slow down. This couldn't happen. Not yet anyway. They had to talk first. "Drake, I–"

He lifted the necklace. Stared at the heavy gold etched with the carving of a wolf's head.

She cleared her throat.

"Why are you wearing this?" Drake asked her, his voice the rumbling mix of darkness and lust that had always been able to make her yearn.

She was yearning already, but she pushed back the need and focused on what the guy was saying. Her necklace. He'd given it to her when she'd turned nineteen. The day he'd told her what he really was.

Werewolf.

That had been the day when her life had started to spiral out of control.

Time to woman up and talk. She swiped her tongue over her lips, tasted him, and managed to say, "Y-you told me...you said a werewolf would never attack me if I wore it." The necklace had been a sign of pack protection.

His strong, tanned fingers closed around the necklace. Then he yanked and broke the gold chain in one vicious tug that seemed to claw across her heart. "I told you," he said, voice even darker, "that this necklace meant you belonged to *me.*"

Ah, right, that rage was burning so bright in him.

"But then you left." A muscle jerked in Drake's jaw. "Disappeared."

Paige backed up a step. When a werewolf this big and angry was coming at you, a smart woman backed the hell up.

"You vanished," his fingers had whitened around the necklace, "when you were supposed to be *mine*."

Yes, a human named Paige Sloan had promised to love him, always. But then she'd stopped being a human, and she'd become the one thing that she knew he hated.

Vampire.

"You don't taste like death," Drake told her.

She flinched at the cold and brutal words. Werewolves always were saying that vamps smelled and tasted like death–that was one of their many insults. So why hadn't she expected that slam from him? Her chin lifted. "And right now, you don't look particularly furry." She'd never actually seen him shift. She didn't want to, either. Paige squared her shoulders and held his gaze. "I guess we're both full of surprises, huh?"

"You can fucking say that again."

Her back teeth clenched together. She hadn't expected the guy to run to her, wrap her in his arms, and immediately swear his undying love. She'd let that dream die a long time ago. But, jeez, did he want to rip her soul out or what? "Look, I know you aren't exactly happy to see me–"

He advanced. She backed up once more. The last thing she wanted was for him to put those big, warm hands of his on her again. When he touched her, her body went into sexual overdrive. She'd gone *way* too long without a lover.

No one but him.

Right. Too damn long.

But lust had to wait. For now.

"Do you know how long I looked for you?" Drake demanded. She could see the edge of his fangs. Probably not a good sign. What was that saying in the vamp world? *When you saw a wolf's fangs, you were about to see hell.* He shook his head slowly and said, "You *vanished.*"

It wasn't like she'd wanted to leave him. But he'd been marked to be the next alpha of his pack and she'd been–

Bitten.

"I didn't think you wanted a vampire turning up on your doorstep." Some of her own anger–the anger she usually worked so hard to keep in check–broke through her fraying control. "Even if I was a vamp that you used to screw."

He pounced. She should have expected the move, but she'd been around humans too long, and werewolves, damn, they could move fast.

In two seconds, he had her on his bed, sprawled amidst the covers, while he held her arms pinned to the mattress. "You weren't a vampire then."

His muscled body pressed against her. No, correction, his *aroused* body pressed against her. There was no mistaking the bulge of his cock.

"You were human then," he said, and his hold tightened around her. "Not vampire, not–"

What she'd been didn't matter. "I'm a vampire now." His sworn enemy. Only…he still wanted her. She'd thought werewolves were supposed to be repulsed by her kind. She'd sure been told that often enough.

The voice from her nightmares whispered through her mind, saying, *"Do you think he'll ever want you again? One look, one taste…as soon as he knows what you are, you'll be dead."*

And she wouldn't be able to rise again.

She waited to feel claws at her throat again. Because she didn't want to see this end, Paige closed her eyes. She'd remember him as he used to be. If only Drake could remember her the same way.

Some dreams just weren't meant to come true.

Paige took a breath, tasted him–strength, power, man–and waited for her second death to come.

CHAPTER TWO

A ghost lay beneath him. A ghost who'd haunted more nightmares than Drake could count.

She was as still as a statue, her features pale and perfect. High, curving cheekbones, a small, pert nose, and lush, red lips made for sin. Her hair–dark as the night he'd always loved–tangled around her face.

And she didn't move. Barely seemed to breathe.

Why?

"Do it," Paige whispered, her voice still that same combination of sin and seduction that had driven him to the edge too many times in the past. "Just…make it fast."

He really hoped she wasn't talking about sex. With her, fast hadn't ever been an option. He'd always needed to take her again and again, to erupt inside of her, to lose himself.

She lifted one eyelid just a bit. Her green gaze darted over him. "You're not…you're not killing me?"

What. The. Fuck. It took every ounce of his will-power to hold back the rage that threatened to swamp him. "Not yet," he managed to snarl.

Paige trembled beneath him. Her slender body had trembled beneath his before, but back then, those little shivers had been from pleasure.

Not fear.

He could all but smell the fear covering her. He hated that smell on her.

"*How.*" Drake bit off the word. How had she become a vampire? Had she chosen this life? Some humans wanted to be vampires. They went out seeking the bite because they wanted to live forever.

Fools. The price of forever was a river of blood and death.

He hadn't thought Paige would be like those desperate humans. He also hadn't thought she'd vanish and leave him aching for her–*ten damn years.*

"It doesn't matter," she told him and both of her eyes opened fully as she gazed up at him. "I can't change what I am."

The scent of her blood filled his nostrils. When he got hold of Michael again, he was gonna give that claw-happy werewolf some marks to remember him by. *You don't touch her.*

Drake caught both of her wrists in his left hand and raised them over her head. She wasn't fighting him, and as a vampire, her delicate form was hiding one hell of a lot of strength.

She just stared up at him, reminding him of all the stupid dreams he'd once had…and lost.

He'd almost left his pack for her. He'd wanted to be human. *For her.*

But now, the beast was in charge. There was no going back. There was only blood, death, and darkness.

For both of them.

He gazed down at her, trying to figure out when she'd stopped being human and become a vampire. She'd been nineteen the last time he saw her. He'd been twenty-one.

Right then, Paige's skin was still flawless and pure, giving no hint to her real age.

What did her age matter? She was right. There was no going back. Not for either of them.

"Are you going to glare at me all night?" Paige asked. "Or do you want to know why I'm here?"

Why she was there…and still wearing his medallion. Or she had been wearing it, until he'd taken it from her neck. It was on the floor now. He'd dropped it when he'd pushed her onto the bed. Paige's neck was bare, and…why the hell did he want to bend down and lick her flesh?

Because I still want her. More than breath. More than life. He saw her, and he needed.

"Why?" He didn't lift his body off hers. Paige would feel his aroused flesh pressing against her. So what? If she wanted a favor from him, she'd pay the price he demanded.

And I demand her.

Vampire or not, she was still his.

Even death couldn't change some things.

"I'm being hunted," she told him in that low, husky voice that made his cock swell even more. He could just see the hint of her fangs behind her red lips. The sight should have repulsed him. It didn't. "If you don't help me, I'll die."

"You're already dead." That knowledge made him feel as if his chest had been ripped open. Since Paige had been human when he'd known her before, she must have been *made* into a vampire.

A rare few, the purebloods, were actually born as vamps, but the rest of the parasites out there? They'd been turned. They were bled until the point of death, then brought back as a vampire.

Drake would kill the one who'd turned her. He couldn't wait to hear the vampire's screams.

"*Don't* say that," Paige snapped at him, then she showed him just how strong she really was. She twisted beneath him and yanked her hands free. A fast roll sent them tumbling across the bed. Then she was on top of him. Her knees straddled his hips, and her hands slammed down against his chest. "I'm as alive as you are!"

Color stained her cheeks. Her breath heaved out. For an instant, they just stared at each other. Then she grabbed his hand and shoved it against her breasts.

"My heart still beats," she told him and he could feel the frantic beat beneath his hand. That fast beat…and that sweet, plump flesh. Paige was curved in all the right places.

"I breathe," she told him and he heard the rush of her breath. "I feel. More than you can imagine, all right? So stop treating me like shit!"

Maybe if she'd stop clawing his heart out…

But then, she was doing that just by breathing. Just by being there. Close enough to take…

So take her. The growl was from his beast, one that was never far from the surface these days.

"You want me to protect you." He held the beast back, barely, because they had a deal to strike. He knew how these bargains worked in the supernatural world. So much could be bartered and exchanged. Flesh. Blood. Sex. Souls.

Sure, humans might be shocked by a deal like this–but then, humans would be shocked to see a man turn into a wolf.

Deal with it.

"You came to me, to my pack," he said slowly, determined not to let his rage escape, not yet, "because you want us to keep you safe." And he would. He–

"No." She shook her head.

Drake frowned. If not for protection, then–

"I want you to kill the bastard after me." Her fangs seemed to lengthen. "I want you to rip his head off, and I want you to make damn sure that he never rises again."

Never rises again.

"You've got a vampire you want me to fight." He'd grown used to battling them. In this part of Alaska, where the cold could creep straight to the bone, where darkness could reign for days and days…this part was home to all manner of supernatural beasts.

The ones at the top of the food chain? The wolves…and the vamps who kept trying to fight them for supremacy. A supremacy they weren't ever getting.

"I've got a vampire I want you to behead." Her breath rushed out. "A vampire named Gabe is the one who made me, he's–"

Drake's claws burst from his fingertips and sliced into the bedding. "He's fucking already dead." As far as Drake was concerned, the vamp–Gabe–had died the instant he put his fangs in Paige.

Her gaze held his, and he saw the worry there. "Gabe is a pureblood. He's strong, he's–"

"No match for an alpha." Didn't she get it? He wasn't the boy she'd left behind. He was a warrior. A monster. A walking nightmare.

Since she'd left him, he'd seen more blood and hell than she could possibly imagine. No, he'd always known the blood and hell...Paige had been the only thing that had been good in his life.

Sweet. Pure.

Then she'd left him, and he'd gone back to the darkness.

She won't leave again.

He stared up at her. He could move her easily enough, but he didn't want to do so. He wanted to keep her just where she was, only he'd like to remove a few of her clothes. Or *all* of them.

But business came first. "What will you do for me?" Drake demanded.

She blinked. Vampires weren't supposed to look so innocent. "I...um..."

He smiled and knew that his own sharpened teeth would flash. "Death doesn't come for free. In the supernatural world, there's always a price."

He heard the slight hitch of her breath. "And what do you want?"

You.

But he wanted to play the game longer and see just what she'd offer him. "What have you got?"

Her gaze fell to his chest, but while she wasn't looking at him, her slender shoulders straightened in a move he remembered. Pride. "I have some money. Not much, but a few thousand that I can pay–"

Drake laughed at that. A hard, deep laugh that sent her bouncing on him. Really? A few thousand to take out a vamp? She didn't quite understand the paranormal market value. Most assassins wouldn't touch a vamp for less than fifty grand.

Unless those assassins were werewolves.

Sometimes we do those hits for free. Depending on the vamp...and the blood and death that the bastard had left in his wake.

But she didn't need to know about the free hits. That knowledge wouldn't work in his favor.

"I can–I can fight with you. Help your pack." Her gaze rose to meet his and a light flush still covered her cheeks. Her voice had hardened, probably because she was pissed by his laughter. "Having a vampire on your side wouldn't be a bad thing."

The laughter faded away and Drake knew his gaze hardened as he said, "I don't want your strength." She'd always had strength, even as a human. A solid core that had drawn him to her. Paige's parents had both been killed when she was just thirteen. They'd only been in Alaska for a little over a year before their accident. Her parents had promised her that they'd all get a fresh start in America's last frontier.

They'd only gotten death.

After their funeral, he knew that she'd bounced around the foster care system and never found a real home. But all that pain, it had never weakened her.

Wolves were attracted to strength.

"Then what do you want?"

Did she realize that her nails were digging into his shoulders? The wolf inside growled.

He liked that.

Time to take what he wanted. Drake stared up at her and said, "I want to fuck you." Endlessly. Again and again until the ache for her, that damn gnawing ache that had kept his body tense and hungry for her–*for years*–finally vanished.

She stared down at him. Swallowed.

And nodded.

CHAPTER THREE

So, what? Did the wolf think that she was gonna pull some kind of shocked, *Oh, no, you can't have sex with me!* routine on him? When she'd been dreaming about him for so long?

Guess again, wolf. If he beheaded that sick freak Gabe *and* gave her the passion that she'd been yearning for, well that was just win-win in her book.

But she didn't want to look too eager. A girl had her pride, after all, and she'd already had to come dragging into his compound looking for some werewolf strength.

Paige swallowed back that eagerness and slowly said, "Well, I guess once we can–"

"Not once, sweet, not even close."

Sweet. He'd called her that, so long before. Only then the word had whispered with affection, and not held the tight, tense edge that honed the endearment now.

"H-how many times?" So she could plan. Savor.

His eyes burned up at her. His cock was also shoving right at the junction of her legs. It was all she could do not to rub against him. If she told him that there'd never been anyone since him, Drake wouldn't believe her.

Even if the words were the truth.

Her body was *starving*. She was already wet for him. Just the touch of his hands had sent a shiver sliding over her. She wanted more. Just how much more would she get?

"As many times as I want," Drake told her, voice rough and dark. "Until you can't breathe without feeling me on every inch of your body."

Her nipples ached. She wanted his hands on them. His mouth.

Did he smell her arousal? Those wolves…

His lips curled in the faintest of smiles. Damn him, he *did*.

His hands rose and tangled in her hair. He began to pull her toward him. Toward his mouth.

Her heartbeat drummed in her ears. They had a deal, and finally, she'd have him.

His lips were so close. She could already taste him on her tongue. *Would* taste him. And he'd taste her. He'd–

A shrill alarm cut through the room.

Sonofabitch.

She blinked, confused, aroused and–

Drake pushed her to the side of the bed and jumped to his feet. "Stay here," he ordered and rushed for the door as the alarm kept shrieking.

Stay? She was a vampire, not a dog. Paige jumped up and raced after him.

He was already thundering down the stairs. More men and women were out now, all racing toward the main level of the house. She joined them, and hoped no one decided to attack the vamp in their midst.

"Fire!" Someone shouted even as she caught the scent of smoke drifting in the air.

Then they were shoving open the front doors and hurrying into the darkness that waited outside of the main house. She saw the flames then, rising quickly, burning right up that thick wall that surrounded their compound. Red and gold flames, burning in a world of snow.

Paige stumbled to a stop even as the wolves fought the blaze. They had buckets of water. Hoses. The water blasted at the flames, but the fire kept attacking all around the compound walls. To the left. To the right.

"*You can't escape me.*" Gabe's words rang in her ears. He'd warned her of this, so many times. He'd said, "*I'll find you and destroy anyone who gets in my way.*"

Someone bumped into her and Paige jerked, then she realized–*I can't just stand here.* She'd seen this type of attack before. It was Gabe's specialty.

Distract and conquer. He'd been using this technique for centuries.

Gabe...or rather, Gabriel, had been born long ago, in the midst of battles and carnage. War was what he knew, what he craved.

When it came to fighting strategies, he liked to think he was a master. The pureblood vamp was always plotting and planning.

The wolves didn't realize that this was just a trick. They were scattering. Each going to a different spot to fight the flames. Each–*vulnerable*.

"Stop!" Paige screamed.

No one listened to her.

More water. More fire.

"*Stop! They're coming for you!*" An attack that had been planned for far too long. She ran forward and grabbed the arm of one woman, a chick with long red hair. "They're coming!"

The woman spun around and her eyes widened. "*Vampire.*"

Yes, she was. "And more of my kind are coming. Move away from the walls! Get *ready.*"

Because Gabe didn't fight fair. He never had.

Thunder rumbled. Someone screamed. No, no, that wasn't thunder. In the wild confusion of the fire, that was someone *shooting*. A man fell to the ground as blood covered the snow behind him.

Gabe always planned so well.

She looked up, her gaze flying along the length of the burning walls. There, to the left. Covered in darkness, she could just see the outline of the shooter.

Only…he wasn't the only one up there.

Paige pushed the woman away. "Get back!" Paige yelled because she knew those guns would be loaded with silver bullets. The fire was just the bait. Carefully placed and targeted to draw out the wolves…

So they could be taken out easier.

She raced forward and leapt up that wall. As a human, she never would have been able to make that climb. The wall was at least fifteen feet high. As a vamp–

Two seconds. That was all it took.

The gunman turned on her. Fired.

The silver bullet tore right through her shoulder. She gasped at the pain, and, somewhere below her, she heard a roar. "Try…harder," Paige gritted out to the shooter as she snatched the gun from him. Then she shot him, right in the heart.

He fell off the wall, tumbling down below.

The vamp wouldn't be dead, not from a silver bullet hit. He'd just be stunned for a while.

More gunshots. More screams.

She whirled around, balancing easily on top of the wall. More vamp shooters had positioned themselves, carefully hiding away from the flames. But the wolves were seeing them now. They were launching at the vamps, trying to take them out.

They just had to take them out *faster*.

Because there was blood on the ground. Injured shifters crying out in pain. And vamps were always attracted to that blood...

Her fangs burned in her mouth as they stretched and sharpened. An instinctive response to the scent of blood. She hurried along the wall's edge, being careful to stay away from those flames. She had her eyes on another gunman. That jerk waited just five feet away, aiming down below. Her gaze darted to the right as she tracked his target. The vamp was–

Aiming at Drake.

No! Drake was rushing toward her, not even looking over at the gunman. "Get down!" She yelled at Drake, and she slammed her body into the vamp's.

His gun fired. The bullet thundered as it exploded from the weapon.

The vampire laughed. "Got the alpha. Fuckin' got him in the heart!"

She drove her fist into his jaw. She heard bones snap and wasn't sure if that snapping was from the breaking of her own fingers or his jaw.

Her gaze lifted and flew to the area below. "*Drake!*" He was on the ground. Not moving.

The vamp's gun had fallen into the snow near the bottom of the wall. Didn't matter. She could deal with this jerk. *He'd shot Drake.* She grabbed for the stake that she kept in her left boot, strapped to her ankle. The vamp was twisting and fighting, and the ledge of the wall was barely a foot across and–

They both tumbled off the wall–falling not toward the inside of the compound, with the werewolves, but back outside.

When they hit the ground, Paige landed on top of the vamp. Even with the snow to cushion them, the thud of the impact shook through her body.

When she sucked in a deep breath, the vampire drove his knee into her stomach.

"Bitch," the vamp snarled. But he wasn't just any vamp. *Henry DeVeau.* She knew him. Had always hated the prick. He liked to torture his victims. The way he'd tortured her. Henry was Gabe's number one attack vamp. A sadistic bastard who deserved to burn forever.

"You thought you'd be safe," Henry spat the words at her as he punched out with his ham-like fists. "You thought he'd save you, but–"

"No," Paige gasped out because, what did she have to lose now? No one else would hear what she said to Henry. The wolves were too busy fighting the flames and the other shooters. "I thought I'd save *him*." Because she'd known that Gabe's attack on the wolves was coming. She'd known that he was going after Drake.

So I wanted to be at Drake's side, to keep him safe.

The bargain she'd made hadn't been about her protection, not really. It had been about his.

But she'd failed him. After only a few damn minutes, she'd *failed*.

Henry's thick brow lowered in confusion. "What? You–"

She had the stake in her hand. She rushed forward–and drove it into Henry's heart. "I *loved* him," she whispered as she twisted that stake. She had once loved him more than anything else in this world, but Henry and Gabe had taken Drake from her. Then, and *now*. "So you burn, asshole, *burn*."

Blood dripped from Henry's mouth, and she saw the light fade from his eyes as the bastard took his last gasp of breath.

And she smiled. A cold puff of air appeared near her face. She was still breathing. Henry would never breathe again.

The other vamps were racing away now, disappearing into the surrounding woods as quickly as they could–and vamps could run, so very fast.

Time to chase.

She'd shown her true allegiance, and if she didn't give chase, they'd all be coming for her head–or her heart.

Paige yanked up her stake. Barely glanced at the blood on the wood and–

Hard arms wrapped her around. She lifted her weapon, ready to take another heart herself.

But Drake stared down at her. His face was stark white, and his eyes glowed with the power of his beast.

His wolf wasn't the only one straining for freedom. Some of the others had already shifted. Paige could hear wolf howls now as the beasts hunted the vampires. Big, furry beasts raced over the snow.

When had they shifted? She hadn't even noticed. She'd been too intent on killing Henry. On getting vengeance because he'd shot Drake.

"Got the alpha. Fuckin' got 'him in in the heart!" Henry had been so certain of his hit. Unlike vampires, wolves couldn't survive a shot of silver to the heart.

So how was Drake still alive?

Her gaze dropped to his chest. A chest he'd clawed open–*to get the bullet out.*

Oh, damn. That was just brutal.

"I thought you were dead." His voice was guttural. His hands locked around her shoulders and pulled her against him. "I saw you go over the wall…"

She shook her head. Her body was trembling. *He's alive.* "I-I was just trying to stop him. I didn't want him to–"

Drake's lips took hers. Not gentle. Not soft. Hard. Wild. Rough.

There was desperation in his kiss, and so much lust.

The sounds of the wolves were all around them. The thudding of their paws on the snow. The howls that broke the night.

It was cold out there, bitterly cold, but she barely felt the ice around her. Right then, she was burning hot.

Drake lifted his head. Stared down at her. "Don't ever do that again."

Um, that wasn't a promise she could make. She'd keep fighting, until the threats to him were gone. She wasn't the running type, not anymore.

He kept a tight hold on her, smearing his blood over her clothes, and he turned to face the wolves who'd gathered around them. Smoke drifted in the air, but most of the flames were out, for now.

"Find them," he shouted. "Hunt them!"

Some wolves were already in the woods, hunting. But vampires were good hunters, too.

"Find them," Drake said again, and his voice cut through the night, "and kill them."

The wolves howled.

Paige knew that the final war between the vampires and werewolves had begun.

CHAPTER FOUR

She could have fucking died.

Drake pulled Paige through the main house, making sure not to let her go, not even for an instant. The woman wasn't getting away from him, hell, *no*.

When he'd looked up and seen her on that wall, with that vampire bastard attacking her...

He'd roared her name.

Then the vamp had shot him. The silver had burned, ripping and tearing through him as he fell to the ground. When Drake had looked up again, it had been to see Paige tumbling right over the edge of the wall.

Drake rounded the corner and shoved open the door that led to his quarters.

"Drake, look, I–"

In an instant, he spun on her. "You knew they were attacking."

Did she look paler than before? It seemed so. Even the red of her lips had faded to a light pink. She stared up at him and gave a slow nod.

Shit. Why couldn't she have lied? He didn't want to know that she'd set him up.

Because then he'd have to punish her.

He headed to the left. He had blood on his hands, and he'd already smeared that blood on her. When he touched her again, he wanted his hands clean.

All he could smell was blood. His blood. The blood of the wolves who'd been attacked. The blood of the bastard she'd staked. And...

Her blood.

She'd seemed paler than before.

He whirled back to face her. As she stumbled, he picked her up and held her close against his chest. *She's a vampire, but she can still die.* The scent of her blood was too strong. "Where's the wound?"

She lifted her arm to her shoulder. Her hair had fallen forward, covering the injury, and he swept the mane back, then cursed at the sight of her flesh.

A bullet had torn through her shoulder.

Why the hell wasn't she healing? Vampires usually healed fast enough when they were injured.

She wasn't healing.

He took her into his bathroom. Put her down next to the shower that could easily hold three people, though he only preferred an intimate two. Then he tore open her shirt and tossed away the scraps of material so that he could see her wound.

But...it wasn't the only wound that he found on her body. There were faint white lines on her flesh, snaking up her stomach. Sliding down her left arm. Scars. Old injuries.

Vampires didn't scar. Those marks...she must have gotten them while she was still human.

He knelt on the marble tile so that his eyes were level with hers. "What happened to you?"

She bit her lip and glanced away. Then, voice whisper-soft, Paige said, "Nothing that matters now."

Every single thing about her mattered.

He put his hand on her shoulder, being careful not to touch the bloody wound. She still flinched.

Because he'd hurt her...or because he'd touched her? She'd once begged for his touch. But that had been long ago.

Another damn life.

Locking his back teeth, Drake gritted, "Why aren't you healing?"

She shrugged and still didn't look him in the eyes.

He reached behind her and yanked on the water in the shower. The water thundered out in a hot rush and steam began to drift in the air. He didn't worry about another attack interrupting them, not then. He'd put extra guards on sentry duty. The vamps wouldn't be getting close again.

They'd just be dying soon.

"Too much blood loss can kill a vamp." He knew because he'd killed his share that way before. A slow, painful death. Some folks deserved that kind of death.

Some didn't.

The vamps who'd killed his family? They'd deserved every single moment of agony that he'd given to them.

"It's almost stopped bleeding," she told him. "I'll be all right." She glanced toward the water.

He put his hand on the curve of her waist. "You need blood." No way to get around that. She'd been hurt, and she'd bled too much. For a vamp to get her strength back and heal, she'd need to drink.

"Yeah, well…" She gave a rough laugh that was nothing like the light, happy peal she'd once had, "Something tells me that wolves don't exactly keep extra blood bags around for the vamp company that comes calling."

No, they didn't.

But if she needed blood…his gaze locked on her mouth. Her full lips. Her white teeth. Her delicate fangs.

A vampire bite is hell. Agony. Pain and degradation.

How many times had he heard that line from other wolves? *Too many.*

So why was he even thinking about offering her his throat?

Because it's her. And because she saved your ass out there. No matter what else she might be doing or planning, Paige had stopped the vamp from firing that silver into his heart. A few more inches to the right, and Drake knew he would've been dead.

She'd saved him and wasn't that worth a few drops of blood?

He caught her chin. Lifted her head. Her gaze found his, finally. The water flowed behind her, and that steam heated the air. "Take from me," he told her. When an alpha gave an order, that order was obeyed. No question.

Her brow furrowed. "Um, take what?"

He caught her fingers–damn, her skin was soft–and lifted them to his throat. "*Take.*" He could handle this for a few minutes. He'd lock down his mind. Pretend he wasn't being used as food and–

She snatched her hand back. Horror had her green eyes widening. "I can't!"

She sure as hell could. "You've got the fangs, sweet, just sink them in." Not like this was her first bite. She must have bled plenty of humans in her time. *Bastards.*

Without blood, vamps would turn to dust.

But she was shaking her head at him. "I-I'll just take a quick shower and wash up. I'll heal soon, and everything will be–"

Well, damn, didn't she want his blood? Now he was starting to feel insulted. "Drink from me." Her whole body was shaking. She needed blood. *Take it.*

He wasn't gonna sit there while she got weaker. He could help her. Her fangs would sink into his flesh, and she'd feed on him. The other wolves would think he was insane for offering his neck to her. So what? Screw them.

This was for her.

Only she was still shaking her head and looking like he'd just shoved a snake at her face. "I *can't.*"

"You got something against shifter blood?" Which wouldn't make a bit of sense. Paranormals had blood that was far more powerful than that of humans.

And vamps were always about power.

Her gaze dropped to his throat. He saw her eyes widen. Saw the flicker of raw hunger on her face. She wanted his blood. No missing that.

Why wasn't she taking it?

"Y-you don't…understand…" Her gaze was still on his neck. "Drinking is…"

His hands curled around her waist. "I don't want to hear about all the men you've tasted." Because he'd just want to give those jerkoffs a whole world of hurt. *Her mouth, on them.* His beast roared. *Kill.* "Just...do it."

Her laughter held a wild edge. "You're not listening to me! I *can't!*" Her voice dropped as she confessed, "Because I never have before."

What the hell?

The words were a lie. They had to be. Drake's hands tightened on her. "You're a vamp. You have to drink to survive."

"Not from a live s-source." Her lips quivered. "I've never...When I drink, I-I use blood bags. I don't take from people! Not directly."

He frowned at her. He'd heard the rumors and whispers about some vamps going all bite-free and trying to blend better with the rest of the world. A newer, more human-friendly vamp.

He'd thought those stories were bullshit.

The vamps who'd attacked him tonight sure hadn't been the blending variety.

"Just...give me a few minutes," Paige told him. She pulled away. Stripped off the rest of her clothes–*sweet hell*–then stepped into the huge shower with its curtain of steam. "I'll be okay."

The hell she would.

She was in his home, back with him, and he was supposed to just stand back while she needed?

His jaw clenched as he gritted out, "We don't have blood bags." Why would they? It wasn't like werewolves entertained vamps. No blood bags on the premises, and there wasn't any damn way to get them right then.

Her body slid beneath the pounding water. Paige sighed softly and the sound was like a stroke right over his cock.

As she turned beneath the spray, letting the water pour down her back, her eyes began to drift closed. Did she really think he was just gonna walk away? He hadn't bothered to put on a shirt when he'd raced outside. No shirt, no shoes. Just a pair of jeans stained with blood. His hands went to the snap.

When his zipper eased down with a hiss, her eyelids flew back open.

Ah, heard that, did you? A vamp's hearing was *almost* as good as a shifter's.

Almost.

"Drake?"

He loved the way she whispered his name.

He dropped the jeans and stepped into the shower. Then he positioned his body near hers. "You're drinking from me." He'd be her first at this, just as he'd been the first to take her body.

But she shook her head. "I don't want to hurt you."

"You won't." He pulled her against him. The water covered them both. Washing away the blood and death. Drake tilted his head to the side. His fingers curled around her chin, and he pulled her toward him. "Just start with a kiss."

Her lips feathered over his skin.

His cock hardened even more–and the damn thing had already been swollen with need.

Her tongue slid out and licked the side of his neck. The small touch sent a rush of hot need surging through him.

He was supposed to be suffering through this. Giving her sustenance, nothing more. Dealing with the pain of her bite–

Only there wasn't any pain yet.

Only pleasure.

"I-I *can't*," she told him again and tried to pull away.

Fuck that.

His hands locked tighter around her. He pushed her back, caging her against the tiled wall of the shower. Then his mouth took hers.

He knew one thing about vampires and their bloodlust…sex and blood were always tied for the vamps.

Sex and blood.

Her mouth opened beneath his. She kissed him back with a hunger to match his. If this was her when she was weak…

He couldn't wait to see her when Paige was back at full strength.

His tongue slipped into her mouth. Tasted. Enjoyed the moan that rose in the back of her throat.

His cock thrust eagerly toward her, pushing hard because he damn well wanted to be inside of her.

Would be...*soon*.

His breath heaved out when he lifted his head. "Drink from me."

The edge of her fangs glistened behind her slick lips.

Drake lifted his hand to his throat. His claws were out, and he sliced a thin line down the side of his throat. The better to tempt his little vamp.

The darkness of her pupils expanded in her eyes. "*Drake.*"

"I want you to drink from me."

Her gaze was on the blood that dripped down his throat. Her fangs were lengthening. "Don't...don't let me hurt you."

What was a little pain? Sometimes, it could even make the pleasure sweeter. He'd learned that lesson long ago, but he just told her, "You won't."

Her mouth went back to his throat. Kissed the skin. Sucked lightly along his flesh.

Damn. He held onto his control with every ounce of strength he had. But her body was wet, soft, and smooth. Her silken legs rubbed against his. Her breasts–tight with those pebbled nipples–pushed into his chest.

Then she licked at the blood on his throat.

His teeth ground together. His cock was so aroused that he felt like he'd erupt any minute.

Only in her.

She moaned low in her throat and licked him again. Again. She sucked his flesh once more, and he felt the score of her teeth on him.

Okay, this is it. She'll slice into me, but it won't last long and–

And her teeth sank into him.

Fuck, fuck, *fuck!*

This wasn't about pain and degradation. This wasn't about a vamp's bite tearing and slicing prey.

It was about pleasure.

Because that was all he could feel then. A white-hot burst of pleasure that seemed to fill his veins and course through his body. So much pleasure that his control shattered in an instant. There was no holding back.

There was only…Paige.

He lifted her up against that tiled wall. Spread her legs.

Her mouth was still on him, lips, tongue, teeth…

His fingers slid over her core. Pushed inside her sex. So wet. So hot. She clamped down on him and held tight.

The water thundered down over him. Steam surrounded them.

In her.

He positioned his cock. Stroked over her clit. Loved her ragged moan.

The head of his cock pressed into her. Her sex stretched, straining around him. He wanted to see her, wanted to pull back–

But he couldn't.

Drake drove into her as deep and as hard as he could. And it was just like he remembered. Tight. Hot. Heaven.

He pulled back. Thrust deep. Again and again. He lifted her up, positioning her so that she had to take all that he gave her. There was no hiding or holding back, not for either of them.

His fingers kept stroking over her clit. The way he knew she liked. The way that would make her–

Scream.

Paige lifted her mouth from his neck. Her eyes were wide, wild, and her lips were flushed red. The scream of pleasure slipped past those red lips even as he felt the contractions of her orgasm around his cock.

So good.

He kept thrusting. Faster. Harder. Rougher. The wolf liked it rough.

So did the man.

She wrapped her legs around his hips. Wrapped her arms around his shoulders.

And she kissed him.

This time, the pleasure was his. A deep, wrenching pleasure that washed over him as he climaxed inside of her. The release blinded him and fucking seemed to gut him as it went on and on, hollowing out his body.

When the climax ended, he didn't release her.

Because he wasn't letting her go, not ever again.

CHAPTER FIVE

Dawn didn't bring light. The polar night had come to Alaska weeks before, and now they were lucky if even a faint twilight would brighten the day.

Just darkness. And more darkness to come.

It was the kind of darkness most vampires loved.

Paige knew that she had never been like most vampires. Hell, she wasn't even a particularly good vampire.

After dressing, she carefully crept toward the bedroom door. When she'd opened her eyes, she'd been alone. The sheets beside her had been cold. *Alone.*

It wasn't like she'd expected Drake to stay with her, just holding her in those quiet hours. Cuddle time wasn't so big with vamps and werewolves, she got that.

But had the guy really needed to haul ass so quickly? Would it have killed him to just stay with her for a little while?

Her hand pressed against the wood of the closed door. She could still taste Drake on her tongue.

And feel him between her legs.

The sex had been as good as she remembered. Actually, way better than good. Drake had always been one fantastic lover and–

Someone was screaming.

The screams tore through the house, echoing, and her body tensed in instant response.

She'd screamed before, for Drake, but those screams had been about pleasure. This time, the cries filling the air were from pain.

Paige yanked open the door. The screams and yells and shouts to "Stop!" had her racing down the hallway.

Faster, faster she went. She bounded down the stairs, taking three at a time, and Paige realized could she smell blood.

Her fangs were already coming out.

"Stop, dammit, stop!" A man's ragged plea.

She rushed down another flight of stairs, one that led to some kind of basement or–

A line of werewolves blocked her path. Paige stumbled to a halt just seconds before she would have barreled into those guys.

The screams continued, coming from a room directly behind that living wall of werewolves.

What the hell?

Her gaze darted over the men. She recognized the two werewolves who'd escorted her in...jeez, had that just been last night?

The smaller one–the guy who'd made the mistake of touching her before–shook his head. "He doesn't want you going inside."

Yeah, well, screw that. "He also doesn't want you touching me." Drake had been more than adamant on that point the last time he'd squared off with this wolf. What had been the guy's name? Mark? Matthew?

Michael. This wolf was Michael.

Drake had been more than clear when he'd said the guy wasn't supposed to touch her again. If Michael couldn't touch her...

Then you can't stop me, wolf.

She marched right ahead. Damn straight that line of wolves backed up. She figured none of them wanted to dare to actually physically try and stop her. "So I'm betting you're just gonna get out of my way." Or else they'd get an ass kicking from Drake.

Then before one of them could grow some balls and *maybe* try to stop her, she sprang forward, leapt right over them, and kicked open the door behind the assembled wolves.

It was a metal door, heavy and huge, but it easily sprang open beneath her booted heel.

Wow. That blood of Drake's had really amped her up. She'd always heard werewolf blood was powerful, but...*damn*. She'd never felt so strong.

The metal door slammed into the wall and bounced back at her, but she dodged it with a little sidestep, and then she noticed that she was in hell.

Or as close to hell as she'd been in a few months.

Cages lined the walls. Cells. Prisons. There was blood on the floor. The coppery scent of blood filled the room. She knew that scent too well. And there, in the middle of the area, strapped to what looked like an operating table, was a vamp that she recognized.

Malcolm Douglas. Another one of Gabe's henchmen.

Guess you couldn't run fast enough.

The wolves had caught him, and now they were making him pay.

"You shouldn't be here." Drake grabbed her arms and turned Paige away from the sight of Malcolm's bleeding body. "Dammit, I told them to keep you away."

"You also told them not to touch me," she said, lifting a brow, "so it's not like they could *really* stop me." Not unless they'd wanted to fight the alpha.

A muscle flexed in Drake's jaw. "You don't need to see–"

Malcolm started to laugh. "Fool. What you're doing to me...we've done so much more...to *her*."

Oh, crap. Ice flooded through Paige's body. Malcolm shouldn't have said–

"We sliced her open..." Malcolm snarled out. She glanced over and saw the wildness in his eyes. "Drained her blood while she screamed–"

Drake lunged for him. His claws wrapped around the vampire's neck and ripped the skin. "I won't make death easy for you."

Malcolm just smiled. His fangs were stained with blood. Despite his screams, she knew he didn't fear death. The guy probably welcomed it.

Hell...had he been screaming just because he knew that she was in the compound? Had he been trying to draw her down here? *So that I'd suffer...and Drake would suffer.*

"Want me to tell you..." Malcolm muttered, "all that we did to her?"

No. She'd never wanted Drake to hear that story. "Drake!"

"Get out of here," Drake ordered without looking at her. His claws sank deeper into Malcolm's throat. Pretty soon, Malcolm wouldn't be able to talk at all.

Paige didn't move. The screams had pulled her in, but she was staying because... "I can help you!" If Drake would just give her the chance.

Malcolm was the one still doing the talking. "She was…waiting," he said, "for you–"

"Take her out, Heath! Now!" Drake snapped and a fair-haired wolf came her way. His hands closed around her arms, but she jerked against him.

Paige wasn't going anywhere. Not yet. "Dammit, Drake, let me–"

"She was near the lake when we found her…" Malcolm's blood dripped onto the floor. "You were supposed…to meet her."

Why couldn't the vampire shut the hell up?

Drake stiffened at the vampire's words. "I went to the lake."

Lost Lake. A fitting name.

She'd lost her own life at that lake.

"You went later." Malcolm's eyes were bright. He liked power. Craved it. Always had, always would. Right then, despite the claws at his throat and the blood around him, Malcolm had the power.

And she had a stake in her boot. So if she could just get away from Handsy Heath, she'd use it and make sure Malcolm never hurt another human again.

The way he hurt me.

"Your alpha…" Malcolm growled, "he made sure you went late…to that little rendezvous…"

His words caused Drake's hold to loosen, just a bit, but Malcolm's revelation didn't surprise Paige. She'd learned this truth long ago.

The old alpha, Jeremiah Quintock, hadn't wanted a human in his pack. He'd thought wolves were far too superior to humans. But Drake had wanted her to be his mate, and he'd been determined to bring Paige into the pack, and it hadn't mattered to him who he pissed off.

Drake had thought he was safe because he was the next in line to be alpha. One day, he'd lead the Alaska wolves. He'd known that, even when they'd dated. So he hadn't thought anyone in the pack would deny him the mate he'd chosen.

But Jeremiah hadn't wanted the next alpha to have a human at his side.

So he'd sent me to die.

She saw the shock on the faces of the wolves around her. Even Heath eased his grip on her. What? Had they all really not known that old jackass Jeremiah had been dealing with the vamps for years?

Because Jeremiah had a taste for blood, too. A taste for blood and death and screams and pain. Not the best image when the werewolves in the pack were trying to show that they were more than beasts.

But Jeremiah had sure liked to play with his prey.

The vamps had gotten rid of the bodies for Jeremiah, and he'd gotten to pretend he was an evolved, strong alpha.

An agreement, of sorts, had been reached between Jeremiah and the vamps. But, sooner or later, all good and evil deals came to an end.

Jeremiah was dead. The old truce was gone. Now the vamps were looking to take back what they thought of as *theirs*.

Their land. Their power.

"You're lying," Drake snarled at the vamp. He'd yanked Malcolm right off the table, easily snapping the restraints that had held the guy. Drake lifted the vamp into the air, and Malcolm didn't even try to break free. He just hung limply, laughing.

"*Ask her...*" Malcolm said, choking a bit on blood. "She begged...for you."

Bastard.

He'd enjoyed it so much when she begged.

I stopped begging. Stopped crying. Stopped letting him enjoy her pain. In the end, she'd been the stronger one. Damn him, she'd been *stronger*.

Heath's hands slackened even more on her. She yanked away from him. "Vamps use distraction as their number one attack method." That's what Malcolm was trying to do then. Why didn't the wolves realize what was happening? "He wants to buy time, to give the others a chance to regroup and come in again for an attack."

Paige inched forward as the wolves glanced around the room. She just needed to get within striking distance. Almost…there.

Drake swung his gaze back to her. "You *weren't* at the lake."

Paige could still smell the lake. That long ago day, the polar night had ended. The darkness had faded and the sunlight had just been about to come her way. Everything had been fresh. New.

She and Drake had wanted to see the sun together.

Then start their lives together.

She'd gone to Lost Lake early because she'd been so excited. She hadn't cared about what Drake was. She'd just loved him.

When she'd heard the twig snap and the rustle in the bushes, she'd thought it was him. She'd spun around with a smile on her face.

Hello, little wolf whore.

"No," she whispered through numb lips as the past and the present fought in her mind, "I wasn't at the lake."

Drake's claws dug into Malcolm's neck. More blood flowed. "I waited for you," Drake told her, sounding lost. She'd been lost, for so long. His eyes were still on her as he said, "I waited for hours. But you never came. You *left* me. You couldn't stand what I was."

A few more steps, and she'd be at his side. "I left," Paige agreed softly. Wasn't that what she wanted him to know?

"She *screamed*," Malcolm gasped out the words. Damn him. *Shut up.* Only he wasn't shutting up. He was saying... "Jeremiah had taken you too far away...and you couldn't hear her. We cloaked our scents, so you never knew we were...at that lake. Then the old alpha came...because he wanted to make sure...she died..."

You won't tempt the boy again. Jeremiah's vow to her. He'd met up with the vamps. In some God-forsaken cabin. A place that had reeked of death and fear.

But by the time he'd gotten there, she'd stopped screaming. She'd realized her screams were only building the excitement for the vamps. They got off on her pain.

So the tears had streaked silently down her cheeks, but she'd stopped crying out. Her lips had clamped together. She'd bit through them to hold back her cries.

Jeremiah had come to kill her. She'd understood that instantly. He'd wanted to be the one to send her to the grave. Personally. Because she'd dared to try and taint his pack with her human blood.

But Gabe...oh, Gabe, he'd always been so smart. He'd known that Jeremiah wouldn't be around forever, and with Drake growing bigger and stronger every day…

A new alpha's taking over. When he rises, I'll have what he wants most. Gabe had whispered those words to her. Then kissed her tears away. *Don't be afraid, love. You're not dying…yet.*

"I wasn't at the lake," she said again as she tried to push the past back into the dark hole in her mind. Drake needed to remember her leaving him. He had to be strong. He couldn't have a weakness.

Gabe was counting on his weakness.

She blinked. Why were her cheeks wet? Dammit, she was crying, and the wolves were all staring at her, dead silent.

As silent as she'd been when Jeremiah had raked his claws down her arm. Then her side.

But Gabe had stopped him before the bastard could rip out her heart.

"She's not yours to kill, Jeremiah." Gabe's taunting voice still haunted her mind. *"She's ours now."*

"We didn't turn her right away." Malcolm's body trembled and his voice shook. "She…got away from us…gave us quite a chase…"

Didn't Drake get it? Malcolm was wasting time with this story. Distracting them all.

Making Drake weak.

Because Gabe wanted Drake to be weak, distracted…*broken* when the real attack came.

She remembered the desperate time she'd spent running. She'd fled through the snow. Hitchhiked. Gotten as far from Alaska as she could.

Hello, Florida.

But Gabe had always been chasing her. He hadn't planned to let her go. Not when she could be such a valuable tool in his battle.

She'd never called Drake after she escaped. Never so much as spoken his name again. Why? Because Jeremiah had still been there, still wielding his power, and if she'd tried to get close to Drake again…

The old scars on her body seemed to burn.

Her heartbeat thudded in her ears. Fast. So fast.

"All vampires aren't sick pricks like him," she spoke quietly, but her voice filled the room. "There are others out there who are different. They're *good*." They'd found her. Hurt. Wild. So desperate after her change. And they'd helped her.

I won't drink from a human. She'd been starving because she refused to drink. But she hadn't wanted to attack another person, hadn't trusted herself to stop once she sank her teeth into prey.

Gabe had told her that she wouldn't be able to pull back after she had her first taste of blood.

"Once you taste the blood, it'll drive you wild. You'll do anything to get more. You'll drain humans, one after the other, and leave their bodies in your wake."

His promise to her, right after he'd turned her. He'd leaned close, pressed a kiss to her cheek and said, *"Then you'll be just like me."*

Never.

Drake had dropped Malcolm. The vamp lay sprawled on the floor while her werewolf stared at her with a face gone white. No, he shouldn't be like this. She hadn't ever wanted him to know all the secrets she carried.

"Paige..." Her name was a ragged sound of pain, torn from Drake.

And Malcolm–his eyes were on her. On her, then Drake. No, not just on Drake...on his neck.

Malcolm's smile said he knew what she'd done.

After resisting for so long, she'd broken down and taken blood from a live source, from *him*. The one who mattered the most.

"Guess I am a monster," she told Malcolm, then she lunged forward. No one tried to stop her. They couldn't. She was too fast then.

In an instant, she had the stake out.

And Malcolm was attacking, too. Not an attack at her, but one aimed at Drake.

He was distracting you. She'd tried to warn him, but Drake had been too busy listening to

Malcolm's twisted tale. The vamp slashed out with his claws, going for Drake's back.

Only she got to Malcolm first. Paige shoved the stake into his chest. "Go to hell, bastard," she snarled. He'd sure done his best to drag her there and–

Malcolm ripped the stake right out of his chest. "Missed...heart...bitch..."

Oh, crap.

"I won't miss," Drake promised as he yanked her back. Then he attacked, slamming his body into Malcolm's. And, no, he didn't miss because one powerful swipe of the razor sharp claws that sprang from Drake's fingers–well, one swipe took Malcolm's head.

And the vampire went to hell.

The silence in the room was deafening then. All the wolves stood, as still as statues, watching her. Waiting.

After one glance, she didn't look at Malcolm again. Her stomach was twisting, her hands shaking. She wanted the nightmare to just end, but for her and for Drake, the end was still too far away. The nightmare wouldn't stop, not yet.

Not until Gabe was the one on the floor, stone dead.

She should say something. Anything. But...

Her shoulders hunched as Paige turned away. The scent of blood seemed to burn her nostrils, and she just needed to get out of there.

Away from the blood and death. *Escape.* She hadn't known real freedom in so long, and she was so tired of being surrounded by death.

Constantly.

Paige shoved the shifters out of her way. Drake called out to her. She didn't glance back, and she sure as hell didn't stop. She'd talk with him–later.

Not now.

I wasn't at the lake.

Her words had been so hollow because, yes, she'd been at Lost Lake. She'd kept her promise to Drake.

And that promise had cost Paige far more than she'd ever expected–her life.

CHAPTER SIX

She damn well wasn't getting away from him.

Paige had fled the compound and raced away into the night. Sure, he could have gotten his men to track her, but this hunt was personal, and Drake didn't want the others chasing her.

If someone hunted Paige, it would be him.

"You can't do this!" Heath grabbed him just as Drake was about to pass through the compound's heavy gates. His eyes blazed with fury. "This could be a vamp trap! She's luring you outside."

Paige hadn't gone through the gates. She'd just leapt over the wall. So fast and graceful. His blood had sure pumped up her power.

As for her bite...it had given him so much pleasure. *I'll have more.* If she needed blood, he'd be happy to be her personal donor from now on.

Her first, her only.

"She's hurting," Drake said and pain, yeah, that was just what he'd seen in Paige's eyes. She'd always shown so much with her green gaze. He'd once been able to look right into her eyes and see her soul.

Heath actually shook him. "She's in pain? Fine. Then let her go off and lick her damn wounds." Heath's words held a sharp bite. "But don't put yourself at risk for her. She's a *vampire.*"

The necklace he'd given to her so long ago, the one he'd stupidly taken from her neck just the previous night, was a heavy weight in Drake's pocket. *Give it back to her.* "She's mine." There wasn't anything else to say.

She was his. And she hurt.

Protect her. An instinct from the wolf and the man.

He looked beyond the wall. So much darkness and icy cold waited for him. But that frigid darkness had been his whole life, ever since Paige had left him.

He wanted more now. He wanted warmth. Light. Paige had always been that to him.

"I'm bringing her back." Drake shoved the other wolf aside.

Heath grabbed his arm. "You can't bring a vampire into the pack." Low words. Gritted. Burning with intensity. "You know you can't do that."

Very, very slowly, Drake turned his head and stared down at his first in command. He'd been friends with Heath since they were both just boys, but that friendship wouldn't stop him from kicking the shit out of the guy. "I'm the fucking alpha." He let the power ring in his voice. He'd fought for the title. Earned it. And since he was alpha, the one they all submitted to... "I can do anything I want."

"Jeremiah–"

Had that bastard really gone after Paige? Set this whole nightmare in motion? His jaw ached as Drake growled, "He's dead." A very lucky thing for the old wolf right then. Because if he'd still been living, Drake would have ripped him apart. "It's *my* pack now." If Heath wanted to challenge him...

Come the hell on.

He was more than in the mood for some ass-kicking.

After he brought Paige back. He had his priorities, and she came first. "Spread the word," Drake ordered. "Any who want to challenge me...tell them to get the fuck in line." When he came back, he'd take them all on.

Because no one was going to keep him from Paige. Not now.

Not ever.

He turned away from Heath and ran into the night. Vampires were fast, but wolves were faster. Especially when they hunted.

He shed the form of man with a crack and snap of his bones. The pain of the shift burned over him, familiar, white-hot, and soon he was running on all fours, with paws instead of hands, and he tossed back his head and howled for the one thing he wanted most in the world.

His mate.

He had her scent, and he wouldn't lose it. He flew over the terrain, ignoring the frigid cold temperature–an arctic chill that he knew would be cutting into Paige. The cold wouldn't kill a vamp, but it would make her body tremble and shake. She'd suffer out there.

She'd already been in pain when she left him.

And the only damn thing he wanted to do was take that pain away.

He bounded through the forest and sent snow flying in his wake. The world was a blur of white, but he could just see the imprints of her footsteps.

He knew where she was going.

Inside the body of the beast, the man cursed.

The wolf ran faster, faster…

She'd never seen him in this form. Before, he'd been ashamed for her to see him transform. He knew what he was…

"Guess I am a monster…" Her words were burned into his mind.

But he'd been the monster. Always. The beast who'd taken what he should never have touched.

He leapt into the air, easily jumping over a fallen tree. Her scent was stronger now.

Strawberries. Sex. Woman. He'd never been able to forget that lush scent.

The small lake was frozen, its surface dark and glistening. Even though it was day, the sky overhead was as dark as the lake. No sunlight.

Not now.

Just cold. Just darkness.

Paige spun at his approach and put her back to the lake. Her eyes widened when she saw him. Swallowing, she backed up a step.

He froze.

Then he changed, for her.

The transformation was brutal to watch. He knew it had to be. His bones shifted and broke, reshaped into a man's body instead of the form that belonged to the beast. The fur seemed to melt from his body. Soon paws and claws became hands and fingers–fingers that had dug deeply into the snow.

"Drake?"

Her hushed voice pushed through the last of the shift, and, naked, he glanced up at her.

Paige rushed toward him. "You shouldn't be here!"

"Neither...should you." He rose before her. Wind whipped against his body, but werewolves always stayed warm no matter what the outside temperature was. The beast burned within.

Paige shivered.

He took a step toward her, but she stiffened, and her gaze darted around the small clearing. "It's dangerous. I didn't think-we need to go back."

Drake lifted his hand and offered it to her. "Then come with me." He knew why she'd run from the compound. Desperation and pain had driven her to flee blindly.

I wasn't at the lake.

But she had been. He knew a lie when he heard it.

"I'm sorry." The words were torn from him. Jeremiah had come to him, told him that he had a message from Paige. *"Your little human said to meet you in two hours."* Jeremiah had smiled and flashed his fangs. *"That gives us time for a hunt."*

And he'd just…gone off with the bastard.

Paige wasn't taking his hand.

Her gaze was on him, sweeping over his body. She hadn't been disgusted by his shift, and she sure didn't appear disgusted by what she was seeing right then.

Lust. He knew that expression well. But he hated the mix of lust and pain in her eyes. He hated to see *any* pain in her gaze.

He'd rather just have the lust.

"Come with me," he said again, and he still waited for her to take his hand. There would be no forcing on this. She had to choose to come with him.

To be with him.

Her gaze swept around the lake. The woods. She inched toward him. The snow crunched beneath her boots. "I-I didn't…you shouldn't have followed me." Her words rushed out. "I just needed a little time…"

"There's a vamp hunting you," he told her. Hell, it was probably a whole gang of vamps now. "You really think I'd just leave you on your own?"

No. Her hand lifted and slowly, so slowly, her gaze met his. Her fingers touched his hand. Tentative. Soft. "I lied," she whispered.

His fingers closed around hers. "What?" But he already knew and if she wanted to confess to him, he'd damn well listen.

He should have met her here, at Lost Lake. He should have told Jeremiah to screw off, that he was still heading out to meet Paige and that he'd just wait for her to show.

If he'd gone then, they would have been married by now. Had children. Had a fucking perfect life.

It was all his fault.

But then he heard the growl of an engine. No, not just one engine. Two. Three.

Coming close.

Too fast.

Far too fast.

Her eyes still held his. "I lied," she said again, then she jerked her hand free from his grip and shoved against his chest. *"Run!"*

The vampires were coming.

"Shift! Turn back into a wolf!" Paige yelled at him. "You can outrun them, you can get away!"

"Not without you." His claws tore through his flesh. He'd be damned if he left her behind.

She shook her head and shoved harder against him. "It's not about me. They don't want me."

But–but she'd told him–the vampire she'd called Gabe–

"They want you," she said, voice stark and sad. Her eyes had never looked bigger. Or sadder. "And Gabe always planned to use me…in order to get you."

He could see the light from the snowmobiles cutting through the darkness. The vamps were closing in on them.

The vamps wouldn't get them, though. Dumbasses. Drake knew this land so well.

Better than any vampire ever could. His beast ran free often. Knew every fallen tree. Every secret bend. Every dark cave.

Every hiding spot.

"Run with me," he told her. Because right then, it wasn't about fighting, even though the beast within was roaring for blood. That moment was about protecting Paige. Getting her to safety.

Then coming back to cut down all the vampires after him.

She nodded, and they took off, racing not around the lake, but right across it. It was icy and slick beneath their feet, frozen solid, and by going straight across that cold surface, they saved valuable time.

The ice wouldn't break. Not for months.

They cleared the lake. Entered the edge of the forest, where the heavy weight of the snow had bent the trees. Because they'd gone right across the lake then leapt into the woods, they didn't leave any footprints behind.

Well, no footprints that would be seen immediately. The vamps would have to search first, scanning every edge of the woods, then if they got lucky, they *might* see the tracks just past the trees but–

But it was starting to snow again.

Hell, yes. The snow came down, brushing against his skin as they ran. The fresh snow would cover any tracks they left behind.

A wolf would have been able to track them through the snow. Vamps were no match for wolves when it came to stalking prey.

No match.

Paige stumbled and would have fallen, but he just grabbed her and hoisted her into his arms. Her weight didn't slow him. He pushed faster. Held her tighter.

He leapt easily over the dead trees, the rough rocks. Faster…

Drake turned abruptly, heading toward the cabin that he knew would be waiting. Small, nondescript, the snow almost hid it completely from view. But he knew the cabin was there, waiting.

The vamps wouldn't be so lucky. Unless they knew the specific location of this safe house, they'd never find it in the darkness.

He punched in the security code, then shouldered open the door. Still holding her tightly, Drake carried Paige inside. The interior was pitch black, and their ragged breathing seemed to echo in the tight space.

"We can't stay here," Paige said, voice desperate. Her nails sank into his shoulder. "We need to get back to the compound. They'll find you here! You can't face all of them on your own!"

He put her down beside him. The cabin was sparsely furnished in this area–containing just a bed and an old table. But looks could be deceiving. Drake bent down and yanked back an old rug, a rug that had covered a trapdoor on the floor. When he'd had the cabin built, Drake had made sure that the trapdoor blended seamlessly with the floor. He pressed against the wood, in just the right spot. With a creak, the trapdoor opened, revealing the gaping entrance that led below.

He'd created this safe house for any wolf shifters who got caught outside the compound during the winter storms. The place was supposed to be a safe harbor for them.

One with all the benefits and security that a wolf needed.

Paige crept down the stairs. He shut the door behind her. Bolted it. Then punched in a series of codes on the alarm pad.

There was a faint hum, then a steel door slid closed above him, covering the wood. Lights flickered on, one after the other, revealing an area twice as big as the cabin above them.

One wall was composed of monitors. A security station that showed all the area around the cabin, just in case any unwanted guests came calling.

There was a bed. A desk. A cabinet full of food.

All the comforts of home and all the security of a mini-fortress.

Just what he'd wanted.

Drake headed toward the nearby desk. He lifted up the radio–one that was wired to the compound. "Alpha One."

Paige made no sound behind him.

Static crackled. "Reading you sir, over."

Drake glanced back at Paige. So still. So beautiful. "Send hunters to Lost Lake. The vamps are out there."

He'd be taking care of this threat. Eliminating the vampires permanently, right after...

After he settled a few things between him and Paige.

"Yes, sir." It was Michael's voice. Drake caught the eagerness in the guy's quick reply. Who didn't enjoy a good hunt?

No wolf he knew.

Drake pushed away from the desk. Stalked toward Paige. She was still shivering but she stood straight and tall. She stared at him like she thought he would attack her.

He did want to pounce.

He lifted his hand and let it skim down her cold cheek. "Tell me about your lies, sweet."

She turned her face into his touch. "You should...find some clothes."

"Why?" Wolves had never been concerned with modesty. "I'm about to fuck you."

Her eyes widened.

Now he was the one lying. With her, it wasn't just fucking. Not just screwing in the dark-or the light. It was more.

Mating.

He took a breath and could almost taste her. "Tell me the secrets you've been keeping...tell me...and I'll tell you mine."

She shook her head. "You know-"

"The vampires were watching the compound. They saw you leave." Obvious. He wasn't a damn idiot. Desperate for her, yeah, but not stupid. "Then they saw me." The vamps had given chase, but they would have been watching from a distance, probably using scopes or binoculars, so it had taken them a while to close in. "And they came out to kill me."

He stepped closer. Pressed his lips against her throat and inhaled her scent. Sex and woman. *His.* "You were sweet bait." He didn't care. The vampires had hurt her. Tortured her. Used her against him. She'd been sent to lure him out in the open.

So the fuck what?

He still wanted her. Always would.

"No." Her word was a sigh as her hands lifted to curl around his shoulders. "You don't understand."

He licked her neck. Her shiver wasn't from the cold that time. "Make me understand." Because he could see a pretty clear picture. *She didn't have a choice.* The man understood that, and he was furious at the vamps who'd done this to her. "You should have just told me, from the start. I could have protected you–"

Her nails dug into his skin. "*No.*"

Surprised by the fury in that one word, Drake lifted his head and stared down at her.

Her breath whispered out as she stared at him. Her eyes were chips of green ice. "This time," she told him, "I'm protecting *you.*"

What?

Then she wrapped her hand around his neck and pulled him toward her. Her lips were open, slightly cool, and her mouth–*perfect.*

His cock was already hard. Like the cold had put a damper on *that.* He ached for her, and that bed was just waiting for them.

One step.

Two.

Three.

They fell onto the bed. His hands fought to remove her clothes even as she kicked away her boots. He wanted *in* her. The truth, the lies–all that could wait. Right then, he just needed her.

The lake…

Waiting…

He wasn't gonna wait anymore. They stripped in a tangle of hands. Fabric ripped. Boots and shoes hit the floor.

He tore her panties and tossed them aside. He pushed open her legs. Found her hot, soft. He pushed her legs farther apart and stared down at her pink flesh. So damn pretty.

Because he couldn't resist, Drake bent his head and put his lips against her sex. Her hips rocked up against him.

"Drake!"

He loved it when she screamed his name. The room had been sound-proofed. No one outside would hear her. Only him.

He licked her clit. Tasted her. So delicious. So good.

So his.

Her hands were in his hair. Not urging him away, no, his vampiress was asking for more.

He'd give her more.

He licked. He tasted.

She came against his tongue. "Drake." A whisper now.

Slowly, he rose above her. Her eyes were wide, shining, and her fangs flashed faintly from behind her red lips.

"You're not a monster." It pissed him off that she'd said those words before. No fucking way. Not her. Not ever. "You're beautiful."

She blinked up at him, and her lips curled in a faint smile. The sight nearly broke his heart.

What was left of the damn thing.

He thrust into her, driving deep, joining them. His hands locked with hers, their fingers threading together. The bed squeaked beneath him. In and out, he thrust. Again and again. Their eyes held.

Their breath heaved out.

Faster, faster now, harder…

Her legs locked around his hips. Her feet dug into his spine when she arched toward him.

His claws cut through his fingertips, but he didn't slice her. *Hell,* no, he didn't so much as scratch her with his claws.

Deeper, *deeper*.

He saw her come again. Saw the flash of pleasure on her face as she eyes seemed to go blind. She jerked beneath him and her sex squeezed his cock.

Yes.

He was so close to coming. He'd explode in her at any moment when she–

"Mark me."

Her husky words had every muscle in his body tightening.

Wolves marked their mates. He hadn't marked her before, he'd been waiting. There was an official ceremony, a marking in front of the pack. He'd wanted to do things right with her.

He'd waited…

And lost her.

"Mark me," she whispered again, and dammit, she was *asking* for his bite. She wanted him as wildly as he wanted her.

He'd never been able to deny her anything.

She arched beneath him, offering herself. His teeth closed over her flesh, right where her shoulder curved into her neck. He licked the skin there.

Mark her.

It was what the wolf wanted and what the man needed.

His teeth pressed into her skin, breaking the skin, and the sweet flavor of her blood flowed onto his tongue.

Even as he tasted her, claimed her, his climax slammed into him. The powerful release crashed through his body as he pumped into her. He lifted his head, stared into her eyes, and, as he drove into her once more, the pleasure tore a roar from him.

Her name.

Drake held her tight, didn't let her go, couldn't. And he kept thrusting. Because he was still hard for her and growing harder every second.

He'd finally claimed her as his own, and no one would ever take her from him again.

***

"How do you lose a werewolf?" Gabe asked as his boots sank into the snow. So much damn snow. Bathing everything in white.

He hated that pure snow.

It looked much better when it was stained red.

So he turned to the right and sliced open the stomach of the incompetent newbie vamp next to him.

The fresh bloods were always so hard to train.

The guy, a blond with too-soft features, immediately fell to the ground, gasping and bleeding with a bright spray of red.

"Suck it the hell up," Gabe snarled at him because the fresh blood's screams grated. "It's not like the wound will kill you." But he was tempted. Oh, so tempted to finish the job.

The foolish bastards around him had let the alpha get away. They'd let the prick just vanish into the wilderness.

"Probably back at his compound by now," Gabe muttered as he spun away and stared off into the distance. "Surrounded by all those mangy wolves."

Gabe had been around a long time. Too long. He'd seen the worst wars and hell that the humans could create.

That hell…it had made him smart. He'd learned from the mistakes of the others. He knew how to pick his battles. Plan his attacks.

He wanted this land. The land that was rarely kissed by sunlight. The land with the savage side that loved his darkness.

The wolves had made a truce with him long ago. Divided the territory. That twisted freak Jeremiah had been all too eager to forge a deal with him.

But the new alpha wasn't the same. Gabe had known that for years. Drake Wyler was different. Not so easily manipulated and controlled.

Drake will come for my head.

Because Gabe had taken the head of Drake's father. His mother. And because…

I took her.

A wolf howled in the distance. A real beast? Or a shifter out for a run?

Gabe narrowed his eyes and stared into the darkness. Jeremiah had wanted him to take the little human. To torture her, to kill her.

He'd had his torturing fun. Oh, he always enjoyed that, but…

Gabe hadn't killed Paige Sloan. Death would have been too easy and not at all in line with his plans.

"Wh-what can we do?" One of the vamps asked behind him.

Gabe's teeth ground together. "She stopped screaming," he gritted out. When she'd finally realized what was happening, when she'd seen Jeremiah and had known *why* she was taken, Paige had stopped calling out for her lover.

He'd actually seen the life fade from her eyes, even while she was still breathing.

That total lack of feeling–he'd seen that look before.

In my own eyes.

So he'd stopped Jeremiah from gutting her. Gabe had bitten Paige, transformed her. She'd fled, but he'd watched her. And he'd always known that the perfect time would come to use her.

That time was now.

"H-he followed her out to the lake, ran right out..." Ah, this came from the still bleeding blond. John. John Mackenzie. How long had he been in the fold? Two years? Three? It was getting hard for Gabe to remember all the fresh bloods. As he stared at the blond, John gave a quick nod. "He chased her out...I saw 'em...through my binoculars."

Because you couldn't get too close to a wolf's lair, not without being scented. So the vamps used technology to supplement their already enhanced vision.

They'd watched. They'd waited. They'd attacked.

The plan had still gone to hell.

"He took her with him." This came from one of the other vamps. The one with the dark eyes and weathered skin. Lorenzo, the Spaniard. "She's probably dead by now."

Gabe laughed. They really didn't understand the wolf at all. He did. "She's probably getting fucked." Because she was the one weakness that Drake possessed. He'd run away from his pack for her. Run into danger for her.

The wolf was addicted, and Gabe had no doubt that, if necessary, Drake would trade his life for Paige.

Snow crunched to the left of him. The vamps around him swore and leapt forward.

Gabe shoved them out of the way. He wanted to see this visitor.

Curiosity had always been *his* weakness.

The white wolf edged from the darkness with his eyes glowing. The beast didn't attack. He just stared at Gabe with that intense gaze.

Gabe smiled at him. "All alone are you?" Because there were no other sounds at that lake. This wasn't a wolf out leading an attack party.

This was something altogether different.

Gabe crossed his arms over his chest. "If you're here to deal..." So many deals, so many years. He knew just how the devil felt. *When will it end?* "Then you're gonna have to shift and talk to me because I don't fucking speak animal."

The white wolf crept forward. His wary gaze darted to each of the vampires.

"Shift," Gabe snapped, losing patience, "or I can just go ahead and kill you now."

The wolf began to shift. Disgusting. Gabe hated the sight of the shifting wolves.

Even though he did enjoy the sounds of those popping bones.

But soon enough, a man stood before him. Fury tightened the man's face and hands. "I know where they are."

Fatal mistake. The wolf was just throwing all of his cards out for them to see. Now, they just had to torture the shifter to get that important information.

No deal. Just pain.

Death.

Some blood.

Snow stained red… It could be so lovely.

"I'll take you there," the werewolf said, "and get you past the security."

Security. So perhaps he *would* be useful after all. The pain could wait a bit. Gabe lifted a brow but didn't move forward. "And you'll do this because…?"

"Because *I* want to be alpha."

Right. Everyone wanted power. But this wolf, with his bitter eyes and snarling arrogance, he wasn't going to control this land.

Gabe wasn't going to sit back and let any animal take control. Not anymore. Those days were over. There'd be no more truces. No more deals.

Only death.

But he smiled because he knew how to play the game. He'd made the damn game. "You want me to kill Drake Wyler."

A quick nod. "That's what you're planning anyway, right? Kill him…and we–we can have the same arrangement that you had with Jeremiah." The wolf glanced over his shoulder. What? Was he afraid the rest of his pack would find out that he was a traitor?

You should be afraid.

"The same arrangement I had with Jeremiah." How the hell did the wolf know about that deal? Gabe cocked his head to the side and studied the wolf with faint interest. "So you want to kill the humans, too? Want to slice them up and hear them scream until their voices break?"

Ah, now that was surprise on the shifter's face. Gabe *almost* smiled.

"He-he did-" A quick swallow and the shifter shook his head. "No, no, I just want control of the pack. The shifters will leave your men alone, I'll make them stay away. You can hunt, you can kill…and I won't do a damn thing to stop you."

The whelp was annoying. "Cause you'll control the wolves…"

"Damn right." The shifter threw back his shoulders and stalked forward. Did he realize how close he was to death? The arrogant ones never seemed to understand, not until it was too late. "I'll keep 'em away. I'll be alpha-I'll be able to do anything and everything that I want."

Provided Drake was dead.

"Do we have a deal?" The werewolf demanded.

Gabe stared back at him. "What's your name?"

"Michael. Michael Flint."

The name meant nothing and that very fact said he was staring at a werewolf no one gave a shit about. "Michael, you're turning on your alpha so quickly."

"Because *I'm* stronger. I'm smarter, I can–"

Gabe barely stifled a yawn. He'd heard this spiel a dozen times. "Take me to him." Then he'd kill Drake, eliminate this werewolf dumbass, and he'd take all the territory in Alaska.

Wolves were always weakest without a leader. Without Drake–they'd be easy pickings for his vamps.

Michael smiled. No, some arrogant fools never saw death coming.

Not until the moment death reached up and yanked their beating hearts right out of their chests.

CHAPTER SEVEN

He'd taken her blood. Euphoria filled Paige's body. She'd been so afraid she wouldn't be able to get Drake to take her blood.

But he had. Her wolf hadn't even hesitated.

He'll be safe now.

She wrapped her arms around him, holding tight. They'd just climaxed again, and the pleasure still hummed through her body.

Then an alarm began to beep, a shrill, deep cry that came from the far right of the room. Paige tensed in Drake's arms because she knew what that sound meant.

They're coming.

Gabe and his vampires had managed to track them through the snow.

You didn't find us soon enough, asshole.

Drake pulled away from her and stalked, naked, to the line of monitors. She followed him, but paused long enough to yank on her clothes as fast as she could.

She didn't see anyone on the monitors, not yet.

"Motion sensor," he said, not looking away from that screen. "Could be anything…"

But the clench in her gut told her that not just *anything* had triggered that alarm.

Then she saw the movement of a shadow. No, not a shadow.

A wolf. A white wolf, running toward the cabin. Paige tensed. "Are we…are we supposed to be having company?" She didn't see anyone else, just that wolf.

"*Michael.*"

While she watched, the wolf began to shift. As the white fur vanished, it almost looked like snow was dripping away to reveal the man's flesh. Then he stood, staring up at the camera. Up at them. In that moment, with him back in human form, she recognized the werewolf.

Paige's hand went to her throat. The faint scratches were long gone by now, but she never forgot anyone who gave her pain, no matter how slight the wound was.

Not until she'd given payback for her injuries.

The old Paige, the girl she'd been, had never thought of vengeance and punishment.

The vampire knew there had to be a rough justice in the paranormal world. Only the strong survived.

She'd survive. So would Drake. She'd make sure of it.

"Why is he here?" Drake demanded. "He should be at the lake, hunting the vampires. He should–"

"He's not alone." Because she'd seen the other shadows. The ones that were closing in on the shifter.

Michael had to hear the vampires. Had to smell them.

But he just kept walking toward the cabin like he didn't have a care in the world. "Does he know how to get past your security?" Her heart was racing in her chest.

Michael headed for the cabin. Another camera zoomed in on his face as he approached the front door. For just an instant, Paige caught sight of the smile that curved Michael's lips.

Hell.

"He brought them here," she whispered as the cold certainty settled in her gut. Michael was going to lead the vampires inside. Right to her and Drake. They would be sitting ducks for the vamps.

Their safe house had just become their prison.

Two of them. Two against–how many vamps?

The shadows pushed toward the cabin. One. Two. Three. Four...

Five?

"He's not getting in," Drake said as he punched a series of codes into the computer. "He doesn't have the right access code. I changed it a few days ago, and, after he hurt you, I didn't give it to him."

Her breath rushed out.

"Never really trusted him," Drake muttered as he reached for the radio. He connected almost instantly with the compound. "Wolf gone rogue at safe house one," he said, biting off the words. "Send back up…"

Michael wasn't smiling anymore. He was kicking at the door. Punching. Guess he'd realized he didn't have the right code to get inside.

"That's steel, bastard," Drake said, voice hardening, "Reinforced fucking steel, and no, I didn't tell your ass about that little feature, either."

Because Drake had known that Michael might turn on him?

Another voice crackled over the radio. "Coming now, alpha. Two teams. Are there–"

The vampires closed in on Michael. They grabbed him and hauled him away from the cabin. Michael didn't fight them. The wolf went with them willingly.

But she could see he wasn't smiling anymore.

Her chest began to burn. She knew what would happen next. Michael might have thought he was working with the vampires. He might have *thought* that...

"Michael brought the vampires," Drake said flatly into the radio, "and, they're–"

Killing him.

Or, they would be, soon enough. Right then, they were holding him down. Slicing into him with their razor-sharp fangs.

Drinking from him.

And making sure that the security cameras saw everything.

"Get the fuck here," Drake snarled and tossed the radio aside. Then he whirled and headed for the stairs.

Paige grabbed him. "You *can't* go out there." A glance at the monitors showed her that Michael was fighting back now. Screaming.

The vampires were still drinking.

Only it wasn't just four vampires any longer. *Six.*

Her breath caught when she saw Gabe. He wasn't drinking from the werewolf. Gabe just stood there, staring up at the cabin.

Waiting.

He'd waited on this one attack for years.

Secrets. She hadn't told Drake everything yet. There hadn't been enough time. There still wasn't.

"I'm alpha," he growled as his gaze burned into her. "Michael is one of mine, traitor or not."

Um, there was a not portion? That guy was a straight-up traitor. No doubt.

"I won't let them drain him," Drake's voice rumbled over the beeping alarm. "Not while I just watch."

No, Drake wouldn't do that. He wouldn't just stand back while another wolf suffered. That wasn't who her shifter was.

She knew that...and that was just one of the reasons she'd known that she had to get close to him again.

He'd taken her blood, but the boost from that blood didn't happen instantaneously. She'd learned from the vampires in Florida–the vamps that weren't twisted freaks–that when a vampire offered her blood to a werewolf, well, the result could be pretty damn amazing.

The wolf could become stronger.

She wanted Drake as strong as he could possibly be.

But the boost took a little time. The vampire blood had to work its way through his body.

I'll give him the time he needs.

"I'm sorry," she whispered because he'd hate what she was about to do.

But, sometimes, a vamp just had to do what she had to do.

Since he wasn't expecting the attack, Paige had the advantage. She grabbed Drake and shoved him back against the wall. The wall had to be reinforced with steel. The whole place was reinforced.

This would hurt. But she had to hurt him in order to save him.

"Paige, what the hell—"

She kissed him. A deep, hard kiss that held all the passion and longing she felt for him. Did he know that she still loved him? That she always had? There'd never been another in her heart. There wasn't room for anyone else. Even with all the miles and years between them, Drake had been the only one she wanted.

He shuddered against her. "*Paige.*" Lust. Need. Fury. All were in his voice. And he was about to try and break away from her. She knew it.

Couldn't allow it.

I'm sorry. The words were only in her mind this time. She brought his lips back to hers. Kissed him again. She knew just what she had to do. Give him an injury that would disable him—for a bit—but allow him to come back even stronger once her blood started pumping fully in his veins.

A tear leaked down her cheek. His arms were around her. He was holding her tight. Some attacks, you never expected.

Paige tore her lips from his. In the same instant, she reached up, grabbed his head, and slammed it back against the reinforced wall. The thud of impact had nausea rolling in her gut.

Her shifter went down with a groan.

She stared at him, aware that her heart just *hurt.* "I'm sorry," she said again. She had to move fast. She knew shifters–no, she knew *him*–and he'd be recovered in three, four minutes tops.

He'd come after her.

He'd go after Michael.

But Drake wouldn't die. Because she wouldn't allow it.

She spun away. Punched in the codes she'd memorized. She'd watched him so carefully, just in case...

The steel slid back. The trapdoor opened. She rushed through the opening but took precious seconds to secure the door behind her.

Her gaze flew around the cabin. She rushed to the left, to the right, and did her best to cover that trapdoor and protect her wolf.

Then she bent down, and her hand slid inside of her boot. Oh, that sweet weapon. Without a stake, she'd feel naked. She never left home–or her wolf's compound–without it. Held inside by special straps, the weapon was waiting for her.

Time to die.

She ran out of that cabin and raced right toward her worst nightmare.

The vamps were feeding. Michael was screaming. And Gabe–Gabe opened his arms to her as if he were greeting a lost lover.

"I've missed you," he said, voice smooth as silk.

Paige's heart raced as she ran into his open arms.

***

Fury filled him as Drake's eyes flew open. *What. The. Hell.*

He leapt to his feet. His gaze went to the monitors, and he saw Paige, *his Paige,* running into the open arms of a vampire.

The fuck no.

He leapt up the stairs and punched in the code to open the door. The steel slid back, and he shoved against the wood.

Only…the wood didn't move.

He shoved again. Harder. The wood lifted, then fell back down with a snap. His eyes narrowed. Paige had put something on top of the trapdoor. She'd locked him in.

His beast didn't like to be caged.

With a roar, Drake slammed his shoulders into that wood. He pushed. He heaved.

The wood broke apart. He leapt up, still shoving–*the bed, she'd put the bed on top of the trapdoor*–then raced for the front door.

He could hear the snarls and shouts and they seemed to burn his ears. The image of Paige running into that vampire's arms was branded into his mind. Why? *Why?*

He rushed outside. Saw the blood on the ground. Michael. Still alive. Barely moving.

Paige–she was…

"Hello, alpha." The taunting voice came from his left.

Drake's claws were out and so ready to claw that SOB apart.

"Did you lose something?" The vampire asked as Drake turned to face him.

The vampire was tall. Blond. Bleeding. And he held Paige in his arms. The embrace wasn't one of a lover, though. One of the vampire's arms locked around her throat, while the vamp's other hand held a wooden stake right over Paige's heart.

"Because it looks like I found something." The vamp smiled, flashing fangs.

Drake saw the other vampires stalking toward him. Was he supposed to be intimidated? Scared?

He was just pissed. "Let her go."

The vampire–he had to be the one Paige had told him about, the one she'd called Gabe-shook his head and laughed. "If that's what you want…she's already served her purpose."

Drake was looking at Paige then. He saw her eyes flare wide in horror, then Gabe spun her around so that she faced the vampire.

"You're free now," the vampire told her, voice soft, almost tender, "because that's what your wolf wants."

Paige struggled against him, clawing, punching–

Drake realized, too late, just what the asshole was doing.

You're free now.

He was killing her.

Drake roared and lunged forward, forgetting the other vampires, desperate to reach Paige, to help her and–

Gunfire.

Bullets. Thudding into his flesh. Burning. Tearing apart muscle and bone.

His blood spilled onto the ground. His legs stopped working. He wanted to reach Paige, but he couldn't.

He was falling.

The snow turned red beneath him.

His claws lifted as he tried to dig out the bullets. So many. In his chest. His back.

He managed to tilt back his head. He could see Paige. She was still fighting with Gabe. The stake was covered in blood.

But she was still alive.

She glanced back at Drake and screamed his name.

He'd promised to protect her. She'd asked him for just one thing.

I want you to rip his head off, and I want you to make damn sure that he never rises again.

Now that vampire was laughing. She was bleeding.

And I'm dying.

No, no, he wouldn't die. He wouldn't go out like this.

Drake called on the beast within. *Wake up.* Drake pushed to his feet. Stumbled. Yanked out the silver in his shoulder and barely felt the burn.

Wake up.

The beast hated silver.

But the wolf loved the woman who was screaming for him.

A vampire came at him, still with a gun in his hand. Fool. *You came too close.* Drake grabbed the gun. Shot the vampire in the chest. Swiped out with his claws.

This time, it was the vampire that fell.

Drake dug another bullet from his flesh. The smoke from his blistering fingertips rose in the air.

Another vampire came at him.

A swipe of his claws and the vampire's blood flowed.

"*Stop him!*" Gabe's scream of fury.

Then all the vampires swarmed him. Even though Drake still had at least three silver bullets in him, he didn't hesitate when they attacked.

He roared and slashed into the chest of the nearest vamp. *Another one down. Bye, asshole.*

The other two vamps–they just turned and ran.

Drake grabbed a weapon that had been tossed aside and turned his focus on the one that mattered. The vampire that was about to lose his damn head.

"*How?*" Gabe gritted as he stared at Drake with fury boiling in his dark gaze. "You can't–you're not strong enough–"

Paige's laughter cut through his words. "He's strong enough…if he's got vampire blood in him."

Drake could still taste her on his tongue.
Mark me.

The wolf had claimed his mate. Marked her. And tasted her blood.

"You bitch." Gabe shook Paige, sending her head snapping back.

Begging for death. Drake fired the gun. It just clicked. No more bullets. That was all right. He wanted to get his hands bloody.

"You did this to him!" Gabe shouted. The guy didn't even seem to see Drake closing in on him. The stake had fallen from his hand. "You made him–"

"Stronger," Paige gasped out as blood dripped from her lips. "I made him strong enough to kill you…just in case I couldn't."

Her words had Drake's body tensing. He'd kill the vamp for her, all right. *A promise is a promise.* Drake grabbed Paige and yanked her away from Gabe. Drake's wolf was snarling, his claws were fully extended, and he was ready to destroy.

The stake broke beneath his feet, and he broke Gabe's neck with one twist of his wrist.

But the vampire just laughed–and his bones snapped back into place almost instantly.

"Try harder," Gabe murmured. There was no fear on the vampire's face or in his eyes. "Come on, let's see what you can do, alpha. Let's see if you can fight as hard as you father did."

His father? What did his–

More laughter from Gabe. Colder than the night that surrounded them. "You thought that you got all the vamps from that attack, huh? Think again, alpha. *Think fucking again.*" Gabe bared his teeth. "Those vamps attacked because *I* gave the order. Only they were supposed to have killed your sorry ass that night, too."

But he hadn't been at home when his family was so brutally attacked. He'd been out, watching Paige as she worked at a little diner. He'd gone to that diner over and over, eager to catch a glimpse of her. That night, he'd finally asked her out. He'd been so excited when he'd gone back home. *She'd said yes!* Then he'd found the blood and the bodies waiting on him.

"Jeremiah let me in," Gabe told him as the vamp circled around Drake. "He knew you'd be the next alpha, and he wasn't ready to let go of the pack. He let me kill them all...and drink all that shifter blood."

Because shifter blood was stronger than human blood. Far more powerful.

Jeremiah had fed his own pack to this prick? *Why?*

"Your bastard alpha was addicted...the same way she wants you to be...to vampire blood."

*He could taste her...*The wolf howled within him, desperate to break free and attack.

Drake sucked in a deep breath. Paige was on the ground. Still, like a broken, beautiful doll. "It's not the blood I'm addicted to," Drake told Gabe, voice growling. The beast was coming out. The vamp was dying. "It's her."

He leapt at the vamp even as the shift burned through him. The vamp would get in a few swipes while he transformed, no way around that, because Drake was weak in those moments when he was locked between man and beast.

But he had to shift. The shift would push the rest of the silver from his body, and the wolf would be stronger than the man.

The wolf would take the vamp's head.

Gabe was smiling as he lunged toward Drake. The vamp's fangs were bared and–

"Think fucking again," Paige shouted, throwing the vamp's words right back at him. Then gunfire thundered. Once. Twice.

She had picked up one of the other discarded guns. But, unlike the weapon Drake had chosen, her gun still had ammunition. She filled Gabe's chest with the silver bullets. He stumbled back, screaming and bleeding.

Not a broken doll, not anymore.

Time to die, Gabe.

In his mind, Drake could see his mother's broken body. His father's pale face.

The shift was over. The wolf growled and charged the vamp. They fell down in a tangle of limbs and claws. The vampire was biting, tearing into the wolf's body, and punching with his enhanced strength.

Gabe was too used to pushing around humans. Too used to torturing them.

Wolves weren't so easy to take down.

"K-killed the alpha…" Gabe gritted out as they fought. "And I'll kill you, too." Blood dripped down his chin. "The vamps are taking over this–"

Drake's teeth locked around the pureblood's throat.

Paige was standing right behind him. He could smell her sweet scent, hear the ragged gasp of her breaths.

This was it. She'd be free. His parents could rest in peace.

But Gabe was still laughing. "Mine…" Gabe gasped, spitting blood. "She'll…always be…mine. The vamps…win. We take…Alaska…"

No, he wouldn't win.

When the wolf's teeth sank deep, the vamp didn't speak again.

He just died.

CHAPTER EIGHT

It was over.

Paige turned away from the sight of Gabe's body. She didn't want to see anymore. She just wanted–

Wolves surrounded her.

Oh, crap, when had they arrived? She hadn't even noticed them. She'd been so intent on fighting Gabe and helping Drake that she hadn't been aware of the wolves. They could move so quietly as they prepared for an attack.

A dozen wolves formed a circle around her and Drake. They stood back. Watching, waiting.

Had they heard Gabe's final taunt? Hell, she *knew* the wolves weren't going to let her stay in the pack, so they didn't have to worry about her taking over their precious territory.

The minute Gabe had transformed her, she'd known that her dream of finding Drake and staying with him–forever–well, it had truly just been a dream.

They might have sex. They might turn to each other in the darkness, but his pack would never accept her.

And she wouldn't ask him to leave the wolves.

She held up her hands and realized they were stained with blood. Her own. Gabe's. "Easy…"

The black wolf near her snarled.

Great. Just–

Drake leapt in front of her. He opened his mouth and howled his fury at the pack.

Paige shivered. She hadn't been afraid when she faced off against Gabe and the vamps. She'd been too pissed. But now, with the wolves circling, hell, yes, she could admit to fear.

These wolves would love to rip and tear her apart. Once they found out the truth about what she'd done, the final secret that she'd kept from them…

They'd want her head, just as she'd wanted Gabe's.

Drake was shifting back into the form of a man before her. The snap and crunch of his bones filled her ears.

But she didn't wait around for him to finish shifting. Paige knew an exit time when she saw one. "Don't worry," she told the wolves–jeez, it sure looked like they were about to rip her limb from limb. "I'm leaving."

She had friends waiting for her. Friends who'd helped her reach Alaska. Friends who'd be glad to welcome her back to the vampire world.

We're not all monsters. She'd learned that. Some vampires were more than just predators. Just as the werewolves were more.

She kept her steps nice and slow. The wolves could probably smell her fear, but a running target–that was prey they'd always instinctively chase. No sense giving them any more reason to want her blood.

"You're not leaving me."

Drake's voice. Guttural. Still more beast than man.

She froze. "The deal's over." Not the conversation she wanted to have in front of a wolf pack. "Gabe's dead." *You're safe.*

He grabbed her hand. Pulled her close. She could smell the metallic scent of the silver hanging in the air. She'd come too close to losing him.

If he hadn't taken her blood…

She swallowed. "Let me go." Dammit, the words were a plea. Because she knew he wanted her, just as much as she wanted him.

I'm addicted to her.

But sometimes, the things you wanted most were the things that would destroy you.

His head lowered toward hers. "I killed for you."

She'd wanted to kill for him. To protect him, she would have done anything.

I did.

"Do you know how your alpha died?" Paige asked him quietly. Maybe he knew some of the details already. There were spies in the vampire covens. For the right price, they'd share any information.

She'd sure offered up enough money over the years for the Intel they'd given her.

Drake frowned down at her. The wolves behind him still didn't move.

"Your old alpha was fed poisoned vampire blood." Jeremiah had thought that he'd get stronger by taking the vampire blood. If he'd been given normal vamp blood, he *would* have become stronger.

But he'd been ingesting blood laced with silver for years. Poison, building up in his body. Eating away at him from the inside.

He'd lost his ability to shift. He'd lost his ability to walk. To talk. To breathe.

Because Gabe had always enjoyed his torture.

"I knew what was happening to him," she said. She'd known for a long time. Long enough to save him. Only she hadn't wanted to save him. She'd wanted him to suffer. "I didn't stop it because I wanted that bastard dead."

A wolf snarled from somewhere behind her.

Screw them all. She turned and bared her fangs right back at the snarling beast. The wolf shut up. Good. Paige exhaled on a low, rough sigh and turned back to meet Drake's intense stare. "But when Jeremiah finally died, I-I knew Gabe would come after you." She shook her head. "But I wasn't gonna let you die. I knew I'd do whatever I had to do...in order to keep you safe."

And she'd done her part. He'd survived.

"It wasn't ever about me taking his head...to protect you," Drake muttered.

No, she hadn't been the one who needed protection.

"You tricked me into taking your blood," Drake said as he towered over her. Eyes so intent. Body naked. Strong. His hand tightened around her wrist. "You got me to drink, so I'd be strong enough to kill the pureblood when he came after me." Because despite what Drake had originally thought, even an alpha wasn't strong enough to take out a vamp like Gabe-not Gabe and his silver wielding buddies. But an alpha pumped up on vamp blood? He could kick ass and destroy any vamp in his path.

The wolves were shifting around them. Transforming into men and women and the snow was falling again.

She didn't look at the dead body on the ground. And Michael-he was groaning and struggling to his feet. Some of the shifters went to help him.

"Leave him," Drake ordered, voice tight with fury. "He worked with the vampires. He led them right to me."

The shifters froze.

"He's banished from the pack," Drake said flatly. A judgment. Cold and brutal. "Leave him where the fuck he is." His head turned as he stared over at Michael. "You're still breathing, so count yourself damn lucky."

When Drake's gaze came back to her, Paige forced herself to meet that hard stare. So much fury. How much was for her? For the vamp he'd killed? And for the traitor he'd had in his own midst?

"You lied to me," Drake said. The words were low and all the more lethal for their softness.

"From the beginning," Paige agreed, her own voice just as soft. But there was no reason for lies anymore. She'd done her job. She'd protected him.

They'd saved each other.

Now they could go their separate ways. He'd go back to his pack. She'd go back to the life she'd created in Florida.

So what if she went back without a heart? She'd been missing that particular organ for years.

Paige turned away. She had to get out of there. Her chest was burning. Aching. Looking at Drake just hurt too much. Her job was done.

Time to leave before he saw through her mask.

I want you. I want to stay.

Some things just weren't meant to be.

But Paige didn't run away. She walked. One foot in front of the other. Slow. Steady.

"Was everything a lie?"

She stopped. Didn't look back. "Not everything." Then because–hell, what did she have to lose? Paige glanced back over her shoulder. "I really have always loved you." From the first moment she saw him. "And I always will."

Then she kept walking. Because sometimes, love just wasn't enough.

Not when you were a vampire.

And not when the man you wanted more than blood was a werewolf.

***

Did Paige really think that she was just going to walk away? *Hell, no.*

Drake watched her as she left him. The snow drifted over her dark hair. Her steps were slow but certain.

Not running…just *leaving* him.

Right after she'd said she loved him? The woman was about to break him.

He inhaled deeply, drawing in her scent. He'd never lose her again.

Never.

"Get rid of the bodies." Easy enough in the wild. "Head back to the compound." Because the battle wasn't over. Not for him.

His gaze swept around the assembled wolves. "Then if there is any one of you who wants to challenge me, take your best shot." He was ready for a fight with claws and teeth and blood and fury. "Because my *mate* is going to be with me, in my pack, by my side, for the rest of my life." Even if his life was shorter than hers.

He'd take what he could get.

Mate. That was what Paige was. She'd been his mate since she was nineteen.

She'd be his until he took his last breath.

Vampire, werewolf–it didn't matter. She was his.

He'd fight for her, just as she'd fought for him.

When the fight was over, he'd find her.

I'll come after you, Paige.

Always.

***

Silence.

Drake stared at the group of shifters who'd assembled in the compound's courtyard. No one spoke. No one moved.

They all stood before him. Waiting.

He wore a pair of jeans, hanging low on his hips, and his claws were out.

His gaze swept over them all. "Who's first?" The wolf inside was already howling.

He'd fight to give Paige a place at his side because he damn well wasn't living without her.

No one stepped forward.

"Who's first?"

They weren't meeting his stare. The shifters backed up, showing submission.

All of them backed up…except for Heath. His first-in-command stepped forward.

First.

But Heath lifted his hands and no claws burst from his fingertips. "I have no quarrel with you or your mate."

Drake grabbed him. Lifted him into the air. "That's not what you said before."

"Before…" Heath swallowed and shook his head. "Before I didn't know what she'd risk for you."

Everything.

"We saw the blood. The bodies. We know what she did."

Fought. Saved him. Saved the pack.

Drake dropped the other shifter. Heath scrambled to his feet. "We'll protect her, swear allegiance to her, just as we do to you."

There was a murmur of agreement from the shifters. Not silence, not anymore.

The murmur turned into a growing roar of approval. Determination.

"So go get your mate," Heath told him, voice fierce now. "Bring her into the pack. Bring her back where she belongs."

Drake's bare feet sank into the snow as he rushed through the crowd. Paige's sweet scent still filled his nose. He wasn't losing her this time. *Not this time.*

Drake ran after his mate, and as he ran, he knew exactly where he'd find her.

***

The frozen lake stared back up at her. So still and cold. Paige was shivering and she was hungry and she just ached.

But she was still alive. Sort of, anyway, and pain was just part of life.

She turned away from the lake.

And found Drake watching her.

She was so surprised to see him that she flinched. "D-Drake?"

He stood next to an old, twisted tree, one bent beneath the weight of the snow. "I was supposed to meet you here," he said, voice rumbling. Intense. Dark.

She shook her head. "Th-that was a long time ago."

He pulled a necklace from the back pocket of his jeans. *Her* necklace. The one he'd taken away that first night.

Her chin lifted.

"Do you know why I gave this to you?"

She did. She'd known him so well back then. "Because you loved me." The words were said with certainty. Once upon a time, a boy had loved a girl.

Once upon a time…

He stalked toward her. Didn't even seem to feel the cold. But then, he wouldn't. Not like she did.

He came toward her and lifted the necklace. "I still do love you, sweet."

She raised her hand and stopped him before he could slide that necklace over her head. "You…you took this from me."

Because of what she was.

Not a girl. Not just a boy.

A vampire. A werewolf.

"I was going out of my mind that night. I'd missed you for so long…" His breath heaved out in a rush. "I hurt, and I wanted to hurt you."

A dark admission.

His head bowed. "I want to make it up to you. I want to make everything up to you."

And there, in the snow, with the lake behind her and too many memories around them, Drake dropped to his knees.

Her breath rushed out. An alpha should never submit to another like this. It wasn't the way of the pack. It wasn't–

His hand clenched around the necklace. "I thought you didn't want me."

She'd always wanted him.

"I never loved anyone else. All those years...the only one to ever touch my heart...was you." He looked up at her. She saw the beast and the man in his eyes. "Stay with me." A plea, from a man who'd never pleaded for anything before.

Paige couldn't speak.

"I can make things right for you. I'll make you happy, I *swear*. Just give me a chance."

She licked her lips and tasted the sorrow from the past. "I'm not the same..."

"You're stronger. More beautiful. And I fucking love you even more than I did before."

Her hands touched his shoulders. Hesitant. Hopeful. "You...do?"

"Yes." Said with a growl. Said as he stared into her eyes. In his gaze, she saw–

The future.

"I want you to be with me, for as long as I walk this earth." Now his words came faster. "I won't live as long as you, I know that. Just give me those years, just give me—"

She sank to her knees before him. Kissed him. Kissed him so hard that they tumbled back onto the soft snow.

And he tasted so good. Like forever. Because that was what she could give to him. Her head lifted slowly. "I can give you more."

If he'd let her.

His brows pulled low. His arms were around her, holding her so close. "You'll stay with me?"

"The pack—"

"They want you to stay. They want you to come home."

Home.

"Fifty years," he told her, "sixty. Give me that, give me—"

She shook her head and saw the stark pain flash across his face.

"*I love you,*" he told her but he sounded…lost.

She knew because she'd been lost for years. "I can give you more," Paige promised him. Because she'd learned so much from the vampires who'd helped her in Florida.

Down there, another werewolf had paired with a vampire female. They'd discovered that if a vampire's blood was shared, the wolf would become stronger.

Aging stopped for the wolf. Death was put on hold.

Jeremiah had thought that he was cheating death by drinking from a vamp, but that blood had been poison.

She'd never poison Drake. She'd give him her blood, and she'd give him… "Forever," Paige whispered and kissed Drake again.

As she kissed him, she heard the howl of wolves in the distance.

She wasn't afraid of that sound. She wasn't afraid of anything. Not anymore.

Because she wasn't lost now. She was home and safe…in the arms of her wolf.

BOUND BY THE NIGHT

CHAPTER ONE

He hadn't expected her to be dead.

Jamie O'Connell narrowed his eyes as he studied the still woman before him. Her body had been placed—very carefully, he had no doubt of that—in the middle of a large bed. White, gossamer curtains billowed around the bed, looking like thin spider webs that had been spun to shield her body.

"This is a bad idea," Sean Whelen, Jamie's first in command, muttered as he grabbed Jamie's arm. "There's a *reason* she's under, man. The woman is evil."

She didn't look evil. She looked…beautiful.

Jamie shook off Sean's hold. The guy swore but stepped back as Jamie shoved away those too-thin curtains and let his gaze sweep over the prize he'd sought for so long.

The woman was pale, but that was expected of her kind. It wasn't like she would have been a fan of sunbathing even before she'd succumbed to the curse that had locked her body. Her hair was long and dark, lustrous and gleaming against the bedding. A silken, white dress covered her, skimming over what he could see were ample breasts and the kind of hips he'd always enjoyed holding tight.

"We're going to die," Sean told him, voice definite. "Probably in the next five minutes. Some horrible, painful death."

Jamie tossed him a glare. "Not helping."

Sean rocked back on his heels.

"And it's not like we have a choice," Jamie muttered. Hell. He didn't want to do this. Waking the woman known as the Blood Queen wasn't exactly something that Jamie had *ever* thought he'd do.

But sometimes, a werewolf could sure get desperate. Especially when the lives of his remaining packmates were on the line.

So he put his hands on her body. *Ice cold.* Figured.

"She's not breathing, is she?" As usual, Sean kept talking.

But this time, the guy was right. "No." That was why she looked…dead. When he'd first heard the story about the Blood Queen, he'd just thought it was bullshit.

He wasn't staring at bullshit.

He'd had to kill his way through half a dozen paranormal bastards in order to get to her. Their blood still stained his clothes. But if the woman before him could really do what he thought, then the hell he'd walked through would be worth it.

His fingers skimmed down the delicate curve of her cheek. She certainly didn't look like the walking nightmare that rumors whispered about in the dark. Her chin was a little pointed, her lips sensual and full—and red. Long lashes cast faint shadows on her cheeks, and Jamie wondered what color her eyes would be.

Since he planned on waking her up real soon, Jamie knew he was about to find out.

He lifted his hand away from her face and claws ripped from his fingertips. "Go outside," Jamie ordered Sean. "Guard the door, just in case…"

"Uh, yeah, in case the crazy bitch gets loose and *kills* you?"

No. He wasn't worried about that. Jamie had this, *her*. "In case we've been tracked. I don't want anyone stopping me. Not until I've put the bond in place."

Silence.

Then Sean gave a low whistle. "You're…really going to do it?"

What, did Sean think he'd gone to all this trouble for the hell of it? Shits and grins?

"You know…you know what will happen to her if you do this, Jamie."

Now Sean almost sounded sorry for the "crazy bitch" in question. Jamie forced a shrug.

"And I know what will happen to me." He turned his head and met Sean's dark stare. "I'll make my pack stronger."

The pack was all that mattered.

He'd returned to the pack just one year before and found them under attack. An attack that had come from within. Men, women—they'd been brutally killed. The pack had dwindled down to just six—*six*—werewolves.

There would be no more deaths in the O'Connell pack. But the pack…oh, yes, the pack would have its vengeance.

His gaze turned back to the woman. *Hello, vengeance.*

She didn't stir.

"Go outside," Jamie ordered again.

This time, Sean obeyed. Jamie heard the shuffle of Sean's boots over the dusty floor and the creak of the old door as it slid closed.

Then he was alone with the prey that he'd sought for the last six months. The instrument of his revenge.

He raised his right hand, and his claws slashed across his left wrist. Blood welled, dripped. Clenching his teeth, Jamie put his hand over the woman's mouth and he waited.

The seconds ticked by as his heartbeat thundered in his ears.

And nothing happened.

Jamie lifted his hand. Blood had smeared over her lips. He leaned toward her. His index finger pushed lightly inside her mouth as he searched for the fangs that *should* have been there.

Only they weren't. The woman had perfectly normal, human teeth. No fangs.

He pulled back. The wound he'd made on his wrist throbbed with a dull ache, but he ignored it. Pain didn't matter. Never had, to him. Frowning, he put his hand on her chest. He didn't feel a heartbeat. Despite what humans believed, the hearts of vampires actually did beat.

Only her heart was ominously still.

His back teeth ground together. "Maybe you are dead," he gritted out.

The Blood Queen had been under a spell for the last fifteen years. A spell, a curse, same damn thing to him.

The blood of a werewolf had put her under — that blood had frozen her body and locked the spell's magic in place.

And the blood of a werewolf was supposed to wake her. *Only she wasn't waking up.*

Hell. So much for his big, secret weapon. Jamie would just have to find another way to destroy Latham and—

She had golden eyes. Dark, deep golden eyes.

"I'm not...dead," she said, her voice a husky purr that actually seemed to roll *through* him, "but you…are." And her hand flashed up. The woman was strong—far stronger than he'd expected—and she grabbed him by the shoulder and yanked him toward her.

Then her mouth, her *very sharp* teeth, bit into his throat.

Instead of being afraid, Jamie smiled and let the Blood Queen taste him.

Drink up, baby. It's your funeral. Because with every drop of blood that she took in these first moments, she was just locking herself to him ever more deeply. Bonding them, body to body, blood to blood, until there would be no escape. Not for either of them.

His claws dug into the sheets as he held his body perfectly still.

Revenge would sure be one bloody bitch.

Latham, get ready to die.

***

Don't kill him.

The whisper slid through the shattered remains of Iona's mind. His blood was in her mouth, flowing like rich bliss over her tongue. His hot, strong body was against hers, and…

Her heart was beating. Hard, pounding beats that seemed to tremble through her. She could feel and hear every single beat.

Her teeth pressed into him. She was probably hurting this man, but she couldn't seem to stop herself. She was *starving*. Had been starving, for so very long.

Pull back. Don't kill.

But it was so hard to keep her control.

Her heart beat was growing faster. She could feel the power of his blood sliding through her body. Giving her strength when before there had been only weakness. There'd been...nothing.

"I think that's enough." His voice was low, deep, and tinged with the faintest brush of an Irish accent.

She ignored his words. Iona hadn't enjoyed her fill of him yet and—

"I said...*enough.*" His hands, big, powerful, caught her shoulders and shoved her away. Her back hit the wooden headboard of the bed, and she blinked up at him.

"If you drain me, then this little deal isn't going to work."

She licked her lips and still tasted him. Maybe it was because she'd gone without blood for so long, but the man—he'd tasted incredible. Fresh. Wild. Spicy.

She'd like more.

When Iona tried to lunge forward, his hands just tightened around her shoulders, and he kept her pinned against the bed's head-board. "Not so fast, baby."

Baby? Her eyes narrowed and she actually managed to focus and look up at his face.

Hard angles. Brutal cheekbones. A sharp nose. Lips that were…sexy.

Her breath whispered out.

There were faint scars on his left cheek. Old. Little ridges that raised the flesh and gave him a tough, dangerous appearance.

She'd always enjoyed danger.

Until that lust for danger sent me to hell.

His hair was dark, even darker than her own. Light drifted through the window on the far right. *Light. Actual light!* And with that light, she saw only pure black in his hair. His eyes — a sharp, intense green — were a bright contrast to that thick darkness.

"You settlin' down?" he demanded and that faint Irish burr rolled beneath his words. Some might not have even noticed that slight accent.

Iona wasn't some.

She was also hardly settling down.

But…how did he hold her back so easily? She'd taken a lot of blood from him during that frenzied feeding. He should be weak.

If he were human, he would be unconscious.

Just what type of creature was he?

His gaze flickered over her. Blood — *his* — had dripped onto her dress.

Her heart beat had finally dimmed. Her heart still raced just as frantically in her chest, but the thunderous booms didn't threaten to burst her ears any longer. Her heartbeat had been the first sound she'd stopped hearing.

Listen, Iona...listen to these last, desperate beats.

Thud.

Thud.

Do you hear them? They're slowing. Soon, they'll stop.

Thud.

And you'll never hear your heart beat again.

As that memory whispered through her mind, a scream broke from her and Iona lunged upward as she battled the ghost from her past. Her nails turned into claws, and she attacked the man before her. She swiped out, catching him across the chest and then tossing him aside.

In the next instant, she was on her feet. The long dress tangled around her legs and she ripped the fabric away from her thighs as she lunged for the door and sweet, sweet freedom.

Get out. The walls wouldn't hold her prisoner any longer. She wouldn't hear the rustle of insects or the scuttle of rats or the whisper of the wind or—

Iona yanked open the heavy metal door, nearly tearing it right from its hinges.

Another man whirled to face her. His handsome face tightened when he saw her and claws broke from his nails. Long, razor-sharp claws that could have passed for knives. Claws that were much bigger and sharper than the talon-like ones that she possessed.

Werewolf.

Rage filled her, blocking all other thought. The room faded in focus around her. She could only see him. The beast. The monster.

Just like the one who'd imprisoned her.

"Die." Her whisper. Her voice was broken. She was broken. But killing the wolf could help to make her whole. This man — this *werewolf* — he hadn't been the one to save her. *Not like the other one.* He hadn't brought her back. So there was no remorse in her, no phantom urge to protect him as she grabbed his head and twisted his neck to the side.

Then she felt claws circle her own throat.

"He can be an asshole sometimes, but I can't let you kill him."

The other man. Irish. And had he said asshole or arsehole? With the Irish thickening his voice, she couldn't tell for sure. Not that it mattered. What mattered was...

Her rescuer had...claws, too. *Werewolf.* Two werewolves.

She freed the fool at the door even as she began to plan her next attack.

"Get out of here, Sean," Irish said.

The one called Sean scrambled back and jerked the door closed as he left.

Her captor kept his claws at her throat and slowly forced her to turn and face him. Blood soaked his shirt and that sweet scent tempted her. Iona's fangs were out, and her body, so long starved for nourishment, shuddered with longing.

Another taste.

If he didn't kill her, she'd get that taste. As weak as she was, even a mangy wolf might be able to take her out.

Maybe.

"I want my taste, too."

She had no idea what he was talking about.

His green eyes seemed to burn into hers. "I bled for you, and now it's your turn."

The claws at her neck slid across her skin. The pain was brief, a prick that she almost didn't even feel, but then he was pulling her closer. Wrapping his arms around her, and because the man was huge—towering far over six feet—he lifted her up against him so that her toes barely touched the ground.

Then he put his mouth on her throat and he…he licked her skin. Her breath shuddered out of her. Iona knew she should fight, but her legs were still weak. She ached. She…

Liked the feel of his mouth on her.

"Mmmm…didn't expect that," the man murmured against her skin.

Her eyes were wide open, staring behind him at the bed that had been her jail cell.

How long had she been there? So long that she'd gone crazy enough to let a wolf put his paws on her.

"Re...lease me..." Her voice was hushed, so raspy. Her throat ached when she spoke, but the blood would heal her. Soon enough. "Or...die."

His tongue slid over her skin. Did he — did he press a kiss to her throat before his head lifted? It felt as if he had. "Easy. I barely took a sip from you." One dark brow rose as he offered her a half-smile that flashed a dimple in his cheek. "While you guzzled me like a frat boy with a new keg."

A frat...? Her eyes slit and she forced herself to speak again, "Re...lease..."

"Right, right..." He dropped his hands and moved back a step. "Happy now?"

Her teeth snapped together. Happy wasn't exactly a part of her vocabulary.

The man raised his hands. "I'm guessing that's a no?"

"Who are...you?" Her voice was a bit stronger now. Good.

"I'm the man who saved your sweet ass." Definitely sounded like *arse* that time.

Her gaze swept over him. "Not...man." Men didn't have claws. Men didn't drink blood.

He shrugged. "True enough. I'm more than just a man." A brief pause. "I'm a werewolf."

"So...you're dead..." A threat because...he *would* be. Vampires and werewolves *didn't* mix. She'd tried that path once upon a bloody time. Hell had been her reward.

"Not quite." That grin came again. His dimple winked. "I'm the hero who just rescued you."

Werewolves weren't heroes. They were the monsters in all the stories. All of her stories, anyway.

"And I'm the guy who can give you exactly what you want."

He didn't know her. How could he possibly know what she wanted? Her lips parted and she sucked in a deep breath. Then she realized what she was doing. *Air.* Wonderful, precious *air.* Her lungs had been starved, for so long. She actually felt a bit dizzy as she pulled in more of that delicious air.

His eyes were on her, watching her far too closely, and then the guy said, "I can give you Latham, and I'll even help you to cut the bastard's head off."

Okay. Perhaps...*maybe*...this stranger did know what she wanted, after all.

She'd let him keep living a bit longer.

Latham. The name had burned itself in her memory. Latham Gentry was the wolf responsible for sending her to hell. "Who are you?" Iona asked again. Her speech was improving by the second. Good thing she'd always been a fast healer.

"My name's Jamie O'Connell."

The name meant nothing to her. It was Irish. So was he. In all her very long life, she'd never met Jamie O'Connell before.

Not until she'd opened her eyes and tasted his blood.

Now that she knew him, Iona realized she'd never forget the werewolf. His memory would stay with her long after he was dead.

"Just give me a little time," Jamie said as he nodded his dark head, "and I'll lead you right to Latham."

She stared at him. The werewolf was trying to offer her some sort of deal. She didn't do deals. "You brought me back." He'd given her the blood she needed to break whatever wretched curse Latham had used on her.

Jamie inclined his head toward her. She figured that was an agreement.

She'd once vowed to destroy the werewolves, to take them out…one by one.

But this man, this werewolf, he'd given her life. Killing him then, well, it didn't exactly seem right. "Count yourself lucky, wolf." She brushed by him and headed for the window. The only window in that narrow room. As she walked into the ray of light that spilled through the glass, the sunlight felt wonderfully warm on her chilled skin.

Most vampires hated the light.

Not Iona.

She'd been in the darkness for so long that she was desperate for that light. She pressed her palm to the windowpane. Beyond that glass, she saw the rough edges of the cliffs that waited outside. Heard the crash of waves. Water seemed to surround her.

Figured, water would be needed for a holding spell.

The werewolf and his damn witch. She'd find them both. Make them bleed and beg.

But first, she had to deal with *this* werewolf. "Good-bye, Jamie O'Connell," Iona said, without bothering to look back at him. Then she slammed her hand through the glass. The window shattered and broken glass rained down on the floor—and fell outside of the window.

Jamie called out her name, but she didn't stop. In an instant, she'd leapt through that window, and she was rushing for her freedom. She was an old vampire, one gifted with powers that few others could ever hope to possess.

She'd been born as a vampire. Born to a father who wanted the power of the gods.

He'd gotten her instead.

She leapt over the rocky terrain. Stared at the water that seemed to howl and snarl below her.

"Stop!"

The dark werewolf, giving chase. She paused at the edge of the cliff.

"What are you doing?" He demanded as he rushed after her. "Do you *want* to die?"

She laughed then, and the sound was as brittle as her voice. Iona glanced over her shoulder at him. "I've been dead for too long." And she wanted to wash away the rot and stench of the hell that had trapped her. "It's time for me to live again."

And when the Blood Queen lived, everyone else should fear.

Lifting her hands high above her, Iona turned back to the crashing waves. Then she stepped off the edge of the cliff and plummeted into the dark water below her.

***

Footsteps pounded behind Jamie as he peered over the edge of the cliff. Hell, that was at least a thirty foot drop. Forty?

The water roared below him.

"Are you going after her?" Sean asked as the younger wolf huffed to a stop beside him.

Her head had just broken through the foaming waves. While Jamie watched, the vampire called Iona began to swim through the churning tide, taking her sweet time as she moved easily through the water.

Amazing.

In-freaking-sane.

Jaw clenching, he gritted, "No." Because, unlike the vamp, he wasn't ready to risk having his body savaged by the rocks and the waves and whatever the hell else waited below.

"She's getting away," Sean said, pointing out the obvious. He had an annoying tendency to do that.

Jamie slanted the guy a hard glance. Sean should be glad the lady was swimming away. Especially considering that the vampire in question had been close to ending Sean's life just minutes before.

Then Sean gave a slow shake of his head and met Jamie's gaze. "That didn't go quite as we planned, did it?"

He re-assessed his grand plan. Iona was a strong swimmer. Correction, she was just plain *strong*. Ten minutes after waking, and the woman was cutting through the water like an Olympic swimmer. Very interesting. Very promising. Jamie smiled and let his anger wash away. "It went even better than I'd planned." The Blood Queen...*Iona*...she'd definitely lived up to the stories that he'd heard.

Iona. Her name whispered through his mind. Beautiful. Seductive. A perfect name for his vampire. Before, he hadn't been able to match that name with a face. Now he knew just what she looked like. It would be impossible to ever forget a woman like her.

He glanced down at the water once more. Then, because he knew where the vampire would go, Jamie turned away from the cliff. Iona thought she was safe. That she was still the paranormal bad-ass that others had to fear.

Once she got to town, she'd see that the rules of the game had changed. She wouldn't be getting away from him.

Not now.

Not ever.

The bond he'd forged with her could never be broken. At least, not if the vampire wanted to keep living.

CHAPTER TWO

As far as hunting prospects were concerned, the small coastal town of Shade, Oregon, wasn't exactly ripe with possibilities. Two bars—both rundown as all hell and faded from time—blasted music into the night.

Just two.

When Iona turned up, Jamie knew she'd head to one of those bars. He just had to make sure he chose the right hunting spot in order to catch her.

The music kept playing. Some young band danced across the stage while girls in low-cut tops swayed in their seats. The alcohol was pouring, laughter floated in the air, and as the darkness deepened outside, not one of the humans there seemed to realize the danger that stalked them.

Humans. They could be so oblivious. Maybe that was why they still thought vampires and werewolves existed only in movies and nightmares.

Jamie tapped the counter and the bartender slid him another beer.

Not just in movies, kids. We're right in front of you. He drained the beer in two gulps.

Now, to just find Iona...

Jamie put his back to the bar and propped his elbows on the countertop behind him. His gaze swept the crowd once more and...

She walked in.

Not still clad in her blood-stained gown, but wearing jeans that curled around her legs, high heels that clicked across the floor, and a tight, black t-shirt that pushed her breasts forward and had three men scrambling eagerly toward her.

Hell.

Iona smiled, and Jamie saw that she was careful not to flash any fang. For the moment.

But then she took the hand of one of the fools who had rushed toward her, and she began to lead the guy back outside. Talk about your easy prey. Jamie was almost tempted to let the dumb kid die.

Almost. Stupidity shouldn't be a crime punishable by death.

He tossed some cash down on the bar and stalked after his Blood Queen.

Bodies jostled into him as he made his way through the bar, but he just shoved those bodies the hell out of his way. In moments, he was outside and the bar's main door slammed closed behind him. The scent of the ocean teased his nose as the wind blew lightly against him. Wind that carried not just the salt of the ocean, but the coppery odor of blood.

His claws wanted to break free. The beast inside roared, but Jamie yanked back on his wolf's chain. Holding tight to his control, Jamie followed the scent of blood, rounded the building and saw —

The kid — some college-aged guy with sun-streaked blond hair — was pressed up against the side of the building. Iona had her hands on his chest. The jerk was moaning and her fangs were in his throat. Jamie's teeth ground together as he rushed toward them.

But before he could grab Iona, she fell away from the guy and hit the ground, hard. Her body began to shake as she wiped her hand over her mouth. "Poi…son…"

The blond wasn't moving. He lifted a hand to his throat and touched the faint wound on his neck. "Wh—"

Jamie lunged forward and grabbed the blond by the shoulder. "Get the hell out of here."

The guy's eyes widened, but, despite the fear Jamie could smell, the fellow shook his head and glanced over at Iona. "She's hurt. I-I should help…"

The dumbass didn't seem to get that Iona had just tried to *eat* him. And now he wanted to play

Galahad. Figured. Hero complexes. Jamie sure didn't suffer from them. "Get out of here, or I'll just knock your ass out." Jamie lifted his fist. One punch, and Galahad wouldn't be waking up for hours.

Galahad swallowed. "I-I—"

Iona was back on her feet. "You *burned* me!" She yelled, then she leapt at her would-be-snack.

Jamie caught her before she could do any permanent damage to Galahad. "Go," he bit off to the fool. "*Now.*"

Finally, Galahad left. Iona twisted and bucked in Jamie's arms, and he was sure that she didn't mean to turn him on. The woman seemed far too furious, but, damn, her curves were fine and when she kept rubbing that ass right over his groin...

His eyes squeezed closed. Fucking her hadn't been part of his plan. This hard lust? No, not the plan. He wasn't supposed to want her so badly. Use her to hunt his enemy? Yes, that was definitely on his agenda. Wanting to strip her and explore that silken body for hours? *No, not the plan.*

His plans just kept changing.

But then she stopped struggling. Iona just seemed to go limp in his arms. Her head sagged forward.

Uh, oh. He wasn't sure just what kind of damage the guy's blood might have done to her.

Jamie knew that he probably should have warned her about that little, ah, issue, but she'd run before he could break the news to her.

"Iona?" He turned her in his arms, moving her so that Iona's chest pressed against his. Her eyes were closed. He bent over her, wondering what to do next.

Her eyes flew open. Too aware. Too...*hungry*. And rather pissed. In a flash, she'd bolted up and her teeth were on his throat. No, *in* his throat.

His breath hissed out, but it wasn't pain that he felt. Her fangs sliced through the skin in an instant, and the only sensation he felt was a burst of pleasure so intense that his whole body shuddered. *More of that. Oh, yeah. More.*

She was drinking from him, and every soft move of her lips had his body tensing even more. Growing harder. His cock was swollen, fully aroused, and hot pulses of pleasure lit his blood as her mouth worked on his neck.

Keeping his hands on her hips, he maneuvered her back, then she was the one pinned against the side of the building. He tilted his head, trying to give her better access because, hell, yes, he was loving this rough ride of pleasure. And the blood that she took...

It links us more.

His fingers slid around to the front of her jeans. Found the snap and jerked it free. Her zipper hissed down.

Her tongue licked over him.

He wanted to touch her skin. Wanted to touch her everywhere so he could discover just how soft she'd be.

Her body trembled against him. "You...you taste so good." Her soft words were whispered against his neck.

He was betting that she'd taste like paradise.

"He tasted like acid, but you..." Now her voice wasn't so whispered. It was snapping. Angry as awareness grew within her. Her fingers curled over his shoulders, and she pushed him back, just far enough that she could see up into his eyes. "You taste like dessert."

Her little, pink tongue slid over her bottom lip. As if she were savoring his taste.

Dangerous. The woman was lethal in more ways than he'd realized.

Her eyes—he could see them perfectly in the dark, a werewolf perk—narrowed on him. "*Why* do you taste like dessert?" Iona wanted to know.

He deliberately let his eyes widen. "Because I'm awesome?"

Her eyes had become golden slits. "What have you done?"

Aw, their hot moment was about to be over. Pity. His hand was still just inside of her jeans. So close to the flesh he wanted to touch.

She seemed to realize exactly how close his fingers were to her sex because she gave a little growl and pushed him back a good five feet.

Not inside her jeans anymore.

Iona yanked up the zipper and fixed the snap in an instant. "You thought to *fuck* me?"

Hoped, not thought, but he lifted his hands and shrugged. "You thought to drain me?" Jamie tossed back.

She growled again. Sexy. "Wolf," she snarled, "I gave you a chance to live. You should have just stayed away from me."

"Can't do that." Time for her to realize just how much her life had changed. "If I do, you die."

She laughed at that. "What? Are you some sort of protector?"

Not hardly.

"Are you going to keep me safe from all the other big, bad wolves out there?"

"No." Flat.

She blinked at that. A faint furrow appeared between her brows.

Jamie rubbed his chin. Time for some fast facts. "The human tasted like crap to you because you can't handle his blood—"

"I'm a *vampire*," said with a long sigh, as if speaking to a clueless child, "I can handle anyone's blood."

He risked a step toward her. His boots crunched on the gravel beneath him. "Not anymore you can't." Okay, she'd flip over this, but he figured it was best to just get it out there. "You see, your body's tuned now. It's only gonna want one thing. Can only accept one thing…"

Her head tilted as she studied him. "Tuned?" Her lips tightened in distaste. "I don't know what you're rambling about."

"To survive, you need blood." It was a simple fact of the undead life for a vampire. To keep existing, a vampire had to take in sustenance. Blood. And, usually, any blood would work to sustain a vamp.

But not for her. Not anymore.

"You were put under a spell," he said this part quietly, with a hint of sympathy, because the spell had been a real bitch for her.

Her hands fisted. "I was there. I remember. You don't have to tell me, wolf."

The woman had more than a touch of arrogance. Probably because, if the stories were true, she actually had once been a queen.

"An alpha werewolf's blood put you under the spell." Here was the dicey part. But, really, what could she do to him? Without just hurting herself in return? "That meant only the blood of another alpha wolf could wake you." And break the spell.

"So you're an alpha. I'm so impressed," she murmured, sounding not even the tiniest bit like she cared. A car horn honked in the distance. The wind kept brushing over them. Near the back of the bar, a chime tossed music into the air. Iona shoved back her hair. "It's not like I haven't met and *killed* a dozen of your kind before."

Except for Latham. She hadn't killed him. If she had, then neither of them would be having these problems right then.

"There was just one little rule about breaking your spell…" Jamie kept his voice flat when his own anger wanted to stir. He had helped the woman. As far as she knew, he was just being a good Samaritan. Had Iona even offered a thank you to him? He cleared his throat. "The wolf that woke you…"

"I *wasn't* asleep!"

He ignored that, for now. She'd sure looked asleep — no, *dead* — to him. "You'd only crave the blood of the wolf that freed you from the spell." He studied her, then said, "'It will taste like wine to you…'" Now he was doing a direct quote from what a witch-in-the-know had told him during his search for the Blood Queen. Before Iona could speak, he finished the last of that witch's quote, "'While the blood of others will never satisfy your hunger.'"

She grabbed him. In all of his years, he'd never seen a vampire move as quickly as she did in that one instant. "You'd better be lying." Her fists had clenched around his shirt. The material was in danger of ripping at any moment.

He gave her a big smile, knowing that his dimple would flash. "Baby, would I lie to you? I'm the wolf who *saved* you."

Her fists clenched even harder as she dug her nails into his shirt.

He kept his eyes on hers. Jamie said, "I'm also the man who'll keep you alive. *My* blood. It's what you need. What you'll always crave." He felt like he was driving nails into the vamp's coffin. In a way, he was. He was also enjoying himself. Iona was about to realize just how much she needed him. "So it's in your best interest to make sure that I live a very, very long life."

The shirt began to tear. "You'll never live as long as me."

Normally, no. But their situation wasn't exactly normal. "I will live as long as you give me your own sweet blood." The beast inside had always enjoyed a taste for blood. And her blood was the most powerful that he'd ever had.

Her gaze held his. "You want *my* blood?"

"I kinda *have* to get it, in order for us both to keep living." He kept his face blank. She couldn't know the real reason why he wanted her blood. That wonderful power boost that he'd get from it. The boost that would make him strong enough to take out Latham.

Because Latham had also been feeding on vamps.

The secret was out in the paranormal world. Thanks to the mating of a few werewolves and vampires, folks had realized that if you wanted a power surge, you had to get very, very intimate with those who'd once been your sworn enemies.

Since Iona had been sleeping during that time of revelation, she didn't realize just how hot of a commodity her blood had become to the werewolves of the world.

Blood as old as hers, as powerful...*and it's all mine.*

Jamie knew his smile had widened. He couldn't help it. Everything was falling into perfect place for him.

"Liar." Barely a breath from her. A breath that was full of burning fury. "One bad human doesn't mean I'm stuck with you. He was probably on drugs. I always hated the taste of drugs in a human's blood."

But she wasn't letting him go, and Jamie wondered if, deep down, she already knew the truth.

Then he caught the scent of blood. Heard the softest tread of footsteps. His head jerked up. His nostrils flared.

Five men. Though not actually men. *Not human.*

Coming their way.

The same knowledge was in her eyes.

"Company," he told her as he drew in the scents of the night.

Her head turned to the left, away from the faint lights from the parking lot and toward the darkness of the woods that waited. Her body seemed to tense against his. "Yours?"

"No." But it was company he'd expected. Just not quite so soon. "Don't worry," he told her, as he pushed her behind his body. She went easily enough, probably more from surprise than anything else. "I won't let them hurt you."

Five against one. He could handle these odds in his sleep.

Especially since he'd taken some of her blood. Hmmm…maybe he could even consider this as a test run. To see just how much strength her blood would truly give him.

The others were coming in fast now. Time to change. Time to show Iona just who — what — she was dealing with in this battle.

The fire of the change swept through his body. It wasn't some light, easy shift. It was brutal. As savage as the beast he carried. His bones snapped. His muscles tore and reshaped. Fur seemed to explode along his flesh. He hit the ground, but when his palms slapped against the cement, they were already transforming into the powerful paws of a wolf.

Iona stood behind him, and the fast pants of her breath echoed in his ears.

The werewolves were coming for her. He knew it. Once the spell holding Iona had broken, Latham's witch would have told him the news. And Latham would have sent out his attack dogs.

Too bad. *You can't have her back.*

Their "company" broke from the trees. Two black wolves. Two gray. One white.

Latham's foot soldiers — wolf soldiers.

Jamie bared his teeth and didn't wait for them to come lunging at him in an attack. He sprang toward them, more than ready to draw first blood.

***

The sounds of the vicious snarls and howls filled her ears. The waves were crashing close by, and the music still blared from the bar, so the humans probably weren't even aware of the bloody battle going on so close to their safe little world.

Iona was too aware.

Jamie wasn't a man any longer. But she knew that, in truth, he'd never been a man. That had just been a surface lie. Werewolves were always more beasts than men.

He was in the form of a big, fierce, black wolf now. A wolf that was easily twice the size of the others he attacked. A wolf that drew blood with his claws and his razor-sharp teeth and seemed to love the savagery of the fight.

No hesitation. No fear.

Two of his enemies were already on the ground.

A third would be out of the battle soon.

It appeared that Jamie was a true werewolf alpha.

Iona turned away from the battle. Alphas had always annoyed her. Maybe because *she* liked to be the alpha, too.

Whatever. She would leave Jamie's lying beast to his own ends. He could handle the others—and she could find a human to eat. *I'll prove him wrong.*

She just needed more blood. There was still a weakness in her limbs that she couldn't allow. When she faced Latham—*oh, I'll see you dead soon*—she had to be at full strength.

A wolf's sharp cry pierced the air behind her. For just an instant, she hesitated and looked back. Jamie had taken out the white wolf. The beast was on his side, and she knew the dark shadow spreading on his coat was blood.

Jamie stood over his fallen prey, with his big body heaving. The wolf's eyes—that same, piercing green—were on her.

I won't let them hurt you. His words whispered through her mind.

As if she needed his protection. Her chin lifted. She'd walk back into the bar. Find another, non-drugged man to sample, and Jamie could fight his little blood battles.

A familiar scent teased her nose. Iona's body stiffened.

Then a rumble of thunder broke the air. Jamie — his wolf — staggered back. More thunder rumbled. No, not thunder, *a gunshot*. Jamie hit the ground.

She was running toward him before she'd even realized what was happening. The other wolves had scattered back, but when they saw her rushing forward, the grey beast tossed his head and howled.

Blood.

And…Iona inhaled deeply, wondering about that other heavy, too thick scent in the air. A scent that was metallic, like…

Jamie was shifting before her. She'd never seen a wolf shift so quickly. Except for one time when her vamp coven had attacked invading wolves with silver. Silver could always force a fast change for a werewolf.

The beast was gone. On the ground, Jamie sprawled as a man. Bullet holes were in his chest. Her eyesight was perfect in the dark, probably even better than his, and Iona saw that he appeared to be bleeding in rivulets of silver.

Liquid silver? Was that the weapon of choice against werewolves these days?

Jamie's claws drove into his own chest, and he yanked out a handful of silver. A brutal move that had the breath freezing in her lungs. Then he did it again, to the other bullet hole.

"Can't...get it all..." His voice was barely human. "Liquid...in my blood..."

Yes, it would be. Unlike a solid silver bullet, the liquid silver would pour through him.

"I'll...die..."

She realized that his head was in her lap. Iona didn't remember sliding her knees under him. Why had she even come to check on him? The shooter could still be out there. The shooter could come for her.

She should run. Leave. Hunt.

Not lean over him and brush the hair from his forehead, but, sure enough, she saw her own trembling fingers sliding through that thick, dark hair.

What is wrong with me?

"If I die..." It certainly looked like the wolf was close to death. Jamie growled, then managed, "So...do you..."

She gazed down at him. She knew what others said about her. She was evil. Wicked. Without a soul.

And maybe some of those stories were true. But in this one instance...

Iona brushed her lips over his. A soft kiss. Gentle. Their first kiss.

It seemed strange to have it here, with blood around them.

It seemed strange to have the kiss after she'd already taken his blood.

But maybe it was fitting.

The kiss was light, but she enjoyed the taste of his lips almost as much as she'd enjoyed his blood.

Perhaps the werewolf could prove to be addictive to her.

And, maybe, she'd show him just how addictive she could be.

Her mouth lifted from his, a few inches. "What makes you think…" Iona asked him quietly, "that I would let you die by any hand other than my own?"

Then she lifted her hand. Brought it to her mouth. Sliced the flesh with her teeth, then offered her wrist to him.

When he drank, she understood that Jamie wasn't like the others. For some reason, he'd touched a part of her that she'd buried deep inside. The human part. The part that wouldn't let a man die before her eyes.

Not a man who'd saved her. Who'd tried to protect her.

I won't let them hurt you.

Funny. No one had ever tried to protect her. Not even her father. No, he'd been the one to tie her to the stake on her twenty-fifth birthday. The day he'd realized she wasn't aging as she should.

He'd tied her to the stake and carried the torch that had started the blaze around her. She'd screamed and begged him to stop. He hadn't.

Too bad for him, she'd been strong enough to break free of the bonds that held her. Burned, savaged, she'd escaped.

Later, she'd gone back for him.

Jamie's hand lifted and locked around her wrist as he took her blood. As far as she knew, only one other werewolf had ever tasted her blood.

That was the werewolf who'd locked her in that horrible house. Made her a prisoner in her own body.

The same werewolf that had been there tonight because, right before the first bullet had slammed into Jamie, she'd caught Latham's scent.

Her gaze lifted to the woods once more. The scent was gone now, but it didn't matter. Latham knew she was free — and she, well, she knew that he'd soon be one very dead wolf.

***

The fool had freed her. Latham raced through the woods, his packmates close to his sides. They were bleeding, and he knew that Jamie would track the scent of the blood.

Jamie thought he was such a fine tracker.

They burst from the woods. Two black SUVs were waiting for him. Latham rushed into the first SUV, the gun a heavy weight in his gloved hand. The silver bullets should have taken out his rival, but Latham had missed Jamie's heart because he'd been distracted.

By her.

The witch was waiting for him in the SUV. Unlike the other werewolves, Latham hadn't transformed into his wolf form.

"Is he dead?" The witch asked. Brian Hennessey didn't look much like a witch. Tall, thin, with small, black glasses perched on his nose, the guy appeared to be a harmless human.

Brian was far from harmless.

The other werewolves were shifting. The others who'd survived anyway—two packmates wouldn't be escaping with him.

Should have gone in stronger.

"No, Jamie is still alive," Latham bit out. "Because he wasn't alone."

Latham knew that once Jamie was out of the picture, the remains of his pack would be easy pickings. Jamie was the strength of that pack. Without him, they'd crumble to nothing.

He wanted them to crumble. Those fools deserved to crumble.

"More wolves?" Brian shook his head and waved for the driver to get them out of there. "I would have thought you'd be able to take them—"

Latham grabbed his arm and let his claws rip into Brian's flesh. "Most witches can see into the future."

No fear flickered in Brian's gaze. "Most witches didn't nearly burn out their power by locking up a born vampire queen for you."

His claws dug deeper. "She's not locked up."

"Yeah, she is. I put that bitch in her cell, I—"

"Not anymore," Latham snarled at him as the rage flared hotter within him. "He got her out." In-fucking-possible. Or it should have been.

Brian paled. "Iona...is free?" Ah, now the fear was there.

The witch was right to be afraid. Iona knew Brian had been the one to cast the spell that bound her.

She'd be gunning for him, too.

But Iona would have to get in line. Latham was ready to rip the witch's head right off. "You said I was the only one who'd be able to get her out." Only he hadn't wanted her out. She just would have fought him then. Tried to take *his* head. So he'd kept her locked up, and every few months, he'd gone in and drained blood from her.

Iona's blood was pure power. It gave him the strength of a werewolf — of five werewolves in fully shifted form — but let him keep the body of a man at all times. Why shift? Thanks to her blood, he always had more than enough strength to break his enemies.

"I-I told you...as a werewolf alpha, you'd be able to bind her body." The scent of Brian's sweat and fear filled the interior of the vehicle. "And if a werewolf alpha locked her body, then only a werewolf alpha could — could free her."

Snarling, Latham put his claws at Brian's throat. "You didn't tell me that *any* werewolf alpha would do the trick! I thought I was the only one! Just me!"

More sweat. More fear. But Brian shook his head. "I never said you were the only one who could free her."

That information would have been important before then. Yet even as the rage pulsed in his blood, Latham smiled at the witch.

Brian's fear deepened. Ah, the witch knew him well.

"Your power's nearly out," Latham said, repeating what Brian had told him. The witch would be regretting those words. "You can't see the future, and that's a pity. If you'd seen it, maybe you could have avoided—"

Latham sliced his claws right across Brian's throat. "This."

Then he shoved open the door and tossed the witch's body into the road.

CHAPTER THREE

The cars had changed. Some were smaller. Some were far bigger. They had computers inside of them. Small screens with maps that showed any area with a touch of a button.

Iona touched lots of buttons.

The radio had what seemed like a thousand channels. The music was crazy. Wonderful. Faster, harder than she remembered.

And the seat beneath her ass? It...warmed. She liked that.

"Yeah, yeah, they attacked outside of the Shore Tavern," Jamie said, speaking into his little phone.

Iona frowned at the phone. The last time she'd seen a phone in a car, the thing had been huge—and in some black bag that plugged into the cigarette lighter. The phone in Jamie's hand was just a few inches long and so incredibly thin.

There weren't any buttons on it. Jamie just touched its screen and things happened.

She liked that, too. She'd have to get one of those phones, soon. Gadgets had always intrigued her.

"We're on the way. Stay on guard, Sean," Jamie ordered and ended the call.

Ah...yes. Her turn. Iona snatched the phone from him. She swiped her fingers over the screen. Music blared. The phone...*flashed*, as if she'd taken a picture, and then some kind of game with little birds popped up and—

Jamie pulled the phone away from her. "What are you doing?"

She wanted that phone back. But her fingers clenched in her lap. She'd always been taught...*don't let others know what you need.* "I'm playing catch-up. A lot can happen in fifteen years, you know."

And it had been fifteen years. Before she'd headed to the bar for a bite, she'd broken into a store and found herself new clothes. After picking up the clothing, it had been time to grab a newspaper in town. As soon as she'd held the paper in her hand, she'd realized all that she'd lost. The date had been big and bold and painful to see. She'd clutched that paper and wanted to rip and tear into Latham.

He'd taken fifteen years of her life away. *Fifteen years.*

In return, she'd take forever from him.

Jamie was quiet for a moment, as if processing her words, then he said, "So you just…slept, that whole—"

Iona turned away from him and gazed out at the blur of darkness beyond her window. "I told you already, I wasn't asleep." *If only.*

"Baby, I was there. Your body wasn't moving. Hell, when I first saw you, I thought you were dead."

She'd wanted to die. For so long.

Iona pulled in a steadying breath and said, "My body was paralyzed." That was how it had felt. She hadn't been able to move a muscle. Not one single muscle.

Her hands shook at the memory.

Kill him. A whisper that came from inside of her.

During that long, long time…Iona had begun to hear voices. She'd lost her sanity, she knew it. After so many years of being frozen, hell, just talking with Jamie still felt strange to her.

"Your body…" He repeated in that faint brogue that Iona wouldn't admit she rather enjoyed hearing. "But…your mind?"

Smart wolf. Maybe he was picking up on the things that she said and the things that she didn't say. "I could hear everything for years. Could smell. Could feel the bed beneath me." For at least the first five years. Was it stupid that she'd been counting the days then? "I heard the bugs and the rats. I heard the crash of the waves and the whisper of footsteps." Latham had kept a guard on her. Always.

A guard that…Iona's head whipped toward him. "Did you kill the guard? The one who smelled of whiskey and cigars?" The odor of his cheap cigars had burned into her over the years.

A grim nod.

She couldn't control her smile. "Good." One less person to hunt and torture. And she *was* going to kill. The thought of killing had sustained her until her mind had finally broken.

Broken…and slid into the dark.

"Did he hurt you?"

The guard? He'd liked to touch her. Touching a corpse. What a sick freak. He'd also liked to burn her with his cigars. Good thing her kind didn't scar. "Did he suffer before he died?" Iona asked instead of answering him.

"No. The death was fast."

"Pity." Her little claws drummed on the leather inside the vehicle. "I would've liked taking my time with him."

"He *did* hurt you." Anger roughened his voice.

And caused her to glance at him with surprise. "Wolf, you sound as if you actually care." A lie, of course, but Iona could admit—to herself—that it would be nice, to have one person who cared.

The vampire coven she'd so carefully created over the years hadn't cared. The ones she'd fought desperately to protect. They. Hadn't. Cared.

They'd left her to wither away.

She'd been so hungry at first. Starving for just a few drops of blood. She wanted to gorge herself on blood now because that hunger was still eating away at her.

But...

But the only blood she seemed to want was Jamie's. *Can't eat him. Not until I find out what he's done to me.*

She would find out, soon enough.

"If it makes you feel better," he told her, the words halting, "I killed the five other guards who tried to keep me from you. No one who left you in that house is alive."

But there were others still alive. Her coven. They might not have *been* at that house, but they'd left her there just the same.

Before she could speak, the vehicle screeched to a sudden stop. Iona jerked forward even as the seatbelt tightened around her and cut into her shoulder. "What the hell—"

"Blood," Jamie snapped out as he jumped from the car.

She caught the scent, too. Heavy. Fresh.

Iona hurried out after him. They were on an old, twisting highway. Jamie had kept the driver's side window down as he drove, the better to follow the "scent" of their attackers, and it sure looked like his nose had led him to their prey.

He stood over a broken body, and the scent of blood called to her.

Then she saw the prey on the ground — saw exactly who he was — and fury rolled within her.

Brian. The witch who had imprisoned her. His throat had been slit, from ear to ear, and blood pooled beneath him.

"It shouldn't have been so easy for you," she snapped, the rage clawing inside of her, raking and ripping open her guts. He'd been on her list. Hunting him, killing him — that promise had gotten her through so many days and nights. To see him like this…

"Those are the claw marks left from a werewolf attack," Jamie said as he bent to better study the body. He shook his head. "Guess Latham got pissed at his witch."

Surprise froze her breath. "You *knew* Brian?"

After the briefest of hesitations, Jamie gave a slow nod, but then said, "Never met him personally, but most paranormals out West, yeah, we knew of him." He glanced up at her. "He's the one who imprisoned the Blood Queen. He kinda got infamous for that bit."

Blood Queen.

The name still hurt, not that she'd let him see her pain. Her father's men had given her that name. When she'd escaped the fire, her father had sent mercenaries — the most vicious he could find — to kill her.

She'd been covered in their blood when she went to destroy dear old dad.

"Guess Latham turned on the witch." Jamie closed the man's eyes. Brian's blue eyes had been wide open.

Hope you are seeing hell.

Jamie stared down at the witch. "After the guy lost his powers, I'm surprised Latham kept him around for this long."

Now that was news. Brian had lost his powers? *Good.*

Jamie rose to his feet. His nostrils flared as he sniffed, probably trying to catch Latham's scent.

Iona grabbed his arm before he could head back to the car. "How did Brian lose his powers?"

"By caging you." His hand lifted. Stroked lightly down her cheek. Heat bloomed within her belly, but Iona refused to let her reaction show.

Fifteen years.

"It's not easy to cage a queen." His hand curled under her chin. "Want to tell me how he did it?"

She remembered screams. Pain. An agony that she'd thought would never end then — *can't move. Help!* "No."

She didn't trust him. There was no point in telling Jamie her dark secrets. Not then.

I must get more blood. Iona knew she had to get her strength back to her maximum level. So she straightened her shoulders, took a long look at the wolf and said, "This is where we part ways."

Jamie stared at her like she was crazy. *I so am.* She knew her own weakness. Fury was boiling inside of her right then, and she was going to let that fury out. Jamie needed to be away from her when the rage broke free. *I should have been the one to kill Brian.*

"Get back into the car, and just drive away," she told Jamie, fighting to keep her voice steady. Iona figured he deserved the warning to get the hell away from her.

Jamie's jaw clenched even as his hand dropped. "We've been over this. You *need*—"

"I don't need anyone or anything." She stepped back. Glanced down at Brian's body. He certainly looked dead.

But then, according to Jamie, she'd appeared dead, too.

Let's make sure.

"Don't worry about Latham," Iona told him as she tossed a quick glance back at Jamie's tense face. "He's next on my list." Latham wouldn't escape their battle alive. "So consider whatever little war that you had with him, well, consider it over."

Jamie shook his head. "This isn't…"

She lifted her hands. "There's something you should know. I'm not just a vampire." If she had been, then Brian would have never been able to bind her. Kill her, yes, but a binding wasn't the type of magic that would normally work on vampires.

Binding. That was what he'd done. Not just a curse or a spell. He'd performed a ritual binding on her. One witch…

To another.

Flames began to flicker above her palms. Not touching her skin, never that, but spinning, burning, right above her flesh. "You need to leave now," she told Jamie.

This time, he backed the hell up.

Smart man.

She stood near Brian's body. Her father had known what she was so long ago. That was why he had tried to burn her. If you wanted to destroy a witch, *truly* destroy her, then you had to use fire.

Iona drew back her hand and sent flames rushing right at Brian's body. "Burn," she whispered as the fire greedily leapt onto his flesh. "*Burn.*"

One down. One to go.

***

She was everything he'd hoped that she would be…and so much fucking more.

Jamie stalked behind Iona, being careful to keep a safe distance between them. He was downwind of her, but with her enhanced vampire senses, he was still worried she'd catch his scent.

He didn't want her aware of him, not yet.

She'd stirred fire.

Vampires didn't control fire. As a rule, they were just bloodsuckers. Sure, they could be super strong, they could live for freaking ever — provided they didn't get staked or lose their heads to a werewolf's claws — but they didn't stir fire from nothing.

Only witches could do that.

The stories had been right about that point, too. Iona wasn't just a Born Vampire. She was a very, very powerful witch.

No wonder she'd been locked up. Caged near the water so the energy from the ocean would work to reinforce the spell. She might just be the most dangerous woman he'd ever met.

That fact only made him want her more.

Perfect. In so many ways. And Jamie wasn't about to let her go. Not when he'd risked so much to find her.

Not when he'd had to make his own deal with the devil to claim her.

So now...yeah, okay, probably not his finest moment, but he was following her through the dark. Keeping his gaze on her as she slipped through the shadows.

Of course, Jamie knew what she was doing. Hunting. Going for another taste of blood.

Not gonna work, baby. You're stuck with me. Did he feel guilty about that? No. These days, he couldn't afford to feel guilty about anything and—

And she was gone.

Jamie hurried forward as his heart raced in his chest. It had only been a moment and—

He was tossed against the side of a dumpster.

"Following me? Really? What must I do?" Iona demanded as she put her hands on her hips. "Rip off *your* head in order to make you stop?"

Taking his time, he stood back up. She'd tossed him about ten feet. Jamie made a show of brushing dirt off his jeans and shirt. Mostly to give himself time to think, then he replied, "You're afraid to rip off my head. Part of you already knows that I've told you the truth." He headed toward her, not trying to keep his footsteps quiet any longer as his feet crunched over the gravel. "And if you kill me, you know that you'll be killing yourself."

It sounded like she hissed at him. He almost smiled but then—then he blinked and Iona was in front of him. She'd closed the distance herself, effortlessly. A distance of ten feet, in less than a second's time. "Let's get one thing straight." She pushed up on her toes. Stabbed a finger into his chest. "I'm not afraid of anything. Or anyone."

Right. She probably wasn't.

And, damn, she was sexy. His gaze dropped to her mouth. Her lips had been the softest that he'd ever felt. He could still taste her on his tongue. The sweetness had been a surprise. From her, he'd expected spice.

"Why…why are you looking at me like that?" Iona asked as her gaze searched his.

He could tell her the truth. "Because I want to kiss you."

Her poking finger jerked back as if she'd been burned. "You mean that you want to take more of my blood. So you can get stronger and so you can—"

He caught her shoulders and pulled her close. Her body brushed against his. *Soft.* He loved the way she felt. "I mean I want your lips beneath mine. I want to taste you. I want to savor you."

She swallowed. "Your brogue is…thicker."

"Yeah, it gets that way when I'm turned on."

Her lips parted.

"I want your mouth," he said again, no longer willing to fight the desire he felt for her. Why bother? They were locked together, even if she didn't realize it.

He was more than ready to start enjoying the perks of the deal.

For an instant, Jamie was sure he saw the flicker of an answering desire in her golden gaze. But then her chin rose as she said, "And I want blood."

The implied *not yours* was clear as she pulled away from him. As he watched her, Iona turned on her heel and headed toward the faint sound of music that drifted in the air.

Yes, she was heading toward big, bad bar number two in the town of Shade. So predictable.

In fact, her move was so incredibly predictable that he'd already told Sean they'd be coming that way. When Jamie had gone hunting for Iona earlier that night, he and Sean had separated. One bar for each man.

Jamie had gotten lucky. He'd found Iona at the Shore Tavern.

But when he'd talked to Sean on the phone, he'd told the other wolf that he'd be coming to meet him. *I knew she'd want to try tasting someone else.*

He knew, but he didn't like it. In fact, it made him feel...jealous?

Impossible.

It *should* have been impossible. Yet Jamie found himself hurrying to keep pace with her. And, moments later, when Iona pushed open the door to the bar, when the bouncer gave her a welcoming smile, and all eyes seemed to greedily stroke her body, Jamie's beast gave a growl.

Back the hell off.

The music was pumping. Loud and—

"The music has changed." Iona tilted her head as she listened to the pounding beat. "I think...I like it better now."

He kept forgetting she'd missed so much in the last fifteen years.

Her hips began to sway. The men began to close in.

Hell. He put his arm around her shoulders.

Those men backed up. *Damn straight.* If they'd come closer, he might have even flashed fang.

"It will be harder to find good prey with you at my side." Her voice was low and husky and her hips were still rocking.

"Too bad. I don't plan on backing off." She didn't seem to realize the gigantic threat that hung over her. Latham could attack, at any time. Yes, she was strong. But so was Latham. And if he caught her off-guard... "I don't want Latham putting you under again."

Her hips stopped rocking. She glanced at him. Anger had melted the gold in her eyes so that her gaze just *burned*. "He won't." Then, with a toss of her head, so queen-like that Jamie had to smile—he'd started to rather like that touch of haughtiness—she sauntered across the bar.

It took him about ten seconds too long to realize that she'd already picked out her prey.

By then, Iona had her hand on the chest of her would-be victim. A familiar victim. The bar was behind Sean, trapping the guy as he stood right in front of Iona.

She chose my first-in-command? Fuck. Jamie stalked toward them. He'd just closed in when he heard—

"I think this could be fun," Iona murmured as she leaned toward Sean.

Sean's shocked gaze darted to Jamie.

"You *aren't* doing this," Jamie snapped. He grabbed her arm. For some reason, he didn't want her touching the other werewolf. He glared down at Iona. "I already told you, it isn't going to work. You can't take anyone else's blood."

"And I told you…I *don't* believe you."

She was making him want to howl. And making him want to toss her over his shoulder and carry her away from Sean. Away from all the other men there.

Her head turned as she studied Sean. "Maybe one werewolf will be as good as another, and at least with him, I'll be sure he isn't on drugs." Her gaze slid back to Jamie. "I'm betting you run a tight ship when it comes to that."

He did. Drugs would make his wolves weak. He didn't allow for weakness. Weakness would just get them killed.

"This way, I don't have to kill any humans...yet." She offered first Jamie, then Sean, a smile that flashed her sharp, little teeth. Then her focus centered on Sean as she said, "So point me toward a private room, and let's just see how you taste, wolf."

Women liked Sean, they sure fell into his bed easily enough. Maybe it was because Sean appeared easy-going, and often...*normal*. A big bonus for a guy who was actually paranormal. Sean was a perfect chameleon. He could fit in with just about anyone, anywhere. Unlike Jamie, he'd dropped his Irish years ago, and, in fact, he could fake other accents—depending on where he was and who he wanted to fool—almost instantly.

Jamie fisted his hands and fought to hold on to his control.

Iona appeared determined. And a little too satisfied with her drinking scheme.

The woman wasn't stopping. Not until she'd tried to drink from someone else. He could fight her, but he knew Iona wouldn't give up. "One sip," Jamie said, his voice clipped. Just one. That would be all she'd need to find out if the blood worked for her.

And if it does work? He couldn't think about that possibility right then. The witch had been adamant. The wolf that woke her would be the wolf that controlled her.

He didn't think Brian had been lying, but since the witch was dead, it wasn't like he could find out for certain.

And I have to make sure she doesn't find out about my deal with Brian. Because if she did...

"There's a room in the back." Sean inclined his head toward a dark, narrow hallway. "Right through there."

Wasn't that just fantastic.

"Lead the way," Iona invited him with a wave of her hand.

But Sean wasn't an idiot. He glanced at Jamie, waiting to see what his alpha wanted.

"Keep your hands off her," Jamie ordered him, voice lethal. "She gets one taste—*one.*"

Sean gave a nod. As a rule, werewolves weren't up for being vamp prey. Only this wasn't a typical situation.

Iona wasn't your average vamp.

Sean headed down the hallway. Iona didn't move, and Jamie was far too conscious of her body near his. Her eyes narrowed as she studied him, then Iona crooked her finger, inviting him closer. His head bent toward her, the move automatic. She rose onto her toes. Her lips brushed against his ear as she said, "I don't need your permission to feed from prey."

He turned his head. Made sure their eyes met. "In order to touch you, *he* needs my permission." Because, dammit, Jamie had already started to think of her as—

Mine.

"Werewolves...always the same." Iona sighed as she eased away from him. "You think that you can control everyone and everything around you." She sauntered toward that dark hallway.

"No." The growl slipped from him.

Iona looked back at Jamie.

"I can't control everything. If I could, there'd be more than six members of my pack still alive." He stalked to her, aggressive, deliberately so. "If I could control everything, my family would be alive. I wouldn't have come home to find my mother and father dead, their bodies savaged. Latham *wouldn't* have killed them." His parents had come to this country because they'd wanted a fresh start. They'd brought their pack over with them. Everyone had been so hopeful, at first.

What could have been sympathy or maybe even pity flashed in her stare. That faint emotion just stirred up his anger even more. Pity was the last thing he wanted from her.

His body brushed against hers. "And if I could control everything," his voice was for her alone, "then I'd already have gotten you naked, under me, and I wouldn't be so wild with lust that I want to rip apart my own best friend…because you're about to put your mouth on him."

The words surprised him with their brutal truth. The lust he felt for her…it was just growing. Stronger and stronger. Almost like he was under some kind of spell.

She's part witch. Maybe I am under her spell.

Under, and falling fast.

"One taste," he told her, "but you're going to regret it."

Her gaze searched his. "There are few things I regret."

He could believe that.

"This won't be one of them." Then she turned, head high, back straight, and marched to the door at the far end of the hall.

He didn't follow her. He didn't want to see her with Sean. "You'll be coming back," Jamie said, the words drifting after her.

And they were a promise. Iona was about to realize that no other man would ever do for her again.

Only me, baby. Only me.

He'd already realized that no other woman would satisfy him.

CHAPTER FOUR

Her fangs had stretched and sharpened as she prepared for the bite. Iona had locked the door behind her — *locked Jamie out* — and now she and Sean were alone together in the small storage room.

"So…how does this work?" He asked her with a nervous glance at her fangs.

She almost rolled her eyes. Really? How did he think it was going to work? "The usual way. I bite you. I drink. *That's* how it works."

Sean was nearly as big as Jamie. His shoulders weren't quite as broad, his muscles not as big. He was probably a few inches shorter than the alpha wolf, too.

But Sean was…handsome. His features were even and smooth and had no doubt drawn plenty of female attention over the years.

Iona realized that she preferred the rough danger of Jamie's hard face. Story of her very, very long life. The bad boys often drew her in.

Then, frequently, they'd tried to kill her.

So she'd had to kill them.

"Give me your hand," Iona ordered.

But Sean shook his head and shoved his hands *behind* his back. "No way. I'm not supposed to touch you!"

For the love of... She grabbed his arm and jerked up his hand. Then she lifted his wrist to her mouth. "Calm down." She could probably try to soothe him. She'd always been good at lulling her prey, when she wanted. Seduce with a look. Kill with a bite.

Been there, done that.

So many times that it rather bored her now.

But, yes, if she wanted, Iona could seduce just about anyone.

Only she didn't want to seduce Sean. She just wanted to find out what his blood would do to her. *Don't burn me, don't.* Because if she was stuck with only taking from Jamie, then she'd be tied to him.

Forever.

Iona parted her lips. Her fangs pressed into Sean's skin, and just like that, with one quick press of her teeth, his blood flowed onto her tongue.

Sean gave a little moan. "Oh, shit, no one said it would feel good." For the first time, she heard the whisper of an Irish accent in his words.

Only...his blood wasn't "feeling good" to her. It felt horrible. His blood tasted rancid, and she was already yanking her mouth away from him and backing up even as her body started to shake and spasm.

"Iona?" Sean called her name as he came toward her. "Iona!"

The door burst in, heaving right off its hinges. Jamie stood in the doorway. His gaze swept around the room, from Sean—and his outstretched hand—to Iona.

When did I curl up on the floor?

She didn't curl. She didn't hide.

I do when I realize my choices are gone.

Because Sean's blood tasted just like the human's, and instead of strengthening her, it had made her feel even weaker.

Now the hunger was ripping through her insides. Hollowing her out.

"I told you not to touch her," Jamie tossed Sean back against the wall. "*I told you.*"

It wasn't the touching that mattered. It was the blood. Blood she couldn't drink.

"Iona?" Now Jamie was the one calling her name.

She forced her head to lift. Made her body rise. She was still shaking, but those trembles couldn't be helped because they came from the hunger and the weakness that filled her veins.

Oh, how the mighty have fallen. So many would laugh to see her brought so low.

Jamie wasn't laughing. He was staring at her with eyes that saw far too much. "Get out of here," he said.

Her lips parted.

"Yank the door back up after you, Sean, and get the hell out," he said, never looking away from her.

Sean hurried to comply.

Jamie didn't touch her. Didn't move another inch. Not until the door was partially up, giving them a bit of privacy, and Sean was gone.

"It didn't work," he said flatly.

Of course, he'd known the truth. Maybe she had, too. She'd just been desperate.

"It makes you sick, doesn't it?" He asked. "When you take blood from others."

Yes. A vampire who could only bite one man? Talk about falling far from her perch of power. She wasn't exactly the big terror of the town any longer.

The faint lines deepened near Jamie's mouth. "I want you to bite me. Take my blood...I don't care. I can give you what you want, always."

He didn't understand. But right then, she just didn't have the energy or the control to *make* him understand.

Fifteen years. For all intents, she'd been dead then. Even if her mind had been crying out in agony.

Now that she was free, Iona wanted to live.

She was about to break apart because she just wanted to let go — to lose her control and take the blood that he offered.

But with vampires, when control broke and blood was involved…

There was a reason she'd been trying to push her vampire coven away from taking blood from live sources. She'd seen the carnage that came from centuries of bloodlust and violence.

When you took straight from a source, when your control shattered, the lust wouldn't just be for blood.

"Blood and sex," she whispered.

Jamie's gaze burned into hers. There was no fear or revulsion or even a hint of hesitation in his eyes. There were just answering hunger. "*Yes.*"

He knew what he was getting with her. No secrets there. And she needed to feel alive again. She'd gone too long in that cold darkness. There would be no holding back for her. *More blood*.

She reached for him. Sank her teeth into his throat.

His blood was perfect on her tongue. Delicious. Addictive. Like a mix of wine and chocolate.

His body brushed against hers.

Pleasure. Close. So very, very close.

Her nipples were tight. Her sex already growing moist. Iona's control was fracturing. She could feel the ripples as they shook through her body.

His hands locked around her wrists. "Don't worry," he told her, the words rumbling against her as her tongue licked lightly at his throat. "I've got you."

Maybe he did.

They were about to find out.

In the next instant, he'd lifted her up. Took two fast steps, and then her back shoved against the wall.

"When you bite me," his words were a dark rumble that had her sex clenching, "I want to fuck."

Not an unusual reaction. The bite did something to prey. Gave them a boost of pleasure. Made them want more.

The vampire could usually control the bite, especially a vampire as old as she was. Could give pleasure or pain.

Her fangs scored lightly over his flesh. He growled. With this bite, she wanted to give pleasure.

His fingers were on her stomach now, under her shirt. His hands were warm and strong and they were sliding up, up, and cupping her breasts. Her breath hissed out as her nipples pebbled beneath his touch. She arched against him, wanting more.

His blood had already made her stronger. So now she wasn't just drinking from him. She was kissing. Licking. Learning what the werewolf liked.

"My turn," he muttered as he lifted her even higher. Strong wolf.

Then he yanked away her top and put his mouth on her breast. He used his teeth to lightly rasp over her sensitive flesh. Her sex ached. So long...

Iona wrapped her legs around him even as he kissed and sucked her breast. She pushed her hips against him. He was aroused. No mistaking that hard bulge that shoved back against her.

Pity his jeans were in the way.

Not for long.

This time, she was the one to jerk open *his* jeans. To pull the zipper down and slide her fingers past the denim. She found him, long, thick, hot, pushing eagerly toward her.

Her tongue slid over the edge of her left fang. She'd had his blood. Now she just wanted him.

His rough breaths filled her ears. Then she heard the sound of a frantic heartbeat. His? Hers? Maybe both. Racing too fast.

"Jamie." Her demand. "Now." She didn't want foreplay that lasted for hours. That could come another time. Right then, she was already clawing at his back. Pushing against him as her control shattered around her. She wanted him inside of her.

Wanted the pleasure to erupt and sweep everything else away.

Then his hands were between their bodies. He had her jeans open, and she had to lower her legs, just long enough to kick out of her heels and jeans. She wasn't wearing any underwear, so she didn't have to worry about—

"Fuck." His hand was between her legs. Pushing into her sex and her head tipped back because she liked the sensation of his fingers sliding in her. Her body was humming, so tuned up that she knew the first climax would hit her soon.

His thumb pushed over her clit.

The climax hit.

She grabbed for his broad shoulders as the release blasted through her. Even as her sex contracted, he was there. Not with those long, broad fingers anymore, but with the heavy length of his cock. Driving into her. Plunging deep.

His neck was inches from her mouth. She had to taste him again. Bloodlust, physical lust, they blurred in her mind and her control fell to the ground. There was no thought. Only need. Hunger that couldn't be satisfied.

He pushed into her, not easy or gentle, and she wanted him that way. His hands were around her hips, forcing her into the air so that he supported her body and he drove into her, again and again with thrusts that stole her breath and made her body shudder.

She clenched her sex around him, squeezing tight.

"Iona…so good…"

She'd show him better than good. She let the bite linger, knowing it would bring more pleasure.

Pleasure. It was what they both wanted. Craved.

He pulled her away from the wall. Wrapped his arms around her so that he held her fully. And his hips still pumped into her. Wolves…so powerful.

Another climax hit her, and this one had her crying out as she lifted her mouth from his flesh. Her breath was choked and the pleasure…it was so intense that it almost hurt.

Her whole body was electrified with feeling. So sensitive that every move of his flesh against hers had Iona tensing.

Then he shoved boxes off a table top. Put her down over it. Her legs dangled in the air.

"We aren't done," Jamie promised, his voice so dark and deep.

She wanted to smile. Couldn't. He'd taken her legs. Hooked them over his shoulders so that she was wide open to him. He took her now, hard and wild, and it was exactly what she wanted. The rush of sensation just wouldn't stop.

Iona didn't care that his claws were out. That they'd slashed across the top of the table. She didn't care that his eyes glowed or that his cheeks had hollowed, signaling the presence of his beast.

She liked the wildness. Wanted it.

His head lifted. She saw the flash of his fangs. Fangs that were even sharper than her own.

Blood and sex—that wasn't just a combination that worked for vampires.

She turned her head to the side, offering herself to him. Only fair…she'd had her turn.

He took the spot where her neck curved into her shoulder. His lips closed over the flesh. His teeth pressed lightly into her. It didn't feel like he was drinking from her though.

It felt as if he were…*claiming* her.

Then he stiffened against her. The hot splash of his release filled her and sent more waves of pleasure pulsing through Iona's body. Pleasure, life, lust…she wanted it all.

This wasn't sleep. Wasn't death. Wasn't whatever the hell had happened to her because of Latham.

Jamie's body was pressed to hers. Flesh to flesh. He was the man who'd brought her from that nightmare. Who'd freed her. The man who'd just given her the best orgasm—or three—that she could remember having in this century.

His scent was on her. Her scent was on him. She'd marked him. He'd marked her.

Her lips began to curl. How perfect.

Werewolves were always so territorial. So driven by emotions and needs. By rage. By possessiveness.

Sometimes, their strengths could be weaknesses. Weaknesses that she could use in her battle.

Her frantic heartbeat began to slow down.

She stared up at the cracked ceiling above her, and her hands were still locked around Jamie. When she went to Latham, she'd be carrying Jamie's scent on her. Revenge, step one.

Not yours, Latham. Never that. Despite what Latham had done to her, she'd escaped. She wasn't the prisoner in his little trap any longer. Not his plaything for eternity. She was free.

And she'd just fucked his enemy.

Payback was coming for Latham, and it had just started…

Wait until I bring my nightmare to your door. She'd make Latham scream, plead, then…die.

***

"Are the stories true?"

Iona didn't glance away from the night sky when Jamie asked the question. She had her back to him. Her legs were drawn up, her arms curled around her knees, and she gazed up at the stars lighting the sky.

When he'd finally been able to speak — and move — again, he'd gotten her out of that back room. Out of the bar and to a safe place. A safe place that had a good bed and fresh clothing for them both. And more comfortable shoes for her. She'd smiled when he'd given her the shoes. He liked her smile. He liked having sex with her a hell of a lot more.

Having sex with her...

Mind-numbing.

The pleasure had been deeper than anything he'd experienced before, and even now, he wanted her again.

If the stories were true, he wasn't the first man to feel this way for her.

"Which stories do you mean?" Her head tilted back, in what looked like an effort to better see the stars.

He sighed and eased down beside her. They were at a house Sean had found for him, a little place in the woods, and though Jamie had tried to get her inside the cabin, Iona had insisted on sitting outside. Sitting outside and gazing up at the stars.

He followed her stare for a moment, then glanced back at her profile. He much preferred that view. "Are you truly the oldest pureblood?" He asked after a moment of just watching her.

Pureblood…the term for vampires who were born, not made. Most of the vamps populating the world had been made or turned. They were humans who'd been bit, who'd taken vampire blood when they were near death, and who'd been reborn as something more.

But Iona wasn't like those other vampires. He caught her left hand. Opened the palm. His enhanced vision easily let him see the small mark in the middle of her palm. Those who were born to the blood often had that mark.

That mark…and a circle of gold in their eyes.

Since her eyes were pure gold, the lady more than met that part of the pureblood requirement.

Her slender shoulders rolled in a little circle. "There could be others out there, probably are. I just haven't met them."

"When were you born?" Jamie pressed.

Her gaze was still on the stars. "Long before men ever thought they'd travel up there."

"Iona…"

Another little shrug. "Around 600 A.D., give or take a few years."

He tried not to let his surprise show.

"I know, I look good for my age, right?" Her lips had curled into a faint smile.

Very good.

He found that he was curious about her. Maybe too curious. "How did you know…what you were?" He'd always known he was a werewolf. When puberty hit, there'd been no surprise when he grew fangs and claws and had the urge to howl at the moon. Surrounded by others of his kind, it had been an easy transition for him.

"I got the first clue when one of my father's warriors stabbed me in the heart, tossed my body in a shallow grave, and left me to die." Her gaze drifted to him. The smile was gone from her face. "Yes, that was my first big clue. He left me to die, only...I didn't."

His hands clenched into fists. "*Why* did he do that?"

Her gaze turned back to the stars. "Have they traveled up there? While I was...under...did they travel more to the moon? Maybe to another planet? I've seen so much in the years I walked the earth, but I've always wanted to go beyond the sky..."

He caught her hand. Twined his fingers with hers in order to catch Iona's attention—and just because he wanted to hold her hand. "They've sent out robots. Rovers. They captured images of planets and stars. Searched and explored." Hell, he'd take the woman on a little NASA field trip if she wanted...*after* they were done with Latham. He'd make sure she learned every advance that had been made in space exploration.

"It hasn't changed," she said, and with her free hand, she pointed to the sky. "Venus waits.

Jupiter shines. The constellations are just as they were. Clothes are different. Music. Technology. But up there...it all looks the same to me."

He squeezed her fingers. "Why did he stab you?"

"Because my hair wasn't gray. Because my skin hadn't wrinkled. Because I wasn't bearing children for my husband."

Her *husband?*

"Did I mention..." Iona murmured, "that my husband was the warrior who stabbed me?"

Sonofabitch. "No," Jamie bit out the words, "you didn't."

"Purebloods usually stop aging around twenty-five. Their bodies just...they freeze. I didn't realize that had happened to me, of course. I learned later that my father and my husband — they thought I was bewitched." Her lips tightened. "Or that maybe I'd even made a deal with the devil."

Blood Queen.

"When I got out of that grave, I made the mistake of running back to my people for help. You see, I still didn't get it. I thought my father would help me. I was sure he *couldn't* have known what Tylar had done. I was so scared and..." Her stare dipped to Jamie's throat. "Hungry."

Because her vampire side would have kicked in with all of the blood loss she'd suffered.

"But my father knew. The attack had been *his* plan. As soon as he saw me, he ordered his guards to prepare the fire."

The fire. Jamie found that he couldn't speak. His hold tightened on her.

"The guards bound my hands. Tied me to an old, rotting tree...put brush around me, and it was my father...he was the one to bring the first torch to start the blaze."

The Blood Queen slaughtered a whole village. That was the tale he knew of Iona's birth. Whispers had told of a Born Queen who'd been so stricken by bloodlust that she'd turned and attacked every person near her.

Only the story that Iona told was much different from what he'd heard. Jamie found that he didn't doubt her account, not for an instant. There was too much pain humming beneath her words.

"I begged for help," she said quietly. Her lips trembled. "So many were gathered around the fire, but no one would step forward to save me. *No one.*"

Now her fingers were squeezing his.

"I'd never known my mother. My father...he'd said that she was attacked by our enemies shortly after my birth. But there were rumors about her. Stories that said my mother could do magic." Her long hair slid over her shoulders as she turned her head and gazed at him. "That day, I used magic, too. The fire should have consumed me."

He knew vampires were particularly susceptible to the flames. Their bodies burned so quickly.

"But I managed to control the fire. I don't know if it was my fear or my fury, but…something broke in me and I felt a surge of power." Her breath sighed out. "I got away. I ran and I ran and then I realized…he'd always hunt me. My father wouldn't stop searching for me because, to him, I was some kind of — of punishment."

"Punishment? For what?" He didn't understand, but he sure would have enjoyed doling out some justice to her sadistic father.

"For killing my mother," Iona said in a soft, sad voice. "Our enemies didn't kill her. I found out that truth too late. She died by my father's hand."

She'd had one sick bastard of a father. Family. Sometimes, you couldn't live with them…

And sometimes you needed to kill them.

Iona kept talking, and she didn't try to pull her hand from his.

Good. He liked holding her palm against his. "My father always wanted immortality. Wanted to rule all the land he could find. He thought my mother could help him, and when she didn't, he made sure she could never use her magic to help anyone again."

He couldn't believe how dark her origins were. A heavy ache had grown in his chest as he listened to her tale.

"It was him or me," she said, and, sure enough, that stubborn chin of hers kicked up. "I knew it, so I went back to my father's land. I slipped inside and made my way up to kill him."

And she had. He knew that, at least, this part of her legend was true.

"I had my knife at his throat, but I couldn't do it." Her head sagged a bit, as if she were shamed by the memory.

Well, hell. *So that part wasn't true, either?*

He'd suspected from the moment her golden eyes first opened that she wasn't the evil bitch that rumor and legend had made her out to be. Now he knew for certain.

And that knowledge made him feel…lost.
What have I done to her?

"He laughed at my weakness and stabbed me with his sword." Her left hand went to her side, as if touching a wound that had to be over fourteen hundred years old. "He was coming to cut off my head. H-he said that would be the way to end me."

Her father had been right. Even a pureblood vampire wouldn't be able to rise from a beheading.

"He'd killed my mother by taking her head. He told me that…"

Had her mother been a pureblood, too? It was possible. Maybe Iona's father hadn't killed her mother because the woman was a witch. Maybe he'd killed her because she was a pureblood and she'd refused to turn him into a vampire? Then the hate had eaten at him, until he'd unleashed his rage on his own child.

"As his blade came for my throat, as I felt my own blood pouring from me, and saw death coming…" Her breath whispered out. "The woman I'd been, she died. The vampire inside of me — she lived. She killed. I took that sword. Snatched it from him. Then shoved it right back into his heart."

Jamie wanted to put his arms around her, so — *screw it* — he did. Jamie wrapped his arms around Iona and pulled her against his chest. She stiffened but didn't fight his hold. Good. He couldn't have fought her then. Her pain was too fresh. Too strong.

He didn't want to ever cause her anymore pain.

Too late for that. You've stolen her life, and she doesn't even realize it.

His jaw locked.

"When his men came and attacked, I fought back. They died. My husband was the first to fall before me." Said flatly, as if she were yanking back on her emotions. "Then I walked away from that land, with their blood covering me."

And the legend of the Blood Queen had been born.

"I learned an important lesson that day," she whispered.

That her father had been better off dead? That her husband had deserved a long, brutal death?

"Even those closest to you will betray you and kill you, if they have the chance." Her head turned, and she glanced up at him. They were close enough to kiss. "Just so you know, I won't give you that chance."

Jamie blinked. "I have no plans to kill you." Keeping her alive was imperative to him. Without her, he *would* be dead.

Her smile was sad, and it called him a liar. "You've been so careful about what you revealed to me. But I know more than you think, and when I sleep, I'll know all."

Because powerful vampires could literally steal people's memories with the act of blood-drinking. Their prey's blood memories appeared to the vampires when they dreamed. Jamie knew that and he also knew that he had to stop Iona from dreaming, at least until their war with Latham was over. But, lucky for him and —*I'm so sorry, Iona* — unfortunately for her, he knew the lovely vampire's weakness. So he had to use that weakness as he asked, "And you're so eager to sleep again, are you? To close your eyes and wake to see that years have passed?"

She flinched. Jamie had hit his target, and shame burned inside of him.

"Eventually," she said, still staring back at him with the eyes that Jamie swore could see into his soul, "I'll have to sleep. There won't be a choice."

He bent forward and pressed a kiss to her cheek. "Eventually, there won't be a need for secrets." They both knew he had them. "My war with Latham will be over." But the end for him and Iona wouldn't come any time soon.

As he pulled in her scent and felt her slender body against his, he had to ask, "Why did you kill the others?" Not the warriors on that long ago night. He would have gladly killed them himself. No, he meant the vampires that she'd brought in to her coven. "Did they turn on you, too?"

A faint furrow appeared between her brows. "What are you talking about?"

"The coven you had in LA. Why did you kill them?"

Stark pain — no, anguish — flashed in her eyes. "They're dead?"

Oh, shit.

But then she twisted in his arms, shoved him back, and Jamie suddenly found himself on the ground with one very, very enraged pureblood vampire above him. *"They're dead?"*

"Yes." Okay, so she hadn't killed them. Big miscalculation his part. If she hadn't done it —

Latham.

"I wondered why they never came for me." The words were spoken with sadness, but fury crackled in her gaze. "I waited for them. Thought they'd betrayed me, too."

Maybe some of them had, he didn't know. All Jamie knew for sure was that, "The compound burned to the ground on the same day that you…disappeared." The flames had lit up the sky. He'd been in LA at the time, young, barely twenty, still too reckless, and he raced toward those flames.

But there had been nothing he could do. The vampire compound had been too far from the main city streets. The fire had been too strong.

Too out of control. For him. And certainly for the human fire fighters who'd tried to battle the blaze.

A tear slid down Iona's cheek.

It felt like someone had just clawed his chest open. He hated the sight of that tear. "I'm sorry. I-I didn't—"

She lunged away from him. Raced away in a flash and disappeared into the woods as she used that super vamp speed of hers.

No. *"Iona!"*

But she wasn't stopping for him.

Swearing, he transformed into the wolf, letting the savage shift sweep over him. Then he was running, following her sweet scent. Rushing through the woods as fast as could.

Can't let her get away. Can't.

But even as he rushed through the woods, her scent was growing fainter. He kept going, knowing she couldn't maintain her enhanced speed forever. She'd still be weak from her imprisonment. She'd still—

He burst from the woods. Heard the growl of a motorcycle. Saw Iona, holding tight to the back of some leather-clad bastard. As the breath heaved from him, the motorcycle shot forward, taking Iona away.

Jamie howled.

The driver glanced back, and Jamie could smell his fear. The man was smart to be afraid. Jamie charged after the bike. After them.

"What the hell is that?" The human demanded. "Too big for a dog…"

"It's a nightmare." Iona's soft voice drifted back to Jamie. Stabbed right in his heart like any knife. "Go *faster.*"

The engine gunned and the bike picked up even more speed as it flew down the narrow road and into the fading night.

For a time, Jamie kept pretty good pace with the fleeing motorcycle. But then the human and Iona vanished.

Vanished…before he could make her realize that the human wasn't harmless. That he hadn't been outside of those woods by chance.

He howled again.

Jamie knew that human's face. He'd seen him before. At Latham's side.

And now that human…one of Latham's army…had Iona.

CHAPTER FIVE

The wolf wasn't following them any longer. Iona's hands tightened around the male. They should be clear, for now.

"Stop," she told him, raising her voice so it would be heard over the roar of the motorcycle.

He didn't stop.

Her hands squeezed him, harder. "Stop."

Did he give a negative shake of his head?

He did. Her gaze searched the road around them. She needed to get to LA, but she didn't need the human, not any longer.

"If you don't stop, I'll kill you." He wasn't wearing a helmet so it would be ridiculously easy to dispatch him. One quick toss and he'd be on the ground. One flick of her wrist and his neck would break.

She might not be able to drink from him, but she could certainly kill him easily enough.

"Someone wants to see you," the human said as his fingers tightened around the motorcycle's handlebars.

Unease skated through her. "Then he sent the wrong messenger." She didn't even hesitate. Iona grabbed the human and threw him off the motorcycle.

Before the bike could crash, she slid forward and took control of the handlebars. This wasn't like the old hog she'd had all those years before but...

But she was a fast learner. Her thighs curved around the body of the bike and she throttled up the speed as she raced away.

The human could live or die. He wasn't her concern.

Her coven — her vampires — they were what mattered. She needed to find out what had happened to them.

***

Greg Coleman rose slowly from the pavement. His ankle was broken, thanks to that bitch. And, also thanks to the vamp bitch, blood soaked the right side of his body where the asphalt had ripped his flesh away.

All that blood, permeating the air, and she hadn't even stopped for a sip. He yanked out his phone. The screen was cracked, but he still managed to make his call.

"You were right," he said when the boss picked up. "She didn't so much as make a move toward my throat."

A growl rumbled over the line then… "Where is she?"

"Driving fast and hot for LA." That was what she'd told him, anyway. When she'd rushed out of those woods—nearly scaring the shit out of him because he hadn't been ready for her; hell, he'd been about to go *in* those woods and scout for her—the vampire had said that she had to get to LA.

He'd told her to hop on the bike. When she had…holy fuck, talk about perfect luck.

"She's alone," he said into his phone as he tried to take a few steps down the road. Every step sent pain pulsing from his ankle. "Probably heading there to see if she can find any of her coven." Not that there were any vamps for her to find there. Well, not any who would be on her side.

Greg stopped walking, sucked in breath, and said, "It looks like she lost the werewolf, so she should be easy pickings for you."

"Yes…"

A twig snapped behind Greg. He whirled around and his ankle gave out, sending him falling right back down. His phone slipped away from him, smacked the pavement once more, and landed just out of his reach.

"Fuck." He clenched his teeth and tried to shove toward that phone. "I need transport," he shouted, hoping the boss would hear him. "Follow my GPS and come get me—*shit!*"

A wolf jumped out of the darkness. Big, black, and with sharp green eyes that promised death. One of the wolf's front paws slammed down onto the phone.

Greg tried to scramble back. He had a gun full of silver bullets...in the saddlebag on his bike. Fuck, fuck, *fuck!* "Stay away from me!"

The wolf stalked closer. It was the same wolf that had followed Iona from the woods. That beast had been hunting them, had come all this way?

The wolf's sides heaved. Saliva dripped from its mouth and it kept advancing toward him.

Greg nearly pissed his pants. He'd never had werewolves come *at* him before. He was part of Latham's team. The pack. Latham's wolves attacked others, not him. Never him.

"Don't!" Greg lifted his hands, trying to cover his face.

The wolf's claws sliced into his left arm. Blood flowed, too quickly.

"Stop!" Greg screamed as he tried to fight the wolf.

The wolf didn't stop. Its eyes glinted. The beast bared its teeth and that green stare locked on Greg's throat. *Death.* Greg saw the promise in that gaze.

Only he wasn't ready to die. And maybe…maybe he didn't have to.

"You want the woman?" Greg threw out and tried not to whimper at the pain from his arm…his ankle…his whole body.

The wolf seemed to hesitate.

"She's heading for LA." Who knew how long it would take for her to arrive? "She's going after her old coven." Greg forced a laugh. "Doesn't realize it, does she? The vamps still left from that coven—just a handful of 'em—they were the ones who set her up with Latham. They were the ones who lit that whole compound up in LA. They didn't want bagged blood and peace with humans."

So he'd been told. He knew nothing first-hand, but he was ready to trade every whisper and bit of gossip that he'd ever heard for a chance to live a little while longer.

"They'll find her. They'll trick her. They'll…" Greg's breath choked out as fear shuddered through him. The wolf wasn't backing off. "They'll take her head—or they'll just give her right back to—to Latham!"

The wolf attacked. His razor-sharp teeth locked on Greg's throat.

"Please!" Greg begged. He could feel the tears pouring down his cheeks. "Let me go…Save her. Hurry...and she could live!" Total lie. That bitch's death was already set.

But the wolf didn't know that, and his teeth lifted away from Greg's throat. The fool pulled back. Turned away. Rushed back into the woods.

And then the beast ran away to play the hero.

***

Nothing remained. The heavy stone walls that had been erected around the perimeter of Iona's home in LA still stood firm, but inside of those walls...

Nothing.

Blackened earth. No buildings. No people. Just...nothing.

A big FOR SALE sign hung on the front gate, swaying a bit in the breeze. The sign groaned as it rubbed against the iron gate. Iona stood about fifteen feet away from the gate, *inside* those cold stone walls, lost in the middle of the one place she'd always felt truly belonged to her, and she refused to cry.

She could almost feel the pain lingering in the air around her. When she closed her eyes, the screams whispered through her mind. Whispered—then burned.

As her friends had burned. Her family.

She'd transformed some of the coven herself. Found the rare few that she'd thought could handle the vampire world. They'd turned others. The coven had grown.

It was all gone now. Ashes.

Her father had wanted to burn her to ashes. Fire was such a good way to kill a vampire.

Her gaze fell to the blackened ground. She'd driven for so long that night had descended on her once more, a black shroud to cover her beloved home.

"Iona."

At first, she thought the call was just a memory. Then she looked up, and, there, just beyond the front gate, she saw Michael staring at her.

He looked as if he'd seen a ghost. She felt as if she had.

Michael. Michael Monroe. The breath rushed from her. One of her coven!

She hadn't transformed him. Another member of the coven — Christine — had brought him over. Christine had found Michael, broken and bloody, the victim of a hit and run car accident. He'd begged Christine for help.

The gate groaned louder as Michael opened the metal bars that lined the entrance. Iona hadn't bothered opening the gate. She'd just leapt over the stone wall.

If Michael had known just what sort of help Christine truly offered, would he still have begged? Or would he have chosen death? Iona had always wondered...

"You should be dead," Michael said, shaking his head as he advanced on her. "All this time...we thought you were dead."

She kept her hands at her sides. Refused to let hope fill her. He was alive, and he'd just said...*we*. Others must have survived, too.

But...but she didn't let the hope take over. Hope had been crushed too many times. "What happened here?"

"Latham," Michael bit off the name of the werewolf at the top of Iona's most-hated list. "When you left us, he came in with his wolves. They attacked during the day and burned the place around us."

Her eyes narrowed. There should have been safeguards in place. Specific vampires and bodyguard humans who protected the area during the day while the vamp coven was more vulnerable. The compound had been set up with security systems, dozens of alarms. The wolves should never have been able to sneak inside and attack.

"How did you escape?" Iona asked him.

But he just shook his head. "I can't believe...I'm so glad to see you!" Then he rushed forward and wrapped his arms around her. He smelled of fresh blood.

Michael had been out hunting. Had his prey been humans? Werewolves?

Her hands touched lightly on his shoulders. "How did you escape?" Iona asked him again. Goosebumps rose on her arms. Something was off, something felt—

A low growl drifted in the air. Iona swallowed.

Michael lifted his head. Pulled back a bit so he could stare down at her. "I didn't escape." He was smiling now. Flashing his fangs. He must have heard the growl, too. Like her, he knew the sound for exactly what it was.

The sound of a werewolf. After all, that deep, rumbling growl was pretty unmistakable. A werewolf was closing in on them.

"I killed the human guards," Michael told her. He was proud. Bragging? "I made sure that the vamps on patrol were given drugged blood. Then I just walked away and let the werewolves have their fun."

Fury had her trembling and more than ready to rip off his head. "Christine *saved* you!"

He shrugged. "Then she got in my way. Tried to get me to be a good, fuckin' little vamp who followed the rules." He shook his head and pulled a stake from his coat. "I'm not the following type."

The wolf was behind him, racing with his giant jaws parted and his eyes trained on the prey that waited.

Michael pressed the tip of his wooden stake over her chest. "I'm guessing all that time, frozen like the dead, slowed you down, huh?" His smile widened. "I'm glad I get to be the one to send you to hell."

She snatched the stake from him, and, before he could even have a chance to fight—*he deserved no chance*—Iona shoved that stake deep into his heart. "You guessed wrong."

His lips parted. His eyes stared at her in horrified surprise.

"No time to beg this go around," she said. "You're dead." Then she walked away while his body fell to the blackened earth.

The wolf was charging right at her. Iona braced her legs to face him.

But the beast started to change. Bones crunched and snapped, and the fur vanished from his body. Golden flesh emerged. Flesh she knew. A face she knew. It would be impossible to ever forget Jamie's hard, dangerous features.

"I was...coming to save you..." The words were raspy and grating as his paws became hands that sank into the earth.

Her head tilted at she studied him. "I didn't need saving."

Jamie looked up at her. His gaze blazed. "That vamp's not the only one after you."

No, she didn't think that he was. She wasn't that foolish.

"A few other vamps were helping him, and they're—"

"Here," she finished with a nod because she'd caught their scents, too. They were just beyond the wall, waiting.

Maybe Michael had been their leader, so they'd let him try for first blood. Would they attack now that they realized she wasn't weak? Would they be afraid—or would they try killing her, too?

"If they're smart, they'll run like hell," Jamie said as he fired a fast glance toward the wall.

If they'd been smart, they never would have betrayed her coven.

Jamie's head jerked to the right. "One's running."

But she already heard other footsteps. Pounding toward them. "And two are attacking." Iona rushed away from Jamie as she ran to face the threat. Fury boiled in her, the kind that just made her want to *destroy*. So when she saw the two vampires charging at her with hate twisting their faces and their hands curled around stakes, Iona didn't hesitate.

She was within range now. She'd just needed to get close enough—

"Good-bye," Iona whispered and flames shot out from her hands.

Close enough to kill.

The vampires screamed as the fire consumed them. A fire stronger than anything they'd probably ever seen before.

My fire. One fueled by rage and magic.

They died quickly, though they probably didn't deserve such a swift death. Not after what they'd done. *Betrayal.*

A hand touched her shoulder. Iona flinched and spun around.

Jamie backed up, lifting both hands in front of him. "Easy, love. I'm on your side."

She wanted to believe that. "The woman…" Iona couldn't look at what was left of her, but she didn't need to. Iona remembered Luanne's face. "She brought the blood to me that last night. Michael and his vamps…they gave me drugged blood." That was how they'd managed to subdue her. She just hadn't realized it at the time.

She'd gone to sleep in her home, and she'd woken in the room that would become her prison, woken just in time to see Latham and Brian. The spell had been cast. The taste of blood filled her mouth—*Latham's blood.* She'd tried to lunge at them, but her body had refused to obey her commands.

If you won't give me your blood, then I'll just take it. Latham's voice. He'd tried to woo her when they first met. Offered her promises of peace between the vampires and werewolves. He'd been handsome. Charming.

But she'd seen the darkness in him.

Latham had only wanted her blood. Her power. He hadn't cared about peace. The werewolf enjoyed his violence and death too much for that.

I would have put him down. She'd planned to kill him, but Latham had struck first. He couldn't kill her, because then he'd never get the blood he wanted from a corpse. And if he let her live, then he'd known she would attack him.

So he'd decided on a compromise.

Bastard.

"Iona?" Jamie eased closer to her. "We should get out of here. Latham knows this is where you were going when you left Oregon."

"And he's coming." No surprise. "When Michael caught the werewolf scent in the air, he thought you were just one of Latham's army."

You thought wrong, Michael.

She rolled her shoulders. Weariness beat at her. She'd driven so far, non-stop, and Iona always felt drained whenever she used her fire and magic.

She risked a look up into Jamie's bright stare and knew he could see her weakness.

"You need to rest," he told her.

True, but not likely.

But when he offered his hand to her, Iona found herself stepping forward and actually clasping his fingers. So many had betrayed her over the years, but…some had been her true friends. *Christine.* Iona could still see her so clearly in her mind. Her warm smile. Her perfect, dark skin. Her kind eyes. "Latham killed my family."

"And mine." Fury vibrated in his words. She could understand that rage. It was no wonder he wanted vengeance against Latham.

They were outside of the gate now. A big, black truck waited for them. She frowned at it for a moment.

Jamie laughed softly. "Ah, love, did you really think I ran all the way after you?"

Love? It was the second time that he'd called her that. She'd just been *baby* before. But Iona pushed the thought aside as he guided her to the vehicle. Her legs wanted to go limp, so she slumped inside, sinking into the soft seat.

She would go with the werewolf, for now. She could always slip away from him later. She could slip away any time that she wanted.

In seconds, Jamie was in the truck with her. With a flick of his fingers, he started the ignition, and they left the heavy, stone walls behind them. Iona squeezed her eyes shut.

"I would have…brought you here," Jamie said, voice hesitant. "You didn't have to leave me."

"I brought myself here." She could protect herself. She'd never needed anyone else to fight her battles. Still didn't. "And maybe I was tired of being used." Because he was using her, too. She knew it. Wasn't it always about the blood?

My blood. My power. The werewolves just kept wanting it.

"Iona—"

"I want to shower." To wash away the ash on her skin. To wash away the death. She forced her eyes to open, and Iona glanced at him. "Find the nearest hotel or just…just find me a *safe place*."

A muscle jerked in his jaw, but Jamie gave a grim nod. He didn't speak again during the ride, and Iona was glad because the ghosts from her past—the vampires she'd lost—their memories were screaming at her as she left her home behind.

***

She was hurting. Not a physical pain. Jamie had checked Iona's body thoroughly and found no sign of wounds.

Her pain went far beneath the surface.

Iona was in the shower, the water pouring down with a heavy thunder that he could hear clearly through the gleaming door.

He had found her a safe place. Not some pay-by-the-hour dump. She'd deserved better than that. The woman was a queen, and he'd gotten her the best room he could afford. Five freaking stars.

He wanted to do anything and everything he could in order to make her pain go away. She'd seen enough pain, more than he'd ever expected.

I want her to be happy.

"I know you're there..." Her voice drifted to him. Not a yell, just a whisper. That was all she needed to do...whisper, and his wolf could hear her. "Come inside, Jamie."

His body hardened at the invitation. Hell, he'd already been hard, from the moment they entered the hotel. Iona had started to strip. Then she'd walked away. Shut the door. Closed him out.

But, now...she was inviting him inside...

He didn't need to be invited twice.

Jamie nearly ripped the door off the hinges when he rushed into the bathroom.

The shower was huge. Easily bigger than the little house Sean had found for them back in Oregon. The place was lined with granite. Some kind of stone bench was in the shower, and, in that shower, two different jets of water poured from opposite walls to slide down over Iona's naked body.

She stood just behind the glass door. Steam drifted around her. Her gaze met his, then she put her hand on the glass.

He could see the small birthmark on her palm. That mark had changed everything for her.

Jamie didn't remember crossing the room, but suddenly, he was right in front of the shower door. His hand lifted and covered hers. Only that thin pane of glass separated his flesh from hers.

Her gaze met his. He could see the edge of her fangs peeking out from beneath her red lips.

"Will it be like before?" Iona asked him. "So much pleasure…it let me forget all the pain."

Her words pierced deep into him. *No more pain.* Jamie lifted his hand. Stripped. Opened the door. Reached for her. His fingers skimmed over the silken flesh that had been heated by the pounding water. "This time, it will be even better."

"Promises, promises…"

He noticed that some of the shadows had lifted from her gaze. *So beautiful that she makes me ache.*

His fingers curled around hers, and he bent to taste her. *Mine.* Her lips parted. Her tongue met his. There was no hesitation in her. Iona knew what she wanted, and she was taking it.

Jamie knew exactly what he wanted, too, and he'd be damned if he ever gave her up.

They were hungry from the start. Wild. Full of lust and need. Their kisses were hard, their tongues tasting. He'd never get enough of her. He *never* wanted to taste another woman. The taste would be bitter. But Iona...

Perfect.

Their hands were greedy and eager. Iona's body was slick from the soap and water. Her fingers brushed over his chest. Over the old scars—some he'd gotten just as a child, long before he could shift and heal—that would always mark him.

Then...she slid down onto her knees before him.

Jamie hadn't expected the move, and he tried to pull back. "You don't need to—"

"I *want* this." Demanding, not asking.

As if he'd deny her anything.

Then her mouth closed around the tip of his cock, and Jamie's knees locked. Sweet fucking hell. Her tongue rasped over him. She took him in deeper as she sucked his flesh. The low moan that Iona gave vibrated along his cock and had him nearly exploding in her mouth.

I made a promise. One he wouldn't forget, even if the woman was trying to make him go blind from pleasure.

He pulled back from her.

She glanced up, her eyes molten. "*Jamie!*"

He liked her demanding. He lifted her into his arms. He'd like her even more when she gave him a chance to taste her.

She kissed him while he carried her out of the bathroom. She licked his lips. Then she moved to his neck. When her fangs slid into his skin, his arms tightened around her.

Can't. Come. Yet.

He had to be inside her before he came, and she—she had to be on her second orgasm by then.

*Promises, promises…*Now he recognized her words for the taunt they were. Iona wanted him to break. He wouldn't, maybe.

He put her on the bed. Hated to move away from her mouth—he loved her bite—but there was a part of her that he'd been dying to taste. Would she taste as good there? *Yes.* He already knew she would.

His hands trailed over her body. Over the soft swell of her stomach. He pressed a kiss there. Then, down, sliding into the silken heat of her sex.

Her legs parted for him. Not far enough. He moved between those sexy legs and opened her even wider.

So fucking perfect.

Jamie put his mouth on her. Tasted her secrets and drove his tongue into her sex. She bucked beneath him, and he grabbed her hips, keeping her just where he needed her to be.

Right beneath his mouth.

Her hands slid over his shoulders. "Jamie?"

He licked her.

And felt her come. *One…the start.*

He kept tasting and licking and her moans filled his ears even as the beast roared inside him. Her pleasure was sweet on his tongue, but it wasn't enough. He needed so much more.

When had she become so important to him? When had she become…

Everything.

He'd been so desperate to get to LA. To get to her. If she'd been killed…

Jamie's hands tore away from her hips just as his claws burst from his fingertips. The claws sliced into the sheets, the mattress.

He heard her gasp, and he tried to yank back the beast. "Won't…hurt…"

His head lifted. He met her stare. Saw his whole world reflected back in that gold.

Claim. An instinct bred into the wolf. When you saw what you wanted, you took it.

An alpha's right. He'd never wanted another this way.

Take.

He pushed his cock into her body. Drove deep and hard and the pure fucking bliss of her had his back teeth grinding together.

Then the animal inside took over. Lust was a frenzy, a desperation within him. He plunged into her, thrusting again and again, but he couldn't seem to get deep enough, couldn't feel her close enough.

He pulled away from her. Turned Iona so that she was on her stomach. Would she—

She rose to her knees. "Ready for more?" Iona asked him, tossing that shining mane over her shoulder.

He was beyond speech right then. His mouth closed around the curve of her shoulder. A kiss at first, but then, because this was the spot that would mark a claiming...

He bit her, even as he thrust into her sex. The pleasure hit them both, sweeping through them, between them, consuming in a white-hot explosion that left him hollowed out, and yet, for the first time in his whole life also feeling...

Whole.

As if he'd found something that had always been missing.

Her.

Jamie pressed a kiss to the faint wound he'd left on Iona's shoulder. The mark of a werewolf claiming. There would be no going back from this, and he wondered just what Iona would do now.

Hopefully, she wouldn't try to kill him.

Her arms curled around him. "I don't want to sleep," she whispered but her words were husky, and he knew that sleep pulled desperately at her.

It pulled at him, too. "I'll stay with you."

Her head tilted back. She stared up at him with eyes so deep and mysterious. "I'm afraid."

He knew the admission had been hard. For her, *hard* was probably one serious understatement.

His arms tightened around her. "It's okay. I swear, I won't let anything happen to you."

The last time, she'd slept for fifteen years.

He inhaled her scent. Realized that she already felt like she was a part of him. "I'll keep you safe."

But Iona gave a sad shake of her head. "It's not the sleep I fear." Her hand slid over his chest. "It's the dreams. What I'll…see."

Because of the blood she'd taken from him. Jamie carefully held his expression, hoping to show only concern for her and not the fear and anger that were suddenly clawing inside of him. Just yesterday, he'd planned to keep her from sleeping. Planned to stop her from using their blood link so she wouldn't see his secrets in her dreams.

But now I want her to know me. Pity his memories weren't the stuff of white knights. Hell, Iona had probably met real freaking knights in her life.

And she'd battled monsters. *Like me.*

"I don't want to find out...you're as much of a monster as Latham..." Her voice whispered away as her lashes began to sag. Her slurred words were a painful echo of his own thoughts.

His eyes squeezed shut. Jamie leaned over to press a kiss to her the tumble of her hair. "I'm sorry." Because he knew exactly what Iona would see in her dreams.

And he knew that she'd want him dead.

But she deserved to know. He couldn't keep secrets from her anymore.

Even if the truth she learned made her go for his throat.

CHAPTER SIX

The bodies were broken. Twisted.

Jagged wounds — claw marks — had ripped into the woman's neck. Her blond hair was matted with her blood.

A man's body rested beside her, his hands still reaching for her even in death. The heavy scent of silver burned in the air.

"Why?" The cry was torn from her...only when she glanced down, Iona wasn't staring at her own body.

No, when she glanced down, she saw Jamie's strong hands. Jamie's body.

Because this was Jamie's memory.

Part of her wanted to wake up, but once the blood memories came, there was no stopping them. This was the way the memories always came for her. She relived the memories, the moments, until the blood pushed her free. So she watched, through Jamie's eyes, as he fell before the people that she knew were his parents. Those memories were there, too, inside of her and —

"You're next." Latham's voice.

He was standing over the bodies. His lips were twisted with hate.

"Why?" Jamie demanded again, the cry like a wounded animal. And — he was.

"Because I'm taking over the pack. He was in my way." Latham glared at the dead man's body and then pointed at Jamie. "You're in my way, too, brother."

Brother?

A knife seemed to slide into her heart, but the heart — it wasn't hers. It was Jamie's. And Latham had just shoved a silver blade into Jamie's chest. Then Latham...walked away.

But Jamie didn't die. Someone else rushed to his side. A wolf she recognized. Sean. Sean took out the blade even as it scorched and blistered his fingertips. But Jamie was still near death. Far too close. Death's cold hands reached out as the world seemed to go dark...

Then she was somewhere else. Her eyes opened. She — no, Jamie was on a bed. "What the hell happened?" His voice seemed to echo all around her.

Sean swallowed and glanced away, as if he couldn't stand to meet Jamie's eyes. "Had to...I had to give you vampire blood. It was the only way to keep you alive."

"Where'd you get it?"

"Latham...he...he has a vamp that he keeps prisoner. She's supposed to be fuckin' strong."

She? Iona's heart burned because she realized this memory...it had been created when Latham already had her captive.

"That's how my brother stays so strong." Jamie *jumped from the bed. Her blood had pushed his strength level higher than anything he'd ever felt before.* "We have to find her. Find her…and kill the bitch. We kill her, and we'll kill him, too."

***

Iona whimpered and turned her head against the pillow.

Jamie's jaw locked. He wanted to shake her and force her eyes to open, but…he didn't want any more secrets between them. No more lies. Iona wasn't what he'd expected. She deserved to know the truth about what happened. About him.

"And when you come for my throat…" His fingers brushed back her hair. "Hell, maybe I won't even fight you."

Because he didn't know who had wronged her more. Him…or his brother.

***

Another time, another place. The memories were coming faster now as the blood pushed her to see more. Learn more.

The pounding of the surf hit her ears even as the scent of the ocean filled her nose. She paced – no, Jamie paced – inside a small beach house. A man sat before him, bound hand and foot to a chair.

The man's blond hair fell over his eyes, but then Jamie said, "Witch, we can do this two ways. I can kill you now, or you can help me." His hands lifted and claws glinted in the dying light. "We can both work together to take out Latham, and you can keep living."

Witch? The man's head rose. Brian Hennessey stared back at her. Pain froze her heart. Jamie had been working with Brian? With the witch who'd bound her?

Blood dripped from Brian's busted bottom lip. "You can't...stop him. He's too strong." Then Brian laughed. "He's gonna take...over every pack...no stopping..."

Jamie kicked the chair and Brian fell backward, slamming into the wooden floor. "He's strong because you gave him magic. You think I didn't hear the story about the vampires you slaughtered? About the Blood Queen that you're holding and slowly draining?" His lips curled in disgust. "I know you're giving her blood to my brother. That's why he's so powerful."

And for an instant, the fast flood of memories were hers, not Jamie's. Iona remembered the prick of a needle in her arm. The slow suction as her blood drained away. Again and again and again as the years rolled away...

Her dark past vanished, and there was only Jamie once more.

"When we take his vamp away, he'll get weak." Jamie crouched over Brian and put his claws to the witch's throat. "Tell me how to find her, and I'll make sure to cut off his little blood supply. Because it's her,

right? Not just any vamp...her. I know she's old, powerful—"

"M-magic." Blood oozed from Brian's throat when Jamie's claws broke the skin. *"Not just a vamp...the Blood Queen is part witch, too. Get her blood, get the power. Latham has the power."*

"Because you helped him!" Fury rolled in Jamie's voice. *"You backed the wrong brother. But you can regret that while you're burning in hell."* His claws sank deeper into Brian's throat.

Brian shook his head, seemingly frantic at the promise of death he must have seen in Jamie's eyes.

Jamie's claws lifted once more. He attacked.

More blood flowed.

The witch broke. "Th-there's a way...end the curse...you can...can control her..."

Iona wanted to close her eyes. Wanted to slap her hands over her ears. But this wasn't her body, and Jamie's hands — they were too busy slicing into Brian.

"Then you tell me that way. Tell me how to control the Blood Queen, and you can help me to kill Latham."

***

"My father was alpha," Jamie said the words, knowing she probably couldn't hear him — not while she was locked in blood memories — but still needing to speak. "I was his second son. Latham...he was my half-brother. Hell, I didn't even know about the guy for the first ten years of my life. He just…showed up one day. His mother had never…she'd never joined the pack. That's why his last name's Gentry."

Latham Gentry. The fucking wolf that had destroyed his world. "He'd been in America, had grown up there." And, later, it would be Latham who convinced the pack that they needed to move across the pond and start fresh in the United States.

"I was a kid when Latham showed up, and Latham—hell, he was a fully mature wolf. He was also a sadistic prick." Jamie shook his head. "Only back then, nobody but me ever seemed to see the evil that burned in him." His fingers were laced with hers. "I tried to tell my father. He wouldn't listen. He was too damn happy to have a strong, new wolf in the pack—a wolf with his blood."

He's fucking crazy. How many times had Jamie said those exact words to his father over the years? He'd *seen* the evil in Latham. Why hadn't the others?

"The years passed. I could see that Latham was growing darker, more dangerous. I could also tell that he was positioning himself to be alpha." *The hell, no.* "I had to leave the pack. I knew…I knew I'd never be able to swear allegiance to Latham." His parents had been furious. Jamie's father had disowned him, still refusing to see what Latham was. *He said I was jealous. Bitter.*

Their father had ignored the truth for far too long.

"When I left, Sean came with me." Sean had been his best friend for as long as he could remember. Orphaned, Sean had always been treated as the runt of the pack when they were kids. But Jamie hadn't let the others ever hurt Sean. He'd fought plenty of battles for his friend until Sean had finally grown big enough to fight back.

When they'd left the only life they'd ever known, Sean had said, *"It's time for me to have your back."* Sean could be a smart-ass, but the guy was loyal. True through blood and bone.

They'd gone out, ready to start a whole new life.

But...something had happened. "Maybe it was you," Jamie whispered to her. "There was talk that Latham had become obsessed with a vampire. That he wanted her for his mate, but she...she turned away from him."

Smart choice.

"The years passed, and Latham just started to grow stronger. Crazier." This was his shame. Jamie hadn't returned to the pack then, despite the stories he'd heard. *My father told me if I left, not to return.* So he'd stayed away, thinking his father would finally see Latham for what he was—

thinking that his father would stop the other wolf.

"But when my parents realized the truth about Latham and tried to fight back, he killed them." The memory was a knife in his heart. "I came back—too late—and found their bodies."

He'd never forget the sight. He'd heard tales of more bloodshed in the O'Connell pack. Tales of torture and death, and he hadn't been able to stay away a moment longer.

"Latham tried to kill me, too, but vampire blood—your blood—saved me." His breath rushed out on a rough sigh. "Didn't thank you for that, did I? No, instead, I just went right ahead with *my* plans. I wanted revenge. I wanted Latham taken out, and I didn't care who stood in my way."

He leaned over her. "I fucking care now."

And he heard the faintest of rustles in the hallway. Footsteps. Someone closing in.

He brushed his lips over hers. "I care now," he said again, and went to face the threat coming for them.

***

"Are you sure about this?" Sean demanded as he glanced around at the two dead bodies that littered the ground. The dead werewolves were slowly shifting back into their human forms.

Jamie straightened his shoulders. She could feel the determination coursing through his veins. "The Blood Queen is inside."

And he'd just defeated a small army in order to get to her.

Sean grabbed his arm. "How do you even know the witch is telling the truth? That whole story about waking her could be a bunch of BS. We might get in there and just find Latham waiting to gut us."

Jamie glanced at him. "Brian burned himself out casting the spell for Latham, and he understands…my brother hates weakness. It's only a matter of time before Latham kills Brian. The witch knows it, even if he can't see his death coming."

Sean frowned. "Can't 'see' it? What the hell are you talking about?"

"Witches can see much in this world, and beyond it. Brian saw how to trap the Blood Queen, and he set the spell so that only a werewolf alpha could free her."

"An alpha like you?"

Jamie nodded. Then they were running down a hallway. Attacking more wolves. Killing their own kind.

As Jamie gazed around, searching for more enemies, Iona realized that she knew this place.

Her prison.

Jamie stopped before a too-familiar metal door. "I'll wake her, and she'll be my weapon."

She didn't want to hear —

"If she wants to keep living," Jamie said as he lifted his claw tipped hand toward that door, "then she'll need my blood. So she'll do what I want."

And she knew…He was just like Latham. Not caring what happened to her. Not giving a shit at all.

Maybe he deserved the same death as his brother.

Then Jamie and Sean were inside the room. Jamie inhaled the scent of the ocean. Saw the wispy curtains. Saw the body lying in the bed. So still.

Dead.

Jamie's stare locked on her prone form. Sean grabbed him again. "This is a bad idea. There's a reason she's under, man. The woman is evil."

No, she wasn't. Sure, she'd done bad things, but only to those who'd come after her. She'd never hurt an innocent. Iona didn't care what the twisted lies claimed about her.

Only Jamie didn't think she looked evil. She was in his head, and she knew that he thought she looked…beautiful.

Insane man. She looked like a corpse.

"Go outside," Jamie ordered Sean. "Guard the door, just in case…"

"In case the crazy bitch gets loose and kills you?"

She felt his annoyance. "In case we've been tracked. I don't want anyone stopping me. Not until I put the bond in place."

Bond. The word trembled through her.

Jamie cut his wrist. It was so strange to watch as he put his wrist – his blood – to her mouth. He tried to *force her to drink. Frustration churned within him when her eyes didn't open. "Maybe you are dead."*

Then she saw her own eyes open. "I'm not dead..." A weak, raspy voice. Her voice. "But you are."

***

Jamie yanked open the door and put his claws at the werewolf's throat. Sean froze with his hands up in the air. Then he demanded, "Fuck me, man, is that how you answer a door?"

"It is when I smell Latham's scent." And his brother's scent was definitely on Sean. Jamie grabbed the guy and hauled him inside. "Want to tell me what the hell is happening?"

Sean swallowed. "He's coming for you." His gaze darted to the bed. "For her."

That had been the plan. Before.

"You've changed your mind, haven't you?" Sean charged. He shoved away from Jamie. "Dammit, I *knew* this would happen. I saw the way you were looking at her in that bar. When she said she was gonna drink from me...shit, you went postal."

Postal? Huh. Jamie had thought that he'd held onto his control pretty well. All things considered. He *had* remembered that Sean was his best friend. So he hadn't shoved his claws into Sean's side.

"She was the big secret weapon." Sean marched around the bed. "You were supposed to use her, not fall for her." Sean's gaze drifted from Iona's still body back up to Jamie. "I guess you are more like your brother than you want to think."

In an instant, Jamie had his friend against the wall, and his claws were out. *"Don't."* There were some lines that he wouldn't even let Sean cross.

"Don't what?" Sean demanded, not backing down at all. "I trusted you. I gave you my loyalty, my life. Latham's a twisted freak, but he managed to walk the thin sanity line until he met *her*. Your brother couldn't have her, and he went batshit. If she wasn't his, then she was nobody's. He locked her up and—"

Jamie's fist and claws drove into the wall as his fury erupted. "He was always batshit! I saw it from the moment he came to the pack. He'd get off on torturing the weak. Hell, he almost killed you when you were only six." But Jamie had stopped him. He'd always had to stop him. *Story of my life.* "You don't remember, but I do. How the hell do you think you became an orphan? He was the one to kill your parents. He was the one who came after you. I told my father. I *told* him, but no one would believe me. Why would a wolf attack his own kind?"

Sean stared at him with stunned eyes.

"Because he's a demented psychopath," Jamie said, answering his own question as he yanked his claws out of the wall and stepped back. "And I am *nothing* like him." He turned away from Sean and glanced over at the bed.

Iona's eyes were open. She was sitting up in bed. Staring at him. Shit.

"You want her just as much as he does," Sean said from behind him, but the werewolf's voice shook with pain and sorrow.

I shouldn't have told him like that. Sean deserved better. To him, Sean *was* his brother, not Latham.

"Remember your big plan?" Sean said and now he was getting angry. So Jamie wasn't really surprised when the guy said — *right in front of Iona* — that, "Part of that plan was that I'd let Latham find me. I'd offer him a deal. Tell him that you'd trade *her* for peace."

Jamie's eyes were on Iona. "That was just a lie to bring him out. To get him to face me. I wasn't going to make a deal." *I wouldn't trade you.* He'd thought to defeat Latham, not to actually give Iona to the bastard.

She just stared back at him. He couldn't read a single emotion on her face or in her eyes.

"I held up my part of the agreement," Sean snapped. "I went to him. Found him while he was torturing some human named Greg. I *told* Latham, and now he's coming to meet you. Latham sent me to deliver a message. He wants you and the vamp to meet him at her old compound, at midnight."

The plan had been to draw out Latham. To force him to face-off against Jamie. Only...Jamie had planned to be riding high off the rush that came from Iona's powerful blood. Finally, a fair fight between the brothers. He'd planned to drink and drink from her.

Then use her to distract his brother so that he could go in for the kill.

I can't. Because what if he was wrong? What if he wasn't strong enough? And if Latham got to Iona...

Iona cut her gaze to Sean. She studied him a moment, then gave a curt nod. "We meet at midnight."

No. Jamie hurried toward her. He leaned over the bed and had to fight to keep his hands off Iona. *Don't touch her when your claws are out. You can hurt her.* "I'll go after him myself. You don't need—"

"I was supposed to be the instrument of your vengeance." She pushed from the bed. Walked right by him. "And now you don't want to use me?"

The blood memories. So she had gotten them all while she slept. No more hiding. His shoulders stiffened. "You know."

Her burning gaze touched on him and said that she did.

"Good," he told her and meant it. "Because I don't want any more lies or secrets between us. I was an idiot then. I didn't know you, and I thought—I thought who you were didn't matter." But she'd gotten under his skin. Into his very blood and soul. "You matter," he said, the words too simple.

A furrow appeared between her eyes. "You expect me to believe—"

He hated that he had an avid audience listening to his every word. Jeez, could Sean not give them some privacy for an instant? "I expect you to believe that I was an idiot. I was bent only on getting my own justice, and I didn't realize the cost to you."

Her breath seemed to come faster. Her eyes blazed. "You *tied* us together. For me to live, I'll have to keep taking your blood."

Shame burned through him. "I'm sorry, I—"

She waved away his apology with an angry swipe of her hand. "And you think I'd just let you waltz out there and face Latham alone? If he kills you, I'm dead, too."

He realized the enormity of just what he'd done to her. Like an apology was gonna cut it. "I don't plan on dying. I'll kill *him*, and when this is over…"

"What? We'll stay together, because you've *bound* us?"

He shook his head. "I'll give you as much blood as you need, anytime you want it. You don't have to stay with me. You can..." He stopped and cleared his throat. *I want her with me.* But he wanted her happiness more. "You can go anywhere you want," Jamie forced himself to say, "do anything you want, and I'll make sure the blood is always sent to you." He'd be her personal donor, for as long as she wanted.

Forever.

She closed in on him and put her hand on his chest. Right over the heart that just seemed to beat only for her now. "And what about you? If you don't get my blood, you won't be the all-powerful werewolf that you so desperately want to be."

"He also won't live forever without your blood," Sean pointed out as he crept closer to them. His voice was controlled now, but Jamie knew the control was an act. *I'm sorry, Sean.* He'd kept the secret about Sean's parents for too long. But if he'd told Sean the truth back then, the guy would have gone after Latham.

And gotten killed.

Sean was just a foot away now. Shoulders up. Head back. Eyes too determined. "All my research showed—"

Iona's head jerked toward him. "*Research?* What research?"

Sean's face reddened. "There's…ah…a few mated werewolf and vampire couples these days. When they share blood, they stop aging. We even found one couple that had been together for seventy years, and the werewolf doesn't look a day over twenty-five."

Iona's gaze came back to Jamie. So much suspicion in that gaze. He hated that look. *I want her trust.*

She didn't appear to be in the mood to give it to him.

"So as long as you have my blood, you get to live forever, huh? I'm betting your *brother*," Iona said the word like the curse it was, "knew all this, too. That's why he just wouldn't take my *hell, no* for an answer when he asked me to mate with him."

"I'm killing him…" Latham would *never* touch her again.

"No, I'll do that. I can fight my own battles, and pick my own mate."

A mate that isn't you. He knew exactly what she meant. His fingers lifted. Curled around the hand that she still had pressed over his heart. "It isn't just your battle. He took my family."

"Mine fuckin', too," Sean snarled.

Jamie flinched.

Iona's small, pink tongue slid over her bottom lip. "I-I know." Her gaze darted to Sean.

Jamie saw the sympathy in her stare, then her stare returned to him.

"I won't let him keep hurting and torturing. I will stop him." Then, he confessed his shame, "As I should have stopped him years ago." Because if he had, then none of this would ever have happened. His parents' deaths. The slaughter of the wolves in their pack. Her imprisonment. "I won't walk away this time."

He was alpha now. He'd been ten when Latham killed Sean's family. Jamie's father hadn't believed his tale. He'd said it was a child's wild imagination.

Latham had been furious with Jamie for trying to reveal his slaughter. His brother had found him, separated him from the others...*As soon as I'm alpha, I'll take your head, brother.* Latham's threat had whispered through his head so many nights when he'd been a child.

But now...*I'm coming to take your head, Latham.*

Jamie had fought to be strong. He had his wolf, a fierce, powerful beast that knew how to battle. How to survive. How to conquer.

And his blood had woken Iona. Only an alpha's blood could have woken her. He *was* an alpha. The power was inside of him, as it had always been. Maybe that was why Latham had hated him so much. Maybe his brother had known that, one day, the life-or-death battle would come between them as they fought for dominance.

That day is now.

"I thought you were different." Iona's voice was so soft now. Not soft because of sadness, but because of the fury he saw blazing in her eyes. "*Why* couldn't you have been different?"

"I *am* different." He pressed her hand harder against his chest. "I'll prove that to you."

But she laughed and the sound cut into him. "There's nothing to prove. I'm in your blood, wolf. I know you."

He pressed his lips to hers. Kissed her hard and deep and wild. Kissed her with all of the consuming passion and lust that he felt for her. "And you're in mine," he gritted out against her lips. "I feel like you're a part of me."

Sean cursed and backed the hell away from them.

Jamie's gaze searched hers. Her breath heaved but she didn't speak.

He did. "You're a part that I didn't even know was missing...the best part of me." His heart.

Then, because it was what he had to do, Jamie stepped away from her. He turned to face Sean. "I'm sorry about your parents. I didn't tell you...because I *knew* you. Even at six, you would have challenged him. You would have died." He hadn't been powerful enough to save Sean. Not then.

And he'd kept the secret, kept it for so many years, because Latham's power had just continued to grow. Jamie hadn't wanted to risk his best friend's life. He'd protected him the only way he knew how...by staying silent.

It wasn't a time for silence any longer. It was a time for vengeance.

Jamie exhaled slowly. "If Latham said midnight, then we're getting there as soon as night falls. We're not going to give him a chance to set a trap." They were only going to let Latham die.

"Of course, there's going to be a trap," Iona said, but her voice wasn't quite steady. "With Latham, there's always a trap. Werewolves in the shadows, vamps ready to betray their own kind, witches with their spells..."

"He doesn't have a witch this time," Jamie pointed out with a fast glance her way. "So there's no power for him there."

"Isn't there?" Iona asked as she swept past him. "Latham doesn't make mistakes when it comes to battle. He killed Brian, yes, but I'm betting that was only because he'd already found another witch who was more powerful. A witch he'll try to use against us in our midnight battle."

The kick in his gut told Jamie that she was right.

"So we need to be ready to fight that witch with our own magic." From the corner of his eye, Jamie saw the flames begin to dance over Iona's hands. "And when it comes to magic, this time, I *will* be holding my own." The flames flared higher. Jamie's eyes met Iona's. The gold in her gaze matched the flames.

Beautiful.

Death had never been so gorgeous. Latham was a fool. Against them, he'd have no chance.

Time for his brother to die.

CHAPTER SEVEN

"I want you to bite me."

Iona blinked at the low, growling words. They were inside the heavy walls that had once surrounded her old home, and the scent of ash teased her nose, a reminder of the fire and death she'd dealt earlier.

Her head turned so that she faced Jamie. Sean was about fifty yards away, perched carefully at the top of the west side wall. A group of trees grew near the wall, partially concealing Sean as he watched...and held a rifle equipped with silver bullets.

"My blood can increase your power," Jamie told her as his gaze searched hers. "You know it can. A werewolf's blood can amp you up for the battle."

So it could. The blood of paranormals always seemed to pulse with power. And she would love to have more power before she faced off against Latham but... "If I take more from you, then you'll just grow weak before the fight."

A muscle flexed along his jaw. "Not if you give me your blood, too."

An exchange. To make them both stronger. Yes, they needed it, but for some reason, when he asked for her blood, it made her feel...used.

So she narrowed her eyes and told him, "The first time I fucked you, I did it because I wanted to make Latham angry. I wanted him to catch your scent on me. I wanted him to know that I was giving my body to someone else." Anyone else. Not just—

Jamie shook his head. "When you lie, a faint line appears right..." He tapped his finger between her brows. "Here."

Iona was so shocked she almost fell onto her ass. As it was, she barely managed to keep crouching next to him without lunging for the jerk. "I'm *not* lying!" She was the *Blood Queen*. Like she'd have some easy tell that gave away her lies.

He stroked the spot between her brows. "There it is again."

Sonofabitch. She had a *tell*. All these centuries, and no one had mentioned it to her before? Wonderful.

"Don't worry," he said as if reading her mind, "I doubt anyone else noticed. I just know because I can never seem to take my eyes off you." His hand fell away. "Just so we're clear, I made love with you the first time because I wanted you more than I wanted breath. That's the same reason I did the second time, too. And the reason I'll do it every chance I get."

Arrogant wolf. "I *did* want to piss off Latham." But…more…Time for her truth. "I also just wanted you."

His eyes seemed to darken.

"Is that what you needed to hear?" She demanded, angry. "That you could make the Blood Queen want—"

"I don't really give a shit about the Blood Queen," he said, the Irish thickening in his voice. "I care about *Iona*. She's the one I want. Not some evil queen who is supposed to give little kids nightmares."

Nightmares? Really?

"I want to give you my blood now because I want to make sure you're as strong as you can be. And, no," he muttered, "you don't have to give me yours. Just take mine. Just…be strong. I don't want Latham to ever hurt you again."

The wolf was sure acting like he actually cared about what happened to her.

And she did need his blood.

Iona lifted his hand to her mouth. Her fangs sank into his wrist, and the image of them—in that horrible room, her on the bed, him leaning over her—flashed in her mind. Then his blood slipped over her tongue—warm, spicy, that delicious taste that was only *Jamie*—and her eyes locked with his.

She didn't see calculation in his gaze. No secrets. Just desire.

His power fueled her, heating her body from the inside out. She drank, taking in that wonderful blood and power. Then her tongue licked over his skin as she tried to soothe the small marks that she'd left behind.

Her head lifted. His taste was still in her mouth.

"I've never wanted another woman the way I want you." Gravel-rough, the words seemed torn from him. "And I've never met another woman who was so far out of my reach."

She was less than a foot away from him.

"If I had to do it all over again, I'd find another way to break the spell. I wouldn't force you to be bound to me."

She couldn't help it. Iona laughed at that. Clueless werewolf. "You really think I'm the one being forced?" Her hand lifted and curled under the hard square of his jaw. "I'm over sixteen hundred years old. I can stir fire with a thought. I'm about to turn your brother to ash…" She smiled at him and knew her fangs would flash. "You're the one who's going to be forced to stay with me, wolf. Do you actually believe I'd ever let my blood supply get away?"

He blinked.

Men. Always thinking it was all about them.

She shook her head and turned away.

He caught her hand. Held her tight. "Love, the only way I'd ever leave you...you'd have to *tell* me to leave. 'Cause otherwise, I'd count myself lucky to be at your side."

She stilled. Then her heartbeat kicked up in a double-time rhythm. Jamie sounded as if he meant the words. She stared into his eyes and searched for the truth.

He *did* mean them.

"What do you want from me?" She asked him, barely recognizing the soft voice as her own.

"Everything." Just as soft, but his words were darker. So deep. "But I'll start with this...give me a chance. Give us a chance. Let me show you that I'm not just a beast."

She already knew that.

"Let me show you the man I can be. Let me—" Jamie broke off, his nostrils flaring. Then he spun away from her. "He's here."

She hadn't caught Latham's scent yet, but she'd take Jamie's word for it. Her gaze darted to the big wall surrounding the old compound. She saw the dark shadows scaling the stones, climbing over the wall. *Coming for us.* Iona counted at least a dozen forms.

"Vampires...werewolves..." Jamie's claws were bursting from his hands as his shift started. "What we...expected..."

Yes, it was. Now it was time to give Latham what he didn't expect. She bared her throat to Jamie. "Bite."

His eyes were more beast than man. "You don't..." He still tried to speak with a man's voice.

"I want you to drink."

His hand lifted. His claws seemed to tremble, then he sliced lightly over her skin. His dark head lowered. His tongue rasped over her wound.

She shuddered against him. Her eyes closed. His lips brushed over her. His claws were at her waist, but he was so careful not to hurt her.

Latham had never been careful with anyone or anything.

A shot echoed through the night. She knew the sound had to come from Sean as he took out prey with his silver bullets. Those werewolves fighting with Latham had picked the wrong side.

Their mistake.

Sean had chosen a position of his own on top of the west wall. A position that let him take out his prey as he wanted, picking them off with his silver bullets, one at a time.

"Get away from her!" Latham's enraged roar. *Showtime.* "You bastard, that's my queen!"

Jamie's tongue licked over her flesh once more. A rough caress. Then he was pulling back. Gazing at her with a gaze that burned with emotions she didn't want to name. "No," he said, voice thundering out just as powerfully as his brother's. "She's mine."

Then he whirled toward Latham. The two brothers charged at one another. Shifting werewolves were on the ground, some in pain because silver bullets had ripped into them, some were just contorting from the force of their transformations.

And the vampires who'd sold their loyalty to Latham were there, standing back because they'd caught sight of her. She heard their whispers...

"Blood Queen..."

"She's back..."

"Back and pissed," Iona clarified, letting her voice ring out and not glancing over at Latham and Jamie even as the scent of blood deepened in the air. "So come closer, and try to take me down, if you think you're strong enough." Then she crooked her index finger at them, daring the fools to come and get her.

Because she needed them closer. They had to be close for her fire to reach them. Just a little closer...

A tall, red-headed vampire made the mistake of lunging for her.

When he was within range of her power, she tossed a ball of fire right at his chest. He hit the ground, screaming and rolling as he tried to put out a fire that just wouldn't be stopped. Only she could stop those flames. Iona wasn't in the mood to stop them.

The other vampires froze.

"Who's next?" Iona challenged.

Bones crunched behind her. More shifting wolves. She turned and saw a big, gray wolf rushing toward her.

A shot thundered out.

The wolf fell, a silver bullet embedded in his spine. There was a shout then, and Iona saw Sean jump down from his position on the wall. He attacked, fighting the wolves that had come for him.

He was fighting — and winning his battle.

Iona's gaze darted to the right. Jamie and Latham weren't in human form any longer. Two big, fierce black wolves were fighting, tangled in claws and teeth and blood. The wolves — they looked just alike to her. She wasn't sure which wolf was winning the battle…or which wolf was Jamie.

"I'm next!" A woman's voice shouted. "And I'm not afraid of that bitch!"

You should be.

The line of vamps parted. A woman rushed forward. A small woman with long, curly, brown hair. She smirked at Iona and fire rose above the woman's delicate palm. "See? I can do it, too."

Ah, so this was the new witch that Latham had picked up. Being right felt so good. "I'm not drugged this time." Iona felt she should point out that little fact.

The witch frowned.

"That's how Latham's first witch got the advantage. The drugs in my system slowed me down…" Iona threw her flames at the woman. The witch's hair caught fire, and the woman screamed as she stumbled back. "I'm not slow now…and lady, *I'm a hell of a lot stronger than you!*"

The witch—minus a whole lot of hair—ran away, shrieking. Easy enough. Too easy. Must be slim-pickings when it came to magic power these days.

Iona lifted her hands into the air. It was time to send a message to the paranormals out there. She didn't want to be looking over her shoulder, worried that others would come and hunt her.

They needed to be too afraid to even whisper her name.

Blood Queen. She could be her, again, in order to be free.

"Run," she ordered the fools still around her. "Or die." Then she called up the magic inside, letting it whip through her and form a circle of fire, a bright ring that closed around her and the two black wolves that fought a life-or-death battle. Everyone else was on the outside, and the fire snapped out at those vampires and werewolves, attacking with greedy tendrils of flame that ignited flesh and sent shrieks into the night.

Most ran. They would be the ones to spread the new story of the Blood Queen's rebirth.

As for the ones who didn't run? The slow? The idiots who still thought they could kill her?

They died.

And then there was only Iona…in the circle with her wolves.

She could kill them both with a thought. Send the fire ripping at them but…

Iona didn't want Jamie to die. *Which wolf?*

She needed to see their eyes. Their scents were too linked then—they were too close to each other. There was too much blood. If she could just look into the wolves' eyes, she'd know her lover.

The claws of one wolf shoved into his opponent's stomach. A long, mournful howl filled the night. The injured beast heaved on his side and slowly, slowly began to transform.

The fur melted from his body. Familiar, golden flesh emerged once more. She knew the strong line of that jaw. Knew the heavy slash of those cheeks.

The other beast snarled into the air, a cry of fury and dominance. Then the beast turned to face Iona.

Not Jamie's eyes. But then, she'd already known her lover was the one bleeding out on the ground.

She lifted her hands and tossed as much fire as she could at Latham. She wanted that bastard to *burn.*

Only, he didn't burn. The flames just sank into his thick fur and disappeared. Tendrils of smoke drifted into the air.

The snap and crunch of his bones reached her ears. He shifted before her, a fast, brutal shift.

She couldn't see Jamie's body behind him. Was Jamie still alive? And why did it feel like someone had ripped out *her* heart?

"I've got so much of your blood pumping in me," Latham snarled as he closed in on Iona and grabbed her wrists. His hold was rough, too strong, so painful it felt like he was about to break her bones. "Thanks to all that blood, your magic can't hurt me, Iona. *Nothing* can anymore."

The fire sure couldn't. But she wasn't about to give up yet. "Then let's just see what my teeth can do..." And she sank her fangs into his throat.

His blood burned her, going down as hot as acid on her tongue, but she didn't let him go. She'd drain him, if that was her only way and —

He screamed and pulled away from her.

No, *he* didn't pull away. Jamie had snatched Latham back. Because her Jamie wasn't dead. He was on his feet and he'd spun Latham around to face him…spun him around and, as she watched, Jamie shoved his claws into his brother's chest.

"She was the distraction," Jamie whispered as he let his brother stagger away from him. "You should have made sure I was dead."

Latham's head swung toward her. He shook his head even as blood pumped from his chest. "I'm…immortal."

"Not anymore you're not," Iona told him. Jamie had been right. Latham was still too fixated on her. Fixated enough to make a fatal mistake.

He'd turned his back on a werewolf who wanted his blood.

Latham's teeth snapped together. "You won't…live…without…*me!*" He rushed toward Iona.

And Jamie's claws slashed over his brother's throat even as the thunder of a gun echoed and a bullet slammed into Latham's chest.

Sean…doing his job and avenging his parents. Overkill could be a good thing.

Iona slowly walked around Latham's body. Jamie stood over his brother, chest heaving, and with blood dripping from his claws.

"Looks like I'm still living just fine," Iona murmured to the dead werewolf. She was living, and Latham had finally gotten just what he deserved.

His eyes were wide open. His face twisted in horrified disbelief. He truly hadn't thought that he'd die.

He'd been wrong.

She stared down into his eyes. She could still see the madness there. Even in death. "I went to Latham..." It seemed like another life. Maybe because it was. "Because I wanted to form a truce between the vampires and the werewolves. I didn't want more bloodshed."

When blood was all they had around them.

She looked away from Latham. Stared up at Jamie. "I wish you'd been in the pack when I came calling."

"So do I."

Her head tilted as she studied him. "What would you have done?"

"Loved you from the start."

She blinked and shook her head. "No, you—"

"I know you don't love me, Iona."

They were standing over his brother's body. It wasn't a place to talk about love. Not the right place. Not the right time. There was too much death here. Too many memories.

And she wouldn't lie. "I don't know what I feel for you." At that moment, she just felt...relieved. *One less monster to face.*

Finally, she was free. Latham would never hurt her again. *Free.*

Jamie's gaze held her own. "Do you think," he asked her softly, "that one day, you might?"

Her eyes wanted to sting with tears. Tears, from the Blood Queen? What had happened to her? Maybe it was the place. The echoes of pain and sadness. *Get away.* She couldn't be there any longer.

Or maybe…maybe it was Jamie. He was asking for things that she wasn't sure that she could give to him. Fifteen years…gone. She wanted to see the world again. See what had changed. Learn how *she'd* changed.

She couldn't talk to him about love then. She needed her freedom.

A freedom that their bond had taken away.

Iona spun around, giving him her back. Then she began to walk away, from Latham and from Jamie. Every step that she took tore at her heart.

What was she supposed to feel for Jamie? Everything had happened too soon. Love couldn't come this way for her.

She needed time. *Time was stolen from me. Now I have to learn to live again.*

Good thing that she was a vampire. Time was on her side. Always.

"Iona!" Jamie's cry stopped her. Not because he yelled after her with fury or desperation. But because he said her name with…love. Maybe he'd been saying it that way for a while now, and she just hadn't noticed.

He'd stopped calling me 'baby' and he'd been calling me 'love.'" Her throat ached. She glanced back at him. He hadn't moved. He wasn't trying to stop her from leaving him. Maybe because Jamie knew that she'd have to come back to him, sooner or later.

The blood would always bind them.

"Do you think you ever might?" Jamie said the words softly, with blood on his flesh, with his claws out, and with his eyes so fierce and bright.

She needed to give him an answer. Iona just wasn't sure what to say. So she didn't speak, but, almost helplessly, she found herself nodding. It was a small movement, and she wasn't even sure he noticed it. Then she saw the hope on his face and knew that he had.

"But I can't stay with you because we *have* to be together." She'd come to hate him then, just as he'd hate her if she forced him to stay at her side. "It should be…we should be together because that's what we want. Because anything else is unthinkable to us." That was why she had to get away then. Latham was dead. The battle over. Now she had to figure out what the hell she wanted. What she needed.

So with her head up and her back straight, she began walking once more. She passed by the dead. Passed a silent Sean. She didn't let her tears fall. After all, she truly was the daughter of a king, and she wouldn't let anyone see her break. Not Sean. And not even the one man who'd managed to touch a heart she'd long thought was ice-cold.

CHAPTER EIGHT

"Are you sure that you're ready for this?" The witch stood over Jamie, a silver knife gripped in his hand.

The tip of that knife burned molten.

"It's going to hurt like a bitch," the witch warned then the guy gave a long whistle. "I sure as hell hope the woman is worth it."

Jamie gritted his teeth. Ray was a smart-ass, some witch that Sean had literally dug up from a hole in Mexico, but the guy knew his magic.

Well, his dark magic anyway.

And he knew how to break the bond that locked Jamie's blood to Iona's.

Two months. Two long fucking months had passed since she'd walked away from him in LA.

He knew where she was, of course, because it wasn't easy to overlook a woman like her.

He'd sent his blood to her. Werewolf take-out. But he hadn't gone to her, because he couldn't offer her the one thing that she needed.

Choice.

He'd taken that from Iona when he gave her his blood.

I can't stay with you because we have to be together. Her voice haunted his nights. And his days. *It should be...we should be together because that's what we want. Because anything else is unthinkable to us.*

Anything else *was* unthinkable to him, and without her, he was going insane. Slowly, moment-by-brittle-moment insane.

He needed her. He wanted her. And, hell, yeah, he'd get his heart cut out for her. *Not because you have to be with me.* Once the spell was broken, she could stay because that was what she wanted to do.

"You have to sever the bond to free your vampire." Ray looked a little too comfortable holding that knife three inches above Jamie's chest.

Sean stood in the background muttering once more about bad ideas and wrong choices. The same song he'd been singing when they first went to wake up Iona.

"Am I gonna live through this?" Jamie asked the witch.

Ray frowned at that. "You expect to live?" He seemed surprised. "I thought it was just about *her* living." He began to lower the knife. "I can't make any guarantees for you."

Sean lunged forward and grabbed Ray's wrist. "Guarantee it." Lethally soft.

Ray swallowed.

Jamie stared at the tip of the knife.

"I-I...he *should* survive. It will hurt, probably worse than anything he's ever felt, but he'll live...and his vampire will be free."

That was what he needed to know. "Cut me," Jamie ordered and his hands fisted, pulling against the heavy chains that held him in place. Silver chains that Ray insisted were necessary.

Not a good sign. But at least he'd stopped feeling the burn from those chains now.

Jamie closed his eyes. Pictured Iona. His beautiful queen.

Then the knife stabbed into his chest, bringing the fires of hell, and he roared her name.

***

Pain exploded in her chest. Burning, white-hot, twisting and cutting and tearing into her flesh.

Iona opened her mouth to scream but found she didn't have any breath. The smell of burning flesh filled her nose even as bile rose in her throat.

What is happening to me?

She'd been on her way to find Jamie. She'd discovered a witch who knew a way to break their bond. Only...

Another burst of pain had her nearly on her knees.

Iona screamed and realized that another cry had echoed her own.

Her head lifted as sweat soaked her clothes. She stared at the house before her, the one nestled off the main road and hiding in the shadow of thick trees.

Jamie's house. The roar she'd heard, it had been her name. His voice.

Iona forced her body to straighten. *Jamie.* Fear and adrenaline rushed through her.

Another pain-filled roar shook the night, and she ran forward. Iona kicked in the house's front door.

Two men—probably werewolves—turned and lunged at her. She knocked them back and followed the echo of that roar down a hallway. Then to the right. Another kick and the door before her flew off its hinges.

A man whirled toward her. Some guy with too-long, red hair. He had a long, wickedly sharp knife in his hand. The blade was glowing red.

Jamie was on a table, chained. Smoke rose slowly from his flesh.

"What are you doing to him?" Iona leapt for him.

Someone grabbed her from behind. "Wait!" A familiar voice shouted in her ear. "He's a witch, he's breaking the bond and—"

And she tossed Sean into the nearest wall. Iona advanced on the witch. "You're hurting him." *Us.* She rubbed her own aching chest. "You're *dead.*" She raised her hands. Let the fire burn.

"Oh, shit," the man muttered as his eyes doubled in size.

"*No!*" Jamie's snarl.

Her head snapped toward him. Surely he wasn't protecting his attacker?

"It's...almost...finished..." Sweat soaked his body. The brightness of his eyes had dimmed. "One more slice, and you're free."

She pushed the man—now she knew he was a witch—away and rushed to Jamie's side. When she saw his chest, she had to bite her lip to hold back her own scream of fury. It looked like the skin had been branded, a dark, fierce red. But she knew the knife was enchanted and the branding wasn't just on the surface.

The brand would go all the way around his heart.

No, not all the way, not yet. Jamie had said that he needed one more slice.

The floor creaked behind her.

Iona spun around and grabbed the knife from the witch's hands.

"Do it," Jamie urged her. "Finish it. Be free…then you can come back to me."

"The witch was cutting out your heart!" She'd found her own witch, a woman who told her this could be done, that this was the way to sever the tie between them.

Take out the heart and the bond is broken.

"No." Jamie shook his head and jerked on the chains. *Silver* chains. The fool werewolf had let himself be locked down with silver chains. "I'll still live," Jamie told her. "Ray's not actually taking my heart—"

Yes, yes, she knew how the magic worked. The enchanted blade both cut and healed at the same time. The witch would cut a circle around the heart, severing its connection to the body. Then, in the next instant, the blade would burn and heal—reconnecting the heart with magic. The severing and healing would continue until a full circle had been cast around the heart.

Brutal. Hellish. Iona knew that the agony she'd felt was just a psychic echo of the pain that he'd experienced. Her witch had warned her of that, too.

When one is sacrificed, the other will feel the whisper of the pain. Just a whisper. The real agony is a hundred times stronger than that whisper.

"A spell." She glared at the knife.

"The knife cuts through the magic that binds you, but he still lives." Did the witch think those words would make her feel better?

She knew their hearts were linked. The blood pumping from her heart linked to the blood pumping from his. To cut their ties, a heart had to be severed.

And Jamie, he was willing to face the agony, for her?

She licked her lips. Felt tears on her cheeks. *Not about breaking. About living.* "You're not like Latham."

He stared up at her. His face was too pale. Her wolf looked too weak. "Told…you…"

She snapped the knife and let the pieces fall from her fingers. The witch gasped and got the hell back.

Sean had picked himself off the floor. He stood back, too. Smart guy.

She grabbed the chain around Jamie's right wrist. Shattered the heavy silver. Did the same with the links that bound his left hand.

"I can feel you…" Iona told him, and brought his hand to rest over her heart, "in here." Even when they were apart, she felt him. Like a caress in her soul, she could feel him touching her.

His gaze searched hers.

"You let him come at you with that knife…" Well, the witch *wouldn't* be coming again since she'd destroyed his knife. "He would have cut me out of your heart." *And taken you from mine.*

Jamie rose. The back of his hand slid down her cheek, and she turned her face to better feel his touch.

"Nothing will ever take you from my heart," he told her. The words sounded like a promise.

He'd been willing to suffer so much...for her.

Jamie sucked in a deep breath. "I can...I can still send you the blood. I can do whatever you want..."

"Kiss me."

He frowned, then shook his head.

She put her hands on his shoulders. Those shoulders of his seemed even bigger than before.

I missed him. "I want you to kiss me, Jamie."

His mouth took hers. Ravenous and wild with its hunger. The same hunger that she felt.

Tears pricked at her eyes. She'd lived so long and had never expected to find a man who looked at the Blood Queen and...loved.

He loves me.

So she kissed him back. Hot, eager, their mouths met. She didn't care about the others in the room. They didn't matter. Nothing, no one mattered to her except him.

His arms locked around her. He pulled her close, right between his legs as they hung over the edge of the table. His mouth was feverish on hers, his hands seeming to touch her everywhere.

"Missed you…" Jamie growled the words against her lips. Then his head rose. He stared at her with the eyes of a beast in the face of a man. "You're…giving us a chance?"

She had to shake her head, and when she did, pain flashed in his gaze. Iona spoke quickly, desperate to make him understand as she said, "No, Jamie, I'm giving us more than a chance." Her shoe crunched over the remains of the knife. "I want to give us forever."

His hands tightened around her. "Be…sure."

"I've never been more sure of anything." Or anyone. He'd been willing to suffer such torture, for her.

And she'd seen more of Jamie's secrets in her dreams.

Him, watching her with not just lust, but longing.

Him…rushing through the day and night as he tracked her to LA, desperate to find her before Latham got to her.

She'd seen a wolf run until his paws had bled. Watched through his eyes as Jamie drove a truck like a madman until he'd arrived outside the dark walls of her old home. She'd felt his fear…until he'd seen her.

Her lips brushed over his once more. He'd woken her up, but not just from Latham's spell. He'd given her life again.

He'd given her love, and it was exactly what she wanted. No, *he* was what she wanted now.

Not because they had to be together.

"Because anything else is unthinkable," she whispered. And it was. Her body and soul had ached for him. She needed him. Couldn't imagine going another single day without her werewolf.

The door squeaked closed behind them, and she knew that Sean had grabbed the witch and gotten out of there.

Good.

Because the Blood Queen had finally found her werewolf king, and she wasn't letting him go.

Not now. Not ever.

Some bonds weren't meant to be broken.

"Forever," Jamie said against her lips. A demand.

Her werewolf had just spoken true…some bonds really were meant to last forever.

They kissed again. She tasted the wildness of his beast. The love of the man.

Forever.

###

A NOTE FROM THE AUTHOR

Thank you so much for reading FOREVER BOUND. I hope that you enjoyed all of the vampire and werewolf stories!

If you'd like to stay updated on my releases and sales, please join my newsletter list www.cynthiaeden.com/newsletter/. You can also check out my Facebook page www.facebook.com/cynthiaedenfanpage. I love to post giveaways over at Facebook!

Again, thank you for reading FOREVER BOUND.

Best,

Cynthia Eden

www.cynthiaeden.com

Also available: **BOUND IN DEATH** - Book 5

She can't remember him...

He can never forget her.

For over two hundred years, alpha werewolf Alerac O'Neill has been searching for his mate, Keira McDonough, a woman who was taken from him and imprisoned by a dark vampire master. He's hunted for her, endlessly, using vampire blood to extend his life. He has become a vicious predator, feared by all the supernaturals. His hold on reality seems to slip more each day because he is consumed by *her*.

Only...the woman he discovers in a small Miami bar isn't the Keira that he remembers. In fact, this woman doesn't *remember* anything. She calls herself Jane Smith, and she has no memory at all of Alerac—or of her own past.

Now that she's been found, Alerac knows that his enemies are going to start closing in on her. Jane may try to act human, but she's not. She's a pureblood vampire princess, incredibly powerful and incredibly valuable. His enemies want to use her, her enemies want to destroy her, and Alerac—he just *wants* her.

If he can't make her remember him, then Alerac has to seduce Jane into loving him once again. Because now that he's found her, he'll fight hell — and every sadistic vampire that stalks the night — in order to keep her safe at his side.

Some bonds go deeper than the flesh. Some go beyond life. Beyond death.

Jane will soon learn that a werewolf's claiming…is forever.

ABOUT THE AUTHOR

Award-winning author Cynthia Eden writes dark tales of paranormal romance and romantic suspense. She is a *New York Times*, *USA Today*, *Digital Book World*, and *IndieReader* best-seller. Cynthia is also a two-time finalist for the RITA® award (she was a finalist both in the romantic suspense category and in the paranormal romance category). Since she began writing full-time in 2005, Cynthia has written over thirty novels and novellas.

Cynthia is a southern girl who loves horror movies, chocolate, and happy endings. More information about Cynthia and her books may be found at: http://www.cynthiaeden.com or on her Facebook page at: http://www.facebook.com/cynthiaedenfanpage. Cynthia is also on Twitter at http://www.twitter.com/cynthiaeden.

HER WORKS

Paranormal romances by Cynthia Eden:
- BOUND BY BLOOD (Bound, Book 1)
- BOUND IN DARKNESS (Bound, Book 2)
- BOUND IN SIN (Bound, Book 3)
- BOUND BY THE NIGHT (Bound, Book 4)
- *FOREVER BOUND - An anthology containing: BOUND BY BLOOD, BOUND IN DARKNESS, BOUND IN SIN, AND BOUND BY THE NIGHT
- BOUND IN DEATH (Bound, Book 5)
- THE WOLF WITHIN (Purgatory, Book 1)
- MARKED BY THE VAMPIRE (Purgatory, Book 2)
- CHARMING THE BEAST (Purgatory, Book 3) - Available October 2014

Other paranormal romances by Cynthia Eden:
- A VAMPIRE'S CHRISTMAS CAROL
- BLEED FOR ME
- BURN FOR ME (Phoenix Fire, Book 1)
- ONCE BITTEN, TWICE BURNED (Phoenix Fire, Book 2)

- PLAYING WITH FIRE (Phoenix Fire, Book 3)
- ANGEL OF DARKNESS (Fallen, Book 1)
- ANGEL BETRAYED (Fallen, Book 2)
- ANGEL IN CHAINS (Fallen, Book 3)
- AVENGING ANGEL (Fallen, Book 4)
- IMMORTAL DANGER
- NEVER CRY WOLF
- A BIT OF BITE (Free Read!!)
- ETERNAL HUNTER (Night Watch, Book 1)
- I'LL BE SLAYING YOU (Night Watch, Book 2)
- ETERNAL FLAME (Night Watch, Book 3)
- HOTTER AFTER MIDNIGHT (Midnight, Book 1)
- MIDNIGHT SINS (Midnight, Book 2)
- MIDNIGHT'S MASTER (Midnight, Book 3)
- WHEN HE WAS BAD (anthology)
- EVERLASTING BAD BOYS (anthology)
- BELONG TO THE NIGHT (anthology)

List of Cynthia Eden's romantic suspense titles:
- MINE TO TAKE (Mine, Book 1)
- MINE TO KEEP (Mine, Book 2)
- MINE TO HOLD (Mine, Book 3)
- MINE TO CRAVE (Mine, Book 4)
- FIRST TASTE OF DARKNESS
- SINFUL SECRETS

- DIE FOR ME (For Me, Book 1)
- FEAR FOR ME (For Me, Book 2)
- SCREAM FOR ME (For Me, Book 3)
- DEADLY FEAR (Deadly, Book 1)
- DEADLY HEAT (Deadly, Book 2)
- DEADLY LIES (Deadly, Book 3)
- ALPHA ONE (Shadow Agents, Book 1)
- GUARDIAN RANGER (Shadow Agents, Book 2)
- SHARPSHOOTER (Shadow Agents, Book 3)
- GLITTER AND GUNFIRE (Shadow Agents, Book 4)
- UNDERCOVER CAPTOR (Shadow Agents, Book 5)
- THE GIRL NEXT DOOR (Shadow Agents, Book 6)
- EVIDENCE OF PASSION (Shadow Agents, Book 7)
- WAY OF THE SHADOWS (Shadow Agents, Book 8)

Printed in Great Britain
by Amazon